If Where You're Going Isn't Home

Book 1

Journey

Max Zimmer

WHAT PEOPLE ARE SAYING ABOUT

IF WHERE YOU'RE GOING ISN'T HOME

"*Journey* serves as a solid foundation for what promises to be a superlative series of novels."

– Cheryl M. Hibbard, ForeWord Clarion Five Star Review

"Max Zimmer writes beautifully. His prose has a natural rhythm and grace that is testimony to his having honed his craft for a long time so that it's no longer just craft but real art. There are many scenes that will stick with me forever."

– Markus Hoffmann, literary agent, Regal Literary, New York

"Other authors create a world and then expect me to believe in it. What makes Zimmer unique is that he writes his story and uses my world to tell it. I didn't want the book to end."

– John Murray, artist and novelist, New Jersey

"I read the first chapter and was hooked. It felt like a movie. The voice is true. The writing is out of this world. A pillow mint on every page. A great journey. Best book I've read in years. This book belongs on every high school English curriculum alongside *The Outsiders*, *Catcher in the Rye*, and *Huckleberry Finn*."

– George Goetz, writer, Massachusetts

"I love . . . love the music lessons. The way Zimmer writes about jazz theory, modality, notes versus tones, numbered notes instead of letters, just wonderful stuff. I want to go back to school for a degree in music."

– Paul Mossberg, rock and blues guitarist, New Jersey

"I want to play Mr. Selby in the movie."

– Ed Selby, professor and jazz trumpet player, New Jersey

"Max Zimmer has written an extraordinary revelation of life in a Mormon community in a way no one else has ever done. He allows Shake to discover both the good and the bad – the sublime and the evil – of the Mormon church and Utah society as he struggles to define himself in terms of his passion for the instrument God has given him. This is not the stuff of Big Love pyrotechnics; this is the real, compelling, and revealing look into the demands of the faith as Shake and his young friends take their first steps into adulthood. But the great craft of this book is that it neither demonizes nor sanctifies its characters. And it neither demonizes nor sanctifies the Mormon church and faith. Zimmer presents his wonderful, quirky, and often hilarious cast with affection for all their foibles and strengths."

– *Rolf Yngve, novelist,* Any Watch They Keep, *San Diego*

"I love Brother Clark."

– *Damon Cooper, teacher, Arizona*

"I wanted to read sections again – slowly – just because the writing is so good I wanted to live in them. Zimmer's detail is unrivaled. Shake's story so perfectly shows the unresolvable nature of inhumanity."

– *Nikolaus Tea, musician and poet,* Red Bandana, *Vermont*

"Jazz indeed. There is a certain and deadly grace about Zimmer's writing now that is hard to put down."

– *Robert Smart, professor and author,* The Nonfiction Novel, *Connecticut*

"As a musician, I felt that the pulse of music in Shake's life, as well as his whole world as created by Zimmer, were so compelling – so real, I forgot I was reading fiction. There's such delight in the details, it was impossible to look away."

– *Fred Simpson, poet and musician, New York.*

THE STORY AND ITS MAKING

Journey is the first novel of the series *If Where You're Going Isn't Home*, a story that chronicles the growth of a boy caught between his dream to play jazz trumpet and the strictures of his father's Mormon faith. As the first book of the series, it takes young Shake Tauffler from the age of almost twelve to fifteen. The second book, *Of the World*, takes him from there to nineteen. In *Not into Night* he reaches the age of twenty-one. The fourth and final book, currently in progress, takes him deep into his twenties.

The genesis of what has evolved into this project is a love story I wrote in the summer of 1978. The story haunted me for several years. What I eventually came to recognize was that its psychic and dramatic setting – what it was like to grow up Mormon in America – had never been put on the map of our collective consciousness in a universal way that readers everywhere, from all walks of life, all religions, all cultures, could reach and experience from the familiar territory of their own lives. To create that setting, I put the original story aside, and began where the story needed to begin – with a boy at the beginning of his duty to his father's faith and his dream to play jazz trumpet. His story – the four-book chronicle of his odyssey – is a story still guided and informed by the love story that gave it life that summer.

If Where You're Going Isn't Home

Book 1

Journey

This work of fiction is modeled in various ways on the author's youth. As in all fiction, while the perceptions and insights are based on experience, the names, characters, places, and incidents portrayed in this work are either products of the author's imagination or used in a fictitious way. No reference to any real person should be taken as literal or factual.

Max Zimmer

Cover photograph "Sunset over Antelope Island in the Great Salt Lake" by Annika Karlsen. Cropped and shaded by permission.

www.photosbylilyanna.com

Cover painting "Red Jazz" by Didier Lourenço

www.didierlourenco.com

Cover designed and executed by Phoenix Design

www..tacomaphoenix.com

Cover inspired in part by Ryan Yost

The religious teachings and customs portrayed in this book are accurate. Based on actual experience, verified by research, they are true to the doctrine and authentic in rendering the culture of the Mormon Church as taught, practiced, and lived in 1950s and 1960s Utah.

Occasional scriptures cited in this work are taken from the Doctrine and Covenants and the Book of Mormon. Both books are official scripture of the Church of Jesus Christ of Latter-Day Saints.

The song Stormy Weather, lyrics from which are cited in this book, was written by Harold Arlen and Ted Koehler.

The General Priesthood Session that Shake and his father attend is based on official church transcripts of the actual Fall 1956 Session.

The town of Bountiful still exists. The sandpit – the long deep gash in the yellow hills above the neighborhood – has been leveled, filled, cut into lots, and colonized with houses and a park. What it was like in the 1950s, and what took place there, exist only as a buried landscape excavated in the pages of Shake Tauffler's story.

ISBN 978-0-9854481-2-7

FOR TONI

And in memory of

MIKE "GUELO" FLOWERS

One of the Boys from Bountiful
1943 – 2012

Contents

Part 1

Sheepherder Music

CHAPTER 1

YOU KNOW before it's over. This sound that takes the human breath of a voice and gives it the shimmer of steel and makes it light and effortless and fly like a bird made of the clear bright ringing sound of steel with all the sky out through the windshield to itself.

It's not enough to hear it.

It has to come from you.

The way you can't breathe just by listening to someone else's breathing. Pump blood just by feeling someone else's heart. Get rid of thirst by watching your mother drink down a glass of her lemonade. It makes you want some too. It has to be you drinking it.

Your breath.

Find out what instrument it came from. Manny and Hidalgo. You can't ask them. They'll tease you if you let them see how much it matters. They'll never tell you.

"What's got you by the tail there, little man?"

"Nothing." And then, feeling the punishing bite of telling a grownup a lie, you say, "That music. On the radio."

"Just now? Just some Mexican jazz. You like it?"

"Mexican what?"

"Jazz. You never heard it?"

"It's from Mexico?"

"It ain't from no hymnbook, that's for sure."

"Where's it from?"

"It's sheepherder music, little man."

"No it's not."

"No? Tell him, Manny. Sheepherder music."

You, almost twelve, the oldest of five, the first born back in Switzerland, four years before you were put on the Queen Elizabeth and brought across the ocean, then on a plane in New York the rest of the way to Salt Lake City, a big plane called a Constellation, where a stewardess helped your mother scrub your vomit out of the sweater some aunt had knit for you. Born four years before you lived in your grandfather's open basement in the big house in the Avenues, with your uncles and aunts and cousins, where blankets were hung from the floor joists overhead to make rooms for the families. From there, a tumbling kaleidoscope of the places you found yourself living, moments in your head you could capture and then let go and then catch again like grasshoppers or moths, the upright piano your mother brought from Switzerland in different living rooms, songs from Broadway musicals one of her ways of learning English, the lessons you took at her side from her thin articulate hands the same no matter what else around you kept on changing. The basement apartment where nightcrawlers came up through the drain in the kitchen sink. The house with two front doors, the house divided down the middle, the half where the welder's family lived and the half where you lived, the room where your fingers nibbled away at night at cracks in the wall your bed was pushed against, where you came home from school one day in the fall to a fire truck, a busted water heater in the yard, the front door open wide, your mother in her striped dress out in front, firemen talking to her. The first Rose Park house on Talisman Drive. The second one, a corner house on another Rose Park street, in whose basement you and a neighbor girl named Louisie pretended you were married. Then La Sal, the ranch down in southern Utah, where they slaughtered a steer each Saturday and passed the meat around and your family always got the kidneys because nobody in America ate kidneys. Four years there, your father the ranch bookkeeper, the retired old workhorse named Rex you used to ride bareback out across the sagebrush till the ranch was a tiny oasis of trees in the shimmer of distant heat, the junkyard of abandoned army trucks across the dirt highway whose dashboard instruments you extracted and traded with your buddies, the tank without a turret in the sagebrush, the mountains behind the ranch bald where their forests ended, the long and intricate and sometimes abruptly scalloped line of distant yellow sandstone that was as far as you could see in every other direction, the piano the choiring heart of the little house where sometimes you woke up to watersnakes in the living room.

School the same kaleidoscope. Kindergarten, the teacher a white-haired woman big as a polar bear, who used to get the class to laugh along with her at the way you fumbled English, who came striding down through the desks when laughing got tiresome to slap the back of your head so hard you saw sparks like lightning in the flash of black. Mrs. Brick. First grade partitioned between three schools you don't remember except for Webster Elementary. Second grade in Rose Park, where you used to come home for lunch to chocolate and cheese sandwiches your mother would heat in the oven to just before they melted, where the Diamond brothers caught you coming home on Valentine's Day and scattered the cards the kids in your class had given you in the slush of the gutter. And then the two-room schoolhouse on the ranch. Third grade in the room from old Miss Jenny. Fourth and fifth and sixth in the other room from Betty Peterson whose husband Chas ran the milkhouse across the big dirt lot from the bunkhouse where all the sheepherders lived. The potbellied stove, the portrait of Adlai Stevenson on the wall, the coal bucket you took out back and loaded whenever your turn came around, the flagpole out in front in the dirt that got turned into a maypole every spring. By fifth grade, and then all through sixth, because of Mrs. Brick, you were winning every spelling bee they could throw at you. And then here, two months ago, in April, to this house in a town named Bountiful, twenty minutes north of Salt Lake City, this brand new house on a paved and guttered circle ringed with other brand new houses. So for junior high you wouldn't have to ride the school bus all the way from the ranch to Moab and back to the ranch again. So you'd be close enough to a school to ride your bike to seventh grade instead.

They let you out of sixth grade early. Your father told them he had to move in April or else lose the house. So they let you and Karl and Molly out of school with two months left and had Manny and Hidalgo use a cattle truck to move your stuff here from the ranch. Karl and Molly and Roy made the trip north through the length of Utah in the deep back seat of your father's Buick while Maggie rode in your mother's lap. You got to ride with the sheepherders, on the bench between them, perched on a bundle of gunny sacks so you could see, smelling hay and sheep feed, keeping your knees away from the trembling black knob of the tall gearshift, watching the buttes and the cliffs and the canyons move slowly past, listening to the radio right there in front of you over the grinding whine of the engine. Moab. Crescent Junction. Green River. Price. Helper. Soldier Summit. Towns you knew from the shopping trip your family made in August every year to Sears in Salt Lake City for clothes for school and Christmas toys. Manny driving, Hidalgo on your other side, the sheepherders talked to each other in Mexican the way your father and mother talked to each other in Swiss. When they talked to you, like your father and mother, Hidalgo and Manny used English.

"Hey, little man, we got your bed back there," Hidalgo saying. "You sleepy, you can go back and take a nap."

"I'm not sleepy."

"We got all your stuff back there. Those magazines with the naked ladies, too."

"I don't have any naked lady magazines."

"Sure, sure. Manny, he'll tell you he don't either, when you ask him."

"Honest. I don't."

"We lose the brakes right now, little man, what you think happen?"

Manny saying something quick and sharp in Mexican to Hidalgo. But you heard chico there in what he said and knew that it meant little kid and you didn't like it. Not after being called a little man all morning.

"What?"

"You see that kind of cliff down there? Where the road turns?"

Manny shaking a cigarette out of the pack of Chesterfields he had on the dashboard while you looked down the road and saw where it looked like it ended. Not a cliff but this bunch of boulders like a family of huge brown elephants. You knew that the road didn't end there no matter how much it looked like it did because the Buick would have been there, stopped, and your father would have been standing in the road outside the open driver's door, wondering what to do, your mother complaining for an answer from the passenger seat.

"Yeah," you saying. "I see it."

"Time we got there," Hidalgo saying, "no brakes, we'd be doing maybe a hundred."

"Would we crash?"

"Would we ever. And all that stuff in back? All that furniture?"

"Yeah?"

"It all come flying. Right through the cab. Smash! Squish us to pieces like three big ripe pumpkin heads. Turn us into pumpkin juice."

You understood it too when Manny coughed out a burst of white Chesterfield smoke and said fuck in the middle of something in Mexican and you got scared and looked at Hidalgo and he shut up but sat there grinning. And then turned his head and looked out his side window. And after a while said, "Manny don't like pumpkin juice."

And then, after the long and growling climb up Price Canyon, after cresting Soldier Summit, after making it around the turn past the elephant family boulders and the road was there again, and the distant back of your father's Buick, there was the song on the radio, and the sound that was playing the song, a sound you'd never heard before, the human breath of a voice giving flight to a bird made out of the sound of steel.

You sat there spellbound. Your breath. If it was an instrument it was one you'd never heard before. But you wanted it to take your breath too, make it the sound you were hearing, a sound you would follow anywhere. And then it was gone, and Hidalgo was saying sheepherder music, and you were saying no, it's not, looking at Manny, knowing from this quiet grin around his cigarette that they were fooling you.

"Sure it is," Hidalgo saying. "Up in the mountains, the moon and the stars all out, the sheep all sleeping, just you and the dog, a little fire going, right, Manny?"

"Keeps away the cougars and coyotes, too," Manny saying.

"That's right." Hidalgo taking a second to lean down toward the dashboard and light his own cigarette. "Makes them peaceful. Takes their minds off their stomachs."

"You hungry?" Manny saying. "Thirsty?"

"No thanks."

"Just say so. Don't want your mom thinking we're letting you starve."

The movie your father took when Manny came to get your dog the afternoon before you moved because your mother said you couldn't bring him north. You drew a picture of him instead to bring along. Rufus sat there, watching you draw, not knowing it was him, not knowing anything until Manny leashed him to the spare tire in the bed of his pickup truck. Manny said he wouldn't change his name, would call him Rufus too, would make him a happy-go-lucky sheepdog. And then he drove away, Rufus barking, leaping back and forth in the bed, and there you were, in your gold-colored swimming trunks and the piece of tarp you used for a Superman cape, half chasing the small cloud of dust that rose up behind the tailgate, your legs confused and irresolute, the same uncertain jerkiness in your arms, up and then down and then up again, half waving, not knowing how to let him go, not sure how to say goodbye. Rufus. The dog you got when he was a puppy not much bigger than the bowl of your two hands. The coyote you cornered and tackled in the yard. The way you pulled his jaws apart until Rufus fell clear. The day it took for Rufus to come unparalyzed enough to eat and walk again.

Later, in Bountiful, when your father runs it on his noisy home projector during a Family Home Evening, the movie will startle and shame you. It will show you what he sees when he looks at you. You wheeling round, seeing the man behind you in the road with the whirring camera to his face, the recognition in your own face that you're being filmed, the half-apologetic try at smiling, then wheeling around again to run a few more stumbling steps in the wake of the dust-blurred pickup. In the film you won't hear Rufus barking. Just see the fierce repeating recoil of his head. Just see you waving while your father records on film what it's like when you think that a dog would know what it means when you wave at him. The scene will feel endless while your family sits there watching. Jazz. A new word. Sheepherder music. A way to comprehend it. Thistle. Spanish Fork Canyon. Springville. Provo. Orem. Out ahead of you, through the windshield of the cattle truck, through the towns going north all the way to Salt Lake City, there was always the green rear end of your father's Buick, heads and sometimes faces in the big rear window.

"Hey. Look over there. Your new house."

Looking where Hidalgo's pointing. The spires of the Salt Lake Temple above the roofs of the downtown buildings in the yellow afternoon sky.

"That's the Temple," you saying, because Hidalgo wasn't Mormon, because maybe he didn't know. "God lives there."

"Looks to me like where Tinkerbell lives."

"Tinkerbell lives in Disneyland."

Manny smoking another Chesterfield. Working the gearshift between your knees to get the truck through another red light of the crawling traffic of the city.

"Who's that gold guy?" Hidalgo saying. "Up on top there? That Jesus?"

"That's the Angel Moroni," you saying. And then catching him smiling away from you. "You knew."

"No I didn't. Promise."

"Yeah you did. You just wanted to make me say it."

Five of you. The places you were born like evidence that you'd lived there while your father looked for footing and learned English himself. Karl almost ten. Born like you in Switzerland. Molly almost eight. Across the Atlantic and then from New York to Utah inside the huge bell she made of your mother's stomach. Born while you lived in the basement of your grandfather's house in the Avenues before your father moved you to the basement of the house tucked under the four-lane double curve that swept around Brewery Hill as it brought traffic down into the city. You remember Webster Elementary not from the classroom you sat in, but from the outside, from across the curve around Brewery Hill when you went out walking with your mother with Molly in the baby carriage, sinister and powerful like a factory or prison, its brick walls black like the hull of a burned ship. Roy just five. Born in Rose Park. In La Sal, you saw him standing in the doorways of different rooms, sucking his thumb while your mother stood over you, out of breath, her pretzel-shaped bamboo rugbeater in her hand, welts rising from your back and face and arms like the brands they gave the cattle. You've heard his fingers hunt for notes and realized he's the one kid who'll ever take her piano lessons and keep going. Maggie. Two this coming November. Born in the hospital in Moab while you were living in La Sal. There was the Indian they wheeled into the hospital the morning your father took you there. His shiny blue-black hair in the sunrise through the glass doors. His leather moccasins at the other end of the gurney. Vomit ran in a steady river out his mouth onto his pillow. You and Maggie the bookends of the family because your mother was done with having kids. Ten years stand between you.

Here, now, in Bountiful, in a town you reach by driving a few miles north of Salt Lake City, past Slim Olson's World's Largest Gas Station, past the stinking yellow haze and always burning torch of the Phillips 66 refinery, past the cattle pens of the Cudahy stockyards, past the monster black machines of the sand and gravel pits carved out of the foothills. A town where your back is to the mountains when you look west toward the Great Salt Lake and Antelope Island and the horizon where the desert starts and goes all the way across Nevada. Bountiful. A town whose name you can't get used to because it doesn't feel finished, just the start of a name, just an adjective. Bountiful. Like naming a town Little. Or Yellow or Shiny or Fat. But you're here, here instead of Switzerland, because of your grandfather. Because he translated the Book of Mormon and a lot of Mormon hymns into the German language. Because during the war he used to cross the border into Nazi Germany to visit the German members in their hiding places there. Because a year before you rode the Queen Elizabeth yourself, the Church officially made him their German translator, and moved him from Switzerland to the big house in the Avenues whose basement became a holding pen for the rest of his family. Soon after the last family moved, and the last of the blankets came down, your grandfather had to leave the big house too, because it belonged to the Church, because he was only renting it from them.

He's short for a famous man. Shorter even than your father but built the same way, stocky and muscular, a small bear on hind legs. In the fenced back yard of the little house where he and your grandmother live, on a dirt-curbed street off the thoroughfare of Seventh East, your grandfather sits in a lawn chair off by himself, not saying much, not drawing attention, but his rimless glasses explode with light when he turns his large bald head toward the small grill where your father, on his knees, rolls hot dogs back and forth across the smoke.

"If Grosspapa's so famous," you say, "how come he doesn't live in a mansion?"

On the way home from your grandfather's house you ride between your father and your mother. A woman is singing opera, high and fast and frantic like someone's tickling her, out of the big chrome grill of the radio in front of you. Behind you, deep in the back seat, Molly holds her sleeping little sister as though in her mothering little arms both of them are safe, Karl's got his head out the window and his mouth open to the wind, and Roy is back there too, somewhere, maybe asleep, maybe watching the tops of the trees and houses pass along the sill of the window above his head. Your father reaches across to pick at something on his arm, then returns his hand to the big black hoop of the steering wheel.

"Is that all it means to you to be famous?" he says. "To have a big mansion?"

You keep your eyes fixed on the speaker grill. The hose fight, the clownish way your father let Molly catch and tag him, the joking around, the horseplay that like a circus bear lured all of you through the afternoon. All of it gone, left behind, put away, like the barbecue grill he scrubbed, the aluminum chairs and card table you folded up, the plates and glasses your mother washed and Molly dried, the mustard and ketchup bottles whose threaded tops your grandmother wiped with a washrag before capping them. He's alone with his family again. His voice is gruff, heavy with responsibility, restless, like you've made him turn around while he's been headed somewhere else. From deep inside his mouth you can hear the soft and regular clacking of his back teeth, a sound that goes with the worried contemplation of some distant peril in his eyes, the always furrowed flesh of his forehead even when he's laughing.

"No."

"Your grandfather is a modest man. Like the commandments teach us to be. Did Jesus have a big mansion?"

Your mother lifts her hand off her thigh and puts it back down again and then turns her head and looks into the wind through her open window.

"No," you say.

"Then why should your grandfather have one?"

"He shouldn't, I guess."

You wonder if what your father's telling you is that your grandfather keeps all his money stored in a bank somewhere.

"He'll have his mansion in Heaven," your father says, "when he reaches the end of his mortal journey."

"So, Harold," your mother says. "He's only a child."

In two years, your grandfather will be dead, of something called a stroke, and at his funeral you'll look across the rim of his casket at the only dead person you've ever seen, and your grandmother will tell you not to be afraid to touch him while the knobbed gray fingers of her veined hand skitter with frightening tenderness across his scalp and ear without him knowing it. He'll look more waxed and buffed to you than dead, like neutral shoe polish was worked into his face and scalp and ears and hands and then brushed until his skin turned satin, like a kid's, no sign that he'd ever had whiskers, like it must have been when he was twelve years old himself, wondering how old he'd be when he'd finally get to shave. Journey. In the front seat of the cattle truck, the big Buick out ahead of you hauling your family toward Bountiful, toward the town where your own will start now that you're almost twelve.

CHAPTER 2

"WHY DON'T you fellows just stay with us tonight."

In the slits of Manny's eyes you can see him take a quick look at your mother. And then he tells your father no. Says him and Hidalgo are going to start heading south, find a motel somewhere, be back at the ranch by morning.

"A motel?" your father says. "I wouldn't hear of it, mister. No, by golly. We can set up the bunkbeds. The boys can use their sleeping bags."

"That's okay. You got your family here. Besides, tomorrow's Monday. Got things to do. Sheep to shear."

Manny looks off toward where the sun is low and red over the roof of a house a couple down from yours, squints to where his eyes are these silver curves like the edges of spoons inside his eyelids, takes off his old straw cowboy hat, takes the bandanna roped loose around his neck, wipes it up across his face and back down again. His hair is glued to his forehead and molded like a cupcake where his hat was.

"Man," he says, and looks down into his hat. "Sure is hot for April."

"I'm sure that Charley won't mind if you fellows get back tomorrow afternoon," your father says. "He probably doesn't expect you until then, anyway."

Manny puts his hat back on, looks at you, grins, and a thousand wrinkles splinter his face and the skin around his eyes.

"Got to get back to Rufus," he says. "Tell him we got you here okay." And then he winks and says, "Tell him you like sheepherder music."

Everything's off the truck, in the house, and your father's all sweaty too, his face shiny in the red light, his shirt soaked to where the temple garments he uses for underwear show through. Out past the curb, Hidalgo lifts the end of the big wood ramp off the street, pushes it in through the back of the trailer, picks up the tarps and blankets and throws them in behind it, swings the two big gates around and latches them. Kids stand around and watch him. Two kids on their toes look through the battered red side boards into the trailer. Another kid looks up at the dark green door of the cab where it says Redd Ranches. Out by the curb off the front of the truck, in her braids, Molly looks at a little brown-haired girl in a yellow dress who's looking her over too. You don't see any kids your age.

"Are you sure I can't convince you to change your mind?" your father says. "You need to eat something too, by golly. And have some breakfast in the morning."

In a driveway across the circle a tall thin man your father's age is washing a dark blue car. In the yard next door a woman with black hair and turquoise pedal pushers waves a sprinkler like a sparkling wand across some pink flowers around the trunk of a baby tree.

"Nah," Manny says. "You don't want to wake up with a couple of old sheepherders in the house. Believe me."

"Yes, Harold," your mother says. "Let them go back. They have done enough for us."

Where he's been standing next to her, his thumb in his mouth, Roy edges closer, deeper into her chocolate-colored dress, creased from the long ride north with Maggie on her lap. You heard it coming too.

"I wasn't asking them anything, Mother. Just offering them supper and a place to stay, by golly."

"So, Harold. I don't even have my dishes unpacked." And then, with sudden modest sweetness, she turns to Manny. "I'm sorry that all we had for you was water."

Yesterday, at the ranch, after Manny drove it over to your house, before the ranch hands and the sheepherders came over and started loading it, you swept the trailer clean of manure and straw, hosed the wood floor and the long slats of the sides to get rid of the smell of the dust. Out in the street, off the back of the tailgate, you watch Hidalgo light a cigarette, shake the match out, toss it away. The kids around him follow its quick arc up and then down to where it hits the street like it's something they've never seen before.

"Don't you worry," Manny says. "You folks enjoy your new house."

He shakes hands with your father. Then takes his hand and cups the top of your head, wobbles it around, and you remember the knob of the gearshift you watched him work all morning on the drive north.

"You're a good helper, little man," he says. "You and your brother. Work hard, know how to stay out of the way."

You lower your head to hide your face. Manny lets you go, turns, heads for the truck, yells something at Hidalgo that makes the woman watering her flowers look his way. Hidalgo yells something back in

Mexican. Shoos the kids away around the truck, trots toward the cab, climbs in, slams the door, sets his arm on the windowsill. Molly comes hurrying back from the curb. Manny starts the engine. It grinds, and then coughs, and then grinds again before it catches, and when Manny revs it up you can feel it, in the backs of your legs and in your feet again. The exhaust stacks shake and their hinged flappers swing up from bursts of black smoke. Manny puts it into gear, the brakes fart, the cab quakes, and Hidalgo looks at you, all of you, on the walk in front of the porch, and raises his brown hand off the windowsill. You wave back. Manny steers the truck wide, using the whole circle, letting the big front tire follow the curb. The tailgate chatters and the tall sideboards of the trailer rock to the side while the growl of the engine works the long truck around the circle. The man washing his car looks up and waves his rag. The woman watering her flowers keeps her face down. When his window comes around, Manny waves, and you wave back at him too. At the mouth of the circle he snakes the cab to the left, and you panic, want to tell him it's the wrong way, but then he swings wide to the right like he heard you, like you were in the cab again, and then watching the truck you get it, that all he was doing was trying to keep from running the wheels of the trailer across the yard of the house on the corner.

And then you remember. How Manny just paid you a compliment and you just stood there stupid instead of remembering what your father always told you. To never let a compliment go unreturned. How people who compliment you deserve to hear something nice about themselves.

"Now come inside, children," your mother says.

You run down the concrete path toward the curb and watch the trailer fall into line behind the cab as it moves off down the street, loud and lumbering, tall as the roofs of the houses on either side. Manny. What you'd say to him if you could catch him. What kind of compliment he'd like and wouldn't look at you like it was phony. You sure know how to shear sheep. You sure know how to drive a truck. From the ride that took you the morning and half the afternoon, you can still feel the steel cab quiver through the gunny sacks under your legs, hear the deep clank of the gears under your feet as Manny's long brown hand works the tall shaft. Hidalgo turns the radio dial. Snatches of voices and songs break through the running static and then vanish. And then he finds it. A song, from out of nowhere, made out of this sound that moves through you so easy you feel like all you are is the shimmering path it leaves reflected across quiet water. Like all you are is the running urge to chase it down. Down the street, the truck turns to the right, down the hill, and the rocking back of the trailer follows it around the corner. And then it's gone. Whatever the compliment would have been. The sound you'd never heard before. The instrument you couldn't name.

"Shake! Come inside! Now!"

For the next three days you help your family settle in. Go with your father to a hardware store in town and help bring home a rake, a shovel, a hoe, a pushbroom, a wheelbarrow big enough to take a bath in. Help him screw hooks along the wall in the garage to hang his new tools on. Rake rocks and dig boulders out of the dirt of the yard with Karl and haul them out back and dump them in the dirt field behind the house. Coming back to the yard you give each other wild rides in the wheelbarrow. Side by side, face to face as you lift boulders too big to lift alone, Karl's appetite for something to hurt or break comes off him like static electricity, and in the field you watch him hurl rocks down on boulders to try and crack them open, watch him look around with a rock in his hand for other things. Out in front, where little kids with slices of Wonder Bread throw pieces into the circle for them, big birds your father said were seagulls turn in a shrieking merry-go-round in the air, out of reach of the rocks that Karl heaves up at them, dancing away from the ones he skitters off across the asphalt.

On the third day your father puts on a suit and tie and heads off to work at a place called Lang Construction. You and Karl finish clearing the yard. The morning is windy and the gray air gritty with dirt that forms tiny marbles of mud in the corners of your eyes. The afternoon turns bright and calm and cold enough for a sweater. And then that night, at supper, your father talks about his day at work, his first day, from the head of the yellow formica table with his family gathered round. He uses his church voice, big and astonished, when he talks about how humbling it is to have this job. From the other side of Maggie's high chair your mother listens, but there's this fretful restlessness in her little smile, the way she always waits for a way to go after him.

"Yes, Harold," she finally says. "It's just too bad."

"What's too bad, Mother?"

"That you have to come home to your family stinking of cigarettes."

"I can't help it if there are men in the office who smoke, Mother."

In the rich smooth cloth of your father's blue suit when he came home from work and you hugged him, you could smell it too, tobacco smoke in there, sharp and sour and new, in the river of all his other smells.

"But didn't you know they smoked before you took the job?"

"No, Mother, I didn't."

"Maybe you should have asked them," she says.

"Ask them what?" Your father puts his fists on the table with his knife in one of them and his fork in the other one. "If they smoke? And then what?"

"Maybe you should have kept looking, Harold."

"I was looking for the best paying job I could find," he says. "I can't help it if it happens to be a construction company. By golly, Mother. I have a family to support."

On your pale blue melmac plate lies the remaining half of your zucchini, hollowed out like a canoe, baked, the hollow loaded with pan-browned hamburger, the hamburger topped with a fresh red stripe of ketchup. Schifflis, your mother calls them. Little ships that people in Switzerland eat.

"Then maybe you can tell them now, Harold."

"Tell them what, Mother?"

"That you don't like cigarette smoke," she says. "That you don't want to come home to your family stinking like an ash tray."

"Yes." He smiles at his plate and shakes his head. "Tell my boss on my first day at work that I don't want him to smoke." He looks up, around the table, and you and the rest of his kids duck your heads. "What do you think, children? Karl. What would happen to me if I spoke like that to my boss?"

Your brother raises his head. Molly and Roy raise theirs to look at Karl.

"You'd get fired," he says.

"By golly," your father says. "Even a nine-year-old boy understands that you don't tell your boss he can't smoke."

"So you have to come home stinking every night because you're afraid to be fired," your mother says. "Pfui! Who needs a job like that? Maybe you should think a little more about your family."

"Think about my family?" His face goes suddenly coarse and red and creased and his voice goes harsh and ragged. "What do you think, Mother? That I took this job for the fun of it? That I took this job to make your life miserable?"

"Are you planning on going to church stinking like tobacco?" She makes a small derisive laugh. "They would look at you like a hobo. A tramp."

"I have a different suit for Sunday. Don't you think I've thought of that?"

"I don't know, Harold."

"Let's change the subject," he says. "You boys can take tomorrow off. Now let's finish supper, by golly."

And now your mother looks around the table, this wounded smiling look on her face, like your father just slugged her but that's okay with her. "Yes, children. Let's eat our supper."

"We can take tomorrow off?" you ask your father.

"Yes."

He doesn't look up from his plate. He's got his knife but uses the edge of his fork instead to cut through the shell of his zucchini.

"How come?" you say.

"We have to wait for the topsoil. It isn't coming until late tomorrow afternoon. We'll wait until Saturday to spread it."

"What's topsoil?" says Karl.

Your father gets the zucchini balanced on his fork into his mouth without spilling any of the hamburger. "Soil that goes on top of the yard," he says, chewing, not looking up. "So we can plant grass."

"What's wrong with the yard the way it is?"

"It isn't soil. It's dirt. Grass can't grow in it."

"Why not?"

"Just take my word for it," he says. He looks at you and Karl with a look like there's something still left he needs to settle. "Take tomorrow off. Now eat before I change my mind."

CHAPTER 3

FOR THREE DAYS you've gone without breathing almost it's been so hard to wait. Wondered what you'd do if you couldn't find a store that had instruments. Now, morning, you put on your brown wool jacket, check your tires, swing onto your bike, and you're gone. You know the way from the trip you took with your father to the hardware store. You charge down the long hill through your neighborhood. You keep your head down because every other kid in town is in school and you're out here alone, in the open, where people could stop and ask your name. The air is cold and wind burns your ears and makes your knuckles hurt. Cars pass you, and trucks, and station wagons, and you hear them come and watch them go without raising the dust you used to have to ride through in La Sal. Soon you can feel their pull. The stores. The street where all the stores are. You lean harder into the handlebars. Stand on the pedals. Start flying down the last street, a big wide street that will turn you left onto the street where all the stores are, one after another, where maybe one of them will be a music store. The dirt and the asphalt along the shoulder are hard to tell apart. You cut the front wheel to miss the gash of a crater. A horn explodes behind you. You yank the handlebars back the other way. In the rubble the front wheel loses hold, stutters sideways, and then the back wheel skids the other way, and then you're on the ground. Ahead of you, a big green car pulls off the street, heaves to a stop so quick its rear end lifts to where you can see its axle. Its brakelights go out, its door swings open, and a woman in a long blue coat is hurrying back your way. You're up, your bike picked up, by the time she gets to you and bends down and takes your shoulders in her hands.

"My God, honey, are you okay?"

"Yes."

Your leg feels like a spear has come up through your shoe and driven its tip into your knee. Your hands burn where you put them out to keep from landing on your face. Your handlebars are twisted sideways to where you'd go in circles if you tried to hold them straight.

"I didn't mean to scare you," she says. "When you turned like that, I thought you were coming out into the street."

"It's okay. I'm sorry."

You want her to leave before she sees your handlebars. Before you have to move and she sees the way your knee hurts. But she still has hold of your shoulders, and her face is right there, close enough to see creases in her thick lipstick, to see how her skin is dusted white the way pork chops look when your mother dips them in flour, how there are fractures in the dust that follow the lines around her mouth like tiny riverbeds. In her almost black sunglasses you can see your own face, the way you're squinting, more than you can her eyes.

"Do you hurt anywhere?"

"No."

"Are you sure?"

"I'm okay."

"Here. Let me look at your hands."

You let her take your hands. You catch your bike against your side. Her deep brown hair drops forward and her coat falls open. Her perfume startles you. The neck of her mint-colored blouse makes you look away. Her hands are so warm they're almost hot.

"Why, they're freezing, honey," she says. "Look how red. Where are your gloves?"

"I'm okay."

"No, baby," she says. "You need gloves." She rubs your knuckles with her thumbs. Her fingernails are the same amazing red as her lipstick. She turns your hands over. Grit covers your raw-looking palms like pepper. She brushes them clean.

"What are these?" she says. "Blisters?"

The ones that were there this morning in the crooks of your thumbs and palms are nothing now but raw red circles. She's looking at you again.

"My God, honey, did you burn yourself or something?"

"No."

"What are they from?"

"Just raking."

"Raking?" she says. "What on earth have you been raking?"

"My yard."

"You're supposed to wear gloves when you're raking, honey."

"I know. I got some."

"Where?"

"At home."

"Where's home?"

"Back there somewhere."

"Are you lost?"

"No."

"Where were you going?"

"To town."

"Here," she says. "Let me brush you off."

She comes around your bike. And then her hands are busy brushing off your shoulders, your back, your butt, down the legs of your pants while you stand there trying not to move.

"That's better," she finally says. "Now you wait here a minute."

"I'm okay."

"You just wait."

You watch her walk back to her car. Her long blue coat moves like the drapes in the ranchhouse with the windows open. Blazing chrome letters across the trunk of her car say Pontiac. When she walks your way again, she's got a big white purse, looking through it, and by the time she gets to you she's holding out a couple of dollar bills.

"Here," she says. "Take this."

You look at her. She shakes her head.

"No, honey. Don't be scared. Here."

You reach up, take the two bills from her hand, stand there not knowing what to do with them.

"When you get into town, I want you to buy yourself a nice warm pair of gloves," she says. "Maybe some wool mittens."

"Okay."

"They have them in lots of colors," she says. "What's your favorite color, honey?"

"I don't know," you say. "I guess blue maybe."

"Then you get yourself a nice warm pair of blue ones," she says. "And the next time I see you, I want to see you wearing them. Okay? If it's this cold? Or you're raking?"

"Okay."

"Now put that money in your pocket. Right there. That one."

You look down at your jacket and put the bills in the pocket she's pointing to.

"Okay," she says. The lines in her face relax. "Okay."

"Thank you."

"You're cute," she says. "You're a handsome little guy."

"Thank you." Your face goes hot again. But this time you remember what your father said about compliments. "You're pretty," you say. And then you say, "Your car's neat too."

She smiles. Her sunglasses keep you from telling what part of your face she's looking at. And then she reaches out and her fingers touch your ear. And then she goes. You watch the tailpipe shudder when the engine starts, a line of smoke come shooting out when she revs it, the brakelights come on and go out again. Her sunglasses appear for a second in the mirror on her door. And then she pulls out and drives away.

You wait until you know she can't look back in her mirror and see you. You test your leg, and there it is, where you left it, the tip of the spear in your knee. You brace the wheel and twist the handlebars to where they're straight again. Swing onto the seat. Put force to the pedal. The pain is so quick you almost lose the bike again. And so you walk. Learn quick that when you walk on the outside edge of your foot you can keep from limping. When you get to the street where all the stores are, you walk your bike along the sidewalk, past the grills and bumpers of cars parked slanted to the gutter, past the dark glass doors and decorated windows of the stores, through women with their purses and their colored sacks, sometimes the shirts and belts of men, while you search the stores on both sides of the street for the store you rode down here to find.

Finally they're almost gone. The white lines of empty parking spaces are angled out into the traffic. This far toward the end of Main Street the slabs of blank cement in the sunlight make the sidewalk feel like the only people who ever come this far are people who are lost. Ahead of you, on down the block, houses and yards start taking over again. You start to feel lost yourself. Lost and stupid. In your knee the spear of pain has turned to mud. In the sun with your jacket open to its heat you can't stop shivering. In the huge windows of an old brick building, on a floor the size of a ballroom, you can see three gleaming cars, and a man at a desk in a corner raises his head just long enough to see that the only thing that has changed outside is you. Ashamed, you look away, across the street, and there it is.

Hinkle Music.

You stop and stand there. The name in black on a white sign, surrounded by music notes, like you could sing its name if you knew the melody. You wait for a pickup and then a van and then a big gray car with a redheaded woman driving before you push your bike across. In the picture window on either side of the door, instruments hang like fish made out of gold, out of silver, out of polished wood, in an aquarium of air. A gold horn, curved double like a huge seahorse with a belly of pearl buttons and rods and flappers, the bottom curved back up and flared to where you can look down into its open throat. A long black skinny one, like an eel, the same kinds of buttons, its end flared too. A violin. A bright red guitar. You look close and see the long silver wires, fragile as spider thread, that hold them from tiny hooks up in the ceiling. The bottom of the window layered with paper songs, the kind your mother has, photographs of smiling singers on the covers, the names and faces faded pink and gray from lying in the sun. In silver letters on the glass door.

Hinkle Music.

You slip your bike between the brick walls of Hinkle Music and the next store over. You crack the door, look, step inside, close the door behind you. You're alone. Alone in a big room with a long wood floor and a glass counter running down a long side wall and a ceiling so high there's room for the long white tubular lights to hang halfway down to the floor and still be where you'd need a ladder to reach them. The air has the dry and sour shoe polish smell of the rooms in the big abandoned house on the ranch with the caved-in roof where nobody had lived for maybe fifty years. The house with the pond whose bottom had the softest mud you'd ever waded in. Where Susan Morrow stood on the bank and took her swimsuit off and showed you what it looked like not to have a penis.

Hinkle Music. You listen. Nothing.

You take a few more steps inside. Hung on the walls and ranked around the floor and on shelves through the glass fronts of the counters are more instruments than you've ever seen. A violin as tall as your father that only a giant could play. Horns with their pipes coiled like knots made out of gold. Thin silver complicated tubes you didn't know had to come apart to fit inside their cases. Cases you didn't know were lined with rich blue velvet. Instruments you never knew existed. Every instrument around you the instrument that could have made the sound you heard in the cattle truck. All of them silent. Like they're holding back from laughing. Like they're waiting for you to guess which one of them it was. You wish you could die and your father could come and get your bike and give it to someone poor.

"Hello, sonny."

CHAPTER 4

THE VOICE brings you around like a rifle shot. The pain in your knee is so quick and sharp you whimper and take the weight off your leg too fast and almost fall. Out of nowhere, behind the counter, a man, an older man who wasn't there before, who wouldn't have had the time to get there if he'd had to come from somewhere else. You wonder if he's been there all along, on his knees, watching you from behind the counter through the glass, since you first came in his door and started to look around and were just about to leave.

"My gosh," he says. "Are you okay?"

"Sure," you say quick.

"I didn't mean to scare you," he says.

He's tall and thin with the same long face that Manny has except that he's not Mexican. But the same half-kidding look where his eyes are just these long curves of wet silver between his eyelids. The same long forehead back to where his gray hair finally starts. The same long nose. The same broad and easy smile that could go a lot broader if it wanted to. Except where Manny's lips are almost black, his are this grayish pink.

"I wasn't scared," you tell him.

In the long gully of his neck his Adam's apple is almost as big as the knot of his green tie. It doesn't move. The slack in the collar of his white shirt makes you wonder if he used to be fat and then went skinny. A baggy light blue vest that looks like a button-up sweater, the sleeves gone, the sleeves of his shirt where the sleeves of his sweater should be, rolled up to just above his elbows. And then you're quick to look back at him, at his eyes, before he can tell that you're looking at everything else.

"Aren't we supposed to be in school?" he says.

"We just moved here." It comes out quick. Quick to where he just looks at you like he's wondering if you're lying.

"Oh," he says. "You're the new kid in town." He lays the biggest hands you've ever seen on the glass top of the counter. His face turns serious. "I've heard about you."

All you can do is stare at him. Look him in the eyes the way you're supposed to look at grownups.

"You have?"

"Why sure I have. The whole town has. I was wondering when you were gonna pay me a visit."

"Nobody knows me."

"You're sure about that."

The woman with the Pontiac. The man who sold your father the wheelbarrow and all the tools. The man who looked up from the desk in the room across the street with the cars inside it could have called. Told him you were coming. To hide behind the counter.

"Yes," you say. "Nobody."

You watch his smile spread back into his cheeks and his cheeks fold back in deep furled lines like tent flaps toward his ears.

"I'm just kidding," he says. "I just wanted you to feel famous there."

"Famous?"

"Every musician should feel famous," he says. "At least for a minute."

"I'm not a musician."

He lifts his hand, holds it up, wags it back and forth. "Sure you are," he says. "You're in my store." He puts his hand on the counter again. "So what can I do for you? What are you looking for?"

"I don't know."

"Just decided to wander in?" he says. "Keep me company?"

It's been in your head, deep inside your ears, for four days now, and you haven't thought about what was going to happen, what to do when you got here.

"I heard this sound," you finally say.

"Sound?"

"On the radio."

"A sound," he says.

You could have thought of how to leave. How to wait for him to look away and then not be there when he looked your way again. How to tell him all the money you had was a couple of dollar bills you were supposed to spend on gloves. A way that wouldn't make him mad enough to run you out the door and tell you to never come back again.

"Yes."

"Okay," he says. "You heard a sound on the radio. Was it a song? Music?"

"Music."

"An instrument?"

"It wasn't singing."

"You know what kind of instrument?"

"No."

"Okay," he says. "That's why you're here. To find out what it was."

"I guess so."

"Do you play anything?"

"Piano."

"So it's not a piano. Or you'd know."

You hadn't thought of that. "It's not a guitar either," you say quick. "Or an organ."

"Well, that's good," he says. "That narrows the field some. Anything else? The name of the song? The kind of music?"

Sheepherder music. The other word that Manny said, bringing the cattle truck down off Soldier Summit, the word you feel stupid now for not remembering.

"It's not drums either."

"Remember the radio station?"

You could have looked at the dial. Looked at the number where the needle was when Hidalgo stopped turning the knob.

"No, sir."

"Okay." Standing up straight. Taking a slow look that moves from the deep back of the long store all the way up to the front. "It's a good thing I know how to play most of these."

"Play them?"

"That's the only way we're gonna find your sound, son," he says. "Your job is to let me know when we get to the right one."

Suddenly this is out of hand. This man just minding his business until he made the mistake of having you walk into his store. In the pockets of your jacket you tighten your hands into fists to hide the blisters.

"You don't have to."

"Why not?"

"It's not important. Honest."

"Sure it is," he says. "It'll be fun. Like a treasure hunt. It's been a slow morning anyway." He looks down through the countertop. "So," he says. "We might as well start here."

You watch him reach inside a door behind the counter. Watch his big hand bring out an open case with dark blue velvet cradling three silver tubes. Watch him set it on the counter, pick up the tubes, fit them together to make one tube, twist them to bring their long thin silver levers and pearl buttons into line. Everything he's doing because you're here.

"Now this is called a flute," he says. "Ever heard one?"

"I don't know."

"Then here goes. Listen."

You watch him arrange his fingers along the pearl buttons, put one end of the tube up under his mouth, draw his lips into the thin gray line of a lizard's mouth. A whistling sound plays a quick hoarse burst of a melody. You watch his fingers move, the levers twitch, the tiny lids of valves snap up and down, wait until he finishes, when he lowers the instrument down from his face.

"Sound familiar?" he says.

If you could just go home. Then he could just go back to what he was doing before you came in here.

"Like whistling?"

"Like the sound you heard on the radio."

"No."

"Close?" he says.

"Not really." And then you think you could have lied. Told him yes. Told him thanks for helping you. Gone back out the door. Grabbed your bike. By now you could be out of sight. But you couldn't. Not because he'd know. Because you can think about leaving all you want and it doesn't matter. Because while he was playing, something changed to where you couldn't leave, even if someone came in and said that your house was burning down or your bike was being swiped.

"What was different?" the man behind the counter says.

"The whistling part."

"Okay," he says. "That's one down." You watch him lay the silver tube across the open case and look through the countertop again. "If a flute's not close, it probably won't be this one either," he says. "But what the heck. Let's take it for a ride."

The instrument this time looks like a midget version of the first one. In his big hands it almost vanishes. With the spider legs of his long fingers he plays the same quick melody, but the sound this time is high and tiny, like a little kid whistling, and he plays it like he's making fun of it, bobbing his head, wagging his shoulders, keeping his eyes on you until he's finished.

"Look at that," he says. "I had you smiling there for a minute."

You can feel it in your face. You look at the floor.

"Come here, son. Come on over. Take a look at this close up."

From where you've been standing since you came in the store, two steps bring you to the counter, where you can take your weight off your knee again. His big hand holds the instrument out in front of you. There's an almost healed cut across one of his fingertips. A thick vein wraps up across the top of his gray-haired wrist into his hand. One of the buttons on his vest is smaller and lighter blue than the other ones. You look back at the instrument and keep your hands in your pockets.

"Silly little thing, huh?" he says.

You look close. Like grasshoppers, like the army truck gauges you took apart in La Sal, it amazes you that something so tiny can be so complicated.

"What is it?"

"A piccolo."

"Is it a toy?"

"A toy." He laughs. "No, it's actually a serious instrument. Grown men pay good money for these little whistles. And then play them in orchestras."

"In orchestras?"

"Yep," he says, shaking his head. "In front of dressed up people. Imagine that."

You understand that it's okay for you to laugh too. Still smiling, shaking his head, he lays the little instrument on the countertop, moves down the counter, stops at a cabinet whose shelves are lined with a hundred different harmonicas.

"It's not a harmonica," you say quick. "I forgot about them."

"Okay," he says. "Not a harmonica."

"I've got one," you say.

"Well. Then you'd know."

You watch him turn to the wall behind him, where polished black pipes in different sizes with their own intricate systems of levers and buttons are hung on padded hooks.

"Okay. Let's see here."

He reaches up, takes down the longest and fattest one, turns around with it, holds it in his open hands in front of you. Close up you can see that the pipe is folded back on itself to look like two separate pipes. Like a bent straw made out of steel, like you could drink soda out of it, a crooked little tube twists out of the end of the shorter pipe.

"So," he says. "What do you think of this beauty?"

"What is it?"

"A bassoon."

"What does it sound like?"

"Like a flute. Just a lot deeper," he says, making his voice go low, a record slowing down when you switch the player off.

"What's that part?"

"This little pigtail here? That's the mouthpiece. That's where you blow."

"It looks weird."

"It's a strange old bird," he says. "Strange and tough. This one's barely used. I sold it to a young man two years ago and he brought it back maybe a month later and swapped it for an electric bass. It's been here ever since. Not real popular. Not something you'd hear on the radio."

"Okay."

He turns around and sets it back onto its hooks. "I could be wrong," he says. "If I am, we can always come back to it. The trouble is that it takes a reed. Like this clarinet here or this oboe. Know what a reed is?"

"A plant." Quick. Like in class. Something you know. "They grow around reservoirs."

"Okay," he says. "This is different. Think of a popsicle stick. You whittle down one of its ends until it's real thin, almost like paper. When you blow on it a certain way, it vibrates and makes a sound. Like a kazoo, sort of."

"A what?"

"Never had a kazoo?"

"I guess not."

"Okay," he says. "Ever put wax paper on a comb and blow on it?"

"Yeah," you say. "It made my lips tickle."

"Okay," he says. "A reed works the same way almost."

"We used to use grass blades."

"Grass?"

"Yeah. We'd put them between our thumbs and blow."

"Really," he says. "Show me how."

Change notes by using your thumbs to change how tight the blade is. You wish you could show him. Show him something you know instead. But then he'd see your hands.

"I can't without grass," you say. "But it works. Honest."

"I'm sure it does," he says. "Now. You've got to wet a reed before you play. So we'll do the simple stuff first. Stuff we can play without going to much trouble."

"Okay."

You watch him look across the store. "Okey doke," he says. "Strings." He goes down to the end of the counter, comes out from behind it, crosses the wood floor, reaches up and takes a violin and a long stick off the back wall.

"Know what this is?" he says.

"A violin."

"Know what it sounds like?"

"I think so."

"Let's make sure." You watch him swing the violin up to his neck and settle it under his chin. Hear the quick chirps when he cuts the stick across the strings. "Might not be in tune, but we'll get the idea."

Standing there in the back of the store, he plays with his elbows out, his eyes closed, his knees going in small slow circles, smiling, a private smile that makes you look away and watch his hands instead. You know the song. Know it from listening to Hidalgo strum through it on his big guitar, slow and lazy, with Manny and George and the other sheepherders out smoking on the porch of the bunkhouse humming along soft, in pieces. In the back of the store you watch him play through the whole first verse. It amazes you that he knows a Mexican song.

"I know that song," you say, as soon as he lowers the violin and the stick. When you see his eyes still closed you think you should have given him more time. He opens them slow like he doesn't want to disturb the rest of his face.

"Greensleeves," he says. "Famous old ballad."

"Greensleeves?"

"My wife's favorite song." He winks at you. "It made her fall in love with me. I play it now and then to make sure she stays that way."

"That's its name?"

"Well," he says, "there's a Christmas version too. What Child Is This. Maybe that's the one you know."

"I just know the one you played."

You watch him hang the violin and the stick back on the wall. "So," he says. "I can tell that wasn't the sound we're looking for," he says.

"No. I would've told you."

"Was it close? Closer than the flute?"

"Maybe," you say. "No." And then you say, "I can't tell."

"Okay. Then we'll keep going."

He starts looking for another instrument.

"What's that?" you say. "That really big one?"

He turns around to face the giant violin you saw standing in back when you first came in. It stands as tall as his shoulders. "Ah," he says. "This." He wraps his hand around its neck. Tilts it forward off its cradle. Spins it back and forth on the long pin sticking out its bottom. "It's what they call a double bass. But it has other names. Contrabass, standup bass, fretless bass, you name it. All depends on who's playing it."

"Who's it for?"

"Whoever comes in and buys it."

"I mean . . ."

"You mean who plays it?"

"Yeah."

"Bass players," he says. And then he laughs. "I see. You think it's played like a violin. Boy, you'd have to be a big fellow to do that. Goliath. Paul Bunyan. Nope. You play it just the way it stands. Like this."

He brings his other hand across the big brown polished belly of the instrument to where the long thick strings run up its long black spine.

When the hooked ends of his long fingers start plucking them, the notes are deep and fat and regular, a steady thumping pulse you can feel deep in your chest. Across the room, from the counter, something makes a quick hard little rattle when he plucks a certain string. It's a rattle you know. The necklace of tiny brown beads hung on the radio knob, dropped down across the metal grill of the speaker, the silver cross at the bottom, the quick and regular rattle the beads made on the speaker grill when Hidalgo reached across and turned up the sound on the radio so you could hear it better.

"Holy cow."

"This is it?" he says.

"Yeah," you say. "No. Yes." You shake your head, start fresh, like taking another shot at spelling a word you were way too eager to spell to get started right. "I mean sort of."

He stops playing and looks at you. "Sort of?"

"Yeah," you say. "It was there too."

"It was there too?"

"With the other sound. In the truck. On the radio."

"You mean playing along?"

"Yeah. Playing along. Together."

"Excellent," he says. "Playing along." He rests his hand on the big round shoulder of the giant violin. "Then I'd say that what you heard was probably jazz."

When you hear it, you suddenly don't have a house to catch fire, a bike to swipe, a father or mother or brothers or sisters, anything outside this store to care about.

"That's what he said. Jazz. I remember now."

"Slow down, son. Who said?"

"The man who moved us here."

"He told you it was jazz?"

"He said it was Mexican jazz. He said it was sheepherder music."

"Sheepherder music?"

"Yeah. That's what he is. He's a sheepherder. He herds sheep. Up in the mountains."

"A sheepherder moved you here?"

"Two of them. Hidalgo and Manny."

"Where did you happen to move from?"

"A ranch."

"A ranch? No kidding. Where?"

"Down by Moab."

"Okay," he says. "I know Moab. Did you grow up there?"

"Kind of."

"Must've been a swell time," he says, "growing up on a ranch."

"I had a horse."

"Your very own horse?"

"They gave him to me. He used to be a workhorse. But they didn't need him anymore. He was too old. So they said I could have him."

"A workhorse, huh? They're pretty big."

"Yeah. I'd have to get him next to a fence to get on him."

"You owned him? You took care of him?"

"Yeah. I'd feed him and wash him and stuff. Help them change his shoes. Put him in his stall at night and let him out in the morning."

"You rode him too?"

"Yeah. Bareback. He didn't like saddles. He wasn't used to them."

"Like an Indian?" he says.

"Yeah," you say. "His name was Rex."

"Rex," he says. "Now there's a name for a horse." He leans the big violin back against its cradle and gives its belly a couple of slaps. "Now. Let's get back to business here. Jazz. I think what we're looking for is a horn. Probably—"

He looks past you toward the front of the store. You hear the door behind you open. The noise from the street.

"Hold on," he says. "I'll be right back."

At the front of the store, a man is closing the door, a man with your father's build, short and husky, a thick brown beard and glasses and a levi jacket your father would never wear. In his hand a black case. From its size and shape you guess there's a guitar inside it.

"Morning, Bruce," says the man you've been talking to.

"Hey, John," says the man with the case.

John. You watch them shake hands across the counter. Then you look away. Make yourself invisible while they do business. Why he'd care about Rex. Why you got carried away. You don't care. A while ago you wanted a thousand people in here so you could sneak away and nobody would care. Now all you want is to have it to yourself again. Stands are racked with sheet music. You keep your hands in your jacket pockets and look at their covers. Patti Page. Carl Perkins. Bill Haley. Elvis Presley. Names you don't know. Faces you've never seen but songs you know your mother would never play. And people you know too. Brahms and Ravel and Chopin. The yellow Hanon book you learned scales and arpeggios from. Soon you hear the ring and slam of the cash register. Them say goodbye. The burst of noise from the street. The front door close it out again. And then he's back.

"Okay," he says. "Horns. My guess is it's one of these. This one's a saxophone. It takes a reed too, so we'll hold off for now. But here's my other guess."

You watch him lift a huge gold horn off a rack on the wall and lower its coil of fat gold pipes down over his head. A thin gold tube lifts a silver bowl the size of half a walnut up toward his face. Up over his shoulder the instrument opens out to a mouth as big as a foghorn on the Queen Elizabeth.

"Behold the mighty sousaphone," he says.

"Wow. It's sure big."

"Wait till you hear it," he says. He puts his mouth against the silver bowl, breathes in hard, pulls his lips tight, and suddenly Rex is letting out one of his workhorse farts behind you. You start laughing. He rolls his eyes your way, plays another note, takes his mouth off the bowl. "What's so funny?" he says, out of breath, stern and hurt, like you're making fun of him.

"I'm sorry," you say, but you can't do anything to keep your face from smiling.

"That wasn't your sound?"

"No." And then you start laughing again. "That was Rex."

"Rex," he says. "Your horse." And then he laughs too. "I've heard some funny names for this thing, but that's a new one. Well, I'm sure old Rex is feeling better now."

"He'd let one go," you say, "and then he'd jump and trot away. Like it scared him."

"Wouldn't it you?" he says. "Have a noise like that come out of you?"

"Yeah." Still laughing. Watching him lift the big instrument like a fancy gold toilet up off his head and hang it on the wall again.

"I was kidding," he says. "I didn't think that was your sound. I just like playing that old thing now and then." He takes a couple of steps along the wall. "Now," he says. And reaches up for it. "Here's the one I meant."

CHAPTER 5

THE HORN he reaches for this time is smaller than the rest of them. Plain where they were fancy. Straight out instead of curved. You think of the tiny bugle one of your cavalry soldiers has. A pipe moves forward straight from the end where you blow it, loops back, then loops forward again and straight ahead and opens out to a flare where the sound comes out. Three tubes with little silver plungers stand in a row at the center and make it different from your soldier's bugle. That and how it's not a toy but real.

"This one," he says.

He threads his hands around the tubes, sets his fingers on the plungers, puts the silver mouthpiece up against his mouth, pulls the corners of his lips back into the lean skin of his cheeks in this small tight smile, points the instrument down toward the floor. And suddenly, after the long whining climb along the ledge of the road carved high in the wall of the canyon above the coal trains down below, you're coming down off Soldier Summit again. The truck picking up speed. Miles of high gray rolling desert through the windshield past the hood. Miles of sky. In the distance the long low silver ghosts of mountain ranges rising and rising again behind each other from land so far away it seems impossible that it could ever end and that you could ever get there if it did. The curve of the world. The way Miss Jenny said there were places where you could see enough of the world to see the way it curved and know for yourself that it was round. The road a long gray winding snake that disappears behind shallow hills and then appears again. On the radio a song made out of the sound you're hearing now. The sound whose pull you feel again, deep down inside, the pull so deep it owns you the way it owned you then, a sound you'd follow anywhere.

He stops and lowers the instrument to his chest. You follow it down.

"Looks like we found it."

You can't talk. Just stare at it. He brings it down in front of you where it lies across his open hands.

"Here," he says. "Hold it."

Your hands come out of your pockets. Lift it off his. In your own hands you can feel its heft. See how the gold pipe that starts from the mouthpiece loops through the three tubes with the plungers. How the plungers are silver caps on silver rods. How the pipe loops through other pipes, then makes its final loop, and from there a straight run forward to where it flowers out in a sudden smooth curve to the polished gold flare where the sound comes out. You look up at his face. Out of all your questions you don't know which one to start with. You look back down at the instrument until you do.

"What's it called?"

"It's a trumpet."

"A trumpet?"

"Yep."

You've heard the word. Past where the instrument lies across your hands you can see his corduroy pants and understand that he'll stand there and give you all the time you want to take.

"Is it made out of gold?"

You hear him laugh. "If it were, son, there's not a soul in the whole town of Bountiful who could buy it. No. It's brass. Like all these horns. They're all brass."

"These are how you make different notes?"

"They're one way. They're called valves."

"This too?"

"This what?"

"This." You use your head to point at it.

"No," he says. "That's a spit valve."

"Spit?"

"Yep. The way you play it, you can't help but blow a little spit into the thing. So every so often you open that little valve and blow."

"Does spit come out?"

"Sure does," he says. And then he says, "Your hands look pretty rough there."

Through the polished gold tubing of the instrument, you see them, the pink bumps of the blisters, the scabbed red patches of the ones that busted, the scuffs of dirt from the road that stayed there after the woman brushed your hands off.

"I'm sorry. I forgot. Here."

"That's okay," he says. "You're not going to hurt it. It's just metal."

"I just forgot. Honest."

"It's okay, son. Look at me."

You raise your eyes.

"Where'd you got those blisters?"

"Raking."

"Raking what?"

"Our yard. To get the rocks out."

"That's what gloves are for, son. To keep you from getting blistered."

"I know."

"Do they hurt?" he says.

"They're okay."

"You're sure."

"Yes."

"Okay." And then he suddenly grins and reaches his big hands out. "So?" he says. "What do you think? Can you see yourself playing that thing?"

You look down at the trumpet, then up at him, then down again. You see the small hook on top where you saw him put his little finger, the ring down lower where you saw him put one of the fingers of his other hand.

"Is it hard to learn?"

"Depends how much you practice. How well you want to play."

"Harder than piano?"

"It's different, son. You only play one note at a time, and you can't sing while you're playing it. But it takes practice the same way a piano does."

"Does it take long before you can play something?"

"Before you can play something well, sure, it takes some time. That doesn't mean you can't play things along the way. Do you know your scales?"

"Yeah."

"Then you've got a head start. The hardest instrument to learn is always the first one. The second one's easier. Especially if you know the scales. After that, the more of them you learn, the quicker you get to learn the next one."

You think of all the instruments he's already played. How easy he could play them. How he could have gone and played every instrument left in the store if he'd had to.

"Are you famous?" you ask.

"Me?" He laughs. "Maybe to my grandkids."

"But you can play everything."

"That comes with the territory, son. You can't do an honest job of selling something when you don't know anything about it."

You turn the trumpet over and look at the other side, at the spindles that brace the tubes apart, at the number 1 and number 3 stamped into the brass of the outside tubes, at the letters USA stamped into the center tube, at the small white tag stuck to the polished brass of the horn part, at the tiny writing on it, at the dollar sign in front of the number 130.

Rufus barking back at you like crazy through the dust coming off the back of Manny's pickup. In the same wild confusion where you knew you couldn't chase him, but couldn't help yourself, you look away quick, at other parts of the instrument, foreign in your hands with all its shiny gold, like something stolen, a man's instrument, a man with a job like your father has, not just a kid like you. You wonder if Manny knew. If he was laughing on the inside at how stupid you were to be thinking you could have one. And then you look up at the man in front of you, from his sweater to his face, a stranger again, a man who thought you were someone else, and you hold the instrument out to him.

"Thanks for helping me," you say.

"That's all you wanted?" he says.

"Yeah."

"Just to know what it was?"

"Yeah."

"You weren't planning on getting one?"

"Not really." You feel your face catch fire. Like you'd just come in here to waste his time. You look at the instrument still there in your hands, and then back up at him, wishing he'd bring up his hands and take it back and hang it on its hooks again where it came from.

"What's the matter, son?"

"Nothing."

"You sure?"

"Yeah."

"You look like you just lost your favorite toad."

"I don't have a toad."

After a minute he says, "You saw the price?"

"No." Your lips fumble. Your eyes slip down and catch on the button on his sweater that doesn't belong there. You break them loose and bring them down again to the instrument you're holding. "Maybe."

"It's not cheap," he says. "That's for sure. But that's between your folks and me."

"Okay."

"Just bring them in," he says. "That's what all the kids do. Frankly, it surprised me to see you here alone, but that gave us time to find what it was you wanted. I'm just glad we did."

Your father laughing that big rolling open clownish laugh at how unbelievable you keep making yourself while his eyes and the rest of his face stay mean. Your mother with her hands to her startled face like you just came up and stabbed her. You standing there with your hands torn up and your knee hurt and two dollar bills in your pocket from some woman they don't know.

"Yeah," you say. "I'm glad too."

"You tell them I'm here till six," he says. "If they can't make it during the week, I'm here all day Saturday."

"Okay." And then you've got the reason you need to get out of his store and on your bike again. You look up at his face and hold the instrument up higher. "I'll go home and tell them."

He still won't reach for it. Just keeps looking down at you past the two dark caves of his big nostrils.

"What's wrong, son?"

"Nothing. I gotta go home. So I can tell them."

He finally takes the trumpet off your hands. You get them back into your pockets and watch him turn around and hang it back on the wall where it was before you came along. You figure you'll wait till he turns around again to say goodbye. But then he just looks at you some more. And then he turns his head and looks at the front of the store where the windows are with the instruments in the air.

"I forgot," he says. "You just moved here. I'm sorry."

"For what?"

"Moving's expensive, son. Your folks had to pay those sheepherders. They don't have the money right now. I should've thought of that. Before I opened my big mouth."

"I can still tell them. For when they get the money."

"My wife keeps telling me I'm getting slow," he says. "Let me see those hands again."

You take them out of your pockets. He takes them and stoops down where he can look at them.

"Must be some yard you've got."

"Yeah," you say. And then you say, "We're getting topsoil tomorrow."

"And you've got to rake that, too?"

"Yeah. I guess."

He lets your hands go. You go to put them back in your pockets. Then you don't know what to do with them. Just let them hang there in the open.

"You look like you don't mind working," he says.

"Not really."

"Ever work for money before?"

"I guess."

"What kind of work?"
"On the ranch sometimes."
"Doing what?"
"Cleaning out stalls. Feeding the steers. Stacking hay bales up."
"Hay bales?"
"Yeah."
"Aren't they kinda heavy?"
"You need to know how to lift them." Remembering what Kent the ranch hand said and the way he showed you. Catch them off guard.
"Who paid you?"
Maybe that's it. Why you can't go yet. He wants you to pay him for finding it. For all his time you took. You wonder if two dollars is enough.
"The ranch hands. Sometimes the foreman."
"I want you to wait right here," he says. "Actually, step over to the counter here and wait for me. I'll be right back."

He goes to the back of the store and through an open door. You cross the floor to the counter where you can give him the two dollar bills. He comes back and lays a black suitcase on the counter. You can tell the leather's fake from where it's worn in places down to frayed black paper. In other places the leather's cut to where you see slices of wood inside the cuts. But the wide bands of scraped and scratched brown leather stitched around the ends of the case are real. Three of the corners have bottlecaps stuck out of them. In the fourth corner there's just a ring and some puncture holes where the bottlecap was. He lays his big hands on top of each other on the lid of the case.
"Yardwork," he says.
You stare at him. Watch his grin spread and slowly make his narrow face go broad.
"Yardwork," he says again.
"Yardwork?"
"That's how this is gonna happen."
"How?"
"It's April, right?"
"Yeah?"
"When people start working on their yards again. You know. Get rid of all the winter stuff. Get ready for summer."
"I guess. Yeah."
"Or," he says. He lifts his hand and unfolds his long first finger in the air in front of you. "Or. And here's the good part. Hire someone to do it all for them."
"Hire someone?"

"Clean out their flowerbeds," he says. "Mow their grass. Plant their flowers. Someone like you."

"Me?"

"Either you," he says, "or whoever beats you there." His eyebrows lift and his voice goes down to where he's whispering. "And that gets us to the other good part."

"What?"

"Your timing. It's perfect."

"How?"

"Your competition," he says. He brings his hand back down and lays it across his other hand again. "All the other kids you'd have to fight for the work. Kids your age. They're still in school. They'll be there another month or so."

"Okay."

"You'll have the whole darned neighborhood to yourself."

"What neighborhood?"

"Yours. The one you just moved to. I'm sure you've got neighbors who'd rather hire a kid like you to do it than have to do it themselves. Trust me. I'm a businessman. Just knock on their doors and ask them."

"They'd hire me?"

"You've got hands, don't you? You're a tough kid. You don't mind working."

"They'd pay me?"

"If they don't, I'll want to know who they are, and where they live."

And then he stands back up, takes his hands off the case, turns it around on the countertop to where the handle faces you. It's wrapped in black electrical tape.

"Open it up," he says.

"Me?"

"You."

You reach up, flip open the gold latch on either side of the handle, then bring your hands back down again.

"That's not open," he says. "Keep going."

You reach for the sides of the lid. Lift it slowly up and back on hinges off the case. He takes the lid off your hands and raises it back the rest of the way. Inside, in a cradle of deep blue velvet, is another trumpet.

"It's a trade-in," he says. "I haven't cleaned it up yet."

The blue velvet is shiny in places where the fuzz is gone. Worn through in other places to where you can see raw wood. The trumpet has the form and size of the first one but immediately looks more intricately made. The smaller tubes are sleeved with silver here and there. Gold and silver braces are held in place with diamond-shaped fittings formed to the curves of the tubes. The fitting for the mouthpiece isn't round but beveled like a small gold nut you could take off with a crescent wrench. What you notice too is how the pipes and tubes and valves are dull with this hazed brown spotted skin and tarnished with bruises the color of watered-down blood. A dent in one of the smaller loops. Patches of black crud collected where someone used to hold it.

"So? What do you think?"

"It looks tired," you say. "Like it just wants to rest."

"It's a little beat up. But it's a good instrument."

"It looks like it's sad," you say.

"It'll clean right up," he says. "Don't worry about that."

Almost like it's ashamed, you're thinking, being out here in the open, in front of the new one on the wall, the way you were ashamed when you saw the little tag.

"Go ahead," he says. "Take it out."

You lift it off its cradle. And then you don't know what to do with it. He leaves the case open, turns and walks to the end of the counter, comes out around it.

"Here," he says. He takes the trumpet, and then your hand, and arranges it so that you're holding the casings for the valves. "Okay," he says. "Let me know if I hurt your blisters." He takes your other hand, tucks in your thumb above your other thumb, hooks your little finger in the hook just past the valves, leaving your three middle fingers positioned on the stems of the plungers. "Now," he says. "That's how you hold it."

"Okay."

"Go ahead. Work the valves."

You feel their light plunging give when you push them down. Feel their easy rebound when you lift your fingers.

"They feel okay?"

"I don't know. Yeah."

"I know it's not as nice as the first one."

"I love this one," you say.

"You do?" he says.

"Yeah. I love this one."

"Okay," he says. "Hold on now." He takes a silver mouthpiece out of a hole in the case, slips it into the small open tube, reaches into his front pocket, pulls out a black felt rag, breathes into it, runs it around inside the mouthpiece. "Now. Hold it up. Pretend you're playing it. Let's see how you look."

You raise it up, put the mouthpiece to the center of your lips the way you saw him do, to where you just feel the hard round ring of the silver bowl. Your eyes follow the slender tube of brass out to where your fingers are, and then past them, out to the rise of the opening, where another small dent keeps the curve of the metal from being perfectly smooth.

"Don't be shy," he says. "Hold it up tight. Look here." You turn your eyes to where you can see him. "Now. Do this." You watch him pull his lips tight across his teeth again, turn the ends up slightly like a lizard smiling, press them together, make this buzzing noise you know how to make yourself.

"Go ahead," he says. "Try it."

It's over almost as soon as you start. Most of what you blow goes out the sides of your mouth. The part that goes through the mouthpiece comes out the other end ten times as big and loud as anything Rex could ever let go, so nasty it makes you yank the trumpet off your face.

"Keep your lips tighter," he says. "Pull them into a little smile. Point them right into the mouthpiece."

This time you keep from blowing your lips off the cup of the mouthpiece. This time, somewhere in the middle of all the nasty stuff, just for a second, it's there, the sound of that steel bird. You look at him.

"Yep," he says. "I heard it too."

"Wow."

"Now you're famous."

"That was me."

"Try it again," he says. "Work the valves this time."

You raise the mouthpiece up again and try to hold your lips together. But the way you can't stop smiling keeps pulling them apart.

He laughs. "Looks like we need to calm down some."

"I'm sorry."

"That's a mighty big grin for a little guy," he says.

"I'm sorry."

"Here," he says. "Looks like we're done playing for the day. Let me take that."

You reach the trumpet out to him, let it go, watch him look it over.

"Don't worry about these dents," he says. "They won't hurt the sound. We can take them out later on, once you've got it paid for."

"How much is it?"

"How does forty dollars sound?"

"Forty dollars?"

"I don't mean right now," he says. He lays the trumpet back on its side in the case and looks down at you. "No kid comes in here with forty dollars in his pocket." And then he smiles. "Remember what we talked about a minute ago?"

"What?"

"Yardwork."

"Yeah."

"Ever hear of something called layaway?"

"No."

"Well," he says, "that's where you give me a deposit, and then a payment every week or so, and I keep it here for you until you get the rest of it paid off. And then it's yours."

"What's a deposit?"

"Anything you can give me right now."

"I've got two dollars. Here. Look."

He looks at the bills in your hand. "Okay," he says. "Two dollars down, thirty-eight to go. Hold onto it for a minute. Let me get my receipt book."

Part 2

Angels

CHAPTER 6

THE AVENUES. Brewery Hill. Rose Park. Like a school, a kitchen, other people and their houses, wherever you lived there was always a churchhouse too. In La Sal it was the long green narrow shack with a tin roof and sagebrush yard that stood on a rise just up behind the schoolhouse.

On Fridays they showed movies there. A clattering projector shot the changing light up the long aisle between the folding chairs, up past all the people watching, onto a large screen on a wobbly stand, the picture rippling and watery sometimes when the windows were open for air. Cowboy movies starring guys like Randolph Scott. A movie about giant ants, desert ants as big as trucks, ants that made the grating shriek of crickets. That night, coming awake in the small back room where you and Karl bunked, you heard them shrieking through the window, loud and close, the back yard full of them, their giant pincers opening to grab and tear away the wall into your room. You started screaming. Knowing they could hear you only scared you into screaming harder. And then Karl started screaming in the bunk beneath you. And then your father came exploding through the door, in the dark, in the temple garments he used for underwear and pajamas, swearing in Swiss, bellowing. Gopvertori! Verdammt nun amal! What's wrong in here!

Your room had this old piece of rug that was purple and green and blue with flowers the size of lettuce heads. In the middle, where every night stood the old round-bottomed steel mixing bowl where you and Karl peed when you needed to, there was this nimbus where the color was almost gone, this circle that was faded almost white where you and Karl would stand in the dark, take aim, and look for the bowl by the ringing sound your pee would make when it found the steel. That night, when your father came crashing in the dark into the room, his foot caught the edge of the bowl and sent it airborne along with all the pee it held. You were screaming at him. The ants are coming! The ants are coming! He didn't care. In the dark he found your legs and then your shoulders, rolled you on your stomach, and held you there while his broad hand came down hard and stinging, over and over and over, on your butt.

They used the churchhouse too for special days like Halloween, and Christmas, where one year, in your own pajamas, holding a borrowed teddy bear, you stood in front of the gathered population of the ranch and sang I Saw Mommy Kissing Santa Claus, scared and bewildered because all the grownups, all your mother's and father's friends, were smiling like everything was okay. That night, singing about seeing him kiss your mother under the mistletoe, Santa was still a real guy to you. You stood there in your pajamas singing and all you could think about was where your father was. All you could think about was telling Santa to leave your mother alone. All you could think about was your mother being this sudden stranger. This woman you didn't know who only looked like her.

The churchhouse here is huge, like the Queen Elizabeth, the vast wall of its dull black hull, the dizzying feel where it plunged deep into the lapping black water. Everywhere you've moved to, everywhere you've lived, there's never been a Sunday as important as the first one. Your mother made sure all of you were ready. Your father made sure he got you all here early. And now you've got time to kill with Karl. The chapel has a high steep roof like the ski chalets in the calendars your father gets from Switzerland. Huge beams run straight up the two steep slabs of the ceiling and touch where they reach the peak the way you draw railroad tracks to where they meet at their vanishing point. The ceiling reaches up and seizes so much space it feels like it has weather. The floor is filled with rows of benches, the wood pale and sleek and polished, for maybe a hundred times as many people as the whole ranch had. In the front of the chapel, below the stand where the leaders sit, below the high pulpit, a gray-haired man plays music, soft and measured, on an organ as big as a sheepherder's trailer. You and Karl move up the aisle slow. The gray-haired man plays a rack of wooden pedals big as oars with his shoes off, in his socks, moving his legs and feet across them like he's doggy paddling.

"How come he needs all those keys?" Karl whispers.

"I don't know."

"How come he's got his shoes off?"

"I don't know."

At the back of the chapel, there's a big picture window, for a room with a door on the side and a sign that says Cry Room. From inside the room you look through the window at the chapel.

"What's a cry room?" says Karl.

"A room where people cry, I guess."

"About what?"

"If someone tells a sad story. Like Mama did in La Sal."

"So if they start crying, they come in here?"

"I guess."

"It's got speakers. Look."

Behind the cry room, tall, massive planks of polished wood make up the back wall of the chapel, planks set with long black hinges.

"They can move this wall," you say. "Look. Hinges."

"What's behind it?"

You go out through the foyer and through a door and there's the biggest basketball court you've ever seen, the polished floor striped white and red, baskets at both ends. Across the court, in the far wall, heavy red curtains are drawn across a stage whose hushed floor you reach through a side door and up four dim stairs.

"I wonder—"

"What?"

How your trumpet would sound from up here with the drapes pulled back.

"If they put on plays or something," you say instead.

Whether to tell your family. You've already thought it out. Not till you bring it home. Not till it's yours for sure. Because if you told them now they'd talk you out of it before you even had a way to pay for it.

"Someone could open the curtain," Karl says. "We'd just be standing here."

"We got lost."

"Yeah," he says. "That's what we'll say."

You remember one thing from your life in Switzerland. On a second story balcony, afternoon, in a high chair, the wooden tray of your little table, your mother feeding you the limp white and the rich gold yolk of a soft boiled egg with a teaspoon from a brown shell, its top cracked off, kids in the courtyard below, playing, riding bikes and tricycles. You don't remember the beginning or the end. Just the spoon in your mother's hand and the live immediacy of her face. After that, the next moment you remember is a stairwell, broad and carpeted, somewhere inside the Queen Elizabeth, a white life preserver in a framed glass case in the wall. You were lost. You take Karl down a long hall lined with classrooms and offices and bathrooms. In one room a small round tile pool is set into the floor. You tell Karl it's where they baptize little kids.

"You could go fishing in there," he says.

"Yeah."

"You wouldn't even need a pole. Just jump in and grab 'em."

"Yeah."

Through the closed window across the pool, you hear seagulls crying, the birds you saw when you got here, big and white and gray, the crying whirl of dirty wings around a small corral of garbage cans at the end of the parking lot.

The Avenues. Brewery Hill. Rose Park. La Sal. Suddenly, standing there with him, the places you've known as home make you put your arm around his shoulder, make you restless for Molly and Roy and Maggie.

"Let's go back," you say.

"Okay."

The foyer is crowded now with people, men and women standing around talking, shaking hands, the air like water boiling with their voices. Suddenly there's a kid in front of you, his hand out, his grin fixed with this weird electrocuted-looking confidence that makes you think that if you shake his hand you'll feel electricity.

"Hi," he says, right in your face, big and loud like you're clear across the foyer. "I'm Mike."

He's wearing this short sleeved shirt with little blue sailing ships all over it and a green bow tie clipped to its collar. His pale brown hair is oiled down, but with wild patches, like a flattop he's growing out that isn't long enough to comb yet.

"Hi."

"You're new, right?"

"Yeah."

"Welcome to the Thirteenth Ward."

"Thanks."

"Are you a Deacon?"

"No."

"Not yet, huh?"

"No."

His grin makes you glance away, at Karl, at the big glass case he's looking at, glass shelves loaded with plaques and trophies, gold statues of men with gold basketballs, bats, bowling balls. You look back at the kid named Mike.

"How about you?"

"Since last November," he says.

"I turn twelve in June."

"You'll be in my Sunday School class. Brother Rodgers."

"Who's he?"

"The teacher," he says. And then he says, "What's your name?"

"Shake."

You see his grin twitch, his hand reach out again and falter, his confidence flicker like the lights in the basement apartment in Brewery Hill whenever the fridge came on.

"No," you say. "That's really it."

"Your real name?"

"Yeah."

"Shake. Okay. What's your last name?"

"Tauffler."

"Mine's Lilly."

And then you don't know what to say because you're wondering why all the little ships on his shirt are ships instead of flowers.

"Are all these trophies from here?" you ask him.

"Yeah," he says. "They are."

"Pretty good."

"Yeah. You bet we are. We're the best."

You break away from the electric hold of his confidence, take Karl away from the trophy case, find your way through the open doors of the chapel. Instantaneously things change. The noise from the foyer is hushed to the mutter of hidden crickets. You can feel the soft and lush and tranquil music from the organ pipes in the carpet beneath your shoes. You move up the aisle. More people sit in the mostly empty benches. A group of girls. Some families. An old couple. They're talking, sometimes laughing, but their voices evaporate before they reach you. You see your mother with Roy and Molly and Maggie in a bench back toward the rear. Nobody knows you. Nobody knows any of you. Your mother raises her hand. Karl heads off in her direction.

You keep looking for your father. And then, across the chapel, up toward the front, you see him, on the edge of a bench by himself, pitched forward, his hands and the forearms of his suit on the bench in front of him. His face is canted so that his line of sight would pass above the stand and land somewhere on the high wall above the organ pipes if he were looking at anything. But you can tell he's not. Even across the width of this place. Even though his eyes are open. The wall is only where he's rested them while he sits there, not aware of you, not aware of anyone, so openly alone you wish you could take your eyes away.

But you can't. His black hair is combed in waves back off his forehead to where you can see this private and wild profusion of gratitude and relief in his quiet smile. Even across the chapel you can see this restless and haunting uncertainty in ridged furrows in his forehead. Along his jaw you can see the skin twitch with the quiet clacking of his back teeth. The Avenues. Brewery Hill. Rose Park. He got you here, where he'll make his stand, like Randolph Scott in the cowboy movies you saw in the churchhouse in La Sal. Will he be enough. The question you can't look away from. The question that reaches down and holds your stomach in its hand and doesn't let you look away. He got you here. This churchhouse where everyone in the neighborhood could live if it just had bedrooms. This place that all along was where he was going. Where nobody knows him yet. Will he be enough. He doesn't know. You can tell. He's your father. He doesn't know.

Chapter 7

"George Doby."

"Here."

Four girls and seven guys sit loose around the bare-walled room on gray steel folding chairs. You remember being the new kid in La Sal, and before that too, listening to a teacher call out the names of kids you'll end up being buddies with, and so you've learned to pay attention to the roll call. The girls sit together in a row across the linoleum floor. George Doby is a big kid in a baggy brown sweater with a rough-boned face and dark brown gleaming hair carved like chocolate frosting into cresting waves. The girl named Ann Cook has the wideset eyes and scattered freckles of a kid you knew in La Sal. The girl named Julie Quist has short blond hair and ringlets like a chain across her forehead. She's the only girl with makeup more than lipstick.

At the front of the room, in brown pants, a salt-and-pepper-looking sport coat, huge black clodhopper shoes with soles that look big enough to let him walk across a river, the man who's calling names leans on his hands on a small table, head down, using a pen to check them off in his roll book. His name is Brother Rodgers. He's got thick black shining hair and a square face tanned this deep red brown. The tops of his ears are so burned they're almost as black as his hair. You can tell he's strong. But you wonder how he got so brown. If he's a farmer. Behind him there's a blackboard. A single tall thin window off his right that looks at the parking lot.

"Chip Keller."

"Yo."

Brother Rodgers looks up at the kid named Keller. A kid who looks like Errol Flynn except for all these freckles and these scared and darting rabbit eyes like there's a time bomb ticking down inside his head and he doesn't know what time it's set for.

"Yo," says Brother Rodgers. His eyes are the silver blue of water reflected off chrome while he stares Keller down.

"I meant here," Keller finally says.

"I know you're here," he says to his roll book. "I know you're all here. I'm just checking your names off. Steve Strand."

In the back of the room the kid named Steve Strand looks cool, his face bored, his hair combed clean from the knife line where he's parted it. When he catches you looking it's only his eyes that let you know. He doesn't say anything to his name.

"Mike Lilly," says Brother Rodgers.

"Here. Oops. Sorry."

"Susan Lake."

The name you've been waiting for. The quiet dark-haired girl on the chair between Julie Quist and Ann Cook. She doesn't say anything either. But from the way her eyes turn down and her hands go restless in the lap of her yellow dress you can tell that she just heard her name. Susan Lake. The last girl you'd want to find you working in her yard. You wish you knew where she lived so you'd know which house to skip tomorrow.

A kid named Johnny Jasperson with a serious face and mud-colored hair. A kid named Bobby West, maybe half a year ahead of you in size, his dark hair combed like Tony Curtis. A girl named Brenda Horn with eyes like an antelope and an expectant smile like something is always about to be funny. Next to you a redheaded kid named Melvin Yenchik. By then you've gone back to Susan Lake, parking your eyes on the floor at her feet, stealing looks up, at her shoes, the thin white leather straps that keep her white shoes on her feet, imagining her fingers lacing the straps through their tiny silver buckles.

"I don't know you."

When you look at him he's got you, staring you down, while you ride out the sudden heat of everyone's attention.

"I know," you say.

"Your name," he says.

"Shake." And then you say, "Shake Tauffler."

"Your real name," he says. "And spell your last one."

"It's real," you say.

You can see it go through his head. Raspberry or vanilla. Rattle and roll. See him think and then decide to drop it.

"It's true," says Lilly. "He told me."

"All right," Brother Rodgers says, and writes it down. "Spell me your last name."

He closes his roll book, comes around the table, lets his head rove back and forth across the class like the turret of a human lighthouse.

"You kids ever look at another church and wonder if it's true?"

Yenchik raises his hand.

"Melvin," Brother Rodgers says.

"No."

"Why not?"

"Cuz all the churches around here are Mormon ones."

"Okay. Let's pretend they're all different. Catholic, Baptist, Methodist. This one, the one we're in, it's Lutheran. All kinds of churches. And you've got neighbors sitting around their kitchen tables inventing new ones right and left."

He pockets his hands, takes a couple of steps across the room, bends forward to look out the window. In the sunlight, the side of his face looks eroded, shelves of dark sandstone.

"In fact," he says, "let's make some up. Say your mom belongs to one called the Church of the Bleeding Quilt. Your dad goes to the Church of the Right Shoe. Your uncle, he goes to the Church of the Holy Nose."

Laughter goes rolling around the room. Susan Lake does this faint elusive smile without letting you see her teeth.

"Now take Bobby here," he says, nodding at West. "What church you think he'd go to?"

"That's easy," says Doby. "The Church of the Pontiac."

"Pontiacs weren't even around then," says West. "Dope."

"Hey," says Brother Rodgers. "We're just making things up."

"The Church of the Huge Sunglasses," says Keller.

"Yeah?" says West. "How about you? The Church of—"

"Easy, Bobby," says Brother Rodgers. "How about George here?"

"The Brylcreem Church," says West.

"The Church of the Same Old Sweater," says Keller.

"It's not old," says Doby.

"It sure is the same," says Keller.

"Hold on," says Brother Rodgers. "We're not doing this to insult each other. What about Mike?"

"The Petunia Church," says Doby.

"The Church of the Pansy," says Yenchik.

"What did I just say?" says Brother Rodgers.

"Sorry," says Yenchik.

"It's okay," says Lilly, smiling this smile like he's old enough to be Yenchik's babysitter, like Yenchik just burped on him. "I'm used to it."

"The Church of the Lost Comb," says West.

"Petunia's his nickname," says Doby. "I wasn't insulting him."

"How about Johnny," says Brother Rodgers.

Nobody says anything. When you look at Jasperson, he's looking at his knees, unhappy. He looks poor, like your buddy Jimmy Dennison from the trailer court in La Sal, but he looks like a kid you can't joke about without him getting mad.

"The Church of the Good Kid," Lilly finally puts out there. West puts his elbows on his knees and his head down in his hands.

"How about Chip?" says Brother Rodgers.

"Keller?" says West. "The High Pockets Church."

"The Church of the Worm Eaters," says Doby.

"It was only one," says Keller. "And I made a buck off it."

"How about the girls?" says Yenchik. "How about Horn there?"

"How about you?" says Brenda Horn. "The Church of the Snoozing Melvin."

"The Church of the Hatchet Face," Yenchik fires back. The look he gets from Brenda Horn looks just like what he said, like she could take her facc and split his skull in half, and then it's him, not Jasperson, who reminds you of the bad kind of luck Jimmy Dennison always had.

"The Church of the Stupid Red Hair," she says.

"That'll do, Melvin," says Brother Rodgers. "You too, Brenda."

From Brenda Horn you cut a quick look at Susan Lake. The church of her white shoes. The church of her hands in the lap of her yellow dress. The church of wishing she'd talk so you'd know what her voice was like. Of being so beautiful it doesn't matter.

"How about him?" says Julie Quist. "Shake?"

"Be my guest," says Brother Rodgers.

"The Church of the New Kid," says Julie Quist.

"Isn't there already a church called the Shakers?" says Lilly, smiling your way.

"The Cowboy Church," says Yenchik.

"Where's your boots?" says West. "Your pistols?"

"The Church of the Git Along Little Dogie," says Doby.

"That's it," says Brother Rodgers, and everyone's got their attention where he wants it, on him, coming back from the window and squaring off in front of the class.

"See what happens?" he says. "Right away things get hostile. You start going after each other. Another five minutes you'd be slugging it out. Say you're all in the same family. Every Sunday, you scatter for different churches, come home all worked up, and spend the rest of the day fighting each other tooth and nail over which one's true. Brenda. Knock that off."

You look at Brenda Horn in time to see her pull her tongue back in but keep her hatchet look on Yenchik.

"And there you are," says Brother Rodgers. "A kid stuck in the middle. To get along, you go to the Church of the Pontiac, the Brylcreem

Church, the High Pockets Church. You try them all. Then, out of nowhere, everyone starts going somewhere else. Bobby, say, gets converted to the Church of the Snoozing Melvin, and he's just as sure it's true as he was a week ago about the Petunia Church."

He rides out another roll of laughter around the little room. This time he doesn't smile.

"Okay," he says. "Let's get serious. Wouldn't you wonder? Wouldn't you want to know what was real and what was smoke?"

His head does the lighthouse again. Nobody says anything. Keller sits there picking at something on his knuckle.

"No," he says. "You don't have to. Someone did all that wondering and questioning for you. Know who I'm talking about? Johnny?"

"Joseph Smith," says Jasperson, dropping his hand.

"Joseph Smith," says Brother Rodgers. "Twelve years old when he started questioning the crazy religious stuff around him. Your age. And everything you just made up is how it was. All these quack crackpot religions swearing they're the one true one. Him just a farmboy living with his dirt poor family in upstate New York. Helping out his dad when his dad can find work. Hey," he says. "Bobby. Melvin. Knock it off."

"He started it," says Yenchik. "He pinched the back of my knee."

"He was falling asleep," says West.

"No I wasn't."

"Anyone falls asleep, I'll handle it. Now. That family we just made up was Joseph's real family. His mom was Presbyterian, his older brother probably some church that believed in splitting logs, his sister, I don't know, maybe some church that believed needlepoint would get you into Heaven. But on Sunday they'd all head off for different churches and come home convinced that everyone else in the family was going to Hell. A week later it'd be something else."

He turns his head to where Brenda Horn is giggling something to Ann Cook.

"Brenda," he says. "What's so funny."

Ann Cook jumps and looks down hard at her lap. You've already figured out that Brenda Horn is one of those girls who can't keep from smiling when she gets embarrassed.

"Why would anyone want to invent a church?" she says.

Brother Rodgers raises his black eyebrows and breaks the brown skin of his forehead into creases. "Good question," he says. "But back to Joseph. By the time he's fourteen he's more confused than ever. All he wants to know is which church is true. One night, reading the Bible, he reads a scripture saying that if anyone lacks wisdom, let him ask of God. So he figures he will."

Brother Rodgers steps back, bumps the little table with his butt, reaches down and grabs the edge with both his hands. Where his knuckles stretch you can see lines of white down inside the brown cuts of their wrinkles.

"So one spring day, he walks off the farm he's working with his dad, goes to the woods, finds a place we call the Sacred Grove, gets down and starts to pray. Like I hope Melvin here does before he goes to sleep."

You look at Yenchik in time to catch his head doing a rebound off his chest. Nobody laughs this time because Brother Rodgers isn't smiling.

"Sorry," says Yenchik.

"Come up here, son," Brother Rodgers says.

Yenchik gets off his chair and comes forward, past you, half the tail of his shirt out the back of his pants.

"You and I are going to do a little acting," says Brother Rodgers. "You get to be Joseph Smith. Hey," he says, standing back. "There's even a faint resemblance."

"Who are you?" says Yenchik.

"Me? The bad guy. Climb up on the table here. On your knees. We'll need to improvise. Pretend it's a place in the woods."

"Like this?" says Yenchik.

"Face the audience. That's what actors do. Okay. I want you to start praying. Out loud."

"For what?"

"For God to tell you which church is true."

"I already know."

"Not if you're Joseph Smith. Start praying."

"In front of everybody?"

"That's right. Never prayed out loud before?"

"No."

"Well, that makes you perfect. Joseph hadn't either. Now put your hands together and close your eyes and go. I'll be right here behind you."

Yenchik turns his head to watch Brother Rodgers go around the table.

"No matter what happens, keep praying. The more scared you get, the harder you'll need to pray."

And then, with Brother Rodgers standing right behind him, Yenchik runs out of ways to slow this down. He takes a wild look around, comes up with nothing, looks down, brings up his hands and puts his palms together, closes his eyes.

"Dear God," he says. "Please—"

Quick as a snake, Brother Rodgers grabs him from behind, covers his mouth with one hand, lifts him off the table. Yenchik's eyes pop open wild. His arms are pinned but his legs start going, running up a hill that isn't there, kicking the table and sending it skidding a couple of feet your way. One of his shoes goes flying. Doby reaches out and catches it. Behind Brother Rodgers' big brown hand you can hear Yenchik hollering like he's underwater.

"Don't yell," Brother Rodgers says quietly. "Pray. It's the only way you'll beat me. It's your only hope."

Yenchik locks his wild eyes on you.

"I'm serious," says Brother Rodgers. "The last thing I want you to do is pray. I'll kill you if I have to."

You nod at Yenchik. Pray. He tries to nod back. You can hear his muffled hollering change its tune.

"You praying?" says Brother Rodgers. Yenchik tries to nod again. Brother Rodgers grabs and holds him tighter. Yenchik starts fighting again. His shirt's out of his pants now all the way, and there are flashes of his white belly, his bellybutton, the band of his underpants where his pants are slipping. "Pray harder," Brother Rodgers says. "I'm still stronger."

This time, hanging there in Brother Rodgers' arms, Yenchik goes limp and his eyes go closed. Brother Rodgers lets his mouth go some.

"Dear Heavenly Father please help me—"

"Harder," Brother Rodgers says. "Your life depends on it."

"Dear Heavenly Father please don't let him kill me—"

Brother Rodgers tightens his hold again.

"Dear Heavenly Father please save me."

"Save me from the forces of evil," says Brother Rodgers.

"Save me from the forces of evil!" says Yenchik.

"Save me from the darkness of the unseen world."

"Save me from the darkness of the unseen world!"

"Save me from the hosts of Satan."

"Save me from the hosts of Satan!"

"Save me from Satan."

"Save me from Satan!"

Brother Rodgers opens his arms back. Yenchik doesn't have far to go, but he drops like a long sack of corn, barely catches himself on the table, stumbles to his feet, stands there dizzy. Brother Rodgers takes him by the shoulders.

"You okay, Melvin?"

"That wasn't fair," says Yenchik. "You're too strong."

"Tuck your shirt in. Who's got his shoe? George?" He rubs the top of Yenchik's head. "Good work."

CHAPTER 8

THE FIRST VISION. The story you've heard for so long it feels like you were born listening to it. Just never like this. After Yenchik gets his shirt tucked in, his pants pulled up, his shoe back on, after Susan Lake's lips are closed again, Brother Rodgers dusts his hands off.

"So that's what happens the minute Joseph starts to pray. He's seized by this invisible force. He can't talk. Think I'm strong? I'm nothing compared to what's got hold of Joseph. I'm guessing you kids get what it was."

Lilly and Jasperson both raise their hands. But West just comes out and says it.

"Satan."

"Yep. He knows what's about to happen. That the hundreds of years he's ruled the Earth are about to end. Anyway, right at the last second, Satan lets Joseph go. He just vanishes. Poof. What happens next?"

Lilly and Jasperson both shoot their hands in the air again.

"Johnny."

"A pillar of light comes down from Heaven."

"Light brighter than the noonday sun. What else?"

"God and Jesus are in the light."

"Too bad we can't act that one out. But imagine it. You're fourteen, you don't have two nickels to rub together, you've just wrestled Satan, and now you're looking at God the Father and Jesus Christ, standing in midair, introducing themselves. Joseph doesn't know what to do. So he does what he came for. He asks Jesus which church is true. Anyone know what Jesus tells him? Ann?"

"None of them?" says Ann Cook.

"Right," says Brother Rodgers. "They're all false. All of them. But the big news Jesus has for Joseph is that he's chosen him to restore his true church to the Earth again. The Church of Jesus Christ."

Brother Rodgers pockets his hands and ambles over to the window.

He steps into the hard sunlight on the floor and you can see hairlines of blazing dust in the creases of his shoes.

"They leave. The grove's just a grove again. Like nothing happened. Joseph barely has the strength to drag himself home. What's the first thing he does when he gets there?" He smiles at the parking lot. "He tells his mom that Presbyterianism is wrong." He shakes his head. "Just walks in and tells her her religion's wrong. That takes nerve."

He ambles back from the window and stands in front of his table. In the wrinkled cloth of his pants you can see his fingers fiddling, with change, with keys, whatever's in his pocket.

"Poor," he finally says. "Humble. Uneducated. Fourteen. Just a farmboy. Here's what I want you to remember. Because he did all the questioning, you don't need to question anything yourself. Because he did all the searching for the truth, you don't need to search for it. Because he heard from Jesus that every other church was false, you'll never need to chase around to anyone else's house of worship. You can just be kids. Just be kids, come to class on Sunday, learn the true Gospel of Jesus Christ, because a farmboy did all the questioning you could ever think of doing, and got all the answers you'll ever need."

On the way out of class, the kid named Doby introduces himself, and then the kid named West.

"Doing anything right now?" says West.

"Going home, I guess."

"Wanna hang out?" says West. "Just for a minute?"

"Sure."

The hangout is out back, through the double glass back doors, a patch of grass just off the sidewalk to the parking lot, where families are crossing the asphalt and getting into their station wagons, where you can see the whale of the Buick between two newer cars. Yenchik and Keller and Jasperson join you. West puts on these big black sunglasses.

"I'm Keller."

"Hi."

"So you're from a ranch," says West.

"Yeah."

"When'd you move here?"

"Last week."

"Where's your house?"

"On this circle. At the end of Crestwood Drive."

"What grade you in?"

"Not any." And then you say, "I was in sixth."

"That's what we're in," says Doby. "What do you mean was?"

You look at him. He's looking friendly. He just wants to know. And so you tell him they let you out early so your family could move here.

"I don't wear my pants high," Keller says to West.

"Yeah you do," says West.

"Your name really Shake?" says Yenchik.

"Yeah."

"Why? You like milkshakes?"

"They're okay."

"Which car's yours?" says West.

You find the green Buick and point it out.

"Tell your dad to get a Pontiac."

"Jeez, West," says Jasperson. "Not everyone has to have a Pontiac."

"Says the guy whose dad drives a Rambler," says West. "Go have a vision, Jasperson."

"Why don't you stop being sacrilegious."

"Rodgers, man," says Yenchik. "He's strong."

What he did to Yenchik. You thinking he'd be crazy too if it wasn't for the way he could pin you down with the steady calm in those chrome blue eyes. If he always does that kind of stuff, you want to ask, but you'd only end up looking newer than you do already.

"He climbs telephone poles all day," says Doby. "You'd be strong too."

"He was a Marine," says Keller.

"How was I supposed to pray out loud with his hand on my mouth?" says Yenchik.

"You oughta stay awake from now on," says West.

Yenchik's face clouds up. He looks off at the parking lot.

"He shoulda used you," says Keller to Jasperson. "The way you love to pray."

The way Jasperson looks uncomfortable, and then looks down at the grass, you can tell he's thinking the same thing.

"That's what he does?" you say. "Climb telephone poles?"

"Yeah," says Doby.

"Wrestling with Satan," says West. "You believe that?"

"You're supposed to believe everything," says Jasperson.

"Satan's tough. He coulda just broke his neck if he wanted him dead. I don't get it."

"God would of made his neck too strong," says Jasperson.

"He coulda clubbed him with a rock."

"God woulda blasted the rock to smithereens," says Jasperson.

"Rodgers coulda busted my neck in a second," says Yenchik.

"What do you mean, I'm supposed to believe everything?" West says to Jasperson.

"You're supposed to," says Jasperson. "You're not supposed to question things."

"I don't," says West. "I just need for them to make sense."

"Maybe you're not smart enough."

"I'm smart enough to know whose ass your breath comes out of," says West.

"Jeez, West," says Doby. "Let up."

You see your mother enter the parking lot with Karl next to her, Roy behind them, and way back, Molly walking at Maggie's baby pace, holding her hand. You wonder where your father is. Not why he's not with them. Just where he is.

"I gotta go," you say.

"See you tonight."

"Are you a Scout?" says Keller.

Cleaning out stables, piling hay bales, saving up money for your uniform.

"Yeah."

"We got Scouts on Tuesday."

"Okay."

The Avenues. Brewery Hill. Rose Park. La Sal. Like here, wherever you lived, you weren't done. You always got dressed up again at night and went back to church for Sacrament Meeting.

"This evening we'd like to welcome another new family to our ward. Harold and Elizabeth Tauffler and their five children. Brother Tauffler, Sister Tauffler, could you stand up, give all of us a chance to get a look at you?"

The names of your mother and father come down like rain from the big speakers in the timbered sky of the ceiling. You keep your head down and your eyes on the rack for the hymnbook in the back of the bench just past your knees. Next to you, your mother shifts Maggie to one arm, and uses the back of the bench in front of her to pull herself to her feet. Without raising your sight, you can hear the rustle of heads turning, the ripple of eyes across the congregation, looking for her. The kids who will be your buddies are out there looking too. And a girl named Susan Lake. You know what they'll see. The combed waves of your mother's black hair off her clear temples. The obedience and bliss and modesty that can infuse her face and turn her smile radiant in an instant. Down the bench, past Roy and Molly, your father rises too, and up at the pulpit, the man you guess is the bishop, a big man in a brown suit, his clotted brown hair half gone and his big face gentle the way it commands this place, gives the congregation time to take your mother and father in.

"Good. Your children too, Harold and Elizabeth. That's right, boys.

Let's stand up. Your sisters too."

And then your whole family, you and Karl and Molly and Roy, have broken the surface of the congregation, the surface of this lake of smiling faces all around you. The bishop goes on talking.

"I hope all of you can join me in welcoming this good family to the Thirteenth Ward and make them feel at home among us. We've been told that Sister Tauffler's an accomplished organist. Well, the Lord's seen fit to bless us, because Brother Sorenson's planning on leaving us this spring."

CHAPTER 9

"YOU'RE JUST a child. How old are you?"

"I'll be twelve in June."

"What did you say your name was?"

"Shake Tauffler."

"Where do you live?"

"Over there. In the circle. We just moved here."

"Isn't there school today?"

"I finished sixth grade where we used to live."

"Do your parents know you're doing this?"

"You can call them."

"What kind of yardwork can you do?"

"Everything. I've got tools."

The doors of the neighborhood open mostly on women. Women whose first glance goes out over your head for someone taller or something more important. Sometimes they're holding bowls or dust rags or dish towels or babies or magazines. Sometimes they're wearing aprons or pedal pushers. Mostly they're in dresses. Sometimes they're older. But mostly they're around your mother's age. Sometimes you hear the waning growl of a vacuum cleaner being turned off. Sometimes the animated company of a tv. Sometimes you hear them cry through the door that they'll be right there. And sometimes there's a door that opens on a man, or on a little kid, who stares at you while you hear a woman cry out from a room inside the house somewhere and ask the kid who it is.

"I'm sorry, sweetie. My husband takes care of the yard."

"Okay. Thank you."

You use their driveways and walkways to let them know, in case they see you coming, that you respect their grass.

"I've got a boy close to your age who does it. I'm sorry."

Standing there wondering if the boy is one of the kids in your Sunday School class.

"Okay. Thank you."

You work your way down the long hill toward Orchard Drive, the border of the Thirteenth Ward, then back up the hill on the next street over. You work the side streets too. The sun burns through your short-sleeved shirt. Heat comes off the asphalt through your shoes. Under this much sunlight the houses look dead to where it surprises you when someone answers the door in an apron and wet hands or there's something going inside like a tv or radio or a baby crying.

"We do it ourselves. It's our hobby. I'm sorry, honey. But good luck"

"Okay. Thank you."

Almost all the yards are immaculate, the grass cut, the sprinklers going, the flowerbeds cleaned out and smoothed and ready for planting. Somctimes you have to stop and wait for a sprinkler to swing the other way.

"I've got rocks to move out back. But they're too big for you."

"How big?"

"Boulders. Bigger than you. Sorry."

"Okay. Thank you."

Your stomach lets you know it's time for lunch. To ignore it you cup your hands and feel the pipes of the trumpet in them and sometimes close your eyes and see it in your hands. By afternoon you've covered most of the streets below your street. You start working the streets that are higher than yours up the hillside.

"I'm sorry, sweetheart. But would you like some koolaid? You must be thirsty."

"That's okay. Thanks."

If you've been to the house where Susan Lake lives. Talked to her mother. You don't know. You figure you must have. To Brenda Horn's or Julie Quist's. To West's or Keller's. If one of the women who told you her husband did the yard was Sister Rodgers.

"How much do you charge?"

It's the oldest and the biggest house whose porch you've climbed, whose door you've knocked on, the only house whose steps are boards. Up on the highest street on the hillside. Behind it, the weeds and the brush take over again, take the hillside up toward the hills behind it and the mountains. It's by itself. On either side a bulldozer has scraped away the even skin of the weeds and opened the dirt and boulders for the basements of houses.

The woman in the doorway asking what you charge is old too. So old it's hard to look at her because she might see how old she is in the way you look at her. In her shadowed doorway her hair is so white its filaments are luminous, and her skin looks thin as handkerchief cloth held up to light, and the light comes from inside her somewhere, like she's in the process of dying, turning slowly into spirit, the cocoon of her body harboring her gradual change into an angel. Tough and raspy, her voice seems to resist the transformation, seems to say she isn't happy about what's happening. Her watery eyes wait for you to answer her, and her thin hand shakes where she holds the edge of her door.

"How much do I charge?"

"How much do I have to pay you," she says.

"I don't know," you say. And then you say, "That's up to you."

"Well," she says. She crabs up her face and squints at you and frowns. "What's your name?"

"Shake Tauffler."

And you stand there and let her look you over while you tell her again where you live, how you just moved here, why you're not in school, that you have your own tools.

"And you don't know how much to charge me."

"No."

"Are you a hard worker?"

"I sure am."

"I've got lots to do."

"Good."

"You know how to trim shrubs?"

"Yes."

"Cut grass?"

"Yes."

"Water things?"

"Yes."

"Tell flowers from weeds this time of year?"

"If you show me."

"Roll a tennis court?"

"I can find out. I can learn."

"Don't bring tools. I've got a shed full."

"Okay."

"You go around back. I'll meet you out there. Lupe," she calls into the room behind her, and you figure she's calling the Mexican woman who answered the door and then went away and got her. "Get this boy a glass of lemonade."

Your father gets home from work that afternoon with a brand new push-around spreader, some bags of grass seed, three garden hoses, two big sprinklers. Earlier, a truck left big square bags of peat moss stacked along the sidewalk, bags the size of the hay bales you used to throw on the trailer as the tractor pulled it slowly through the stubbled fields. He changes into his yard clothes, comes outside with his big portable radio, lays out an extension cord, tunes it, and you get to work to the sound of an orchestra. You listen for a piccolo. You've got a way to buy your trumpet. By sunset you and your father have done both yards. A sprinkler down on the lower part of the back yard sweeps a high sail made of a hundred thin jets of water back and forth. Through the water, red in the sunset, you can see all the way to the Great Salt Lake and the long black ridge of what your father says is Antelope Island.

His face and arms are blotched with peat moss where his sweat has turned it black and muddy. His shirt and hair are covered with dust that the sunset turns red too. It's on your arms and teeshirt and probably all over your face like his.

"That's it," he says. "Now we wait and see."

"For it to grow?"

"Yes," he says. He turns his big face west through the lazy sparkling sail of the water into the flaming sky where the sun has gone down behind Antelope Island.

"Is it okay if I get a job?"

"Doing what?" he says.

"Taking care of people's yards."

Now he looks at you. "What makes you think that people would hire you?"

"I don't know."

"They don't even know you."

"I can tell them."

"Why can't they do it themselves? Don't you think they have their own sons?"

"Not all of them."

"What do you plan to do with the money?"

"Save it." And then you say, "After I pay tithing."

"It's never too early to start saving for your mission, you know."

"I know."

"You have to pay fast offering too. Don't forget that."

"If I got a job could I keep it?"

"I don't see why not."

"What if I already had one? Could I keep that too?"

"What do you mean? Do you have one?"

"Yeah. If it's okay."

"What is it?"

"This old house on the street up the hill." And then you say, "She's old too. She's got a big yard and a tennis court."

"When did this happen?"

"This afternoon."

"Does your mother know?"

"No." And then you say, "I forgot."

Your father's face goes vexed.

"How much is she paying you?"

"Twenty cents an hour."

"That isn't bad," your father says. "Just remember who you are."

"I will."

"So," he says. "Let's clean up. Put these tools away. Then see what's left for dinner."

"We could use the sprinkler."

"For what?"

"To wash off."

He looks at you. Then he looks at the sprinkler. Through the blotches and lines of peat moss you can see the ridges in his face relax.

"By golly," he says. "Let's do it."

CHAPTER 10

TWENTY CENTS an hour. A dollar sixty a day. Eight dollars a week. Minus ten percent for tithing and you're left with seven dollars and twenty cents to take downtown each Saturday. That night, in your room, you calculate things out. You need forty-four dollars. Four for tithing. Two for the gloves you didn't spend the woman's money on. Thirty-eight for the trumpet. You stare at the numbers. Less than six weeks. You sketch up a calendar for the rest of April, all of May, and into June. You do everything again and it comes out the same way. Before your birthday.

Her name is Mrs. Harding. Her rambling back yard is a jackpot. Flowerbeds choked with clusters of limp stems and shriveled leaves and colorless flowers. Ragged shrubs and bushes and trees. Meandering stone paths with weeds in the cracks of dirt between them. Jigsaw patches of grass between the paths, the grass long and tired and yellow, stunting the early shoots of green. Things need water. In a back corner a chainlink fence two stories tall surrounds the red dirt of the first tennis court you've seen. Smeared ghosts of white stripes mark out what you guess are boundary lines. In the other corner the shaky plank doors of a shed swing back on a dark museum of hoses and ancient tools. Most of the tools are mysteries of spiderwebs and rust. The Mexican woman she called Lupe shakes rugs and dustmops over the railing off her wide back porch.

In the morning Mrs. Harding appears on her porch to show you what to do. She has you start by cleaning and sharpening her tools. Hobbling, faltering, using a black cane to keep herself from falling, she leads you around the yard and tells you where and what to use them for.

In the middle of the morning Lupe brings a glass of lemonade out to the shed. For lunch she's there with a glass of milk and a deviled ham sandwich and a damp washcloth for your hands. That afternoon she shows up with two glasses of lemonade.

"Come outside," she says. "Sit with me."

On a bench outside the shed you use the washcloth to wipe the oil and rust off your hands and then drink down your lemonade.

"Don't drink so fast," she says. "It's not good for you."

"I'm sorry."

"Here. Hold out your glass."

She pours half her glass into yours.

"Thank you."

"It's okay," she says. And then she says, "What made you come here?"

Her face is plump like the rest of her and her rich brown skin is the smoothest you've ever seen. Her dark eyes are so steady and deep and kind you could fall right into them and know you'd be okay.

"My dad bought a new house. Down on the circle."

"No. I mean to this house."

"I needed a job," you say.

"So you just come knocking?" she says. "You didn't know nothing?"

"Nothing about what?"

"Nothing about Mrs. Harding."

"I didn't know this house was here till I got here."

She holds you for a minute with her smile.

"You're new here."

"We moved here last week."

"Where from?"

"From a ranch in southern Utah."

"A ranch," she says. "That must have been a nice place for a boy to live."

"We had sheep and cattle," you say. "It was fun. They gave me an old workhorse."

"Ahh. Sheep. I bet you had some Mexicans working there."

"Two of them moved us here. Manny and Hidalgo. I got to ride in the truck with them. I gave Manny my dog Rufus. He said he'd make a good sheepdog out of him. He said he wouldn't change his name."

"Can I ask is your family Mormon?"

"Yeah," you say. "Yeah. We are."

She looks down into her glass. And then a quick wince goes through her face that makes her frown and narrow her eyes and raise her face and look off toward the bulldozer parked on the dirt next door. Then she looks at you, smiles, lowers her eyes.

"Mrs. Harding's a widow. Mr. Harding died long ago."

When you don't say anything she reaches over and pats your knee.

"I'm sorry her husband's dead," you say.

"They had four children," she says. "Four boys. All four of them are dead."

"Wow. That's sad."

"Her last son Paul, he lived here and did the yard before he died a year and a half ago," she says. "He was in his forties. You see where the branches of the shrubs and bushes are cut? Those are his cut marks."

"I saw them."

"Those dusty cars in the garage? You see them? The Cadillac convertible, that was her husband's. That fancy Mercedes Benz sports car was Paul's."

"I guess I'd keep them too."

"She was always proud of her yard. It didn't always look like this."

"What happened?"

"You're the first kid to come knocking. In the two years since she lost Paul."

"Maybe all the kids around here are rich," you say, thinking of Jasperson and Yenchik, knowing you're lying. "Maybe they don't need jobs."

"Mrs. Harding," says Lupe. "She's thrilled that you came to her."

She looks you straight in the eyes and smiles. Then puts her cool hand up to the side of your face. "I'm Lupe," she says. "Now we both have to get back to work."

At the end of the day Lupe brings a large tin basin of warm water and a towel and washcloth and fingernail brush out to the back porch for you. Mrs. Harding appears again to inspect you before she releases you for home.

That night you put on your uniform and head to the churchhouse for Scouts. Scoutmaster Haycock, a big friendly redheaded man, teaches you how to fix an electrical plug, and afterward, you and Keller and West and Doby and Jasperson and Strand head for home together. You tell them you've got a job. You tell them what you're doing. You tell them where.

"You work for that old bag?" says West.

"She's not a hag."

"Man," he says. "You got guts. She's scary."

"Why?"

"She poisoned all her kids. When they grew up. One after the other."

"Yeah? How come she's not in jail?"

"She used this stuff where they couldn't tell what it was."

"Yeah? Why?"

"She got scared they were planning on poisoning her. So they could get her money. Because she wouldn't die."

"Is she rich?"

"She's loaded. From her old man. You been in her garage?"

"Yeah."

"She still got that Gullwing?"

"I thought you were a Pontiac guy," says Jasperson.

"No," says West, looking at Jasperson. "I like Ramblers too."

"She's got a Cadillac and a Mercedes," you say.

"Yeah. Like I said. A Mercedes Gullwing."

"What's a Gullwing?"

"Its doors swing up. Like seagull wings. She got it for her last kid. He used to drive it around."

You stop. He looks and then turns and stops too. You wonder if this is where you'll have the fight that will set you off on the road to being buddies.

"She didn't poison him."

In the dark street you can feel it more than see it, the way he's looked you over, the way he's wondering too if you'll need to fight to go from here.

"If you can get me in her garage," he says, "I'll show you how those doors work." And then he says, "I'd love to see that thing up close."

For the first week you work under the urgent crossfire of two possibilities. The first that Mrs. Harding will die before you get all the money made you need. The second that Mr. Hinkle will change his mind, or get tired of waiting, or not remember you, and sell the trumpet to someone else. One of the possibilities is always there, standing guard, while you rake leaves and twigs and haul them up to the hillside beyond her yard. Sometimes both of them are there to keep you working. And sometimes you stand guard yourself, at the edge of her yard where her gray shrubs break and the rubble of the neighboring excavations starts, holding a rake, pruning shears, pretending you've got work there, keeping up a presence, letting the man in the bulldozer know her property's occupied, letting him know he's being watched. Sometimes he waves. With your face tough and warning you wave back.

Every morning Mrs. Harding comes out to show you what to do. At the end of the day she appears again to make sure you're clean before letting you go home. During the day, as long as Lupe's bringing you lemonade and a sandwich, you figure Mrs. Harding's still okay. And on Friday, after you've washed your face and ears and neck and shown her your scrubbed nails, she counts eight dollar bills into your hand.

"I didn't work a whole week," you say. "I didn't start till Tuesday."

"I know that," she says. "But it took you a day to find me. You deserve to be paid for that."

"Thanks, Mrs. Harding."

"Thanks nothing," she says. "You earned it."

The next afternoon, after your Saturday chores, you pedal downtown again and stop for a pair of gloves at J.C. Penney's. The most expensive pair they have are leather, big enough for your father's hands, and only cost a dollar forty something. You buy them for Father's Day. You wonder what the woman with the Pontiac would want you to do with the change. In front of Hinkle Music the same instruments hang on wire threads behind the windows. This time, in direct sunlight, the glass is streaked and the instruments are frosted with a film of blazing dust. Below them, the same sheet music lies fanned across the windowsill, the faces of the singers ghosts where they've lost their color to the sun.

A woman and a girl with a single dark brown braid down her back stand at the register. The girl holds a case for what you guess is a flute. In his glance from behind the register the absence of any recognition makes you look quickly at the floor. You remember wondering the last time you were here how you could leave. The chatter and ring of the register and the latch of the drawer. "Those pads should last her all the way to Carnegie Hall." The voice you remember. The snap of the woman's purse. "Thank you." You open and hold the door for them. The burst of noise from the street and then the quiet store with its quiet instruments. You look up and there's the same wide beaming grin you remember from the first time you finally made the sound.

"Well," he says. "I'll be a monkey's uncle."

"I got a job."

"I figured that's where you've been. Yardwork?"

"Yep."

"I knew it."

"I've got a payment too."

"That's what jobs are for."

"Here."

You put five dollar bills on the counter and lay two dimes in the lap of the top bill.

"Next week I can start bringing you more. Two dollars more."

"Seven twenty instead of five twenty?"

"Yes. Every week."

"Every Saturday?"

"Yes."

He slips a pencil out from inside his sweater vest and does some scribbling on the back of the receipt the woman left on the countertop.

"Second Saturday in June."

"Is that okay?"

"I'll make sure it's ready. Want a look at it?"

"No thanks."

"You sure? Long way to come just to make a payment."

"Yeah. I can wait till I'm done."

"So how's the job? Got lots of customers?"

"Just one."

"One? Must be a heck of a yard. A farm or something."

"Yeah. It's this rich old lady with a big old house and a tennis court."

"A tennis court? What's her name?"

"Mrs. Harding."

He smiles. "Margaret Harding?"

"I don't know her first name."

"That's who she is," he says.

"I didn't mean to call her old."

"Don't worry," he says. "She'd be the first to say it. She's no non-sense. Quite a woman."

"Do you know why she's rich?"

He looks at you, sharp and quick, his eyebrow raised, his face all of a sudden weathered like Manny's always looked in winter.

"Her husband made a fortune selling mining equipment out at Kennecott Copper." He pauses, looks down at the backs of his hands, straightens up again. "He didn't want a local girl. He wanted himself a city girl. So he went to Chicago and found her. A singer. City through and through. And beautiful. Raven black hair. Sang like an angel. He brought her back and married her. They had four kids. For some sad reason, all of them died young, in their forties. The last one, Paul, just a year or two ago. She's outlived every one of them."

"Someone said she poisoned them."

You watch his face go hard and weathered so that the skin reminds you of gray sand cut by wind into thin ledges.

"I told them it wasn't true," you're quick to say.

"Who told you that?" he says.

"A kid in my Scout troop."

"A Scout. He should know better."

You look down, ashamed for having West for a buddy, scared, won-dering if you've just lost your trumpet.

"It doesn't matter," he says. Turns his head away from you. Looks outside for a minute. When his face relaxes again it looks old.

"Are you Mormon?" he asks.

"Yes."

"Me too," he says. "She wasn't. So there were always rumors. Some worse than others. Makes me sad. I'm talking about my own people."

"I told the kid it wasn't true."

He smiles. "It broke her heart," he says, "seeing her boys die. Poisoned. That takes the cake."

"I'll tell him again."

"You know, when she came here, she threw herself into the community. Didn't stop to figure it out. Just made friends with everyone. Gave these wonderful parties. Invited everyone. I played at some of them. She'd turn that tennis court into a dance floor. Hang Japanese lanterns around. I'd play right there at the end of the court with my band. She knew she was rich. All it meant to her was sharing it."

"Would she sing?"

"Sometimes. She wasn't a showoff. Anything but. People would have to beg her. Two notes into any song and she'd have everyone's attention. Someone to Watch over Me. Stormy Weather. She could turn your bones to butter with her voice."

"Are those songs?"

"They tried to convert her at first. You know. The way we're taught to. She was polite to the point of being apologetic. But she was happy being Catholic. People couldn't handle that. It killed them. Guess it made them feel like they'd failed the Lord. And then the rumors started." He looks down at his hands. "Some of the worst rumors were started by people who danced on her tennis court." He looks at you. "Stormy Weather?" he says. "Yes." He looks toward the front of the store. "They're songs."

You want to know who it was who started them the way you've been keeping the bulldozer from getting too close to her property.

"Still kept giving parties. Still kept her head up. I'd go to church and hear one thing. I'd go to her parties and see another. Same people. Those rumors finally made a hermit out of her."

"Who were they?"

He studies you. You let him see the face the man in the bulldozer sees.

"I shouldn't be telling you this," he says, his voice the one you remember. "You caught me off guard there. Anyway, it doesn't matter. She's outlived most of them, too."

"They're dead?"

"Most of them," he says. "May the good Lord forgive them. I'm just glad she doesn't have to hear the new ones."

"She won't."

"We've got business to do," he says. "Let me get my book. You sure you don't want to see that trumpet?"

"Maybe next time."

"You tell her John Hinkle said hello. Tell her . . . no. Just tell her I said hello."

"I will."

"She wouldn't want you to know anything I've told you."

"She won't."

"She wouldn't want anyone else to know it either. Understood? This is just between us musicians."

You feel your face go hot with a sudden confusion of pride and duty.

"Yeah."

Comb out and trim the yard. Cut the withered branches, the branches too gone to know it's spring, out of her shrubs. Rake out her tennis court. Fill the drum of the roller with water and smooth the clay where a long time ago Mr. Hinkle played and Mrs. Harding sometimes sang and people left the footprints of their dancing. And every Friday the dollar bills. Eight of them. You hold them, look at them, feel the astonishing way that things can turn into other things. Cutting and clipping and raking and mowing and planting into dollar bills. Dollar bills into the scarred black suitcase and dull brass pipes and valves of the trumpet in the worn blue velvet of its cradle. The trumpet into the sound. How something you do can turn, methodical and blunt as arithmetic, into something you want. At home, under your mother's persistent watering, green starts to haze the yard around your house, and your father carves a bed for rosebushes in the dirt along the concrete walk from the curb to the porch. And every Saturday afternoon the ride downtown.

CHAPTER 11

THE FIRST TIME you see Susan Lake's teeth, the first time you hear her voice, is the day Brother Rodgers asks you to imagine how your lives would be different if it wasn't for Joseph Smith.

"Different how?" Keller finally says.

"If he never existed. If he was never curious enough about religion to pray about it."

"But he was," Jasperson says, quick, sounding nervous.

"I'm asking you to imagine."

"You're asking me to deny my testimony," Jasperson says.

Brother Rodgers puts up both his hands. "Just give me a chance, Johnny," he says.

"I wouldn't have the Priesthood," Jasperson says.

"Good. What else?"

"That's not good," says Jasperson.

"I meant your answer," says Brother Rodgers. "What else? Mike?"

"We wouldn't be here," Lilly says.

"Be where?"

"In this room."

"Where would you be instead?"

"I don't know. Just not here."

"How about you, George? Where do you think you'd be?"

"I don't know," says Doby. "Anywhere."

"Pick somewhere," says Brother Rodgers.

Doby looks helpless. "You mean like Paris or someplace?"

"Paris is good. Especially in springtime. Melvin?"

"I'd be here," says Yenchik. "Cuz of my dad's job."

You've already gone back. Through La Sal. Through Rose Park. Through Brewery Hill and the Avenues. None of them. It would be all the way back to Switzerland if it wasn't for Joseph Smith. You never thought of it. Just lived wherever you've lived. A kid in Switzerland.

Where the way your mother and father swear wouldn't just be funny words but real swear words.

"Susan?"

"Here?" says Susan Lake, smiling at Brother Rodgers, hoping her answer's okay, and that's when it happens, the first time you hear her voice or see her teeth. One word. You reach out and catch it, the small uncertain bird of her voice, and put it in a cage where you can hear it anytime.

After class, out in the parking lot, you and Doby and West look at a brand new turquoise Thunderbird blazing in the sunlight to where your eyes start to water when you look at the paint and chrome too long.

"Too bad it's a Ford," West says.

"Yeah," says Doby.

If you didn't believe in Joseph Smith. How it would just be Doby and West out here. It would be like not believing in your life. It would be like you were just an optical illusion, out here in the parking lot with West and Doby, two guys you didn't know, looking at a Thunderbird you'd never know was here.

"What's up?" Doby says.

"Nothing."

On your first day in class with them, it didn't matter, because nobody meant anything. Now they're your buddies. Now you've started losing who you were without them. Doby big and comfortable. Next to him, you feel lean and tough and quick, like you're partners in a cowboy movie, or like you're a fighter plane and he's an aircraft carrier you can land on after shooting down some Japs. West more like you, lean and tough and quick too next to Doby, the way things need to make sense and fit together right, his hunger for cars like yours for a trumpet. You don't feel like partners with West. More like an even fight. Like both of you are fighter planes.

"Okay," says Doby. "Nothing's up then."

"I was just thinking something," you say.

"What."

"If this place ever closes."

"The church?" says Doby.

"Yeah."

"It's a church," West says. "Not a Las Vegas casino."

"I mean like an airport," you say. "Or maybe a factory."

"Sure it gets closed," says Doby.

"When?"

West and Doby look at each other. And then West says, "At night. When nothing's going on. Like after Mutual."

"Why?" says Doby. "You wanna sneak in and use the girl's bathroom?"

"I just wanna know if it's ever closed."

"I wish that old lady you work for would leave her garage open," says West.

"Who told you she poisoned her kids?"

"Everybody."

"Yeah," you say. "Anyway, it's too late. She sold the Gullwing."

West looks at you. "She did not."

"Yeah. She did."

And early the next morning, as soon as your father closes the garage and backs the Buick the rest of the way up the driveway and then heads off for work, you and Karl are up and dressed and heading out across the field behind the house and then down through the crooked and knotted trees to where the orchard breaks out on the churchhouse.

"What if someone sees us?" Karl says.

From the downhill edge of the orchard the parking lot ahead of you is vacant. White stripes mark the blank asphalt with dark patches and fragile trails of oil centered between them. Across the lot, the big brick back of the gym stands up like the wall of a cliff, still in shadow this early from the foothills that rise behind you. Just beyond the gym the roof of the chapel vaults up above everything around you and places its peak like a mountaintop in sunlight that won't reach the ground where you're standing for a few more hours.

"Stop worrying all the time," you tell him. "Nobody's up yet."

"Papa is."

"He's already gone."

"What if the bishop comes? What if he lives here?"

"Just act normal. All we're gonna do is check the doors."

"Won't it look like we want to get in?"

"We'll just act like we left something here from yesterday."

"What?"

"Nothing," you say.

"What if they ask?"

"Okay. My bow tie."

"We're gonna lie to the bishop?"

"He's not gonna come. He doesn't live here. Nobody does."

"Okay."

"Ready?"

"We're not gonna go inside?"

"No. Just check if the doors are locked."

From where you're standing you can see two doors. A double door in the back of the gym and another set of doors in the one-story part off the chapel where the classrooms are, the glass doors where you and your buddies hang out.

"You ready?"

"Just nervous."

He'd just be a kid in Switzerland too.

"Here. Gimme your hand."

You start in back and then along the side and finally around the front where the big doors are. Karl looks out for the bishop. He tells you not to leave fingerprints. Where you try a knob or handle you wipe it off with your shirt. But the place where everyone believes in Joseph Smith is closed. Every door locked hard and fast. On the way home, up through the orchard, then back across the gray bulldozed rubble of the open field where your only camouflage is the morning shadow of the foothills, you try to get used to it. Closed. Like a store or a movie house. Like there were only certain times you could believe in Joseph Smith. Like there were only certain times you could count on him to keep your life here real. To keep you from being a kid in Switzerland. Every door. All it did was feel like it was always open.

At work the next morning you ask Mrs. Harding if you can borrow the key to her garage.

"Is there something in there you need?"

"I want to cover up the window with a gunny sack or something. The window in the door on the side."

"Why would you want to do that?"

"So people can't look in there and see the cars." And then you say, "They're really neat cars."

"Good Lord. Do you think someone might do that?"

"There are a lot of men next door."

"My goodness."

"You'll have neighbors pretty soon too."

"Yes," she says. "I will have that, won't I."

"You never know."

"How clever of you to think of that."

"Want to take a look at it?"

You don't want to see it again until it's paid for. Until Mr. Hinkle can bring it out of the back of the store for good. You know he'd let you take it out, hold it, look at it until you went blind, lock your hands around it the way he showed you how to work its valves until he had to pry your fingers off to close the store, do anything you want. Anything but take it out the door. No. You know what it would feel like. Too much like something you might not get to see again. But you want him to keep asking. So every time you make a payment you wait. Count eight singles out onto his counter, take eighty cents change when he fishes it out of the register drawer, watch him find your page in his notebook, wait for him to ask if you'd like to take a look at it. And every time he does you tell him what you always do.

"No thanks. Next time maybe."

It kills you to say it, this close, just a room away from where he's keeping it for you.

"All right then," he always says. "Tell me how Mrs. Harding's doing."

CHAPTER 12

JOSEPH SMITH. If it wasn't for him, if he hadn't questioned everything, or gone into the woods to pray, or wrestled Satan, missionaries would never have come knocking on your grandfather's door. When you try to imagine the life you would have lived, imagine yourself on a street somewhere in Switzerland with other kids for buddies, you can't, because you keep turning into some other kid yourself. It just comes to you and cuts through what you're doing, and then goes again, and leaves you doing what you were before it came along. Quick as lightning cutting a line through the dark. For the instant it's there, that blinding filament of jagged light that sets its flashbulb fake white fire to everything, whatever you're doing isn't real, and then it's real again like nothing happened. Except that you know it did. Where for an instant you were the bright ghost of a kid you didn't know in Switzerland.

"Why'd he tell people?" West says.

"Wrestling the Devil?" says Brother Rodgers. "Having God the Father and Jesus Christ come to him? A kid? Think you could keep a secret like that? Nobody believed him. Everyone hated him. Even churches forgot their differences." Brother Rodgers lets the dark turret of his head sweep across the class. "They couldn't agree on Jesus Christ," he says, "but they could on Joseph Smith. They all hated him." Out through the closed window a seagull shrieks. "But after a while he went back to being just a kid. He horsed around, got in fights, probably chased girls. Just growing up stuff. Yes."

"Did he keep going to church?" says Strand.

"I don't know."

"Jesus told him they were all crap," says Yenchik.

"Watch your language, Melvin."

"Crap's not a swear word."

"It's close enough."

"He couldn't just stay home on Sunday," says Doby.

"I don't know. But he's seventeen now. Time to get serious. In bed one night he starts praying. Repenting for all the kid stuff. All of a sudden his room lights up like it's noon inside the house. In the light stands the Angel Moroni."

The angel made out of gold, you're thinking, standing on one of the two tall steeples of the Temple, blowing his long horn out across the valley, Hidalgo teasing you that it was Jesus.

"That night, while he hovers there with the bedroom blazing, the Angel Moroni tells Joseph about the Golden Plates."

"That he translated," says Jasperson.

"We'll get there," says Brother Rodgers. "Any questions so far?"

What Joseph Smith's house looked like that night, you're wondering, walking by outside, with all that light inside it.

"Okay," Brother Rodgers says. "The Golden Plates are buried in a stone box in the side of a hill close to where Joseph lives. Fourteen hundred years ago, before he was an angel, Moroni buried them there himself. He was dying. The last of the ancient American prophets. The last white man in America until Columbus came along. The plates contained the fullness of the gospel. It was time to dig them up."

Brother Rodgers clears his throat into his fist. The sudden growl brings Yenchik's head up off his chest.

"That night the Angel Moroni opens Joseph's mind to let him see the plates inside the box. Buried along with them are two stones. The Urim and Thummim. They're what Joseph will use to translate the language engraved on the plates into English. Yes, Brenda."

A kid in Switzerland, you're thinking, who'd never seen Susan Lake. But that would have to be some other kid. Brenda Horn lowers her hand. She's got that crinkled look around her eyes like she needs to laugh but knows she can't.

"What did you say they were called?" she says.

"Urim and Thummim." Brother Rodgers turns around and writes it on the board. "There. I think that's right. Okay?"

"What does it mean?" she says. Next to her Ann Cook has her head down and her mouth covered.

"It's an ancient name. I'm not sure. It's just what it was called."

"What did it look like?"

"Two stones. Held in wire rims. Like a pair of glasses your grandma would wear. Then a breastplate. Like a knight would wear to protect his chest. Then a bracket to hold the stones to the breastplate, so that when you put it on, the stones were right there, in your face, and you could look down through them. Johnny."

"Could he see through them?" says Jasperson.

"More than just see. They were seer stones. God made it so Joseph could look at a plate full of ancient hieroglyphs and know what he was reading."

"So the stones would turn the writing into English?"

"That's right. Yes, George."

"How come it had two names?" says Doby.

"It's just what it was called," says Brother Rodgers.

"Was one stone the Urim and the other one the Thummim?"

"Whoa. We're still in Joseph's bedroom. The Angel Moroni tells him he'll show him where the plates are buried. Let him dig them up and take a look."

Brother Rodgers looks at you and your buddies. The metal beetle noise that's been coming out of Keller's pocket stops.

"The Angel Moroni doesn't want to rush things. He knows how poor Joseph is. How hard Satan will work to tempt him. Make him think how rich the plates could make his family. Joseph has to get to where he can look at the plates and only think about glorifying God."

His turret head moves back and forth across the room. Susan Lake has on this light blue dress with white stripes and a white belt. Some of her brown hair spills into its white collar without her knowing it.

"What happens next?" he says.

"He takes Joseph to where the plates are buried," says Lilly. "The Hill Cumorah."

"That's right. While the Angel Moroni watches, Joseph clears off the grass, digs away the dirt, gets to a big flat rock, works it out of the way. There they are. The way Moroni left them. The first time they've seen the light of day since he buried them fourteen hundred years ago."

"Were they rusty or anything?" Doby says.

"Gold doesn't rust, George. But you can bet God took care of them. They were good as new. Bright and shiny."

"Was that Urim and Thummim thing there?" says Brenda Horn.

"It was. Now. Imagine Joseph standing there. Seeing them for the first time. What do you think went through his mind?"

Brother Rodgers puts his hands together while he waits. But none of you is about to guess what went on in the mind of Joseph Smith.

"The Angel Moroni was right. The second Joseph sees the plates all he sees is gold. He goes to grab them and run home. But the Angel Moroni isn't about to let that happen. The instant Joseph reaches for them he gets knocked back. Bam!"

Brother Rodgers shouts the word, throws his arms back, staggers back against the little table. It skids and goes crashing into the blackboard. Everyone jumps. He gets his feet back under him, reaches both hands up, strokes the sides of his hair.

"No," he says. "It wasn't the Angel Moroni. Or the Devil. It was the hand of God this time. Anyone here ever been shocked?"

West and Jasperson and Lilly and Julie Quist raise their hands.

"That's the closest I can come to describing it," he says. "I got electrocuted once. I was up on a pole just hooking up a line. All of a sudden this seagull flies in from behind me. Catches me off guard. I throw back my arm to bat it away and hit the power line with my wrist."

He takes off his sport coat, lays it on the table, undoes his shirt cuff, pulls the sleeve back, holds his forearm out.

"See that?" he says. You look. The deep brown skin is split with the shiny hairless streak of a smooth scar maybe six inches long. "That's what a few thousand volts will do."

"Holy crap," says Keller.

Brother Rodgers steps over to the girls. They pull forward. And then all of them except Julie Quist draw back and look away. The way Susan Lake screws up her face makes you wish you could show her the scar where a steer pushed the long nail of a gate latch deep into your thigh. Brother Rodgers stands back and buttons up his cuff. "That's where it went in," he says. He opens his hand. "See this line here?" He points to a thin white crooked line that doesn't have any business being in his palm along with the other lines. "This is where it came out. I had hold of another line. Lucky for me I had on gloves. They had to take me off the pole. I was out cold. The doctors said my heart stopped." He raises his sport coat up behind him, lets it drop over his arms and across his shoulders, and then he's standing there like nothing happened.

"Were you dead?" says Julie Quist.

"No. Your heart's just a pump. You've still got oxygen in your blood. It has to stop for a while to kill you." He looks at the closed door. You hear it too. The shoes and voices of released classes out in the hall.

"Anyway," he says, "that was what Joseph got. His heart wasn't pure. The Angel Moroni had him put the lid back, the dirt back, smooth it over. Then he sent him home to think it over for another year."

After class, out back of the churchhouse, you and West and Doby and Jasperson watch families head for their cars and station wagons.

"Man, if I had a vision," says West, "I sure wouldn't go blabbing it around."

"Why not?" says Jasperson.

"Why?" says West. "You would?"

"Probably. I wouldn't be scared about it."

"Okay," says West. "I had a vision last night."

If you blabbed about your trumpet, you're thinking. If you wanted your trumpet just because it was colored gold. If you wanted it for something other than the way you could make that sound with it. If you'd get electrocuted if you touched it.

"You shouldn't make fun of things," Jasperson says.

"I'm serious," says West.

"No you're not. You're being sacrilegious."

"You saying I can't have a vision?"

Your heart stops. The dark hair, the light blue dress, the white belt, a little brother by the hand. The Lake family. Her father and mother. Her mother the chorister, the redheaded lady with the big happy lipsticked mouth, the big white teeth, the big voice, the baton. You remember knocking on her door. Of all the ladies who answered all the doors you knocked on, whose faces you searched for some hidden similarity to Susan Lake, you thought she was the safest, the last one on earth who could be her mother. When you knocked on her door and she answered, there was the sound of a piano, someone playing a scale, slow and hesitant, like stepping from one unsteady rock to the next to cross a moving river. You stood on her porch and listened to her tell you that her husband took care of the yard. She was smiling when she said sorry. Smiling like she was telling you good news instead of bad. The way it turned out, she was, or there you'd be, mowing the grass, on your knees in a flowerbed, when Susan Lake came walking home from school. Your heart starts up again. You watch the four of them reach a white station wagon that matches her belt and shoes.

"If you really had a vision," Jasperson says, "you'd be too scared to tell anyone. You just said that."

"Well, I had one," says West.

"What was it, then?"

"Your sister appeared to me."

"Shit, West," Doby says. "Don't talk like that. You've got the Priesthood, man."

"Cool down, man. I didn't say she was naked."

CHAPTER 13

OVER THE NEXT few weeks spring comes on full. Everything in Mrs. Harding's yard explodes. Next door, on both sides of her property, cement trucks appear, and then lumber trucks, and then men with saws and hammers. You see how your own house was built. How the naked skeletons of the rooms rose from the basement walls. How the wires and pipes were run. In each house, in the thicket of vertical studs, a white toilet stands exposed, where the people who live there one day will go to the bathroom. A truck takes the bulldozer away. With the bulldozer gone, with the work centered on the house itself, you relax. Your hands get tough. Your arms and neck and face turn red and then gold and then brown.

The grass around your house, under your mother's constant watering, keeps filling in and darkening. Your father brings a power mower home with a Briggs & Stratton engine. He shows you how to use it while you stand there knowing how it works already. How he wants the edger used along the curb and walk and driveway. You go to work. And then you're done and on your bike. And late in May the Saturday comes when you don't need to wear your jacket to pedal into town.

"One more payment," Mr. Hinkle says. He closes his notebook slower than usual. "Guess I need to get it ready."

"Get what ready?"

"Your trumpet." He gives you a questioning look. "The reason you come in here every Saturday. You're down to four dollars."

"What do you have to do to get it ready?"

"Clean it up. Get the valves lubricated. The slides greased. Try to fumigate that case a little."

"Can't I do that?"

"You mean take it home the way it is?"

"Yes."

"Sorry," he says, lifting his hands off the glass and putting them down again. "I can't let it out of my store like that."

"I don't care."

"It's not how I do business."

"Honest. I don't care."

He shakes his head. "It'll be ready for you next Saturday."

"Then can I watch?" you say. "So I'll know how to do it?"

"You're not just another customer, are you."

What you see in his face makes you look down quick at the counter.

"My typical customer comes in here, picks something out, pays for it, and leaves. Done. Clean and simple."

You take your hands off the counter. The smear marks on the glass where you had them make you wish you had a rag.

"And then there's you. You come in with this sound in your head."

"Sorry."

"And now you're asking me to go against my policy. Let a dirty trumpet go. And when I say no, you want to know if you can watch me work."

"I don't have to."

"Nobody's ever been in my back shop. Nobody's ever asked me if they could."

"I'm sorry."

"Look at me, son."

When you look back up at him he's smiling.

"You still can't tell when I'm kidding."

And then you're smiling too, all over your face, like heat from a campfire.

"Get here a little earlier next week," he says. "Around noon."

"I will. Thanks."

"Bring something to eat. A sandwich."

"Okay."

It isn't long, still before your birthday, before they make your mother the organist, before the sound of the pipes is because of her moving hands, before people entering the chapel for Sunday School and Sacrament Meeting are ushered in on the lush disciplined reverence of her preludes. Chopin. Ravel. Brahms. Schubert. She keeps her shoes on and ignores the rack of pedals underneath her. She holds her back straight and her arms level and her eyes on the white baton of Iris Lake, the unlikely mother of Susan Lake, while the congregation sings its loud and always lagging way through O My Father and Onward Christian Soldiers and all the other hymns you've known so long you can't remember when you didn't. In her poised and obedient almost schoolgirl face is nothing to give away what went on your first night there as soon as your father got the family home from Sacrament Meeting. No trace of the rage she aimed at him for having gone and told the bishop she could play the organ. By the next Sunday, the skin of your father's face had absorbed the strenuous red bedeviled coarseness it always gets, and was clear again, clear and expansive, his smile ready for his neighbors. None of it showed on any of you. Nothing to give away how the air in your house could burst in a million fiery slivers of splintered glass. All of you ready. All of you dressed. All of you with your shoes polished and your faces washed.

It isn't long before your father has some jobs himself. Teacher for the Adult Gospel class. Another job singing the bass part in the choir to Iris Lake's baton. Another job, called Ward Teaching, where he goes and visits four families assigned to him one night a month. Your family gets Ward Teachers too. Brother Jeppson, big and heavy and half bald, who wears the same plaid sport coat to your house that he wears to church. One night a month, after dinner, he shows up with an older kid named Billy Hess to ask the circle of your family gathered around the living room how you're doing, and give you a little lesson in something like tithing or modesty or love or faith. Billy Hess just sits there with his tall glossy dark brown pompadour and his skinny tie and sport coat until it's time for everyone to kneel around the coffee table and listen to Brother Jeppson pray.

You sit there studying Billy Hess without him knowing, wondering what he's like when he's somewhere besides your living room, what grade he's in, what he'd be like for a friend. You try to picture your father kneeling at the coffee tables of the families he's assigned to visit. You wonder what older kid he takes along with him. You know that you have to have the rank of Teacher in the Priesthood. That you have to be at least fourteen. Brother Jeppson teaches math at the high school, and sells Electrolux vacuum cleaners, and it isn't long, still before the Saturday you bring the trumpet home, before your mother has an Electrolux of her own.

"Because an Electrolux is the best vacuum that you can buy."

"Was it expensive?"

"Yes, Shakli. But it will last for twenty years."

At the kitchen table your mother uses a teaspoon to scoop asparagus sauce off Maggie's chin and mouth while you eat a bowl of Cheerios before heading out for Mrs. Harding's.

"Wow," you say. "I'll be old."

"Yes," she says. "You'll be done with your mission, and with college, and you'll be married and have a good job with a nice income." She looks at you and gives you that rare and startling smile where pride and sweetness melt away the bonework of her face and leave it soft and formless. "And maybe your father and I will have a little grandchild."

"How long do Hoovers last?"

"Oh, Shakli. No more than four or five years, maybe."

You take another spoonful of Cheerios. Four or five years. You wonder what kind of trumpet player you'll be by then. If your wrists will be thicker. If you'll have hair on them. How it would change things if she'd bought a new Hoover instead.

"How come Papa hates the Nazis?" you say.

She's turned toward Maggie again but you can see surprise lightly tighten the skin in the side of her face.

"He saw what they did," she says. "How evil they were."

"Was he in a concentration camp?"

"No. Don't be silly. They were only for Jewish people."

"So what did he see them do?"

"He saw them take people from their homes. Children from their parents. Babies from their mothers. Old couples from each other. Just to slaughter them. He saw how they took anything they wanted. How they destroyed cities with their bombs and tanks and guns."

"Was he a soldier?"

"He was in the Swiss Army. He had to help keep Hitler out of Switzerland."

"How about you?"

"I saw things too, Shakli. I don't like to remember them."

"You saw bombs go off?"

"I could hear them sometimes. Boof! Boof!"

"That's what they sounded like?"

"Oh, Shakli. You could feel the ground move."

"How come you heard them? Wasn't Switzerland neutral?"

"When the Americans came to bomb Germany. Basel is close to the border. Sometimes they would make mistakes. They would think they were already in Germany and bomb the railroad stations. Sometimes on the way home they would just drop their leftover bombs."

"Didn't they care if they killed anybody?"

"I don't know, Shakli. There were times I would have you in the baby carriage, out walking, and the sirens would go off. You could look up and see them coming. Oh, Shakli, it was terrible. The sky would go dark with them. And I would have to run with you in the carriage for the nearest shelter. And then Boof! Boof! Boof!"

"I'd be in the carriage?"

"Yes."

"All I remember is you feeding me a soft boiled egg."

"You do?"

"Yeah. On this balcony somewhere."

"Leimenstrasse," she says, and looks away from Maggie, and her face goes delicate, her eyes distant and perceptibly brightened by what she sees there, her smile soft but sharpened barely by something you understand is romance or the memory of some other innocent thing. Without expecting to, or wanting to, you see for an instant the woman your mother is. Just the woman. The way her forehead and eyes and nose and mouth and chin and cheeks compose her face. The way other people look at her and see how purely and quietly beautiful she is. Not a mother or wife or an organist. Just a woman. The way your father must have seen her, in a dress on a street in Basel somewhere, before he knew anything about her, before you came along and she became a mother, hurrying a baby carriage toward a shelter while sirens howled and the iron clouds of bombers moved across the engine roar of the sky. A woman on a street in Basel somewhere, a woman on a balcony, if it wasn't for Joseph Smith.

"I remember the little balcony," she says. And she looks at you, and smiles, and you realize she wants to stroke your face, but her hand is busy with the spoon on its way to Maggie's already opening mouth. "You were my baby. My first born. I was so happy."

Chapter 14

Mr. Hinkle comes through the door from his shop in back and sees you standing there. "Boy," he says. "Right on time."

"I did most of my chores last night."

After washing up on Mrs. Harding's porch. After letting her count eight dollar bills into your open hand. After rushing home. Before dark you had the yard mowed all around the house. You emptied the last few catchers under the blazing sky of the sunset over the Great Salt Lake. All you had left this morning was edging and clipping and hosing down the concrete. You don't tell Mr. Hinkle you got downtown more than an hour ago, burning off time by circling the blocks off Main Street, returning after every circle to look at the hands of the clock in front of a corner store called Bountiful Drug.

Mr. Hinkle wipes his hands with the small gray dirty towel he brought with him from the back and lays it aside. You notice the stains in the skin around his fingernails and wonder if he started without you. He catches you staring and holds them up where he can see them too.

"I was changing the pads on a sax," he says.

"I can wait."

"I'm done. Come on back."

"Can I give you the rest of the money first?"

"Sorry," he slaps his forehead with the butt of his hand. "Wouldn't want to cheat you out of a payment."

For the last time, you flatten out eight singles on his counter, watch him fetch his notebook, find your page. He picks up the singles, counts them, holds some of them back out to you.

"I only need four of these," he says. "That's what it says here."

"The rest is for a book."

"A book? A lesson book?"

"Yeah. Except for eighty cents."

"Okay. Leaves us three twenty for a book." He opens his register drawer, counts five singles into it, lays the last three singles on the sill above the drawer, and fishes out a dollar's worth of coins. "We'll get to the book later," he says. "Here's your change for now."

For the last time, you hold out your hand for your change, the eighty cents you'll give your father for your tithing, the eighty cents he'll turn around and give to the Church for you. He closes his notebook and grins at you with this frank and satisfied admiration. He holds his big hand out to you across the countertop. "Congratulations. You did it."

"Thanks." Your tanned brown wrist is plunged like a stick into his big warm knuckled hand.

"Now. Let's get to work."

And for the first time you follow him down the counter to the door in the back of his store to the room where your trumpet is.

"Here we are. Go on in."

"For sure?"

"Go."

The room is tall, like the store, cluttered, the shelves around the dull walls a tumbling junkyard of instruments and their pieces. A high wood workbench takes the center of the room. A few tall stools stand lost around the bench. The air has the leather and oil smell of the tackhouse back in La Sal and the metal smell of the army trucks whose dashboards you picked clean. Mr. Hinkle moves the saxophone and some tools and little bottles off to the side. He goes to one of the shelves and closes an open case. You've already spotted it. He lays the case on the bench and pulls a stool up next to the one he was using.

"Here. Take this one."

Then, from his stool, you don't know what to do except sit there and look at it.

"I kept the case open to let it air out," he says. "It was kinda musty. But that's all I did."

"Okay."

After a minute he says, "Well, it's yours. If you bought it just to sit there and stare at it all day, I guess that's fine."

"I'm sorry."

And then your hands reach for latches you can't believe belong to you, spring them open, lift the lid back.

"Remember the first time you saw it?"

From next to you his voice is close and soft.

"Yeah."

"Remember how you said it looked?"

"No."

"Sad?"

"Oh. Yeah."

"Pick it up."

You lift it out of its blue cradle.

"It's got nothing to be sad about."

"I know."

"No. I'm serious. First, it's a much better trumpet than the student one I got hanging on the wall. It's a Bach. A Stradivarius. One of the best trumpets you can buy. See? Look here. On the bell."

His long finger indicates a spot where the horn starts to open out to the flare. You lean forward. At the tip of his finger you see the word Bach engraved light and shallow in the gold.

"Like the composer," you say.

"Like the trumpet company," he says. "One of the best."

"Wow."

"Another reason it's got nothing to be sad about. It's been around. It's gone out and proved itself. These stains? It earned them. They're what you call its stripes." And then he says, "That's an army term."

"It's not supposed to be shiny?"

"No, son. I know that's what people think and want. For something like this to look all new and shiny. I can tell them they're wrong till the second Tuesday of next week but they'll still want me to sell them a cleaning kit. You don't shine a trumpet. You keep it clean but you don't shine it. You understand?"

"I guess."

"If it was a beauty contest, a shiny contest, the one on the wall out there would win hands down. But it's about sound. And you can't put a shine on that." After a minute he says, "It'll be a few years before you're good enough to know what you've got here."

"Do you know the man who owned it?"

"Yes," he says. His face darkens just long enough for it to have been the shadow of a passing bird if you'd been outside. "He wasn't a bad trumpet player."

"Did he play jazz?"

It takes him a minute again. "Yes. He did."

"Was he in your band?"

After another minute he laughs. "We were amateurs."

"Did he play at Mrs. Harding's?"

"A long time ago," he says. And then he stops and cocks his head and says, "I've got a customer. Don't go anywhere."

You lay the trumpet on a couple of rags, pull the open case forward, lower your nose into it. The velvet carries the rich sweet smell of old tobacco smoke you could always smell around the bunkhouse and the sheepherders. The smell in your father's suit when he comes home. Inside the smell are a thousand mysteries that make you dizzy. You sit back up. Under a blue velvet lid are a handkerchief and three of those sticks with cotton ends your mother uses to clean the snot out of Maggie's nostrils. You're holding the trumpet again, wondering what it will feel like when you get the feeling that you own it, when he comes back in.

"I put up the out to lunch sign," he says. "Maybe they'll leave us alone now."

Guiding your hands he shows you how to disassemble it. Unscrew the caps that hold the valves in the cylinders and then draw the silver plungers out. Ease out the slides that make up the ends of the loops. He tells you what everything's called as you take it off the instrument.

"This is the valve cap. It's how you get to the valve."

"Okay."

"This is the piston guide. The piston's inside here."

"Like an engine?"

"Pretty much. This here's the spring barrel. Brings the piston back up when you let up."

"Okay."

"These are the tuning slides. The main one. And then each valve has its own. You use them to make the notes go flat or sharp. You know what that means. From your piano lessons."

"You can do that?"

"Just slide 'em in and out some."

"Okay."

When you're finished, your trumpet lies on the bench in pieces, disconnected gold and silver bonework. You're surprised at how light and thin and finely tooled the pieces are.

"Good. Now we'll clean it up."

He comes back from the sink with a small bowl of water and a couple of white rags and a handful of sticks like the ones you found in the case. Under his close instructive scrutiny you wet the ends of the sticks and use them to reach and clean away the spots of crud where the man who owned it held it. Use the rag to wipe the ends of the slides and the shafts of the plungers. Wet the other rag and wipe everything until the cloth comes away this tobacco-colored amber. He hands you a towel. When you're done, the stains and bruises are there, but they look burnished now, like they belong, like they were how it was supposed to look.

"Okay," he says. "Let's eat before we put it back together."

"Okay."

"Where's your sandwich?"

"I forgot it."

"Here. Take one of mine. Tuna or olive loaf."

"I'm not hungry."

"I understand," he says. "Okay. I'll eat for both of us."

And with the smell of tuna and then olive loaf in your nostrils, you learn how to oil the piston guides, the pistons, the spring barrels, line them up and slip them down inside their casings. How to film the tuning slides with Vaseline and fit them back in place. How to put a drop of oil on the rag, hold the spit valve open, slip the oiled spot underneath it, clamp it down on the rag so the tiny pad inside the valve can soak up oil. How to keep the grease and oil light the way he keeps repeating. How to wipe everything down again. How to make it yours. How it feels to have the feeling come to you, wave after wave after wave, that it's yours.

"Now let's get you a mouthpiece."

"It's already got one."

"That one's a little big for you," he says. "We'll start you out smaller."

CHAPTER 15

IN YOUR new house, in the only unfinished part of the basement, the part that hasn't been made by linoleum and knotty pine and an acoustic tile ceiling into a room, the part where the furnace and water heater are, where the floor is still cement and the walls are studs and the ceiling exposes the boards that hold up the kitchen floor, your father makes himself an office. He lays a flat unvarnished door across two filing cabinets to make himself a desk. He brings home an office chair with wheels, a big gray Royal electric typewriter, and a metal stand that wobbles when he types and rocks sideways when the carriage slams back to start another line. He clamps an adjustable lamp to the door and works under the white light of two long fluorescent tubes. He buys an address book with a metal lid and a slide that lets him pick a letter from the alphabet and then open the lid to the page where the people go whose names start with that letter. He has a carpenter build shelves across the studs of the wall where the stairs come down. He lines the raw shelves with books, books about the history and doctrine of the church, books whose authors are General Authorities whose names you mostly know. He calls the place his den. He does his Sunday School lessons there. He starts to fill up his flip-up directory with names and addresses and numbers.

On the wall that leads down the stairs he hangs framed photographs of mountains and valleys he cuts out of calendars from Switzerland. He tapes photographs of the Temple and the Mormon Tabernacle Choir to the brown steel wall of the furnace where he can see them when he lifts his head. When you go down the stairs you get a tour of where he came from. When you get to his den you get a tour of the place that was his destination. When you tell him what he's done, the way he's hung his photographs, he looks surprised at first. Then he turns his office chair to look at the wall of the furnace and the photographs he's taped there.

The engine inside his typewriter keeps humming.

"I didn't realize it," he says. "But you're right, by golly."

With this helpless instantaneous shyness you realize that you're standing there in the rare moment where you've got his full attention without having done something stupid or wrong to get it.

"Is the churchhouse always open?"

"Not always. Why?"

"It feels that way."

"No," he says. "I'm sure they lock it up when it isn't being used."

"Do you miss Switzerland?" you say.

"Sometimes," he says. "Yes. Of course I do."

"Are you glad we're here?"

"Absolutely. No question."

"Why?"

"Because of the things the Gospel promises us. Things we couldn't have in Switzerland."

"Like what?"

"The promise to always be together," he says. "To always be a family."

"Weren't we a family in Switzerland?"

"Of course," he says. "I'm talking about the hereafter. Eternity."

"You mean when we're all dead?"

"That's right."

"We won't be a family then?"

"No. We would just be children of our Heavenly Father."

"You mean you'd have to give us back?"

"Yes."

"Like you borrowed us?"

"You could say that. Yes. Like something I took temporary responsibility for."

"Would we know each other?"

"Oh, yes. We just wouldn't be a family any more."

"Wow."

"That's why I brought you here. What did you think? That we came here to get rich?"

"I thought you wanted to get us away from the bombs."

"The bombs?"

"The bombs and the Nazis."

Weariness briefly relaxes his broad face. "The war was over by then. I had practical reasons. But I came mainly so that we could be together as a family for eternity. Only one church can make that promise."

"Ours."

"That's right. And there's only one place where you can make that promise. In the Temple. Do you remember being there?"

"No."

"Soon after we got here. Just after your sister Molly was born. We went there to be sealed together as a family for all eternity."

"I don't remember."

"You were too young."

"I just thought we'd always be together."

"We will be now," he says. "But only if each and every one of us follows God's commandments."

"What if we don't?"

"Imagine we're at a train station at night in the middle of nowhere. We don't know where we are or what's around us. And when the train comes, you've wandered off, and nobody can find you."

"Couldn't you get the train to wait?"

"This is a very important train," he says. "I can't just go to the conductor and tell him I have a lost boy. It doesn't wait. It can't. That's why we all have to follow the commandments. To stay together. Because in the darkness all around us are evil spirits. The agents of Satan."

"What's an agent of Satan?"

"Let me tell you a story about your grandfather. During the war he used to sneak into Germany to check on the members there. In a restaurant one night he ordered a bowl of goulash. When they put it on the table in front of him, a small voice told him not to eat it, but just to run his spoon through it instead. When he did, in the meat and sauce were all these tiny fishhooks."

His mouth full of them. Snagged in the flesh of the insides of his cheeks. His tongue like a pincushion.

"Was it the Nazis?"

"Perhaps. In any case it was an agent of Satan. There are many."

"Is this like a train station?" you finally say.

"Is what?"

"Where we live now."

"Yes. I suppose you could say that."

"Is everywhere we've lived like a train station?"

Something lights up his face and makes his eyes look tired. He smiles. A sheet of paper rises a few inches off his typewriter. A book lies open on his desk. Parts of paragraphs are underlined in red. A ruler lies across the book. A red pencil lies in the crack between the pages. You've made it last as long as you can, the warm calm of his attention, and now you can feel it restless, chill some, a wind picking up, being drawn away.

"I suppose you could say that too," he says. "Yes."

"Are train stations always open?"

"Important ones are. In cities where the trains come and go all night. Why?"

"I just wondered."

There in his den that night the furnace and water heater and typewriter felt like the deep and powerful engines you'd feel if your house was a train. Behind you was the finished room your brothers share. Where Roy went to sleep the way you did in La Sal, to the hurried cadence of Karl rocking away in his bed across the room, and Karl fell off to the rolling clatter of the train wheels of your father's typewriter carrying you through the night too fast for the agents of Satan to catch you. Your sisters in their room upstairs next to yours. In the big bedroom, the one at the end of the hall, your mother fell asleep by herself after reading the Deseret News. That night, with everyone in place, you looked out your window at the houses gathered round the circle in the moonlight and understood why the churchhouse felt like it was always open. It was like gravity or geography or the sky. To hold everything in place. To keep the houses of your neighbors in formation. And you understood too why sometimes it had to be closed. Karl. Molly. Roy. Maggie. Your mother. The doors locked all the way around. The haunted part of what you saw in your father's face.

You take your trumpet case and follow Mr. Hinkle out of the shop to the store again. He brings a tray out from underneath the counter. He picks out mouthpieces and has you tighten your lips while he leans down and checks the way they fit you. He asks you how they feel.

"They're like kissing steel girls," you say.

"What do you know about kissing girls?"

"Nothing."

"Girls," he says. He wipes the last mouthpiece with his handkerchief and holds the next one out to you. "Girls are something you'll have to look out for."

"How come?"

"Trust me. Hold it. Let me take a look."

Standing there, your lips pulled tight, you don't tell him about the dark and quiet girl named Susan Morrow in La Sal who sat two rows away and two desks up and lived in one of the trailer houses where the uranium miners and their families lived. Or Susan Lake. The second Susan now you've been in love with.

"That's it," he says. "C5. You get older, you may want a bigger one, but for now, that's your size."

"Okay."

"Okay. Now for a lesson."

"A lesson?"

"Just a quick and dirty one. Some little things to practice before you meet the Professor. You don't want to show up not knowing anything. Come on. Back in the shop."

The first thing he teaches you back in the shop in the back of his store is how the middle C on a trumpet is the B flat on a piano.

"That's why they call it a B flat trumpet. Here. Let me show you."

He pulls the brown quilt off the big upright piano deep in the back of his shop, opens back the lid, and runs the fingers of his right hand up and down a C minor scale.

"Tuning's held up. Amazing. Now. Listen."

He plays the B flat, the black key, just below middle C, and plays it again while he watches you.

"Now. Let's find that sound on your trumpet. Don't use any valves."

You finally manage to blow a sound but it's way too high and squealing.

"Relax your lips some. Don't blow so hard."

When you manage to blow a sound again it matches the one he played.

"Okay. That's a little sharp. Here."

He takes the trumpet and pulls the big slide out a quarter inch or so and hands it back and has you play again.

"Okay. That's good. That's your middle C. You can read music. So when you see that middle C in your book, that's the sound you want to hear. You memorize that sound."

"Okay."

"Okay. Air flow. Don't blow from your throat. Let the air flow from your diaphragm. Down here below your stomach. Flow from your diaphragm up through your trumpet, all the way out the bell, one long unbroken pipe. Try it. Just blow."

How it sounds, the hoarse rush of your breath through the hollow tubes, how it feels, open and continuous, like it could go for miles out ahead of you if your lungs were bottomless.

"Good. Next is buzzing. Here. Just try it with the mouthpiece. Buzz down low and then up high. Nice and even."

Your face goes hot from the sound you make when you try it.

"It takes practice. Keep at it. Next is attack. Attack is how you hit a note. This is for your tongue. Like this. Tu tu tu tu. Try it."

How it feels like you're doing a machine gun. Shooting Japs and Nazis in the sandpit.

"Not that hard. Just flick your tongue behind your teeth. Keep the air flow going. Okay. Take everything slow. Slow and even. Control is everything."

"Okay."

He teaches you how to do it too with the back of your tongue. Ka ka ka. The machine gun bigger. The bullets fatter. The Japs and Nazis tougher.

"This is stuff you can practice any time."

"Okay."

"Okay. That's enough. Don't push it. Now. Do I have a teacher for you."

"A teacher?"

"The Professor. I'll write his number on your book. Let him know you're coming."

CHAPTER 16

THE CASE makes the long ride home, between your hands, tied and cross-tied with twine to the handlebars, your legs steady and your steering watchful. Your heart wants to bust out of your chest. You can't keep your lips from riding off your teeth. Your machine gun tongue from killing Japs and Nazis. Main Street to Fourth North to Orchard Drive to the long hill of Crestwood. In their yards people turn their heads from what they're doing. You've got something too. Something you earned. You're one of them. You belong here. On Monday you can take it to work and show it to Mrs. Harding. Tell her how you paid for it. Finally tell her Mr. Hinkle says hello. Lupe too. And on Monday you can call the number Mr. Hinkle wrote in pencil on the cover of the lesson book he took off a rack and gave you. The Professor. What Mr. Hinkle said they called him. You'll have the money to pay him now that you've paid your trumpet off. By the time you're home your face hurts trying not to grin.

In the garage you untie the twine, take the case, start heading up the stairs. Karl and Roy look your way from where they're watching tv in the basement recreation room. "What's that?" Karl shouts. "I gotta pee first," you shout back. Through the wall of the stairs you can hear your father typing. You've got something too. In your room you lay the case on your bed and open the lid. It's there the way you left it. You run across the hall to the bathroom and drain the ache out of your bladder. You rinse your hands and open the door and run smack into your mother. Up above the collar of her dress her lips are stitched together in a tight red line and her eyes have this hard hurt appetite for retribution that has always meant that you've wronged her in some way she can't forgive you for. Her rugbeater face. But instead of the rugbeater, the bamboo wand with the bamboo pretzel at the top, she's got your trumpet in her raised hand.

"What is this?"

"A trumpet."

Behind her, through the open door to their room, Molly and Maggie sit watching from their rug, surrounded by crayons and paper.

"Whose is it?" she says, her voice still measured but charged like a cloud with lightning. "Where did you get it?"

"I bought it."

"Yes," she says. "You bought it. Where?"

"At a music store."

"Yes. At a music store. How much did you pay for it?"

"Forty dollars."

"Yes. Forty dollars. For this junk."

"It's not junk."

"Yes. It is junk. Just look at it."

"It isn't. It's a Bach."

"Bach," she says. Spit comes out with it. "Do you think I'm a fool?"

"No."

"But you let someone make a sucker out of you."

"Please don't hurt it. Please."

"I should smash it to pieces," she says. "But then you couldn't get your money back."

"And you wouldn't have any teeth left."

She looks at you amazed. You feel your whole face trembling trying not to look away.

"What did you say to me?"

"Please don't hurt it."

"Harold!" she yells. She keeps looking straight at you. For a crazy instant you wonder if you're supposed to answer her. "Harold!" Then suddenly she turns and walks off down the hall. "Harold!" she screams down the stairs. "Harold!" And then she stands there waiting. In the folds of her dress where she's holding it behind her you can see your trumpet. It pulls you up the hall. Your father finally comes rising into view.

"So," he says, loud and annoyed, his red face furrowed, his breathing hard. "What's the matter up here?"

"Tell him," your mother says. "Tell him what you did."

Your father looks down at you.

"I bought a trumpet. With my own money."

"This piece of junk." She brings it out from behind her. Your father looks at it, vague and reluctant, like a nuisance he'd like to avoid.

"Where?" he says.

"From a store."

"Yah," your mother says. "A junk store. Tell him how much."

"Forty dollars."

"Where did you get forty dollars?"

"From Mrs. Harding."

"Why would she suddenly give you forty dollars?"

"She didn't. I earned it. I made payments."

"Yah!" your mother says. "Behind our backs!"

"You made payments?"

"On Saturdays. After I got paid."

"Payments to whom?"

"To the music store."

"What music store?"

"The one downtown."

"Hinkle? Hinkle Music?"

"Yeah."

"Hinkle Music?" your mother says. "Where I buy my music?"

"Yeah."

She puts her hand to her mouth and looks at your father.

"Mr. Hinkle sold you this?" your father says.

"Yeah."

"What did you tell him that would make him sell you a trumpet?"

"Nothing. Just that I wanted one."

"And he just sold you one?"

"Yeah."

"What lies did you tell him?" your mother says.

"None!"

"You must have told him something! Did you tell him you were an orphan? That you didn't have parents?"

"No!"

"So why would he just sell you a trumpet?" your father says.

"Because I wanted one! Because I had money!"

"No!" your mother says. "Because he doesn't know you! He doesn't know you like we do!"

"So, Mother," your father says. "Take it easy."

"I won't have this piece of junk in my house! We have a piano!"

"What's he supposed to do with it? Throw it away?"

"He can take it and get his money back!"

You feel yourself start crying. "No!"

"How much did you say?" your father says. "Forty dollars?"

"It was my money!"

"This is the best you could do?"

"It's a good trumpet! It doesn't matter what it looks like!"

"Obviously not to you. Your mother's right. You have to take it back."

"Please don't make me!"

"I won't have it in my house," your mother says. "That's final."

"I can keep it somewhere else!"

"I'm sorry," your father says. "You have to return it."

"I earned it! It was my money! I paid tithing on it!"

"You have to learn not to throw your money away."

"Please let me keep it!"

"You have to go with him, Harold. We can't trust him."

"He knows he has to come back home with forty dollars."

"He'll lie to us! He'll go to one of his friends and borrow forty dollars!"

"Please let me keep it!"

"I'll take him later. Right now I have a Sunday School lesson to finish."

"I won't stay in this house another minute with this piece of junk! Do you hear me? Not one minute!"

"Then give it to him! Give it to him so I can go and get this over with!"

CHAPTER 17

IN LA SAL, at bedtime, while your father worked late at his office in the ranchhouse, your mother gathered all of you around her in her bed to read to you. Stories from a set of storybooks your father bought called Uncle Arthur's Bedtime Stories. Stories where kids did the loving and kind and generous things that Jesus wanted kids to do. With her head on her pillow and the book in her hands just above her lighted face she would lie there and read one or two of them while her Swiss voice, fluid and musical, held everyone's attention. There was one you would never forget because it made her cry before she could finish reading it. It was about two buddies. One of them got hit on his bike by a car and was hurt so bad every bone in his body was broken. He was wrapped in casts and bandages from head to toe. The night he was going to die his buddy came to the hospital. They knew that Jesus was coming that night, to take him back, but with all the bandages and casts, they were afraid that Jesus might not know him. So they decided to raise his hand. If his hand was raised then Jesus could find him. So his buddy lifted the cast that held his arm together and arranged a couple of pillows to keep it in the air. Then his buddy sat down next to the bed to wait for Jesus with him. In the morning, when the hospital people came in the room, his hand was still raised, and he was dead, and his buddy was sound asleep in the chair, and you knew from the story that Jesus had come and found him.

You remember your mother's voice, rising and catching and then caving in before she got that far, the book clutched open on her nightgown, her dark hair splayed across her pillow, her face in wet and red-eyed turmoil while she waved you all away.

"Oh, children," she said, "I can't go on. It is just too sad."

Maggie wasn't born yet. But you remember Karl and Molly and Roy, there on her bedspread, chastened faces around her in the shadows, just out of reach of the light of her lamp. You remember lying in bed that night, wondering how the story ended, listening in the dark through the racket of the crickets for your father to enter the house. You remember stealing into their room in the morning, finding the book on her nightstand, reading the last few lines of the story for yourself to see what your mother read that made her cry.

Across the circle, working his yard, Woody Stone watched you come home on your bike just minutes ago. Now he waves when your father backs the big Buick out into the circle. On the ride downtown, classical music quiet on the radio the way it always is, your father takes streets you've been using every Saturday. Crestwood Drive to Orchard Drive. Orchard to Fourth North. From the passenger seat you can look out the open window and see what you looked like, pedaling along, from the back, to cars that came up behind you while you tightened your grip on the handlebars and tried to hold your course in the gravel and dirt on the shoulder. You can hear the pinging music of pebbles as they fire out from underneath your rolling tire. You can feel the jar of the handlebars in your wrists. You can see how stupid you looked. You stare into the wind to dry your face so you won't have to rub your eyes and turn them red. Fourth North to Main. All the way down Main past the building with the windows and the man in the corner sitting at the desk. Your father angles the Buick against the curb in front of Hinkle Music. Instruments that never get played hang on spiderweb wires in the dead air behind the windows. Your father turns the key to the place that turns the engine off but lets the radio keep on playing.

"Please let me keep it."

"You know what your mother said."

"I know."

"She brought that piano all the way from Switzerland so she could teach you how to play it. Did you stop and think how this would hurt her?"

"No."

"It's like a slap in the face."

"I can learn the piano too."

"You don't practice now."

"I'll practice. I promise."

"When you've learned the piano," he says, "we can talk about a trumpet. We can help you buy one if you're still interested. A brand new one."

"Please let me keep this one."

"I'm sorry. It's settled."

In La Sal they wouldn't give you Rex until you had a bridle. They wouldn't give Jimmy Dennison the other workhorse they were retiring, the black horse they called Nigger, until he had a bridle too. You did all kinds of jobs for the money, you and Jimmy, side by side, cleaning corrals, breaking bales of hay into the troughs, washing down steers, picking corn and lettuce, and then, when each of you had half the money earned, your parents went and bought you a bridle for your birthday, leaving you suddenly with money you didn't need. All Jimmy Dennison had was a mother. She didn't have the money to even fix the wormholes in his teeth. And so you gave him yours, so he could put it together with his and buy his bridle too, so you could get Rex and Nigger together, so you could be like a kid in one of Uncle Arthur's Bedtime Stories.

Your mother found out that afternoon. Showed you the empty bandaid box you'd been using for a bank. Screamed at you for being a sucker when you told her what you'd done with it. For letting Jimmy Dennison and his mother play you for a fool. Said you had to get your money back. Went crazy with the rugbeater when you told her no. That night your father drove you up past the school to where the trailerhouses were.

You remember looking through the windshield at Jimmy's trailerhouse down the road. Out through the windshield now, two guys walk past, older guys, maybe high school guys, one talking, one laughing. The one laughing looks sideways at the window, then looks ahead again, still laughing, like what he saw was nothing. All you have to do is kill things. Like that night at Jimmy's. Kill all the wild things in your head. Make this just a thing you have to do so that all the other things will settle into new positions where they'll all make sense again. Like you've never been here. Like everything that happened here was nothing. Like Mr. Hinkle was a sucker too, for helping you find the instrument that made the sound, for writing down your payments in his little book. Your throat feels sore and your lungs hurt from trying not to cry from the way your father says it's settled.

"Okay," you say.

"In a couple of weeks you'll receive the Priesthood. You'll be a Deacon."

Like Lilly and Keller and Jasperson and West, the look there, on their faces, the look of the Priesthood, the look of human steel, the look of soldiers in God's army while they walk the bread and water trays around the quiet chapel to your mother's organ music. The look of every guy or man who has the Priesthood. What it feels like. If you'll have it.

"I know."

"The Priesthood isn't for children."

"I'm not a child."

"Then you'll have to prove it."

"Prove it how?"

"By respecting your mother, by golly. By putting childish things aside."

You look down at the case between your knees and then at the door of the glove compartment.

"Now," he says. "Let's get this behind us."

You pull up the handle, put your shoulder into the heavy door, put your right foot out for the ground. He picks a book up off the bench next to his leg and opens it on the steering wheel.

"Aren't you coming?"

"It's important for you to handle this yourself."

"Please."

"I'll be out here if you need me."

"What should I tell him?"

"That you've thought it over and changed your mind."

"What if he doesn't believe me?"

"Then you haven't done a good job."

"What if that's not a good enough reason?"

"Then tell him something else."

"Like what?"

"I don't know. Just remember what your mother said. To leave her out of it."

You remember him saying the same thing the night he parked the Buick down the road from Jimmy's trailerhouse. You telling Jimmy you needed the money back for shoes. Jimmy telling you it was okay. Saying he knew it was your mother. Saying he knew because of the red mark on your neck back by your ear. And then suddenly you're scared. Scared that in spite of everything he tells you, everything he tries to teach you, you'll never get things right. So scared it hurts your throat to hold it back and keep it from coming through to where you start crying again in front of him.

"Go now. Before he sees us."

"Okay."

"Before he starts to wonder why we're sitting here."

He's behind the counter, his back to you, his arm raised, dusting the instruments up on the wall with a feather duster. Oboe, you remember, and then everything you put him through makes him look bleak, an old man in a strange store, someone you never knew. While you wait for him to turn around you remember the way your knee hurt the first time you were here.

"Is something wrong?"

"No."

He puts the duster slowly on the counter. In your hand you can feel the hard raw curled edge of the electrical tape that someone wrapped around the handle.

"I wouldn't know that from your face."

"I need my money back."

"Your money back," he says. "Why?"

"I just need it back."

"Is there a problem with the horn?"

"It's okay. I just need my money back."

"How come, son?"

"I need it for my brother." And then you say, "He's sick."

He studies you again. And then he says, "Your brother's sick and needs your money."

"Yes." And then you say, "I'm sorry."

"Tell me what's wrong, son."

"I like playing piano better."

"Anyone but you could come in here and tell me that."

"I just need my money back."

"Your folks?" he says.

"No. Me."

"Your folks sent you back here?"

"No."

"Tell me the truth, son."

And then you can't look at him.

"It was your money," he says.

"They say I threw it away."

"What did you tell them?"

"That it wasn't junk. It was a Bach."

"They called it junk."

"I told them it wasn't."

"Good for you."

"I just need my money. Please. My dad's waiting."

"Your dad? Where?"

"At another store. I mean at home."

And then, helpless, you watch him turn his head toward the front of the store where the windows are.

"That him out there? In the Buick?"

"No."

"I'd like to meet him."

"No. Please."

"Don't worry, son. I don't bite."

He comes around the counter and puts his arm around your shoulder and ushers you out the door ahead of him. And then on the sidewalk he lets you go and crosses the curb to the open driver's window of the Buick, where your father's head is, lowered down, reading the book on the steering wheel.

"Good afternoon."

Startled, your father looks up, closes the book, leans forward and reaches for the door handle, but Mr. Hinkle already has one hand on the windowsill, his other one out for a handshake. You watch your father recognize that he's trapped. Watch him sit back, put his own hand out the window, bring his big public smile quickly to his face. You almost start to cry again when the two of them shake hands.

"Good afternoon, sir," your father says.

"I'm John Hinkle. I own the store you're parked in front of here."

"I'm Harold Tauffler. What can I do for you?"

"Is this your son?"

"Yes."

"He wants to return a trumpet he bought here earlier today."

"Yes. That's why he's here."

"He wants his money back."

"Yes. I know that."

"Well, Mr. Tauffler, I'm sorry, but there's a problem."

"Call me Harold. Please."

"All right. I'm John. You see, Harold, it's a used trumpet."

"Yes."

"We've got a policy. Had it since we opened. We don't give refunds on used instruments. Guarantees either."

"I see."

"Here's the problem. I've spent the last five minutes trying to explain that to your boy here. He doesn't understand. He keeps telling me he needs his money back. Says his brother's sick. Maybe you can help me out."

"Yes sir. What would you like me to do?"

The ridges in your father's forehead and the lines around his mouth are deep and red and strenuous and make his friendly smile look almost desperate. In his cheeks you can see the recoil of his back teeth clacking.

"He's pretty determined," Mr. Hinkle says. "He really wants his money. He won't take no for an answer. Maybe he'll listen to you."

"Yes. How can I help?"

"Talk to him. You're his father."

"Of course."

Mr. Hinkle turns his head to where you're standing on the sidewalk.

"Come here, son," he says. "Your dad wants to talk to you."

You come up past the big chrome grill and the long green fender toward the window.

"What?"

"Did Mr. Hinkle explain to you why you can't have your money back?"

"Yes."

"Then you need to listen to him."

"Okay."

"You can't ask people to change their rules just to suit you."

"Okay."

"You can't ask people to make exceptions."

"Okay."

"Okay, son?" Mr. Hinkle says. "You understand now?"

"Okay."

"I'm sorry, son."

"That's okay."

And then Mr. Hinkle turns back to your father.

"Thanks, Harold," he says. "I appreciate the help."

"Anytime. I'm sorry he caused you trouble. He's taught better."

"He's got a fine trumpet here. A real fine one, if that's any consolation."

"Yes. That's fine."

"Now, if he'd bought a new one, we'd have a different story. But he didn't. He couldn't afford a new one."

"I understand."

"Since he was buying it himself."

"Yes. I understand."

"Nice meeting you. I hope your other boy gets well quick. Hope it's nothing serious."

Part 3

Childish Things

CHAPTER 18

IN THE GARAGE, in the Buick, you listen to the hot restless idling of its engine, the rumbling loud and crowded by the walls and ceiling, the hoarse whirling of the radiator fan and the whining of the belt and pulleys, the tapping and knocking coming from deep inside the engine. Noises you only hear when the Buick's in the garage, the engine running, its raw heat welling up around you, the way you could only tell how really big and powerful Rex was when you were in the stall with him. How much air it took for him to breathe, how much heat came off his damp fur, how big his teeth were, how his big lips felt like nubbled velvet rubber when he used them to snort the oats out of your hand.

"We can't bring it inside," he says. "We have to find a place for it in here."

You look out past the long green hood of the Buick, past the trembling chrome spear of the hood ornament, at the boards of the shelves you helped your father build across the back wall, a wall of stuff the Buick could crush. All your father has to do is pull the lever into drive and push the pedal down. But the engine doesn't even know it's here, doesn't know the Buick is caged like this, doesn't know it isn't on the highway where it could be doing seventy, where it could blast through the wall in front of you like it was made of paper.

"I can find a place," you say.

He doesn't say anything. Like you could matter. Like you could help fix something you weren't old or smart enough to fix. You see his hand move forward slowly and finally turn the key. You hear the engine stumble, lose momentum, stop.

"There," he says. "Under the bottom shelf. Behind the Christmas boxes."

Where you looked for wrapping paper for his gloves for Father's Day. Without the engine running, in the backwash of exhaust, you can hear his restless complicated breathing.

"I'm sorry," you say.

"Don't worry. We'll handle this together."

The sudden change in his voice makes you turn and stare. There, in spite of everything, the benevolent warm surrounding look in his big face, the look you've seen him extend to other people, there for you. Like you're okay. You scrutinize his face for something else. You want to bawl and have his arms reach out and take you in, want it so bad you look away, look down, look by accident at the trumpet case between your knees, look quickly at your hands instead.

"I'm sorry."

The way your voice goes high, almost out of reach, like a kite string suddenly loose and racing through your fingers, the way it makes your throat hurt.

"Now you know what can happen when you act like a big shot."

The edges of your fingernails still gray. A fleck of something black under your thumbnail.

"I wasn't trying to be a big shot."

"You walked into that store thinking you were smart enough to buy a trumpet on your own. Your mother or I could have told you to find out about their refund policy first."

"He wasn't trying to gyp me."

"Did he tell you that you couldn't get a refund?"

"No."

"Then he wasn't completely honest with you, was he?"

"If I'd asked he would have told me."

"Where were you planning on practicing?"

"I don't know."

"Did you think about how loud a trumpet is?"

"No."

"How it would disturb the house?"

"I could have practiced somewhere else."

"Like where? At one of your friends?"

"I don't know. The sandpit maybe. The field."

"The sandpit." In his brief soundless laugh you hear how stupid you've come across to him again. "That's what I mean by big shot. Not thinking of anyone else. Not thinking about the consequences of your actions. Do you understand?"

"Yes."

"Good. Now put it away until I decide what to do with it. I'll go talk to your mother."

The part you're not smart or old enough to fix. The part your father has to do. Upstairs, doing something, ironing maybe, rinsing lentils for dinner, waiting to see the money ever since you and your father left to get it back. Your forty dollars. The feel of Mr. Hinkle positioning your hands. The feel of his big hands shaping your fingers around the gold cylinders of the valves. The part he had to do for you. Lie. Make your father look stupid. Shame makes you cringe so hard you almost cry when you see the two of them again, Mr. Hinkle and your father, two men making you understand that you have to keep your trumpet.

The part you can do for him. Stay away from his store. Not go back. Ever. You almost start to cry again.

Your knees on the concrete. Pulling the Christmas boxes out from under the bottom shelf. Sliding the case back in against the wall, how it looked, this thing you wanted, the taped handle, the bottlecap imprint in the bottom where the foot was missing, this sudden foreign thing. Sliding the boxes back in front to where you couldn't see a trace of it, you could hear their voices, muted at first, the warbling music of their wordless bickering, then finally hard and sharp enough to penetrate the ceiling like it wasn't there.

"So, by golly! It's been taken care of! Enough!"

"I don't believe you!"

"I told you! He wouldn't give us a refund!"

"You should have just demanded one!"

"It's his policy! By golly! He has the right to decide what his policy is!"

"I don't care about his policy! I know I should have gone!"

"What would you have done? Break into his cash register?"

"If only you had some backbone!"

"It has nothing to do with backbone! It's his policy!"

"Where is it now? Is it in this house again?"

"It's been taken care of!"

"Where is it?"

"I told you! It's taken care of!"

"I don't believe you!"

"Then go to the Devil! To hell with everything!"

"Yes! To hell with everything! Except your precious Sunday School lesson!"

CHAPTER 19

WHY YOU couldn't keep it. Why it had to make your mother crazy. What she knew that Mr. Hinkle didn't. In bed, you keep your knees pulled up and your body curled around your stomach and the covers tight around your neck but nothing you do can keep you from whimpering when you breathe, your throat from hurting, the questions from reeling around inside your head. It's his now. You traded it away. For the way he had to fix things with your mother. In the Buick you searched his face for something else he'd want to trade you for. You had other stuff. Your bike. Your box of arrowheads. Your scout knife. He didn't want them. He wanted Mr. Hinkle. The sound you heard on the radio. The workbench where you learned how it came apart and went together again.

You keep your eyes fixed on the wall because when you close them you're standing in this place where everything used to be, this place where you're a hot shot and a sucker and Mr. Hinkle is a crook, this place now gutted and left bewildered by some fire, this place where your mother pokes through the ashes with her rugbeater. Because all you can see is the trumpet, burnished and blind in its cradle, buried under the lid of its case on the concrete floor below you. Why it was childish. Why it was junk. You keep your eyes fixed on the wall because when you close them the mattress comes to life and the questions start to reach into your stomach.

Sometime toward morning you can feel yourself start losing hold. Breathe without whimpering. Let up your grip on the covers. Stretch out your legs again, take your eyes off the wall, roll over on your back, feel the hold of the mattress give. He can have it. You don't need it. You don't want it. Asshole. It slips into your head from out of nowhere. You flinch, and then you don't dare move, just hold your breath and wait, wait for something to come exploding through the ceiling looking to hurt you. Nothing does. You hold still longer. Then slowly start to breathe again. Nothing. Just the word in your head as cold and luminous and stark as the moon in the high black shell of a winter night. Asshole. You can call your father one and live. And in that discovery you let it go for good. Don't want what you can't have. Don't want anything they can take away from you. In his shop, behind his counter, surrounded by instruments, while Mr. Hinkle stands there showing a customer some harmonicas, you say goodbye, take yourself out of his life, leave him there the way he was before you came along. And finally tears cut down across your face and pool inside your ears and you can fall asleep.

For the next three years, while he made his yearly trip to the Hill Cumorah to dig up the box that held the Golden Plates and have to bury them again with the Angel Moroni watching, Joseph Smith kept himself busy. He moved to a town called Harmony in Pennsylvania to work for a man who thought there was silver around. He started his own mine. He fell in love with his landlord's daughter Emma. Her family had heard the stories about wrestling the Devil and having God and Jesus Christ appear and didn't want him near their daughter. So Joseph gave up the silver mine and stole her back home with him, to New York, close to the Hill Cumorah, where he married her and picked up farming with his father. At the end of the fourth year he met the Angel Moroni at the hill and dug up the plates again. This time he didn't have to bury them. This time, when he reached for them, he wasn't thrown back by some electrocuting force. This time his lust for their shining gold was gone.

"The plates could've been made of tin for all he cared," Brother Rodgers says.

"Maybe by then he liked silver better," says Keller.

Brother Rodgers ignores him, takes a picture off the table, holds it up. The Golden Plates. A stack of wrinkled-looking gold pages half a foot tall and held together with three tall rings like a looseleaf without a cover. You've seen pictures of them before, all painted by artists, because by the time cameras were invented, Joseph had translated them and the Angel Moroni had taken them back to Heaven. It makes your knees itch how Susan Lake can sit and look at them like Brother Rodgers wants her to. Like it's her first time.

"These could have been the Tin Plates, or the Paper Plates, or the License Plates when he looked at them." Brother Rodgers pauses to let West laugh. "He wouldn't have noticed. He was finally pure. This time the Angel Moroni let Joseph take them home."

"How about that thing with the stones?" Doby says.

"The Urim and Thummim," Lilly says.

"He took those too."

"Have you got a picture of them?" says Brenda Horn.

"Nope. Wish I did. Steve?"

"Gold's really heavy," Strand says from in back.

Brother Rodgers smiles. "Someone's been doing their science homework. Joseph was a strong young man. I'm sure the Lord gave him any extra strength he needed. Anyway, word got out he had them. Everyone wanted them. Robbers, shysters, mobs, professors of religion. So Joseph took his wife and the plates and headed back to Pennsylvania to hole up with her family. This time they didn't mind. They even helped protect him when word got out again to the mobs and robbers and professors of religion. Bobby."

"How come he told people?" says West.

"Told people what?"

"That he had all this gold."

"Maybe it wasn't him. He had a family. A wife. Maybe they went out and talked."

"But they wouldn't of known unless he told them first."

"Think of this." Brother Rodgers pockets his hands like it's just another stupid Sunday. "A small house. Full of people. You come home with a set of heavy gold plates you're supposed to translate and a breastplate and stones to do it with. That's not something you can just put in your pocket like a frog. Sooner or later, your family's gonna know."

"He could of hid them before he got home. In a field. Or in the cellar."

"He had to translate them. Could he do that in a potato cellar? Out in a turnip field?"

"Yeah," says West. "I guess."

You can feel Jasperson getting fat as a wallowing pig on getting even with West.

"And what would he say when he had to take time off from farming to translate?" says Brother Rodgers. "What excuse would he use?"

"Yeah. Okay. I get it."

"Okay. It's been a year and a half since he brought them home. He hasn't done much translating. He's been busy protecting them. And he needs the scribe the Angel Moroni told him they'd send him. Someone to dictate to. Anyone know what that means? Julie?"

Julie Quist brings down her hand.

"It's what a boss does to a secretary."

West lets out a snort. Brother Rodgers' face goes hard as rock but he keeps his eyes on Julie Quist. She looks confused and worried.

"What does it mean exactly, Julie?"

"The boss says stuff and my mom writes it down." And then she says, "My mom's a secretary."

Brother Rodgers looks hard at the floor. Then he looks up and starts off again.

"One day a schoolteacher shows up. His name is Oliver Cowdery. He's heard. He's there to help. They set up a working arrangement at opposite ends of a long table. They hang a curtain from the ceiling to cut the table in half. Joseph, he'll sit at one end with the plates, and read what he sees in the stones. Oliver, he'll sit at the other end, write down what Joseph says. The next morning, Joseph straps the Urim and Thummim on, and they get to work."

He picks a soft black leather book up off the table.

"When they finally get done, what they've got is the Book of Mormon. This."

He holds up the book. The book your grandfather took and translated from English into German, not with a Urim and Thummim, but with the fiery little spectacles that always hide his eyes in sunlight.

"Melvin," Brother Rodgers says.

"What'd he do with the plates?" says Yenchik.

"The Angel Moroni came and got them and took them to Heaven with him."

"How about that thing he used to translate them?"

"That's gone too. Up in Heaven."

In La Sal, in the dirt cellar underneath the house, a two-cylinder engine sat in the damp dirt in one of the dim back corners, left there by someone you didn't know, there when you moved in, caked with dirt and rust, shrouded in spiderwebs. You used to wonder what it had come from. Your mother stored her potatoes and jars of apricots on the other side of the cellar away from it.

One day you and Jimmy Dennison took your father's crescent wrench and vice grips and a screwdriver, headed down into the cellar, pulled the engine out of the corner to the center of the dirt floor, and started working the bolts loose.

You remember feeling like you were tampering with the house. Your mother was taking her afternoon nap when you started. Later, you could hear her footsteps, follow them from the living room to the kitchen and back, and then you were listening to her give Karl a piano lesson. Each bolt took forever. But you got them, one by one, all of them around the head of one of the cylinders. And then you worked the tip of the screwdriver around the edge until you broke the seal. And then you lifted the head free and looked inside. When you talked again you were whispering.

"What's that?"

"I think the piston. The top of it at least."

"What are these?"

"I think the valves."

The valves and the top of the piston were crusted with something hard and black.

"How come this part isn't all rusty?"

"I don't know. Maybe it couldn't get in here."

And then you turned the engine on its end and started working the bolts out of the underside. For some reason they came more easily. Karl's piano lesson was over. You heard Maggie crying and your mother soothing her. Soon you were pulling away a deep steel pan. Oil thicker than pancake syrup and black as liquid licorice started oozing out through the broken seal into the dirt. The pan came clear. You looked inside the engine. You'd expected everything inside to be as caked with rust and dirt as the outside. Everything looked brand new. Everything wet and slick and gleaming with oil where it was nested in the iron housing. Like the engine had never been used. Like the day it was put together. Both of you moved back to get your shadows out of the light.

"Wow."

"Man."

When you took an accidental look at the wormholes in Jimmy Dennison's front teeth, and he knew it, he remembered to bring his top lip down to cover them. From upstairs, you could hear your mother playing, singing her Broadway songs. And then you went to work, dismantling the engine, gutting it, turning the bolts loose, hauling out the slick parts, amazed at how new they felt and looked, aware that what you were doing was permanent, something you could never change back to the way it was, put together again.

Yenchik reminded you of Jimmy Dennison from the start. The same way of never being lucky. The same look of some bad cloud ahead of him. He made you feel sorry and scared for him the same uncertain way. After class, out in the bright sun, all the chrome and glass and paint in the parking lot blazing, Jasperson waits for West to get his sunglasses on.

"I guess Brother Rodgers told you," he says.

"Told me what?" says West.

"About hiding the Golden Plates like a frog in your pocket. Or in a field."

West looks at him. Jasperson looks back. West doesn't look away. Jasperson tries to stare him down except that he can't see West's eyes.

"You really screwed yourself," Keller tells him. "The way you laughed about what Julie Quist said."

"I couldn't help it," says West.

"I almost cracked up too," says Yenchik.

"What's with you today?" says Doby.

You shrug. "Not much," you say. "How about you?"

"Nothing. You just look pissed."

"I'm not pissed."

"I do something?"

"I'm not pissed. Honest."

CHAPTER 20

ON MONDAY everything at work is the way it was on Friday. At the end, when you're done, there's the same basin, the same lukewarm water, Lupe ready with the same towel, Mrs. Harding standing there the way she always has, making sure you go home with your hands and arms clean and your hair combed and the dirt brushed off your knees and shoes. And there's the same feeling, the feeling that she likes you, that she's proud of you, not from her face, not from anything she says, just something you feel immersed in while you dry your hands and arms.

All you have to do is act like the same old kid you've always been. Act the same and things will stay the same. It surprises you how easy it is to act like you did when you knew what you were here for. How easy it is to act like where you're going when you get on your bike and wave goodbye to them is home.

Anywhere but home. On Monday you head for West's and sit around his room reading hot rod magazines. On Tuesday you head for Keller's and laugh your way like morons through his sister's yearbooks. On Wednesday and Thursday you just keep going. Out of the useless neighborhood of all the useless people you know from church. Out roads where you've never been. Anywhere but home till it's late enough to know your father's there.

After work on Friday, after you hand Lupe back the towel, Mrs. Harding steps forward the way she always does, a little wobbly, the way that always looks like she's trying to balance herself on the edge of a board. You hold out the hand you've always put out for her while she counts eight dollar bills into your palm. You're standing there wondering how much of it the Professor would have wanted for a lesson. And then you're standing in the rubble on the shoulder of a street, staring at two dollar bills, the rush of the woman's perfume in your nose, the idling Pontiac behind her, the loose green neck of her dress that makes you look away.

"Dear?"

You look up quick at her face expecting her to tell you what to do with it. And when you see Mrs. Harding, the stern questioning attention in her pale eyes and delicately creased face, you realize how close you just came to giving everything away, to letting her see everything.

"I'm sorry," you say, your smile quick, already in place. "Thank you, Mrs. Harding."

"Didn't I count it right?"

"No. It's right."

"Then what is it?"

"I was just daydreaming. I'm sorry."

And then you watch the hundreds of intricate lines in her face arrange themselves into a new expression, shift like the hundreds of colored facets in the turn of a kaleidoscope to form a new pattern, from sternness to a rare small smile.

"Money can do that to people," she says. "Make them dream."

"Yeah," you say. "I guess."

"Now put it away, dear. Before you dream it away."

Saturday morning. For the first time since you moved here your bike won't be taking you into town when you get the yard done.

Nowhere to go. But nowhere is everywhere.

"I'll be home to do the shoes," you tell your mother.

In the shadowless pale light under the straw brim of her big hat her face looks like it's in an aquarium. You don't wait to answer her singsong string of fretting questions. You pull your bike out. Come rocketing out of the garage, up the driveway, across the hump, up and out of the circle.

For the first time on a Saturday it isn't where you're going. It's where you need to get away from. And that makes nowhere everywhere.

CHAPTER 21

IN SUNDAY SCHOOL, now that the Golden Plates are translated into a language you can read, Brother Rodgers can take you through the story they tell. The Book of Mormon story.

"Okay. Lehi was a prophet of Jerusalem. The city had become wicked and needed to be destroyed. God told Lehi to take his family and leave so he could burn the city down. Lehi and his family wandered the wilderness for eight years. They finally came to a land that gave them everything to eat they needed. They named it Bountiful. It bordered on a big sea. Yes, Brenda."

"Did they name this one after that one?"

"I'd say so."

"Where was this place?" says West.

"Somewhere around Persia. Nobody knows for sure. But Lehi had three sons. Laman and Lemuel and Nephi. Nephi was the youngest. He was also the most righteous. God would talk to him too. At the big sea God commanded Nephi to build his family a ship."

"It was a submarine," says West. "Made out of stones."

"No it wasn't," says Jasperson.

"Let me tell the story, boys. Laman and Lemuel were rebellious. Sometimes God would have to reveal himself to them through Nephi. They'd repent but soon start griping again. Nephi finally finished the ship and everyone got aboard. When they hit land again they were somewhere in South America. Chip."

"Why South America?" says Keller.

"Why?" says Brother Rodgers.

"Why not North America?" says Keller. "Like Columbus."

"South America's where God led their ship. Lehi eventually died. The descendants of Nephi became the Nephites. They remained righteous. The descendants of Laman and Lemuel turned wicked. So wicked, in fact, God had to punish them. He cursed them with a brown skin and made them a loathsome and dirty people. They got to be known as the Lamanites. Everyone good so far? Any questions?"

How many telephone poles he's climbed. If he's kept count. Susan Lake. You used to sit here and wonder what song.

"Okay. Over several centuries the Nephites and Lamanites grew into great nations with armies that spread across South and Central America and into North America. Sometimes they got together to fight this powerful outlaw tribe called the Gadianton Robbers. Most of the time they fought each other. The Nephites always won. After Jesus was crucified, for the three days he vanished from his tomb, he appeared to the Nephites to establish his church among them. The Lamanites who accepted him and were baptized had their skin turned white again."

"They turned white again?" says Doby.

"As white and delightsome again as the Nephites were," says Brother Rodgers.

"How? When they were baptized?"

"I don't know."

"Maybe they went underwater brown and were white when they came up," says Keller.

"Yeah," says Yenchik. "Like all it was was mud."

"I don't know how. Eventually the Nephites got arrogant. They started taking credit for winning all the wars instead of giving it to God. They finally ended up becoming more wicked than the Lamanites. So God started siding with the Lamanites. They started winning battle after battle. The once great nation of the Nephites was slowly annihilated. Yes."

"What's annihilated?" says Yenchik.

"Wiped out," says West. "Killed off."

"The Lamanites drove the last of the Nephites into New York State. The last great battle took place around a town called Elmira. It wasn't there then, Elmira, and neither was New York, but the land was called the Land of Cumorah. Mormon was the leader of the last of the Nephites. He tried to turn his people back to righteousness before it was too late. But they wouldn't listen. Yes, the Mormon the Book of Mormon got named after. That what you wanted to say, Johnny?"

Jasperson's already got his hand back down and his face hangdog.

"Yeah."

"So Mormon went to the King of the Lamanites and asked the king for mercy. The king refused. In the last slaughter, Mormon himself was killed."

Susan Lake. Her dress brown, a black collar, black trim around the ends of her sleeves, a black belt with a brass buckle, two rows of black buttons up the front, the collar low enough to see all the white skin of her neck and where her collar bones are. Her face raised and spell-bound. You used to sit here and wonder how long it would take to get good enough to play for her.

"Moroni was Mormon's one surviving son. He wasn't an angel yet. The last white man in North and South America until Columbus. Four hundred years after Christ was crucified, four hundred years after he appeared to them, it was over for the Nephites."

Brother Rodgers looks at the window. Something outside makes him walk over and take a closer look. But then he turns to the class again.

"So that's it. A thousand years later, when Columbus arrived, he was greeted by brown-skinned people. He called them Indians. But they were Lamanites. When the Spaniards came and conquered them, the Aztecs and Incans were Lamanites. When the army went west and ran into Apaches and Comanches, they were fighting Lamanites. When Brigham Young came here and found the Ute Indians, he knew they were Lamanites. Descendants of Laman and Lemuel, the sons of Lehi, a prophet of Jerusalem."

Done talking, Brother Rodgers leans back against the wall and folds his arms, ready for questions, and all you can think is the way his deep tan makes him look like an Indian too.

"So all the Indians are Lamanites," says Strand.

"Yep. From here to the tip of South America. The Pacific Islanders too."

"Cochise?" says Keller.

"Yep."

"Sitting Bull?"

"Geronimo?"

"Tonto?"

"Yep. Every one of them. Steve."

Strand brings down his hand. "Tonto's Italian. Like all the actors who play Indians."

"No he's not," Yenchik says.

"You're probably right about most movie Indians," says Brother Rodgers. "But Tonto's an Indian in real life. His real name is Jay Silver-heels."

"The Pacific Islanders?" says Strand. "Like Hawaii and Tahiti?"

"Yep."

"What about Mexicans?" says Keller. "They came from Jerusalem too?".

"Their ancestors did."

"So they're brown because they're cursed?" says Strand.

"No. Their ancestors were."

"So how come they have to be brown?" says Yenchik.

"Like I said. Once they accept the Gospel, the curse is lifted, and they'll become white and delightsome again. God makes that promise in the Book of Mormon."

You sit there and try to picture Manny once the curse is lifted. Once he believes in Joseph Smith. White again the way he was always meant to be. The eroded deep brown skin of his face the color of yours. The long backs of his lean hands as white as your mother's when he reaches for his piece of bread or the little paper cup of water from the tray you're holding. You try to make him delightsome. Hidalgo too. Picture them sitting out on the porch in front of the bunkhouse, wonder what they'd be doing, what they'd look like, if they were being delightsome. And Lupe too. If she believed in Joseph Smith.

For the first time since your first time here you raise your hand.

"Yes. Shake."

"Maybe that's why the Indians were so good at killing white people," you say.

West laughs. Then everyone starts laughing. You sneak a look and there she is, Susan Lake, looking your way, smiling, looking at you from the nest of dresses where all the girls are clustered laughing, because of you, just looking at you and smiling. The Righteous Brothers. The Platters. You look back quick at Brother Rodgers. He's waiting for you.

"What do you mean?" he says.

The girls go quiet first and then the guys. And then finally Yenchik.

"You know," you say. "Settlers. Pioneers. White people."

"Why's that?"

He still doesn't get it. This dirty nervous anger floods your head.

"Because they had all that practice killing Nephites," you tell him.

He looks down frowning at the floor. You watch the veins and muscles flex in the deep brown skin of his forehead. When he looks up again he knows exactly where to find you.

"That was a joke, right?"

"No," you say. And then you say, "Maybe."

And then you're staring back at him, at his steady chrome blue eyes, knowing you'll win, knowing you can sit here and stare at him forever, because he's got somewhere else to go.

"Niggers were bad too," says Yenchik.

Something flexes and cracks behind Brother Rodgers' eyes. He holds your stare another few seconds before he cuts his eyes away.

"Okay, everybody," he says. "Let's move on."

"What're you doing this summer, Doby?" says West.

"Don't know yet. Just glad school's out."

"Yeah," says Keller. "Never have to see Tolman Elementary again."

"How about you?" says Doby.

"Dunno," says West. "Wish I was old enough to work in a gas station."

"My dad's gonna try to get me work at his machine shop," says Yenchik.

"Doing what?" says West. "You can't run tools."

"Cleaning up," says Yenchik. "Stuff like that."

"I'm gonna work for Old Man Tuttle," says Jasperson. "Beans and peas. Then for Charley Bangerter. Cherries and apples."

"How about you, Tauffler? You gonna keep working for the old bag?"

West turns his sunglasses your way. You see the ghost of your head in each of the dark lenses.

"I guess so."

"Get me a job taking care of her Gullwing."

"I told you. She sold it. It's gone."

"Yeah. And I still think you're fulla shit."

"Have it your way," you say. Then, because nothing matters, because you can't think of anything you've got to lose, you say, "Up your ass."

You're ready for the quick pissed step he takes in your direction. He stops where your bulging face in his sunglasses reminds you of seeing yourself in the sunglasses the lady with the Pontiac was wearing. And then he grins.

"Don't push your luck, Tauffler."

"Who needs luck?" you say, watching yourself grin back. "It's just you."

CHAPTER 22

TRAINS. YOU'VE WATCHED them from the crest of the sandpit up behind your house, out west across the valley, following the thin black distant line of the tracks that run north through the towns and yellow marshlands along the Great Salt Lake. Freight trains. Black snakes that pull themselves in a straight line along the length of the valley. You've heard the hoarse whistles of their horns, their short restless barks, their long sustained moaning cries, and remembered the coyotes at night around La Sal.

You knew it wasn't settled. On Tuesday night, walking home from Scouts with Keller and West and Strand and Doby and Jasperson, all of you in your uniforms, it comes up again.

"My dad says they made it out of stones," says West.

For how cool and smart he is, keeping Brother Rodgers on his toes, Strand has this laugh that comes out in a loud explosive snort at first, like he's been holding his breath, before it settles down into a regular laugh. He's got this tiny comb that he fishes out of his pocket sometimes to comb the same small patch of already combed short hair on the back side of his head. After the first snort, after the regular laugh, he says, "Stones. Good one."

"No," says Doby. "I heard that too."

"You mean rocks?" you say.

"Yeah."

"That's stupid," says Keller. "You ever seen a rock float?"

"He said it was like a submarine," says West.

"That's nuts. It'd sink."

"God could make anything float he wanted to."

"How come rocks?"

"There wasn't any wood around," says West.

"You're wrong," says Jasperson. "It says wood. Right in the Book of

Mormon."

"Where'd they get wood from?" says West.

"From trees."

"There's no trees there. It's just desert."

"They had olive trees."

"They're like apple trees," says West. "All stumpy and twisted. You can't build a ship out of 'em."

"Sounds like you need to read your Book of Mormon, West."

"Sounds like you need to kiss my ass. Assperson."

"Sounds like you need to wash your mouth out. Westicles."

You're in the street in front of the Burnhams' house. You and Doby and Strand and Keller let West and Jasperson swap a few slugs in the dusk. Then pull them apart. West looks like his nose is about to bleed. Jasperson stands there shaking like a leaf, looking hurt, at the edge of crying. A couple of feet away the lamp post suddenly lights up, and Sister Burnham's there, in her picture window, holding back her curtain. Jasperson picks his scout cap up. Doby hands West his. You get going. The lamp goes out behind you. Strand brings out his comb. And in the dark a couple of houses later the ship comes up again.

"What made it go if it was a submarine?" says Keller.

"I don't know."

"Submarines need motors. They didn't have motors back then."

"I guess God made it move," says Doby.

"My dad says it didn't have windows either," West says.

"How could they see where they were going?"

"They were underwater. All they could of seen was fish and seaweed."

"Did they have lights at least? Stuff to read?" says Keller.

"My dad didn't say."

"It wasn't a submarine. It had sails. The Book of Mormon says so," Jasperson says.

"How far you ever ridden your bike?" you suddenly say.

"I wouldn't be caught dead on a bike," says West.

"Far from where?" says Doby.

"Home."

"I used to ride to Tolman Elementary."

"You gonna ride it to junior high?" says Keller.

"Maybe. Unless there's a bus."

"There's not," says West. "My mom checked."

"So what're you gonna do?" says Keller. "Take a submarine?"

Nowhere is everywhere. After work every afternoon that week you wash up in the basin on the porch while Mrs. Harding stands there waiting. And then you show her your fingernails. And then you say goodbye and go. Just never home. Down the long hill. Last week's eight dollars in your pocket. Money you don't know what to do with. Money you don't want. Money your father can have. Where the hill ends, where nowhere starts, you swing your bike onto Orchard Drive, away from town, north toward where the houses thin out and orchards and fields take over, knowing you have to save half the strength of your legs to get home again for supper.

On Thursday Lupe brings a washcloth and your afternoon glass of lemonade and doesn't leave when you thank her. Just stands there like she's waiting for you to drink it.

"You okay?" she says.

"Me? Yeah."

"You sure."

"Yeah. Why?"

"No. Nothing."

"I'm okay."

"Just asking," she says. "All I can do."

And on Friday Mrs. Harding is there on the porch again to count eight dollar bills into your open hand.

"Thank you, Mrs. Harding."

For the first time ever she touches you. Reaches out and puts her fingertips under your chin to bring your face up. You've looked for the young Chicago singer when you've let yourself look at her. There was always the luminous white hair in the way. Always all the intricate wrinkles in the tissue of her skin. Always the raspy voice. Always the way her hands shook. Always the way you were scared she might see how old she was in the way you looked at her. All the years. You weren't old enough to make sense of that many years in someone's life. But in her eyes now you can see her. As if she came and got you and brought you back herself to when she sang. Her eyes roam your face. You let yourself look at her too because all you're seeing now is how young and beautiful Mr. Hinkle told you she was then. She takes her fingertips out from under your chin, reaches up and fixes something she doesn't like about your hair, brushes your ear.

"He looks fine," she says to Lupe. "I don't know what you're fretting about."

"Just a feeling," says Lupe. "Sometimes I'm wrong."

You don't know how to get to them, the tracks the trains use, only that you'll get there if you ride west long enough. You ride away from Mrs. Harding's house down the long familiar hill through your neighborhood. Keep using roads that keep the afternoon sun ahead of you. Cross the four-lane highway that runs along the west of town and keep going, following the cratered shoulders of valley roads, roads you never knew would be here. You ride straight through the craters. Stand up off the seat and let the bike roll through them. The tracks are farther away than they ever looked. Too far by the time you get to them to ever make it home in time for supper. When you look back you can't find your neighborhood until you see the white gash of the sandpit in the hills above it.

Your father's alone in the kitchen the way he likes to be when he cleans things up from supper, in his short sleeved shirt and apron, wiping down the kitchen table with a washrag.

"So," he says. "You're home."

"Sorry." In your pocket, the sixteen dollar bills are in your hand, eight from a week ago, eight from today, damp and limp and warm from the ride, the last part up the long hill, your legs gone, the yards in dusk, the air red from the low sun, the long oblique shadow of a kid pedaling a bike laid out on the asphalt ahead of you.

"Where were you?"

"I went to the railroad tracks."

"Out in Woods Cross?"

"I don't know what town."

"Woods Cross. That's quite a ride."

"I didn't know till I got there."

You wait for him to rinse and then wring the washrag out, hang it over the spigot, dry his hands, take his apron off and hang it on the wall hook next to the washing machine. You hand him the folded bills. His hands are pink and his fingertips wrinkled from the dishwater when he takes them.

"What's this?"

"My pay. Two weeks"

"All I need is your tithing," he says. "Two weeks? Sixteen dollars? So a dollar sixty."

He takes out two bills and holds the rest of them back out to you and reaches into his pocket for change.

"You keep it."

"Your money?"

"Sure."

"You want me to put it in the bank for you?"

"Sure."

He looks at you. You can see the fretful weariness in his face, the weight in his eyelids, how rough the ridges and furrows in his forehead are while he tries to figure out what's going on. In your breathing, you can feel the rough shiver from the last hard uphill pull, from being scared of standing here.

"I don't understand," he says.

"I don't need it."

"What do you mean, you don't need it?"

"I just don't. You can have it."

"Shakli? You are home?"

You turn around and she's there. In the fitful way her eyes run across your face is the same pained searching uncertainty her voice had. She's dressed in a homemade muumuu. You can tell from her tousled hair that she's been in bed reading.

"I'm sorry," you say.

"He went for a bike ride," your father says. "He got a little carried away."

"We're just glad you're home. Are you hungry? Come! Let me heat you some supper!"

"I'm okay."

"But you have to eat, Shakli!"

"So, Mother. He can eat later. Come. Let's all sit down."

"Yes, Shakli," she says. "Come sit with us."

You take the chair across from her. Your father takes his usual chair. He looks at the bills in his hand and puts them down. Around you the house is quiet, like the rest of it is vacant, like only the three of you live here, like the rest of the chairs around the table are for company.

"Tell him," your mother says.

"I will, Mother. I will. Just give me a moment."

"Should I tell him?"

"We made some phone calls tonight," your father finally says.

A boulder of ice starts forming in your stomach.

"What phone calls?"

"Your friends, to start with."

"You called my friends?"

"We were worried," your father says. "What do you expect?"

"Yes, Shakli." There's pity in your mother's smile now. "We were just worried."

"Which ones?"

"That's not important," your father says. He looks at your mother and then starts picking at the dark scab of a sore on his husky forearm. Revulsion flashes deep in your mother's face but by the time she looks at you it's gone.

"We called Mrs. Harding too," she says.

"You called Mrs. Harding?"

"Yes, Shakli."

"Why?"

"Why?" Your father smiles and shakes his head at how stupid he thinks the question is. "Because none of your friends had seen or heard from you."

"What did you tell her? What did she say?"

"We didn't speak to her," your mother says. "Only to a Mexican lady."

"Lupe?"

"Yes," your father says. "I think that was the name she used."

"Why did you even bother her? I was done working."

"So," your father says. "Settle down."

"All I was doing was riding my bike."

"Tell him, Harold."

"Tell me what?"

"She had some sad news," your father says.

"What?"

"Mrs. Harding passed away tonight."

"What?"

Your mother looks harshly at your father. "So, Harold. He's a boy. Use language that he can understand." And then she looks at you and says, "Mrs. Harding is dead."

"Dead?"

"Yes, Shakli."

You look at your father. "Mrs. Harding's dead?"

"Yes." He opens his hands and looks at them. "I'm afraid so."

"I just saw her. She paid me and everything."

"Yes, Shakli. Sometimes it happens that way."

"She can't be dead."

"You must have been on your bike ride," your father says.

"Maybe she just passed out. Maybe she's okay now."

"Oh, Shakli."

"Did you call back? I bet if you do, she's okay now."

"She's gone," your father says. "We're sure."

"How do you know? I just saw her. I was just there." You reach for the folded bills next to your father's arm, slide them out onto the table. "Look. Here's the money. Here's my pay."

Your mother's eyes look like they're floating. One of her hands comes gliding across the table, looking for yours.

"We had to lose someone too, Shakli. Someone much younger."

Your brother Felix, the baby they had right after you, before Karl, who died when he was two weeks old from an ear infection. Maybe she wants to be even now, you and her, with Mrs. Harding dead.

"Yes," your father says. "Sometimes we just have to accept things."

"No," you say. "I just saw her. Really."

"Three or four hours ago," he says. "You said it yourself that your ride took longer than you expected."

Standing there in the weeds and dirt off the side of the road where you could see the steel rails come from a long way south, cut through the asphalt like it wasn't there, and then keep going north, along the lake where you could see them from the sandpit, keep going north forever, trailing the long hoarse wailing cry of the horns. The way she brought up her hand to fix something she didn't like about your hair. The way they felt like paper where her fingers brushed your ear. The way she looked on the tennis court, singing, while people danced, while her paper lanterns burned, while Mr. Hinkle stood there playing in the shivering glint of the cymbals. Now, while your mother sits there with her eyes wet and her hair mussed, while your father sits there looking for something in his hands, while it starts happening, while this hollow aching wilderness starts opening up inside you, you look everywhere but at them. At the apron on the wall, the washer, the box of Tide, the cabinet where the clothespins are, the back door, the empty yellow chairs, at the deep red almost black night outside the window. At your mother's open hand, her rugbeater hand, waiting for yours. And finally down, at the table, where you try to keep from crying, where hundreds of tiny wire boomerangs are caught in the yellow formica between your hands.

"How can someone just be dead?"

"She was old, Shakli. She lived a full life. It was time."

"Why?"

"Only God can answer that."

"Look at us, Shakli," your mother says. "Please. We're your parents. We love you."

"So, Mother," your father says abruptly. "You don't need to beg."

You look up at her. Gratitude organizes her wet face. She uses her open hands to wipe her cheeks. Your father clears his throat.

"It looks like you might still have your job," he says.

"My job?"

"The woman we spoke to. She said she'd see you Monday."

"Monday?"

"Yes. The regular time."

"Do you think you can still work there, Shakli?"

"I guess."

Your father puts the palms of his hands on the table. "So. Are we finished here?"

Obediently, your mother goes to compose herself, reach up to smooth her hair, give you a fond contented smile that floods you with this restless itching need to get away again.

"Thanks for telling me."

"Here," your father says. "Don't forget your money."

"I don't want it."

"Don't be foolish. You earned it."

"That's okay," you say. "You keep it."

"This is about that trumpet, isn't it," your father finally says.

Across the table, your mother sags back, brings her hand to her mouth, gives you this look like you've come out of nowhere and slugged her.

"Yes, Shakli," she says. "After everything we do for you."

"So, Mother. Just let him go. As usual, this is the thanks we get."

Chapter 23

THE NEXT morning, dumping the catcher onto the pile of clippings at the edge of the field, you see the backs of Mrs. Harding's shoes while she led you around the yard the first time, stark enough to take your breath and leave you staring. Later, running the wheel of the edger along the curb in front of your house to cut the dark groove of dirt your father wants, the blade hits a buried stone. You keep cutting the blade back and forth across it like it's something you need to kill to get even with. The times where things just come to you. The Everly Brothers on Keller's transistor radio. If she liked them. A white Thunderbird convertible. If she ever had one. If she wore a scarf and lipstick when she drove it. The soft liquid chill of ice cream. What flavor she liked. What color her hair was when it wasn't white. In Sunday School the next morning, on Father's Day, you wonder if her father was a big tough Chicago guy. If he gave her rides on horses when she was a little girl. She's dead. People know. You watch your mother talk to Sister Avery and know what they're saying from the way they touch each other's forearms. They don't announce it. She wasn't Mormon. But people know. The poor woman. It's so sad what happened. At least she's where she can accept the Gospel now.

Your buddies are careful not to say much. Out in the parking lot, unable to help himself, West comes close, and then backs off when you step up.

"Come on," you say. "She poisoned herself. Say it."

"All I was gonna ask was what happens to the Gullwing. Sorry. Geez."

"I told you. It's gone."

"Asswipe," Keller tells West.

"Yeah," says Jasperson.

"Yeah? Go drink some mouthwash, Assperson."

"Better mouthwash than soap," says Jasperson. "Like you could use."

"Oh wow. That really hurt."

After Sunday School, your mother serves sauerbraten, mashed potatoes, Brussels sprouts, grape juice, your father's favorite dinner. Karl and Molly set the linen tablecloth of the dining room table with china and silver. You take your places. In her Sunday dress your mother still has the angel look she carries home from church, as though the music she played still lingers in some place where only she can hear the way the pipes breathe. The smile she sends around the table just before your father starts to bless the food is radiant and naked.

His prayer is long, even for him, as he expresses his gratitude for his wife, the kids who made him a father, the opportunity to raise his family in Zion, the fullness of the Gospel, his friends, every other thing he's blessed with, then turns around and asks God to bless the poor, the sick, the old, the less fortunate, the leaders of the church, every father everywhere. On and on, oblivious to the heat rising off the platters of his favorite dinner, to the threat you can sense with your eyes closed, the failing angel of your mother across the table while Maggie mutters and fusses next to her. Everyone says amen. Your mother's still smiling but there's nothing angelic in the way she reaches for the sauerbraten. Everyone eats. Your father, still humbled from his long prayer, praises the way the food tastes, tells you all how thankful he is for his wife, how fortunate all of you are to have her for your mother.

"Did that lady you work for die?" says Karl.

"Let's not remind him," your mother says. "Let's have a nice dinner."

"You still got a job?"

"Yes."

"Is she going to Heaven?"

"That depends," your father says.

"On what?" says Karl.

"So, Harold. Let's enjoy our dinner."

"On whether she finally accepts the Gospel in the Spirit World," your father says.

"Thank you, Harold. Thank you for listening to your wife."

"She's already there," you tell Karl.

"How do you know?"

"She told me so."

"She's in Hell," says Karl.

"Enough," your father says.

After dinner, the tablecloth in front of him cleared of food, cluttered now with his napkin and steel tumbler, the handmade crayon cards that Karl and Molly and Roy brought home from Primary, your wrapping paper, your father pulls on the gloves, holds them up, examines them.

"Gloves in June." His grin broad and his voice big. "By golly. This is what I call thinking ahead."

"Do they fit?" you ask.

"Yes," he says. "Perfect."

"They're fur lined," you say.

"Yes. I can tell."

Around the table Karl and Roy and Molly watch him. Your mother takes Maggie's spoon away to keep her from running it back and forth across the wooden tray of her high chair.

"Do you like them?"

"Very much," he says. And then he says, "Of course, I'll appreciate them much more by the time January gets here." He pulls the stitched brown fingers loose, one by one, takes them off his hands, reads the tiny label stitched just inside the wrist. "Calfskin. By golly. I'm not so sure I deserve them."

"So, Harold. Don't start. We're having a nice time."

You look across the table. The angel in your mother's face is thin as tissue paper, fragile as a moth or butterfly in your father's hands.

"By golly, Mother. I'm just trying to express my gratitude."

"Yes. They are nice gloves."

"One of the nicest presents I can remember getting in a long time."

"Yes. Now that is enough."

He lays the gloves on the paper you wrapped them in. "Of course, my biggest present comes next week," he says. "When I'll have the opportunity to ordain my firstborn son into the Priesthood."

And suddenly you're conscious of Karl and Molly and Roy. Their cards around your father's elbows. The money you left on the kitchen table. Your pay. Your father could have driven them to town. Your mother could have helped them pick things out.

"They're from all of us," you say. "The gloves."

Your mother looks at you surprised and then with this tolerant sweetness.

"Yes, Shakli," she says. "That is very generous."

"They're not from me," says Karl.

"He's right," you say.

"Shakli," your mother says.

"She's in Hell," says Karl. "With all the other hags."

CHAPTER 24

LUPE SAID Monday. And so you've stayed away all weekend in spite of the constant pull of the house. You had no business there. On Monday you do. On the porch in front of the back door the coiled braid of the mat is the rag doll of a sleeping snake. Lupe comes out when you knock. She's wearing a black scarf, tied in back like a bandana, and her nose and eyes are red, but she's still the same old Lupe. She tells you it was a stroke. You nod. You figure you can look it up in your father's dictionary. She tells you a man came from Chicago Saturday, on the plane, and talked to her about the house and everything, and yesterday he took Mrs. Harding back to Chicago on the train. They'll be selling the house. They want you to keep the yard up.

"On the train?"

"Yeah." And then she says, "Kills me that I can't go to her funeral."

"They can do that?"

"Sure they can. They can put anything on a train."

"Who was he?"

"A cousin. Maybe a nephew. I don't know for sure."

"Was he nice?"

"Nice enough. Mostly business." And then she smiles. "He gave you a raise."

"A raise?"

"He don't know he did." She looks around. And then whispers, "I told him Mrs. Harding pay you ten dollars a week."

"He believed you?"

"Do I look like I could lie?"

"Wow. Thanks."

"I got one too," she says. "Don't tell nobody."

You get to work. Soon there's a panel truck parked in front of the house, painted green and yellow, the side decorated with a yellow sailing ship, the name Mayflower. Three men take cardboard boxes and rolls of paper inside. Another truck shows up, backs up the driveway, raises a long black bin off its back, eases it onto the concrete, lowers its frame again and leaves. Later, a station wagon pulls into the driveway behind the bin, four Mexican women get out and carry mops and brooms and buckets inside, and soon you see them bringing armloads of stuff out the side door. Sometimes they skirt the bin and put things in the station wagon. Lupe brings you lemonade. Her face is shiny. Points of sweat sparkle in the sunlight like diamonds on the dark gold skin where her nose flares out, and you can hear her breathe when she asks you how you're doing.

"What's a stroke?"

"When your brain stops."

Occasionally, over the course of the morning, the men from the panel truck come out on the back porch, smoke, relax against the railings, look around, like the men used to do on the side porch of the ranchhouse outside your father's office, waiting for him to finish counting their pay into envelopes. Questions fill your head, questions for Lupe, and when she brings you a tuna sandwich for lunch, and a banana and a glass of milk, you're ready for her.

"Are those women your friends?"

"Two of them are my sisters."

"Are they throwing that stuff away?"

"The stuff in the big box?" she says. "Yeah."

"How come?"

"They don't want it in Chicago. Why? You want it?"

"No."

"Help yourself if you do. It's going to the dump."

"What are those men doing?"

"They're packing."

"What are they packing?"

"Everything that's going to Chicago."

"Was Mrs. Harding pretty?"

Lupe looks at you shocked, and then she looks away, and you can see her brown throat move, and then she looks down at your sandwich.

"Her pictures were."

Stuff she looked at in a store. Stuff she thought she'd like. Stuff she tried on, stuff she bought and then brought home, stuff people thought she'd like and bought for her. Stuff that mattered to her, for a year, for longer, for just a minute or maybe a day or two. Every piece had its time when it held her attention, however brief, for its beauty, for what it could do, for being a gift, maybe just for the moment it sat in her lap unwrapped. Armload after armload, when you glance across the yard at one of the Mexican women, you see what the house was like inside, what it held, what decorated it and cluttered it, what it was made of. When you walk past the bin, you could easily grab the top, stand on the big steel beam that runs along the bottom, and look inside, like the men from the panel truck keep doing. That afternoon, when the panel truck leaves, you pick the cigarette butts out of the flowers and dirt around the porch.

On Tuesday, the panel truck is there again, across the street this time, to make room for a moving van that runs the length of the front yard. The wall of the van is painted like the panel truck except that everything is big. From the back yard, you can hear the men shout, hear them laugh, hear their boots hit the ramps with the weight of Mrs. Harding's furniture, feel the way the ramp would flex when you were helping Manny and Hidalgo empty out the cattle truck.

In the afternoon, Lupe comes out of the back of the house with one of the men from the panel truck, crosses the yard, unlocks the side door, takes him inside the garage. A second later you hear him whistle low and long. You wonder if it's the Gullwing or the Cadillac. Lupe comes to the tennis court where you're pulling weeds.

"That man?" she says.

"Yeah?"

"He's going to pack the garage. He went to get boxes. When he comes back, I want you to go in there and watch him. Make sure everything goes in a box."

"Okay."

"Don't touch nothing. Just watch. That way he can't say it was you. Come get me when he's done so I can mark the boxes down."

"Okay."

"Come get me too if you see something funny."

"Okay."

She watches him come out of the back of the house with an armload of collapsed cardboard boxes, a roll of paper, a fat roll of tape looped around his wrist like a bracelet.

"Can't trust men around tools. Like kids around cookies."

You remember the old paint cans, the empty oil cans, the brushes, the dirt-caked parts of cars in the corners and along the walls.

"What about the junk stuff?"

"I told him what's junk. It stays."

"What about the cars?"

"They go on Thursday."

The long silver Mercedes. The layer of dust where you can almost see this sheen of dull gold where its dark curves catch the light from the naked bulb up in the dark rafters.

"Can I ask you for a favor?"

"Sure," says Lupe.

"My friend wants to know if he could come and look at the Mercedes."

"Yeah?" she says, tough, like she's still talking about the man you're supposed to guard. "Who's your friend?"

"Bobby," you say. "He loves cars." And then you say, "He knows he can't touch it."

"He can look all he wants," she finally says. "Just wait till it's cleaned out in there. Say tomorrow afternoon."

That night the men lock up the moving van and leave it there. All of them drive off in the panel truck. You pick their cigarette butts out from around the porch again. The next morning, the day you turn twelve, the men are back. They load up the boxes from the garage. Save Mrs. Harding's mattresses for last. They slide the ramps up underneath the trailer, and close and latch and padlock the doors, and you watch black smoke explode and then surge from the stacks when they fire up the engine, ease the van away from the curb, slowly drive away. The panel truck follows the van down the street like a calf behind its mother.

That day, for the first time, Lupe and the women eat lunch outside, on the back porch, and Lupe brings you milk in a paper cup and a sandwich on a paper plate.

"No more dishes," she says. "No more table, no more nothing."

"Okay."

She looks at the house next door. Two men have been on the roof all morning, laying shingles, the hollow crack of their hammers nailing them in place.

"You have to wait to get home to wash up now," she says.

"That's okay."

You already know. You saw the big tin basin come out earlier. Lupe's eyes go narrow, roam across the yard behind you, linger on the tennis court, then come down on you again.

"Ever hear of Yuma?" she says.

"Yuma?"

"Little desert town in Arizona. Way down in the corner by Mexico and California. It's where I'm from."

"Where you were born?"

"Born, raised, went to school."

The way she looks after she says it leaves you silent, standing there, holding your plate and cup, wondering if you're supposed to tell her where you're from.

"It's my sisters," she finally says. "We just been telling stories."

The next day West shows up maybe an hour after lunch to take his look at the Gullwing. He's standing in the driveway, unsure of himself in the middle of everything going on, when you look up from raking the tennis court and see him. You pull the door back on the dull nose of the Gullwing and then the door on the Cadillac. He comes a couple of steps closer and stops.

"Happy Birthday," he says. "You sure this is okay?"

"Thanks. Yeah. She said you could look all you want."

Inside the garage you flip the switch for the light bulb in the rafters. With the doors open to daylight you can only tell it's on where the bulb itself is reflected through the dust on the glass of the windshield. West stays outside. Gets down on one knee and studies the front end, gets up and studies the long dark silver hood and the long swells of the fenders, moves to the side, gets down again to follow the length of the silver body back toward its rear end in the deep shadow at the back of the garage. He gradually makes his way inside, where his eyes follow the even seam between the hood and fender, where he kneels in the dirt to study the front fender, the wheel and the tire it houses, the slotted vents in the body back of the fender, the seam where the door is cradled in the body before he stands up again to follow the line of the door up into the roof.

"You can see how the door works," he says. "It lifts up. That's the handle. Wish I could show you. I didn't know it would be this dusty."

You've stayed in the back corner to give him room. You've never seen anyone look at a car this way. This close and slow and serious at things you never knew were there to look at.

"How come?" you say.

"Don't ever touch a dusty car. You'll scratch the paint. Ever seen where some moron's gone and wrote wash me on a dirty car with his finger? Even after you've washed it you can still see wash me because it's scratched into the paint. It's there for good unless you compound it out."

When he starts talking again it's to tell you things about the Gullwing you'd never know from seeing it here, garaged and still, the way you'd never know Rex and the shifting feel of his big powerful muscles from watching him sleep standing in his stable. Things that are only suggested in the residual smell of oil and gas and exhaust in the garage the way the smell of hay and sweat and horseshit suggested what Rex could do.

"How fast can it go?"

"Over two hundred."

"Wow."

"You know me and Pontiacs," he says. "This is the one car I'd put over a Pontiac."

"How much are they?" you say.

"I don't know," he says. "I know I'll never own one."

Out through the open door, in the daylight, you watch Lupe throw a glance at the garage as she crosses back from the black bin to the house.

"Is that the lady who said I could come look?"

"Yeah."

"I'm sorry about all the shit I said."

"She never poisoned anyone," you finally say.

"I know." And then he says, "Nobody who'd buy a car like this for their kid would turn around and poison him."

"She was a singer a long time ago. Back in Chicago." And then you say, "That's where they took her back to. On the train."

"Dead?"

"Yeah."

"What'd she sing?"

"Whatever they sing in night clubs. Love songs."

"What's gonna happen to these?"

"Back to Chicago too. A truck's supposed to come tomorrow."

"They're hauling them?"

"Yeah."

"You oughta wash 'em down some," he says. "At least the door handles. They gotta get inside to get 'em on the truck."

"I'll do it."

"I gotta go," he says. "Thanks. Tell her thanks too."

Late that afternoon the truck that dropped the trash bin off two days ago comes back. You've never seen a truck like it. From the cab back, the rest of it is nothing but a skeleton, a long black frame of beams and rails. A man in gray coveralls gets out and guides the truck up the driveway back against the bin. The truck lurches, the brakes grunt, and the driver gets out, wearing the same gray coveralls. He leaves the engine running while his helper looks back and forth inside the bin.

The street is busy with little kids. From the back of the driveway, you watch the men in coveralls unroll a black tarp across the length of the bin, tie pieces of rope from holes in the tarp to hooks in the black steel walls. You hear the hard dirty racing idle of the engine and breathe the sharp hot smell of diesel smoke. The driver uses levers to tilt the frame high off the truck and then slide it down until the back of the frame hits concrete. The helper hooks a cable to the front of the bin. The driver pulls another lever. You hear a high howling fluid squeal over the sudden deep pull of the engine as the bin connects with the frame and slowly rides the rails up toward a shrieking pulley. The rising bin seems to grow till it looks twice the size it did. Finally the pulley stops, the engine slows, and they drop the bin level and chain it into place. The driver hands Lupe a clipboard and a pen. Lupe studies what the clipboard says and then signs it.

For the first time, you see how the whole back wall of the bin is hinged, like a tailgate, so that the bin can be raised again and dumped, like you saw at the place out west where you went with your father once with a trunkload of junk from La Sal your mother didn't want in the house, the place where seagulls filled the sky and bulldozers rode smoking hills of garbage. The driver and helper slam the doors of the cab. You follow the back of the truck down the driveway. Follow it when it turns onto the street.

This time you're not confused. This time you don't go off half chasing it. This time your father's not there with his camera. This time you know. This time you just stand there while the black bin, set high on the back of the smoking truck, rides off down the street. This time this sound starts coming out of you. And then someone grabs you, and it's Lupe, and she holds you up against herself while the sound keeps coming, up your throat and out of you, this sound you've never made before, this long hard quiet groaning sound that feels like it will never end and let you breathe again.

CHAPTER 25

THREE DAYS AGO it was your father's turn. Tonight it's yours. Your mother starts off by cooking your favorite dinner, breaded pork chops and spaghetti, and afterward, your father gathers the family in the living room and talks about your upcoming journey through the Priesthood. Then everyone stands around the piano and sings while your mother plays Happy Birthday. Then the wavering light from the kitchen, the blazing cake, the smoking wicks of twelve extinguished candles while Karl asks what you wished for and Roy asks if he can have a frosting rose. There are homemade cards from Karl and Molly and Roy. Then presents. Your mother hands you the first one. Shorts and socks. The second one is a bankbook, like the one she and your father have, and for a minute you're scared, wondering why they wrapped their bankbook up for you. Your father watches from the far corner of the couch.

"It's your very own savings account! Look, Shakli! Look inside!"

She backs away, back toward her seat on the couch, while you open it. On the first page there's your name. On another page there's a stamped imprint for a deposit of fourteen dollars and forty cents. Bountiful State Bank. The old man in the blue and gray uniform guarding the front door. The high counter with openings like old-fashioned battleships had for cannons where women sit and trade papers back and forth with customers. The big steel wall of the safe in back with the thick steel door.

"Do you like it, Shakli?"

Your mother perched on the edge of the couch, her fingers locked together on her knees in a single interlaced hand with two wrists, her face flushed.

"My money's there?"

"We deposited it last Saturday," she says. "Do you like it?"

"Yeah. For sure."

It amazes you how suddenly official and important your money is, in a bank, with people to tend it, a guard to watch over it.

"Better than the kitchen table, by golly," your father says.

"Thanks, Mama. Thanks, Papa."

"Oh, Harold, he likes it! I'm so happy!"

"The start of your missionary account."

"We have another surprise for you," your mother says. "Are you ready?"

"Sure."

She leaves the room. Karl looks at your bankbook. Molly sits on the carpet with Maggie between her legs like they're riding a pony together. Roy sits nested up against your father. Your mother comes back. You know what it is the second you see it, in her arms, before you see the handle where it pokes up through the paper, before she crosses the room to set it on your knees and wait for you to hold it there, before you feel its heft, its hard round corners through the stiff skin of the wrapping paper. She backs away again.

"This goes with it." Your father rolls to his left and pulls an envelope out from between his leg and the armrest. "Here," he says, handing the envelope to Roy. "Bring this to your brother."

"We didn't know," your mother says. "We're sorry."

"So, Mother. Don't apologize."

"It's okay, Mama."

Roy hands you the card and then stands there. "What is it?" Karl says. "Open it."

"I will. Go sit down."

The card is signed in your mother's Swiss handwriting, fresh, chaste, the way she learned to write in school. The folded typewritten note inside it is your father's. Dear Son. As you embark on your journey now, great things will be expected of you, and great responsibilities will be trusted to you. You will be called to serve the Lord in many ways. To be His instrument. Every talent He has blessed you with, everything good He has given you, has a single purpose. To further His work. Let me quote just a short scripture. 'Hence when you go on making gifts of mercy, do not blow a trumpet ahead of you, just as the hypocrites do in the synagogues and in the streets, that they may be glorified by men.' I want you to know how proud I am of you.

It's signed your loving father. Under his scrutiny, you fold the note, put it back inside the card, put the card back in its envelope, look across the room at him.

"By golly," he says. "Open it. It's not going to unwrap itself."

"Yeah," Karl says. "Open it finally."

He's on his knees, on the carpet, something derisive and mean in his eager face, your bankbook still in his hand. You sit there desperate for a way to slow this down.

"Say you're sorry you called her a hag."

"I'm sorry. Open it."

"Say it. I'm sorry I called her a hag."

"Oh, Shakli, let's not ruin our nice time."

"Yes," your father says. "Let's not bring up old business."

"Say it."

"Okay. I'm sorry I called her a hag. Now open it."

"Say you're sorry you said she was in Hell."

"Come, Shakli, open it. Don't be mean to your brother. We all want to see!"

You see it in his eyes. The mean satisfaction of having your mother on his side. The way this will have to happen.

"Say it. Or nobody gets to see it."

Karl throws a look at your mother. Then back at you, the satisfaction gone, just the meanness there now.

"I'm sorry I said she's in Hell. Okay?"

Don't want what they can take away from you. When you head for work on Thursday it's back in place, behind the Christmas boxes, its tarnished history caged away, part of the house again. At work, Lupe and the Mexican women shake mops and rags in clouds off the back porch, throw buckets of dirty water around the roots of bushes. You see them at the upstairs windows, and at first you think they're waving, but the circles their hands describe don't stop when you wave back, and then you see the rags they're using to shine the glass. Lupe has you come and eat with them on the porch, where you try to figure out which two her sisters are, and listen for the word Yuma to surface in the rapid babbling of their passionate and happy Spanish. That afternoon a truck shows up for the Gullwing and the Cadillac. Lupe opens the garage door and takes a man with a clipboard inside.

"They're filthy. I ain't touching 'em."

Out in the yard, hearing him talk to Lupe in the garage, you get off your knees with the clippers ready in your hand.

"Mr. Swift said to leave them this way," you hear Lupe say. "He said they'd just get dirty on the road."

"That's too bad. I only haul clean cars."

"Oh yeah? Is that why that big trailer out there is empty?"

"That's none of your business. Clean cars only."

"So we make a deal," you hear her say. "You get clean cars, but not to put on your filthy trailer. You wash the trailer, we wash the cars."

"My rig ain't filthy, lady."

"Yeah? Then you show me. Let's go take a look."

Outside, listening in the sunlight, you can barely hold yourself back from running inside, jamming the long blades of the clippers deep into his gut.

"Okay, lady. But you gotta sign here that they're dirty."

"They're dusty. That's all I'm gonna sign."

"Dusty then. Whatever you say."

"And I don't want you touching the dust and making scratches in the paint. The door handles are clean so you can get inside to do your business. But that's all."

Just outside the garage you smile. Happy you told her what West said. Happy she let you wash them. Happy you gave her something she could use on the man.

On Friday morning, there's a note from your father at your place at the kitchen table, reminding you of your interview at six that night with Bishop Byrne. Sometime that afternoon, at work in Mrs. Harding's back yard, you watch a sparkling white Chrysler pull into the driveway. A woman in high heeled shoes and a white suit with a gleaming head of blonde hair is let into the house. A while later Lupe comes outside with her. You watch her try to keep her pointed heels from sinking in the grass while Lupe shows her the back yard and the tennis court. She opens the trunk of the Chrysler and takes out a sign and hammer and heads out front. Soon after she's gone, the Mexican women haul suitcases and bags out to the station wagon, and Lupe comes out back, locking the door, looking for you. She opens a manila folder and hands you an envelope.

"Your first real paycheck. Guess you can have your dad cash it for you."

"I got my own bank account."

"Well," she says. "What a little man we have here."

"Are you going back to Yuma?"

"Yuma?" She laughs. "No. I'm living with my sister. In Salt Lake. On Third West. Close to the high school."

"Okay."

"You'll be getting paid in the mail from now on," she says. "Every two weeks."

"Okay."

She takes a long look at you, and then your hair, and then she looks up at the sky, and for a minute you can see the skin draw tight around the corners of her mouth, and dimples appear in her chin. Then she takes another piece of paper out of her folder.

"Here."

It's a photograph, an old one, five Negro men in tuxedos and bow ties and shiny rippled hair, all of them smiling, a couple of them with lines for moustaches, one with a pair of drumsticks in his hand. A woman whose dress leaves her shoulders naked at the center of their gathered faces, a woman with an open white flower in her dark long wavy hair, eyes that take you in and make you king of anything you want, a smile you never thought could have been this clearly beautiful, her hands still sleek and graceful where they lie crossed in the lap of her dress.

"You asked if she was pretty."

When you look up, tears are leaving thin silver streaks down the brown skin of Lupe's cheeks, and the yard feels like it's exploding, quiet and astonishing, wave after bewildering wave of the summer light around you in the leaves and flowers of the woman in the photograph.

"She liked you." Lupe looks away quickly. "She said your name."

CHAPTER 26

IN THE FIELD behind your house, on a bank of dirt after racing your bikes around the winding track you've started to wear into the weeds, you and Johnny Blackwell pick stones off the dirt between your shoes, toss them at a half-buried can a few yards away, a can too rusted and crushed to tell you what came out of it when it was opened. It's Saturday afternoon, three days past your birthday. Tomorrow morning, men your father knows will circle around you, lay their hands on your head, give you the Lower Priesthood, the Priesthood of Aaron, and when they do, you'll feel the power of the Holy Ghost.

The Holy Ghost. Its power will pass from their hands, down through your head, into the temple of your body, into your bosom. When it does, you'll know, because you'll feel a burning there. That's what you were told by Bishop Byrne at your interview last night, in his splashed and dappled housepainter's clothes fresh from a job, from behind the big desk in his office at the churchhouse. Now, picking stones, you ask Blackwell what it feels like. You figure he should know. He's thirteen and a half. He's been a Deacon since before you moved here. At church you've watched him pass the Sacrament.

"What it feels like?" Blackwell says.

"Yeah."

"I don't remember."

"Does it itch?"

"I guess. Maybe."

"Does it burn?"

"I'd remember if it burned."

"Bishop Byrne said it burned. In your bosom."

"He told me that too," says Blackwell. "Guys don't even have bosoms."

"How come he'd say that then?"

"Cuz that's the way they talked back in the olden days."

"Is it like electricity?"

"No, stupid. It's not like electricity."

What Blackwell will always be is the first friend you made in Bountiful. No matter what else happens. No matter if you get to hate each other. Back in April, looking for yardwork, you knocked on the door of a house just off the circle from your house, and when it opened, there he was. His mother wasn't home. He brought you in and showed you his model aircraft carrier and his father's army rifle. He let you use his slingshot to fire small steel marbles off his back porch at big green ripening flowerheads across the yard. He said he was home from school because his mother had to take him to the dentist when she got home from Safeway. It didn't matter then that he was a grade ahead of you or in an older class in Sunday School. But you've made other friends since then, and Blackwell knows it, and it gripes him, and he uses it to hold you to the obligation that he was the one who welcomed you to the neighborhood.

"You ever felt electricity?" you ask.

"Yeah. In science. They made us hold hands. Then they turned this crank on this machine."

"So what'd it feel like?"

"It tingled like crazy. On the inside of your wrists. Right here."

"I meant the Holy Ghost."

You know you're not the first. That it's happened to him before. That this passing way, this way when you're new to the neighborhood, is the only way he has friends. Doby and West and Keller saw his plastic aircraft carrier and his father's army rifle and shot his slingshot too. And then moved on. You hang out with him to prove that you're not like them. To keep passing the ways he tests you. To keep him from calling you another traitor. To keep from feeling bad for him. A few feet away, in the dirt, your bikes rest on their pedals and handlebars. Yours has the handlebars turned over, the fenders off, the seat low. Blackwell's is stock. It's even got a headlight, a fake gas tank, a battery-operated horn that sounds like the lambs back in La Sal when the sheepherders put rubber bands around their tails to cut the flow of blood off. The sound when you hit the can is dirty and soft and only barely hollow.

"I don't know," he says. "Just different. Stop asking me."

"You didn't feel anything."

"Sure I did."

"No you didn't."

"If I didn't, I wouldn't be passing the Sacrament, would I?"

"So what'd it feel like?"

"I keep telling you. I don't remember. Just different."

"How?"

"Like jacking off is different."

"Jacking off?"

"You don't know about jacking off?"

You look at him. Smiling, he tosses a stone he's been holding, watches it miss the can, looks out across the field and then up into the hills. You know the smile. Lazy, mocking, there to make you feel stupid. Because you beat him. Because you always beat him. Because he's older and bigger and has a better bike and can never figure out why you're faster. Because he's flabby and big and keeps his seat and handlebars too high. Because you can make him go wobbling off the track into the weeds, his legs out, his loafers pedaling the air like someone swimming with their shoes on, when he tries to block you from going around him on a curve.

Sweat mixed with hair tonic clots his hair down the back of his neck and makes his skin look oily more than wet. Behind him, across the field, you can see the back of your house. The black perforated shell of the incinerator barrel where you burn your family's trash stands just off the edge of the yard where the neighborhood ends and the field starts. You fish through the dirt between your shoes for another small stone. The dirt is like dry grease, like the black dust out of a pencil sharpener, where your slick fingers start turning the stone.

"You ever see the guts out of a steer?" you say.

"The guts out of a steer?" He says it like you're crazy.

"They're huge. Big and green."

"How do you know?"

"They used to shoot one every week where we used to live."

"A steer?"

"Then they'd hang it up and gut it."

"How?"

"Just cut its stomach open so all its guts come rolling out."

"No kidding?"

"Nope."

You're there again, you and Jimmy Dennison, sitting on the top rail of the fence around the big corral, the spears of your long sticks already whittled sharp. The wood of the rail where you sit is weathered to where it feels like velvet. A couple of men herd a single steer into the corral, herd it close to the hoist, three tall poles like the tripod your father has for his camera, a pulley at the top where the poles are roped together. The rifle, waiting for the steer to get in close to the hoist, stop, hold still. The lash of its head, the give of its knees, the slow roll of its dead body onto its side, the men tying rope around its back ankles, hauling it out of the dirt and up until it hangs there, upside down, underneath the pulley, its neck limp, turning in the air. You remember running the kidneys home.

"What'd they do with them?"

"Just leave them. They'd skin it, then take it away to butcher it, and leave the guts there for a while. That was the fun part."

"Why?"

"They were like these big balloons," you say. "You could poke holes in them." You toss the stone at the can, watch it miss, skitter a couple of times. "These big long stinky farts would come out."

"You're lying."

"They were loud. Sometimes they'd whistle."

"What'd you poke them with?"

"Spears."

"You didn't have spears."

"We made them."

"How?" Blackwell says. "Outta what?"

You look ahead, across the field, to the brown eroding cliff on the other side, where the long hill is partially carved away for the dirt road over to Old Man Tuttle's house and his fields of peas and beans. Up the hill, just past the top, the back side of the hill is gone, carved away for the dirt bowl of the sandpit. On the floor of the sandpit stands a big black elevated hopper big enough to make you wonder what it would be like to have a room made out of steel. There's a steam shovel too, a yellow cab on rusted tracks, its bucket resting like a knuckled fist on the dirt.

"Tell me what jacking off is," you say.

Coming from Blackwell, you know it's dirty, like Danny Archuleta was back in La Sal, wanting to be a doctor or an artist just so he could see women naked.

"You tell me how you made spears."

"You first."

"Ask your dad if you want to know."

You know what he means. He means your father's got an accent. He means your father's just another ignorant foreigner who won't know what you're asking him.

"You tell me," you say.

"I'm not your dad."

The way your father acts when Blackwell comes over. Sits him at the kitchen table. Asks him if he wants some lemonade. Talks to him like Blackwell matters. Like everything Blackwell says is funny enough to make you sick from laughing, smart enough to make you want to write it down, like Blackwell and him are men while you're a kid. Maybe it's because they both already have the Priesthood. Because they both already have the look. Like Lilly and Jasperson and Keller and sometimes even West.

"Maybe I'll ask your dad instead," you say.

"Maybe you won't."

"Maybe I'll tell him where I heard it from."

"Maybe you won't."

"I just figured it might be like electricity."

"Yeah." His cheeks pull back in this greasy smile again. "Jacking off's like electricity."

"No. Getting the Priesthood."

"It is," he says. "Like the electric chair. They strap you down and put their hands on your head and start talking, and all of a sudden, a zillion volts go through you, and your clothes start smoking and your eyeballs pop, and you're jumping like a monkey, and you start crapping and peeing at the same time."

You're a big fat stupid prick, you want to say, but you don't, because it's the honest truth, and if you said it, he'd know you didn't really want to be his friend.

"Wanna race again?" you say instead.

"Up yours."

"Wanna go up and do the sandpit?"

"Up yours."

"Up yours too. I'll find out what it feels like tomorrow."

When you get it. You know its ranks. Known them so long you can't remember when you didn't. A Deacon now, a Teacher two years from now when you turn fourteen, a Priest when you turn sixteen. The ranks of the Lower Priesthood, the one they call Aaronic, each rank with its set of special keys, each rank with the power to do more things in the name of God. You've looked ahead to them the way you've looked ahead to school, to getting pubic hair some day, to having your wrists grow thick enough to where your thumb and finger won't touch when they reach around them. Things that will come along. Things you'll do with your circle of buddies in the larger circle of everyone you know. Somewhere along the way, maybe before they make you a Teacher or a Priest, you'll have passed enough of Blackwell's tests to not have to be his friend. You'll have found a way to tell your father he doesn't need to laugh at Blackwell's phony jokes without having to tell him what Blackwell thinks of him. Without having to tell him the way Blackwell stares at your mother's chest, like he's looking at someone in a magazine who can't look back, when she sets a glass of lemonade in front of him.

You've still got everyone's shoes to polish before your mother dishes up a Saturday night bowl of lentils for everyone around the table where the small pink rubbery wheels of hot dog slices are visible just beneath the dark gold surface.

"I gotta get home," you say.

"Yeah," says Blackwell. And then, when you've picked up your bikes and brushed the dirt off your seats and handlebar grips, he says, "You're my friend."

You look at him. There's nothing mocking in his face, or dirty, nothing that says you're stupid. Just his face.

"Yeah?"

"No. I'm asking."

"Yeah. Why?"

"For sure," he says.

"Yeah."

He looks away, past your shoulder, pulls his lips into a tight circle like he's about to whistle, squints his eyes. Then he looks down at his handlebars before he looks back up at you.

"You don't feel anything," he says.

"Not anything?"

"Naw."

"The Holy Ghost?"

"Naw."

Sometimes the shovel will start to cough black smoke, move forward on the shrieking rust of its tracks into the far cliff, raise its huge bucket dripping with dirt out of the slowly caving wall it leaves behind, swivel around, dump the bucket into the open top of the hopper. Sometimes a truck will appear, a dump truck, pull up between the four tall legs of the hopper, wait for the door in the bottom to open, when dirt will come in a steady gush out through the bottom in a slow exploding cloud of dust, to where the truck is gone, to where you wonder how the man who works the door can tell when the bed is full. When the truck drives off, dirt will sift off its hood and fenders, clods will drop off its roof and burst when they hit the ground, and when you wave, the driver will sometimes pull his horn, its sound hoarse and fat and steady, like the horn on the Queen Elizabeth when you stood there, next to your father on the deck, looking through the wet steel bars of the railing into the dark and the rain for what he said was the Statue of Liberty.

CHAPTER 27

OUT THE WIDE aluminum-framed window of your bedroom is the circle where you used your bike yesterday, coming home from racing Blackwell, to chase seagulls into taking flight off the asphalt. This morning the circle's quiet, the houses closed, the hoses coiled against foundations, the yards vacant except for the rainbird sprinkler in the Allers' yard, chopping high arcs of water out across the bruised grass. But you can feel it from yesterday. From the forceful hellos pitched across the circle by the men. From your mother, straightening her back, taking off her sun hat, lifting her dark hair, using a white handkerchief to wipe her neck. The fierce momentum of the neighborhood. The sense of something relentless, ambitious, insistent on its forward motion, impossible to stop, something that will sweep you up this morning, make you part of it.

You find your father in the kitchen. He's wearing an apron over his dark blue suit, melting down a gob of Crisco in a frying pan, tilting the pan back and forth to skid the clot across the hot steel surface. You smell the vapor and listen to the Crisco spit as it leaves its trail of oil across the pan. An open box of eggs and a package of baloney sit on the counter next to the stove. His large portable radio, on the windowsill above the sink, is tuned to a program called The Spoken Word. The Mormon Tabernacle Organ plays quietly in the background. The Mormon Tabernacle Choir, like the murmur of an idling engine deep inside a ship, hums the tune of a wordless hymn behind the rich smooth voice of Richard L. Evans. From the Crossroads of the West. From the Shadow of the Everlasting Hills. You watch your father break the eggs, shred slices of baloney across them, cover the pan with a lid. You set two places at the table. You pour two glasses of milk. The heady smell of frying eggs and the thick and meaty aroma the heat releases from the baloney find your nostrils. He carries the pan to the table and slides two grease-slicked eggs, inlaid with brick-red shards of baloney, onto each plate. The two of you sit down. He spreads the morning's copy of the Church News out across the table just beyond his plate.

You pick your moment carefully. You know he doesn't like to be disturbed when he's reading about the church. You wait while he reaches out to turn the page and uses the edge of his fork to carve away another wedge of egg.

"Papa?"

He lifts his head, turns your way, and you can see, from how the lines in his broad face have come into relief, that you've already triggered his aggravation.

"Yes, son."

"Do you feel any different after you're ordained?"

"I should hope so. You'll be a Priesthood bearer. An instrument in God's hands."

"Do you feel anything when it happens?"

"If you're worthy of receiving the Priesthood, you'll feel the power of the Holy Ghost."

"How do you know if you're worthy?"

"If you feel the power of the Holy Ghost, you're worthy. If you don't, you're not." He turns to the Church News again. "By golly. I thought you could figure that out for yourself."

"So you won't know if you're worthy until it's too late."

And now when he looks at you he's more alert.

"What do you mean too late?" he says.

"I mean if you get the Priesthood and you don't feel the Holy Ghost."

"I don't understand."

"I mean you'll already have the Priesthood, but you won't be worthy of having it."

"You should have decided by now if you're worthy or not. If you don't know, you'd better tell me now, so we can call the whole thing off."

"I wasn't talking about me."

"I should hope not."

"But what if you're not worthy?"

"Then you've accepted the Priesthood under false pretenses."

"Does something bad happen?"

"Something bad has already happened. You've been false with the Lord."

"Do you get punished? Like electrocuted or something?"

"Stop talking nonsense. You just won't have the Priesthood. We can ordain you a hundred times, but if Heavenly Father doesn't think you're worthy, it won't mean anything."

You watch him read. Wait till he reaches up to turn another page.

"Where's my bosom?"

He's got the page in the air when he stops and stares at you.

"Bishop Byrne said I'd feel a burning in my bosom."

"Yes. He's correct."

"So where is it?"

"It's in your chest," he says. "In the same area where your heart is."

"Does it really burn?"

"In a manner of speaking, yes."

"Did yours?"

"Yes," he says. "Of course. Now eat your breakfast. We don't have time to waste."

"What if mine doesn't?"

"Your job is to make dead certain that your heart is pure," he says. "The Holy Ghost won't enter an impure vessel."

"Will all my friends be there?"

"No. Just the brethren who will help me ordain you. So don't make a fool of yourself. This is the biggest day of your life."

"I know."

"Your hair is sticking up in back. Did you forget to comb it?"

"No."

"Try combing it again. Try to do a better job."

"Okay." Thinking of Strand. His tiny comb. "I will."

Outside, in the driveway, you watch the Buick come idling out of the garage, wait for its massive nose to clear, use the strap to pull the door back down while your father holds the Buick from rolling forward. You know what's happening in the house. The sound of the engine rousing your mother and brothers and sisters awake. Molly waking slowly to her soaked nightgown, to pee puddled around her by the rubber sheet your mother keeps under her regular sheet, to the fresh rekindled fire in the raw skin around her butt and legs and stomach. From the passenger seat, backing up the driveway, you see what your father always sees through the windshield when he leaves, your waking house in the shadow of the foothills. Behind the blank plane of her bedroom window over the garage, Molly's face is there, a ghost head in the glass, watching, her ghost hand raised in a wave she isn't sure of making. You wave back. In the parking lot of the churchhouse your father noses the Buick into a stall, moves the gearshift into park, sets the brake, turns off the engine. Where it has cleared the foothills, the morning sun sets the streaks in the windshield on fire, turns the pits you didn't know were in the glass to piercing sparks of light.

"Just a minute."

You let go of the door handle, sit back, look at him, and in the harsh sunlight watch his face work as he gathers what he wants to say. He turns to you.

"I want you to know how proud I am of you."

The sudden heat in your face makes you look down.

"This day means a great deal to your parents. I think you know that."

"Yeah."

"It's also a proud day for your brothers and sisters."

"Okay."

"Now that you'll be a Priesthood holder, they'll look up to you. You'll have to set an example for them."

"What should I do?"

"Live the commandments. See that they live the commandments. By golly. I'm surprised that you should have to ask."

"How?"

"Admonish them when you see them doing something you know they shouldn't. Encourage them when they're doing what you know is right."

"How do I admonish them?"

"Talk to them."

"What if they don't listen?"

"Then you'll have to try a different approach."

"Should I spank them?"

"Don't talk nonsense. Especially today."

"I wasn't."

"Of course you shouldn't spank them. If they don't listen to you, then tell your mother, or tell me. But I'm holding you responsible for giving them some guidance."

"Okay."

Nothing but guys and men inside. Everyone in the neighborhood with the Priesthood. Without their wives, their girlfriends, their kids, their sisters, their little brothers, they barely take up half the chapel, gather in the benches toward the front. Lilly and Blackwell. Billy Hess. Other high school guys. Guys up in their twenties, looking to get married now that they've done their missions, and from there, every man around your father's age, every other father, all the way to Charley Belnap, the oldest man you know, white-haired, a permanent explosion in his milk-starred eyes, his moist lips red and shiny on the inside, restless, looking for something he can't remember the words to. Keller and West and Strand and Jasperson. Every face the look of human steel except for you and Charley Belnap.

There's no prelude. In your mother's place a short tough-looking man named Bill George who does welding for a living plays the organ just enough to get everyone through the opening hymn. Bishop Byrne does some business from the pulpit. And then he says your name and announces your ordination. In the bench in front of you, a man turns around, gives you a nod and a grin, and then looks at your father next to you before he turns back around again, where you can see the band of fresh white skin laid bare by a new haircut across the back of his neck.

Your father and five other men take you down the hall away from the chapel to a classroom. Four rows of metal folding chairs stand idle and disordered on the brown linoleum floor. Someone closes the door. Chairs are moved back. They leave one chair at the center of the room. You're directed to sit down. Your father takes his position behind you. The men join him. They make you the center of a standing circle. You feel his hands cup your head. You think of the Brylcreem your hair will leave on them. You feel the weight of other hands as they're stacked on your father's, this increasingly heavy sandwich of palms and fingers, fingers that look for purchase on your scalp, rest against your ears. You close your eyes. Their hands feel suddenly precarious, like they might slip off, and so you sit there with your eyes half open, adjusting the muscles of your neck to hold their shifting weight. You watch the shirt of the man in front of you expand and collapse with his breathing. Wrinkles run across the white cloth. The head of a horse is stitched in yellow thread into his dark green tie. When you think of Rex you look at his belt instead. In the thin loop of the buckle, the gold is chipped away in places, and there are hairline cracks of white in the leather around the distended hole where the point of the buckle comes through. You look down at his knees. You smell the sour ambrosial early morning smell of the men around you, of their breath, the bite of their aftershave still wet and sweet. You concentrate on the damp twitching in their palms and fingers. Where it will happen. Where you will feel it if it does. You hear your father's voice, somber, full of import, as he says your whole name.

"Shake Wilford Tauffler."

And then he stops and clears his throat and you can feel his fingers look for traction on your head. You hold your breath and get ready, try to clear your bosom, try to give the Holy Ghost all the room you can, before you hear his voice again.

"We, the Elders of Israel, in the name of the Holy Ghost and by the power of the Holy Melchizedek Priesthood vested in us, hereby lay our hands upon your head to confer upon you the Aaronic Priesthood, which holds the keys of the ministering of angels, and of the Gospel of repentance, and of baptism by immersion for the remission of sins, and to ordain you a Deacon in the Church of Jesus Christ of Latter Day Saints, and confer upon you all the rights, powers, and authority pertaining to this office and calling in the Aaronic Priesthood, in the name of the Lord, Jesus Christ, Amen."

Part 4

Lessons

Chapter 28

"OKAY. LET'S TALK about baptizing dead people."

Brother Rodgers stands up front, doing the lighthouse turret thing with his head, sweeping it back and forth across the dangerous boulders of your heads. He's had to get your attention twice already. Once when your hands were curling their fingers around the pipes and valves of a trumpet that wasn't there. Then when you were looking at Susan Lake's shoes. Since then, he's had to do the same with Keller for playing with his Chinese handcuffs, with West for trying to grab them, so you're not the only one who's had your face on fire. Baptizing dead people. This time everyone's attention is where he wants it.

"Anyone know what I mean by that?"

"Baptism for the dead?" says Jasperson.

"Anyone know what Johnny's talking about?"

"Yeah," says West. "But you don't really baptize dead people."

"So you're listening." Brother Rodgers winks at West. Jasperson looks deep into his lap to try to hide a dirty grin. One of the girls titters. All four of them, even Susan Lake, wear little smiles, but only hers looks the way a smile might look in the middle of being kissed. Brother Rodgers pulls his leather-skinned hands out of his pockets, folds his arms across his chest.

"Bobby's right. We don't go to cemeteries, dig them up, baptize them, then bury them again. What do we do instead? Mike?"

"We get baptized on their behalf," says Lilly, bringing his hand down, looking like he just gave the answer of the year. On their behalf. You know that West and Doby are doing what you're doing, mocking the angry crap out of Lilly in your head. And then Brother Rodgers turns his face on you. You brace yourself, but he just keeps looking, his burned face quiet, impossible to read, and then he turns away. He was only using you to park his eyes while he figured out where he was going next. You wonder if your face will ever be that way. Thick and solid and blank to where people won't be able to look through your skin and skull to what you're thinking.

"Okay," he says. "What two things do you need to get baptized?"

"Water," says Keller.

"That's one. What's the other one?"

"Someone who's got the Priesthood," says Doby.

"That too. Just not what I had in mind."

"Nose plugs," says Yenchik. Brother Rodgers looks down. Susan Lake picks something like lint off the knee of her dress and releases it like a delicate booger to drift to the floor.

"Okay. Nose plugs. Not what I was thinking. Bobby?"

"The baptism speech," says West.

"That too. Not it either."

"The Holy Ghost," Doby says.

"Him too. Guess I should have thought about this question more. Julie?"

"A white dress?"

"Okay. I thought I was asking something simple. Let's start over. We've got water. What else?"

The image so quick and clear that you flinch hard enough to make the metal of your chair squeal. Susan Lake, being lifted from the water, water spilling off her face, brown hair soaked flat along her head and down her neck, the thin fabric of the white dress stuck like peeling skin from a sunburn to every inch of her body. Your hand shoots up, on its own, without you thinking, to give some other meaning to the way your chair squealed.

"Shake," Brother Rodgers says.

"Someone to baptize," you say.

"Tell me more," says Brother Rodgers.

Like he can see through your eyes and watch her too, stepping out of the arms of the man who baptized her, wading waist deep across the font toward the steps where her bare feet will lift her dripping hair and body out of the water, as close to naked as you've ever pictured anyone.

"You need a body," you say. It kills you to use the word.

"That's so easy," Keller says. You can hear him jealous. Feel it from Jasperson and Lilly.

"Finally. I was starting to think we'd be here till a week from Tuesday. Okay. Water and a body. In the Spirit World, where we go after we die, do we have those things?"

"Not a body," says Keller.

And now Keller's used the word, but it's nothing now, just another word in a spelling bee like hubcap or asparagus.

"No water either," Lilly says. "Everything there's made out of spirit stuff."

"So what does that mean?"

"You can't get baptized there," says Brenda Horn, like it's something too obvious to even be worth saying.

"And if you can't get baptized?"

"You can't get into Heaven."

"Okay."

And then he gives you the picture. How for centuries millions of people lived and died without the chance to hear and accept the Gospel. How people still die today in places like China and Russia and India without the opportunity. How when they die they go to a place called the Spirit Prison. How there are missionaries there, dead missionaries, there to teach them the Gospel, so that they can accept it and get released from the Spirit Prison to enter the part of the Spirit World called Paradise.

"But just accepting the Gospel isn't enough," says Brother Rodgers. "They're still stuck in the Spirit Prison. Johnny. What are they waiting for?"

"Someone to be baptized for them," says Jasperson.

"That's right. They're waiting for you to use the gift of your physical body to free them. Millions are waiting for each of you."

You see them, your share of the dead, centuries of people crowded in the dark cavern of some infinite stone prison, looking at you from behind the iron bars, their faces skittish in the crossfire of hope and fear and hunger you catch sometimes in Roy's and Molly's faces.

"Who knows what genealogy is?" says Brother Rodgers.

"My mom does genealogy," Julie Quist says.

"Everyone's mom does it," says Jasperson. "They do it in Relief Society."

"But what is it? Ann?"

"It's when you try to find out who your relatives are?"

"Your dead relatives," Brother Rodgers says. "And the big reason we try to find out who they are is to baptize them. That's why you see your mothers doing all that work, looking up names, writing letters, going to the library."

Your mother too. Letters to Switzerland to track them down. Dim little photographs of your angry stern-faced ancestors. And now Susan Lake's hand is up, her fingers limp, her palm this pale rose, the skin probably damp if you could touch it.

"Yes, Susan."

"How do we know if they've accepted the Gospel?"

You listen to her question sustain itself in your head like a piano with the pedal down, smell the dizzying trace of some exotic musical perfume in her voice.

"We hope they can find a way to tell us. If they can't, or we're not listening when they do, we baptize them anyway. Mike?"

"What if they haven't accepted it?"

"The baptism's still good. It doesn't expire. It'll be there when they do accept it. That's why we have to make sure we baptize everybody."

"Everybody," says West.

"Everybody we can track down."

"Everybody that ever died."

"That's the goal."

"That's a lot of dead people."

"It's a big job," Brother Rodgers says. "But I'll tell you. If only one out of every hundred thousand people accepts the Gospel, and the gift of baptism, that one person is worth every one of those nine hundred umpteen thousand ninety nine other baptisms. You'll know. They'll make their gratitude known to you."

Questions flood your head. Who tracks down all the dead Chinese. All the Russians and Negroes and Mexicans who don't have mothers finding what their names are. If Hitler and the Nazis and the Japs get baptized too. What happens if they're Catholic or Buddhist and want to stay that way. If they can give their baptism away to someone else. If they can sell it.

"Shakespeare's dead," says Yenchik.

Brother Rodgers looks at him. "That's right," he says. "He is."

"I'd like to be baptized for him."

Brother Rodgers smiles. You sit there wondering the same thing. Where Yenchik came up with Shakespeare. Yenchik looks around and sees it on everyone's face.

"Why not?" he says.

"Anyway," Brother Rodgers says, taking a long breath, "you're probably wondering why you're learning about this today. Next Saturday, we'll all be going to the Temple, where you'll be baptized for the dead."

"Us?" says Doby.

Across the room, Brenda Horn and Ann Cook pull faces at each other, faces like they're on the edge of puking.

"That's right. As long as it's okay with your parents. Melvin, you're a little young yet, but we were able to sneak you through."

"The Temple?" says Jasperson.

"That's where they do baptisms for the dead. In a big font in the basement."

"Won't we need Temple Recommends?" says Lilly.

"Not like your parents. This is just the basement. You'll need Temple Registration Slips. But we took care of that. I vouched for you to

Bishop Byrne. Don't worry. You won't be seeing any dead people. It's not a mortuary. All you'll know is their names."

"Yeah," Ann says to Brenda, "but they're still dead."

"If you don't feel like going, that's okay. Nobody's forcing you. But it'll be fun. Like a field trip. And you'll be doing something the Lord will bless you for doing. Besides," he says, "we're stopping at the Frostop afterward for burgers and malts."

"What time?" Lilly asks.

"Eight in the morning," says Brother Rodgers. "You'll need to bring a towel and a fresh set of underwear." And then he looks from face to face. "I want you to spend this week praying for the people you'll be baptized for. Praying they'll accept the gift you're giving them. You're responsible for them."

CHAPTER 29

IT ISN'T the burgers and malts. It's that the Lord will bless you for doing it that makes it mandatory. That and your father that night when you tell him.

"He's right. You'll be responsible for them."

"Them?"

"Yes. Them."

"More than one?"

"Everyone's going to a lot of trouble to baptize you for the dead. They wouldn't go to all that trouble to baptize you only once."

If you were only baptized once, you're thinking, you'd want it to be for Mrs. Harding, but only if she wanted it, and while she was here she never did.

"How many?"

"Maybe ten or twenty. It varies."

"That many?"

"It depends. What's important is that you try to remember their names, so that you can keep praying for them."

"Do they write them down for you?"

"They don't have the time for that. It's up to you to remember them."

The Temple. The mysterious granite heart of Temple Square where all the secret things go on that would get your father killed, struck dead, if he told you what they were. Where you can only go if you've paid your tithing, lived the Word of Wisdom, obeyed the commandments, and got Bishop Byrne to give you a Temple Recommend, a piece of paper that works like a fishing license or a ticket for a ride. Where your father and mother go sometimes with their little blue suitcases filled with their secret clothes. That night, your family on their knees around the coffee table while your father goes droning through his prayer, you silently ask God to help you remember names you don't yet know. After school, knowing that God helps only those who help themselves, you use the telephone book to practice. You pick ten names, read each one out loud, close your eyes, repeat it, then look out the kitchen window and name as many as you can remember. Every day ten new names. Two. Five. Seven. Then eight before you have to look. And by Friday you're up to twelve.

Three cars are there on Saturday in the lot behind the churchhouse. Julie Quist's mother with her white Cadillac. Doby's mother with her Chevy Bel Air. Brother Rodgers with his brown Ford station wagon. He passes out your Temple Registration Slips. Tells you to show them at the door of the Temple.

"Nineteen?" says Keller.

"What?"

"Look here. It says nineteen. They got me down for nineteen baptisms."

You look. The blank line where someone wrote the number 19. Yours too.

"They're gonna baptize us nineteen times?" says Keller. And now everyone's looking.

"I'll drown."

"That's crazy."

"How come so many?"

"I can't hold my breath that long."

Brother Rodgers puts out his hands like he's warming them over a campfire.

"Calm down. They don't hold you under. Just this quick dunk for each name. And then you get to catch your breath. They'll go slow if you need to. Nobody's gonna drown today."

Nineteen dead people. You ride in the back of the Chevy, with West and Yenchik and Keller, a fresh pair of jockey shorts rolled up inside the towel on your lap. Doby sits with his mother up front with Perry Como on the radio. Strand and Lilly and Jasperson ride with Brother Rodgers. The girls ride in the Cadillac. You imagine being one of them, in the back seat, shoulder to shoulder, arm to arm, leg to leg with Susan Lake instead of Yenchik. Nineteen of them. They could have told you what their names were.

"I hope I get baptized for somebody famous," says Keller.

"Like who?"

"I don't know. Like President Eisenhower maybe."

"He's still President, you moron," says West. "He's still alive."

"Oh. Yeah. Then President Roosevelt."

"Did he die yet?" says Yenchik.

"I think so. I'm not sure."

"I wanna be baptized for Wild Bill Hickok," says West.

"Billy the Kid," says Yenchik.

Your hero from the cowboy movies they showed at the ranch in the long tin shed they used for the churchhouse. "Randolph Scott," you say.

"Captain Hook."

"Albert Schweitzer."

"King Louie the Fourteenth."

"You'll be rich, man."

"I get Custer," says Doby from the front seat.

"I get Moses," says Yenchik.

"He's already a Mormon, you idiot."

You convoy south through Bountiful, then along the foothills past the Phillips 66 refinery and the Cudahy stock yards and Slim Olsen's 43-pump gas station, up the long climb of Victory Road, past the State Capitol, and then down the hill from the Capitol into downtown Salt Lake and Temple Square. Somewhere along the way, Doby won the fight to put KNAK on the radio, and the four of you sing ain't nothin but a hound dog out the rolled down windows while his mother glides the Bel Air into a parking space.

Brother Rodgers leads you through one of the gates in the tall gray prison wall that goes all the way around the city block that houses Temple Square. Julie Quist's mother heads for the gate on the other side toward the department stores. Doby's mother says she'll just roam around the grounds, enjoy the flowerbeds, look at the statues, spend time in the Tabernacle and Assembly Hall. Brother Rodgers takes you to a back entrance in the granite wall of the Temple. You follow him down stairs, along corridors, to a locker room where you change into your clean underwear and get dressed all in white and leave your feet bare. And then you're standing in the biggest and fanciest room you've ever seen.

"Okay," says Brother Rodgers. Dressed in his regular clothes, in his shoes, it makes the rest of you look like you're wearing pajamas. Under the soles of your feet the polished stone is cool and slick. "You girls will be baptized for women. You boys, for men. Boys, you'll go first. When you're done, go back through that door to the locker room, take a shower, get back in your street clothes. They'll come get you for the confirmations. Now go sit up there and wait till I call your name. And keep it quiet. This is the house where the Lord lives."

Your face burns. The boys are going first because he saw you watching Susan Lake last Sunday. He wants you gone before her turn comes up. You sit between West and Doby. The room looks like a palace room. Tall carved columns reach to the huge beams of the high ceiling. Behind the columns are huge windows with domed tops. You imagine another century, a country in Europe, a ballroom, couples dancing, men with white wigs and velvet jackets and knee pants and long white socks, women with their hair up, long dresses with butts like geese following them as they float across the floor to a Schubert waltz. What keeps it from being a ballroom is the font that stands in the middle. It looks like the biggest soup bowl in the world. Under the font, set into a big round shallow hole in the floor, stands a circle of twelve gold steers, big as life, big as the steers in La Sal. Their gold heads and fierce eyes and curved horns face outward. Their gleaming bodies strain against each other. The font stands on their haunches and reaches halfway to a chandelier that hangs from crossed beams in the high ceiling. There's not enough room to waltz. A staircase with a gold banister goes up one side of the font to a platform like a lifeguard uses. Another staircase comes down the other side.

Three men, dressed in white shirts and pants, are talking on the platform. One of them sits at a small desk and looks through a big flat book like the one your father brought home from work for your mother's genealogy. You figure it for the book where the names are written down. The names of the dead. You wish you could look at them now.

"Man," West says.

"Yeah," you whisper back.

"If this is the basement, it must be really neat upstairs," Doby whispers.

"Wonder what's out those windows," West says.

The tall windows are lit but clouded so you can't see through them. Their pale and steady light reminds you of aquarium light, and you imagine fish, big fish with eyes like cows, moving lazily back and forth through long blades of seaweed on the other side.

"I don't think it's the outside," you say.

"Not if this is the basement," West says.

"That's weird," says Doby. "Windows on the inside."

Brother Rodgers throws a look over his shoulder. The three of you go quiet. You wonder if they're here, in spirit, back against the walls behind the columns, waiting to hear their name called when you wash their sins away. And then you realize they're still in the Spirit Prison. One of the men on the platform descends into the font. Another man calls Brother Rodgers over, leans down, tells him something. Brother Rodgers turns around and calls for Strand. Strand climbs the stairs to the lip of the font and then descends. The names are too quiet to hear but you can still count nineteen dunks. When they're done with Strand, he climbs dripping out the other side, goes down the stairs, leaves footprints of water across the floor. Brother Rodgers calls for Jasperson. And then for Doby. And then for Lilly. And then for you.

"What's your name, son?"

The water is warm. Where it circles your waist it feels sharp, like the edge of a knife, like it could cut you in half if it closed around you. The man in the water with you has the big chest and beefy arms and half-bald head of a gym teacher. His rolled-up sleeves are soaked to his armpits and the thick blond hair on his forearms is plastered to his skin.

"Shake."

"Shake? Like a milkshake?"

"Yeah."

"It's not a nickname?"

"No."

"What's your last name?"

"Tauffler."

"Shake Tauffler," he says to the man sitting at the desk on the platform.

"Okay. He's here. Go ahead."

"Okay, Shake. Let me have your hands. Hold your wrist here with this hand. Like this." His big hands mold your small hand into place. "Use your other hand to hold your nose. When I take you under, hold on tight. I'll hold you here." His big left hand grabs yours where you've got it wrapped around your wrist. "Don't worry. I won't drop you. I'll have my other hand on your back. Like this. Just like when you were baptized for yourself."

"I remember."

"Okay."

He raises his free right arm. You take a breath, hold it, clamp your nose, look at the tiny hairs on his big knuckles.

"Brother Shake Tauffler, having been commissioned of Jesus Christ, I baptize you, for and in behalf of . . ."

"Hermann Geissler," the man at the desk calls out.

". . . Hermann Geissler, who is dead, in the name of the Father, and of the Son, and of the Holy Ghost. Amen."

It happens quick. His arm comes down, you feel his big firm hand between your shoulder blades, his other hand pushes you back, and you hold on, think of Mr. Hinkle, let your knees go, let yourself fall, and the water barely closes over your face before his hands reverse direction, lift you back to your feet again. He's already talking as the water runs out of your ears.

". . . commissioned of Jesus Christ, I baptize you, for and in behalf of . . ."

"Johann Geissler."

". . . Johann Geissler, who is dead, in the name of the Father, and of the Son, and of the Holy Ghost. Amen."

". . . for and in behalf of . . ."

"Peter Geissler."

As your body and breathing find the rhythm, you realize the names are alphabetical, like the ones you practiced in the phone book, and you can't believe your luck in having come across that way to practice. Hermann. Johann. Peter. You wonder if all the Geisslers were related, if they were brothers, grandfathers, uncles, sons.

". . . for and in behalf of . . ."

Hans Geldstock. Oscar Genstiefel. Names, dead names, names that sound like they're from Europe somewhere, names you couldn't spell if your life depended on you spelling them, names you don't have time to memorize before you're tipped back, back to where you'd fall if you didn't have someone holding you, before the water closes over your face again. You lose track. You lose count. Their names are lost. All you have are their sins, the sins you're being used to wash away, sins whose residue you can feel in the water around you like the dirty foam that collected along the eddies and behind the rocks in the creeks around La Sal, foam you were told the Indians used for soap. Drinking. Smoking. Fornication. Adultery. Gambling. Cussing. Stealing. Rape. Murder. Sins you don't know the names to. Sins you have to assume, have to pretend are yours, name after name, before you can be cleansed of them. Finally, your eyes closed, on a dark and knotted street in some village deep in the long ago past of Europe, you see them, ragged, thin, almost skeletal silhouettes in the moonlight, shambling along the cobblestones, shuffling toward you, hollering for you, in voices you don't understand but know you don't have to be afraid of. Men. Dead men. Their names are lost but their faces are there around you, gleaming wet, half-collapsed, grotesque, water dripping off their hair, their eyes fierce, their lips raw, their mouths like caverns they can't close, their teeth down to stubs set like tiny brown diamonds in their black gums, their breath so hot and wet and sweet you have to hold your own to keep from gagging.

And then there's a woman there, a farm woman, a woman so big and fat and round and so suddenly there you're amazed you didn't see her coming. She stands there, smiling down at you from her round and enormous face, while the men tear her farm blouse down off her shoulders, while the glowing skin of her billowing breasts spills out into the moonlight. You're scared. You don't get it. What they want from you. What they have in mind. And then you do. Their eyes your eyes. Their lips your lips. Their teeth your teeth. Their names your name. The woman's colossal breasts your reward. Standing back, their crabbed hands on your back and shoulders, they push you forward, gently but with terrifying strength, to where her breasts are everything you see, to where you're close enough to reach them, close enough to push your face deep into them, like water, drown before you're ever brought up again for air.

"Okay, Shake. That's it."

His hand releases yours. Water blinds you when your eyes come open, but off to your right they're watching, West and Yenchik and Keller, Brenda Horn and Ann Cook and Julie Quist and Susan Lake, Brother Rodgers, knowing where you've been, seeing what you saw, your mouth open and gulping air.

"You okay?"

"Yes."

"Good. Just go ahead and take the stairs there."

You use your hands to skim the water off your face, glide across the font toward the tile stairs, feel your regular weight come back into your legs as you rise dripping, holding the gold railing, out of the water. You hear Brother Rodgers call for West. And then you're in the shower, naked, running the water hot, using a bar of Ivory to wash away the residue of the font.

On the way home, in the back seat of the Bel Air, none of you talk much. Doby's mother has the radio on some Frank Sinatra station. Next to you, Yenchik does the whole ride quiet, picking at his thumbnails. By the time you're in line at the Frostop on Highway 89 your hair is dry again. Yenchik takes his paper-wrapped burger and banana malt and goes off across the parking lot toward a patch of yellow grass on the other side. You look at the other guys, unwrapping their burgers around a picnic table, decide to follow Yenchik, sit down next to him on the curb.

"What's the matter?"

"Nothing."

"What."

He looks down for a long time. When he looks up again his cheeks are wet and his eyes are red. He puts his burger down on the concrete ledge of the curb and uses the butt of his hand to wipe his eyes.

"None of my baptisms counted," he finally says.

"Why?"

"You can't tell anybody. You gotta promise."

"Okay. I promise."

"I peed."

You just look at him. "Holy crap."

"I know," he says. "I couldn't hold it."

"But Brother Rodgers had us all go to the bathroom first."

"I did. It doesn't matter. It happens when I go underwater."

You picture being Yenchik, in the font, peeing away in secret while you're being baptized for the dead, knowing as long as you're peeing that none of them count.

"You shoulda stayed home."

"Yeah," he says. "And what would that of looked like."

"You coulda said you were sick."

"Probably nobody else's counted either. At least who went after me."

"How come?"

"You can't get baptized in pee."

And all you can think about while he sits there wanting to be dead is who went in the water after him. Who got baptized in his pee without knowing it. Besides Yenchik, Keller and West were left when you were done, and you heard them call West's name while you were coming down the steps on the other side. That left Keller unless Yenchik went after him. So Keller was a maybe. But all the girls for sure. Ann Cook. Brenda Horn. Julie Quist. Susan Lake. Over and over, name for name, her nose clamped shut to where she couldn't have smelled it even if she'd known it was there to smell. You look back across the parking lot, at the picnic table where they're sitting off the highway, talking away, giggling in the sunlight. You watch Susan Lake just barely bow her head and raise the straw for what she's drinking to where her lips pucker when they reach for it. And then you don't know what to think except what you'll do with your hot dog and chocolate malt.

"Man."

CHAPTER 30

YOU LEAVE it there, behind the Christmas boxes, under the raw unpainted boards of the shelves, while you work through the rest of June and then July and August on Mrs. Harding's yard. While sometimes the white Chrysler parks in the driveway and the woman comes on her heels to bring people wandering through the yard, married couples mostly, sometimes just men, men dressed in suits who look at the tennis court, the garage, the back of the house. You leave it there, in the dark rich mysterious smell of its threadbare velvet cradle in its black case, while you pull your father's mower out on Saturday and join the bawling orchestra of all the circle's mowers. While you clear and sweep the garage and put things back in place again. You leave it there, still able to curl your fingers and hook your thumbs and feel it in your hands, while you discover the amusement park called Lagoon a few miles north of Bountiful in a town called Farmington. While you ride the Whip and the Rockets and watch them hose Jasperson's cotton candy vomit out of the Hammer.

You leave it there, with the lesson book with the phone number scrawled in pencil on the cover, while families move in and start to live in the finished houses next door to Mrs. Harding's. While your paycheck comes every two weeks from an address in Chicago. While you write them back to tell them you need to go to school, and there won't be much yardwork left, and what there is you can catch in an hour early every morning. While they write you back and tell you thanks but they're leaving your pay the same. While your mother frets that you're being overpaid, that you've fooled them somehow, lied to them, no matter what their letter says.

You leave it there while Scoutmaster Haycock and one or another father load you into their station wagons to take you swimming at Wasatch Springs. In the cavernous room with the pool as big as a basketball court, you watch for flakes of plaster coming off the high white disintegrating ceiling, rub your eyes to get rid of the burning rainbows that circle the bulbs of the high caged lights, stay away from Yenchik when he's in the water, ride the soft horse of Blackwell's shoulders while you try to pull Keller or West off Doby's shoulders.

For Blackwell, Scoutmaster Haycock, a big guy, redheaded and friendly and sometimes goofy, a guy who never gets mad at anything, is the luckiest guy in the world. Under the neck-high blouses and sweaters and dresses she wears, his wife has the biggest breasts you've ever seen awake, breasts that stand off her chest like the breasts a man would have if he filled a bra with cantaloupes and dressed like a woman for Halloween. From her face, prim and hawklike, always happy and oblivious under the high plumage of her black hair, it's like she doesn't know she even has them, or what they do to Blackwell.

One Friday in the pool at Wasatch Springs you ask Blackwell if he wants to try the diving board with you. He tells you no. When you stay after him he tells you it's because he's got a boner and needs to keep it underwater. For a second you're sharply aware of the water between you, the way it conducts things like electricity and heat, the way it connects things.

"A boner?" You look around. There's nothing but Scouts. "Who from?"

His eyes slide off to your left the way they do when he doesn't want to tell you something.

"Haycock," he finally says.

"Haycock?"

"His old lady," he says. "I can't help it."

"She's not here."

"I get a boner just from him. Sitting in Scouts."

"In Scouts?"

"Looking at him. Knowing where he's had his hands. He's talking about knots or something and I'm wondering what it's like inside his eyeballs."

"You're kidding."

"Then there's his ears," Blackwell says.

"His ears?"

"I see him taking and sticking her nipples in 'em. Both of 'em. At the same time."

"How come he'd want to?"

"Just to prove he can."

"What's she doing? While he's sticking her nipples in his ears?"

"Does it matter?"

"How's he supposed to breathe?"

"I don't know. A snorkel maybe."

"You're crazy."

"I can't help it."

"You get a boner from Haycock's ears."

"Don't tell anybody. They'll kick me out of Scouts."

"I won't."

"I'd just tell them you're lying. I'd tell them you're the one who gets boners."

"Don't worry."

You leave it there, while September comes around and Yenchik finally gets ordained a Deacon and your circle of buddies is whole again, because you don't know what to do with it. You don't know how to read the history of its tarnished and bruised and dented brass. You don't have anything to help you understand what your mother was after when she gave you back the trumpet she hated for your birthday, the trumpet she called junk, or what your father meant when he wrote not to play it like a hypocrite.

How that night, after Karl said he was sorry, while your family waited, you snapped the latches and pushed the lid back. How it suddenly came exposed. How your family drew in close. How down in your stomach you could sense malevolence in its brass.

"What is it?" Karl saying. "A bugle? Let's see it! Take it out!"

"Yes, Shakli! Take it out! Let your family see it!"

How you remembered Brother Rodgers and his electrocution scars when you reached for the gold cluster of its three valve cylinders. How you took a firmer hold, then lifted it off its cradle, held it up for them to look at.

"It's a trumpet," you saying, seeing Molly's questioning shy face and then Roy's as they stood there looking.

"Play it!" Karl saying.

"I don't know how."

"Try it! Lemme try!"

How infused with happiness your mother looked. How shining wet her eyes were. The way she clutched her hands together. How long it would last. What you could say or do without suddenly turning her. How you still don't know. And so you leave it there. Leave it the way you leave the photograph of Mrs. Harding in the place you found to hide it.

CHAPTER 31

AFTER THE opening hymn, the opening prayer, business from the pulpit, the chapel empties, and everyone heads for the classroom of their rank. They're called quorums. You and your buddies head for the room where the quorum for the Deacons is. The high school guys for the rooms where the quorums for the Teachers and Priests are. From there, it's the quorums of the Higher Priesthood, the Melchizedek men, men who've gone through the upstairs part of the Temple and traded in their underwear for temple garments like your father wears. Guys back from their missions, guys just starting families, guys like Brother Rodgers in their early thirties, head for the Elders Quorum. Guys around your father's age head for the room for the Seventies Quorum. Old Charley Belnap gets helped to the carpeted room where the High Priests meet. Sometimes, when the door's left open, when you've already started listening to Brother Clark, you can see Charley Belnap being shuffled by outside, flanked by a couple of men like he's been arrested by the FBI.

"I know you boys have heard this story before." Brother Clark leans back in his metal chair. "And you'll hear it again, because it's the foundation of the church. Well, we've got a new crop of Deacons in here, and they need to hear it too. Besides, it won't hurt you boys to hear it again."

Where your Sunday School class has girls, where everyone's in the seventh grade, your Priesthood class is only guys and has older kids than you, kids who are thirteen, eighth graders like Blackwell. The other difference is your teacher. Brother Clark is the fattest man you can ever remember seeing. His wife and three daughters are smaller, but for their height, they're all about as round as him. He's got the deepest voice you've ever heard and the biggest most hairless head you've ever seen. Below his eyes his face goes broad and bellies out and his mouth looks like someone had to decide where to draw it. And that's the way his whole face is. A cartoon face where the only things that are made to move when he talks are his mouth and eyes.

You hear the older Deacons call him Pear Head. Pear Head Clark. You never do. You like him. Like how you can always count on him to show up in the same big hide-colored suit and the same black tie. How calm he is. How he never has anything to prove. How he just comes in and sits down behind the little table and takes you through half an hour of information as factual and impersonal as arithmetic. How he takes every question he's asked the same considered way no matter how dumb it is. The knot of his tie is always out of sight beneath the layered bibs of his extra chins. His bulk makes the table look like a lunch tray. He never uses anyone's name. He teaches Driver's Ed at Bountiful High School. In four more years, when you're made into a Priest, when he teaches you how to drive, you'll probably have to call him Mr. Clark.

"It wasn't the answer Joseph Smith expected," he says. "That he'd been chosen to restore the true church."

"How come it had to be restored? Was it old?"

You hear some of the older Deacons snicker while Brother Clark looks at Yenchik and then around the room.

"What I want to make clear to you older boys again," Brother Clark says, "is that you don't laugh if someone asks a question you happen to know the answer to. Not so long ago, you were asking the same questions, and you were free to ask them."

He looks at Yenchik.

"Good timing, son. That's right where we're headed. Yes. Old things can be restored. But there's another way to restore something." He looks down and picks a book up off the table and holds it up over his head. "What did I just do?"

The only thing hard about Brother Clark is his way of asking questions. Sometimes he's looking for an answer. Other times he just puts a question out there, like lobbing a ball straight up that he plans to catch himself, as a way to keep his lesson going. Sometimes you can tell from this barely visible way the blond traces of his eyebrows move. But all you can do for sure is wait.

"You picked up that book," an older Deacon finally says.

"Let's let the younger boys answer," Brother Clark says mildly. "Where was the book to start with?"

"On the table," says Jasperson.

"Is it still there?"

"No."

"So how is the table different?"

"That book's not on it any more," says Keller.

You catch Blackwell gloating across the room like you and your buddies are morons he never wanted for friends in the first place. Brother Clark brings the book out over the table and glides it in for a landing exactly where it was before.

"Okay," he says. "Now what did I just do?"

"You put it back." It's Doby taking his turn at being lame.

"What if it had been a church instead?" says Brother Clark.

After a while the fingers of his one hand start tapping the back of his other hand.

"You restored it?" says Doby.

"What had to happen first? Before I could restore it?"

"You had to take it away?"

"Okay," he says. "Now we're where we need to be."

And he goes on to tell you about the Great Apostasy. How when Jesus was crucified he left his Church to Peter and his other Apostles. How soon after Peter died the Church fell into Roman hands. How the Romans made it the Church of Rome and turned it into an instrument for wealth and power. How Jesus saw that the Church of Rome no longer resembled the church he'd left behind and so he decided to take it back to Heaven.

"Now here's the big question," he says. "The one that's real important for you boys. How do you take a whole church back to Heaven?"

He lets his eyes travel across the room. You can feel everyone restless. Wondering like you if he's looking for someone to raise his hand.

"Do you physically take the house of worship?" he says. "The cathedral? Pull it out of the ground and fly it off to Heaven? Which, of course, God could do. But is that what you do?"

He looks back and forth again.

"Do you take the benches? The organ? The pulpit? The statues? Just pack everything up and haul it off?"

You hear a long rolling growl from Jasperson's stomach a couple of chairs away.

"Of course not," says Brother Clark. "God doesn't have any use for that stuff. So what is it you take when you take a whole church back to Heaven?"

Brother Clark picks up the book again, looks at the title, puts it down.

"Let me use an analogy. I go to a uniform store and buy a police uniform. I go to a badge shop and have them make me a badge. I buy a holster and a gun. I buy myself a ticket book. I go home and put everything on."

Brother Clark gives you a minute to see him as the fattest cop you've ever seen.

"And then I have some friends do the same thing. And then we all paint our cars black and white, and write Police on them, and get sirens, and put red lights on the roofs. And then we build a place and write Police Station on the door. We even get a welder to build us a jail cell."

He gives you another minute to put everything else together.

"Now. You're out driving with your dad. He's going a little faster than he should. I come up behind him. I turn on my lights and siren. He pulls off the road. I come up to his window with my ticket book and tell him I'm going to ticket him for speeding."

This time he pauses long enough for you to see his hairless head with a cop hat on, his big face in the driver's window of your father's car.

"What do you think your dad would do?" He looks you and your buddies over. And then he nods at West. "You."

"My dad?" says West. "Probably laugh."

"Why?"

"Because he knows you're not a real cop."

"Would he laugh at a real cop?"

"No," says West. "He's not nuts."

"Well, hold on, now. I've got the car, the uniform, the ticket book, the badge, the gun, the police station, the other fellows in the department. Isn't that all real?"

"No. Yeah. I guess."

"Then why would your dad laugh at me? What's the difference?"

"A real cop's got the right."

"The right to what?"

"To give tickets."

"Okay. So what's missing is something I can't buy, or build, or paint on the side of my car. It's my right to give your dad a ticket. Now. Give me another word for right."

His eyes cross the room again, his big face neutral, not looking to see if he's persuaded you of anything, just looking to see if you understand some fact he's given you, like what you're supposed to do about a stop sign. "Authority," one of the older guys finally says. Brother Clark takes a look at him. Then his eyes come back to where you and your buddies are clustered.

"Let's hear that word from you younger boys," he says.

"Authority." Jasperson and Lilly say it right away. The rest of you give it the straggling tail of an echo.

"All of you. Older boys too."

"Authority." This time it hits the huskier register of the changed voices of some of the older Deacons.

"Good. Now. Let's go back to where we were. When Jesus told Joseph Smith he had to take his church away, what exactly did he take?"

Jasperson's hand shoots up.

"Yes."

"He took away its authority."

"Its authority to what?"

"To be his church."

"There's a name for that authority. What is it?"

Jasperson's face goes off looking for something he forgot. Brother Clark starts tapping his hand again.

"The authority to baptize," he finally says. "Pass the Sacrament. What's it called?"

"The Priesthood." It comes out of Keller like an exploding grenade.

"The Priesthood," he says. "The power to act in the name of Jesus Christ. Bless and heal the sick. Raise the dead. Perform miracles. Preach the true Gospel. Enter the highest degree of glory. To do the things Jesus himself did while he walked the Earth."

This is how he'll teach you to drive. How he'll explain the purpose of a yellow light or the reason for an arm signal. How it won't have anything to do with what you think.

"The Priesthood." His face is placid, his eyes observant, only his lips in motion. "That's what he took away from the Holy Church of Rome. The church we know as the Catholic Church. He let them keep their cathedrals. Their statues. Their artwork. Their gold. He took the one thing that gave those material things their meaning. The very Priesthood you boys now hold."

Keller raises his hand.

"Priests in the Catholic Church aren't really priests?"

"Not in the eyes of God."

"What about when they baptize somebody?"

"They can do that. They can bless a bowl of water and sprinkle it on a baby's head. They can tell you your sins are forgiven. They can feed you wafers and wine and tell you it's the real flesh and blood of the Savior. But that's like me giving your dad a speeding ticket."

"What about all the people who believe them?"

"Suckers," one of the older Deacons whispers, loud enough to get Brother Clark's immediate attention.

"No, son," says Brother Clark. "They're not. Most are well intentioned people, good people, people who just don't know better. Say a stranger comes through town. I happen to catch him speeding and pull him over. He doesn't know me from Adam. He'll think my ticket's real. He'll pay it. The fact that he doesn't know I'm a fraud doesn't make him a sucker."

He turns back to the rest of the room.

"Let's say I start a church instead of a police department. With enough friends, enough money, I can build a big cathedral and decorate it with gold and marble. I can hire Michelangelo to paint God and Adam on the ceiling. I can put an organ up in the balcony and hire someone to play Johann Sebastian Bach all day. I can wear a fancy robe. I can put Jesus on a cross and hang him up in front. I can make up some commandments and tell you the only way you'll see Heaven is if you live by them. I can tell you to sit in a closet and admit all your sins to me if you want to stay out of Hell. And what will you do?"

In the subdued room, while everyone sits there wondering if he really wants an answer, you can picture everything he said, even hear the organ.

"Go ahead. Laugh. You know what I do for a living. Without the Priesthood, the only thing I'm authorized to do is teach kids the difference between a brake pedal and a gas pedal. But there are people who'll believe me. They'll come to my cathedral. Listen to me preach. Take my wafers and wine and think it's the flesh and blood of Jesus. When I tell them I can save them, take away their sins, they'll take my word for it, put money in my basket."

He looks around the room again.

"They aren't wicked or stupid. They're people who want to do right by God and their fellow man. But I couldn't save them any more than I could write them a speeding ticket."

Yenchik's head has started coming down and bounding off his chest. Brother Clark waits until Yenchik hits a rebound hard enough to scare himself awake, jump so hard his chair shrieks when he realizes he's got Brother Clark's attention.

"Son, you need to stay awake and listen. When you go on your mission, you're going to be expected to teach this stuff to people."

"Sorry."

Brother Clark lets him go and casually takes in the rest of you.

"That's how it went for fourteen hundred years. For fourteen centuries the world went on without the Priesthood. The lights were out. Millions of people lived and died in dark ignorance of the real truth."

"That's why we have baptism for the dead."

You look at the floor wishing Jasperson would keep his eager mouth shut sometimes. You hope Yenchik doesn't start crying, remembering how he peed.

"Didn't they have other churches?" says Lilly. "Like Lutherans and Methodists?"

"Sure they did. They were pretty much irrelevant. Tell me something. Can you go out and act in the name of Robert Clark?"

Lilly starts up with this small bewildered smile and then goes stiff. "No," he says.

"Can you show up at my job and teach kids how to drive?"

"I can't even drive."

"Can you go to my house and walk in like you own the place?"

"No."

"Can you tell my daughters to do their homework?"

"No."

"Can you tell my wife what to cook me for dinner?"

"Not unless you told me what you wanted."

"What if your friend there told you to?"

"You'd have to tell me."

"What if your friend there told you I told him to tell you?"

Lilly looks at Keller. Keller looks the other way.

"I'd have to know he wasn't lying," says Lilly.

"That he really had the authority to tell you. On my behalf."

"Yeah."

"So you're saying," Brother Clark says, "that the power to act in the name of Robert Clark has to come from Robert Clark. Or from someone he's given that power to."

"Right."

"The power to act in the name of Jesus Christ. Where does that have to come from?"

"From Jesus Christ," Lilly says. And when Brother Clark keeps waiting he says, "Or someone he already gave it to."

"Good." Brother Clark lifts his face to where it almost clears the knot of his tie and then brings it down again. "Okay. It can only come from Jesus Christ. From there, that power has to be handed down, from one anointed person to the next, by the laying on of hands, in an unbroken line that can be followed back from every one of you to Christ himself."

Somewhere back in Switzerland, you're thinking, your father sat in a chair too, a pile of hands on his head, waiting to see what it felt like. Brother Clark raises his book again.

"For fourteen hundred years this entire planet had less power than each of you boys has in the little fingernail of your left hand. It had Shakespeare. Mozart. Kings and presidents. Nations and civilizations. Armies. Thousands of churches. Hundreds of cathedrals. But all of it together didn't have the power you boys hold in just that little fingernail. Least of all the Catholic Church for fourteen centuries. Not even the United States Army today."

He lowers the book again, brings it back to the table with focus and deliberation, like he's showing you a science experiment. You remember your father saying the same thing about one hair of your head. That one single hair of your head had that much power. You wonder if Brother Clark said fingernail because he didn't have any hair himself except his eyebrows.

"The power you boys hold is the greatest power on Earth," he says. "The responsibility for holding it is just as great. The Church of Rome had to learn that lesson hard. By losing it."

And then he sighs and pushes himself off his chair until he's standing. One at a time he picks his feet off the floor and shakes his pants legs like there are bugs in them.

"See you boys next week. We'll get to those other churches too sometime."

CHAPTER 32

YOU BUY a wire basket for your bike and bolt it to the handlebars. You put the fenders on again to keep rain and slush from painting a stripe of road dirt up your back. You work on Mrs. Harding's yard starting out at six. Nothing's growing anymore, just dying, and most of the work is cleanup work, pulling up the shriveled stems and unresisting roots of flowers you planted back in April, sifting dirt through your fingers to catch withered leaves and petals as transparent as the shucked skins of snakes, the husks of insects with their legs crossed like tiny zippers over their bellies, the dark kernels of dead beetles.

Nobody's up that early except the fathers, leaving for work, and so you work quietly, stealing clippings and leaves and rubbish out the back of the yard to the hill. Sometime after seven you use the hose to rinse down your arms and hands, change from the pants and shirt and shoes you keep in the shed to your school clothes, and make the ride to school, your books in the basket with their spines faced forward to keep the wind from blowing back their covers and rifling their pages. After school you pedal home, change, head for the orchards, where you and Jasperson pick peaches, then pears, finally apples for Charley Bangerter.

Mostly you ride alone. Doby's has a busted fork, West thinks he's too cool to ride a bike, and Lilly thinks he's too old. Keller and Yenchik usually get rides from their fathers and you don't want to ride with Blackwell or show up with Jasperson.

The school reminds you of Webster Elementary when you lived in the half of the house below Brewery Hill, where you went to kindergarten, where Mrs. Brick used to set off lightning in your eyes when she cracked you in the head. Colossal where it stands, old, set back on the field of a big front yard across from the head of Main Street, three stories of tall windows set in rows in massive walls of faded yellow brick. Racks against the side wall where you park your bike. Hallways inside where the classrooms go on and on. Wood desks carved with initials and hearts and stars and swastikas and sometimes idle lines that go nowhere. Fluorescent lights hung from high gray ceilings. Windows raised to random levels for air. The blinds raised too, splayed and cockeyed, half of them crooked. The dark green dusty expanse of the blackboards behind the desks for the teachers. Heavy rolls of maps hung on brackets up over the blackboards in History and Geography.

By eight o'clock, after a stop in the bathroom to comb the wind out of your hair, you're in your first class, History, where you've started to notice a girl who brings an instrument case to class with her three days a week, keeps it on the floor next to her shoes. She never says anything. Just sits there writing what Mr. Kapp puts on the blackboard in her open notebook. One day you work up the nerve to make it look like an accident that you're there when she comes out of class and bumps you with her case.

"I'm sorry," she says.

She wears glasses. Round black glasses that match her round face and the round way she wears her hair, red like fresh rust after rain, short around her face. In the lenses of her glasses her eyes are round too, and make you think of the necklace your mother has, the one that opens like Manny's pocket watch, where there are tiny round pictures inside of her father's and mother's faces, except in her glasses the pictures are her eyes. Her mouth is round too. A pink plump oval smile framing her white teeth. The rest of her is skinny, like you, milky blue veins like yours in the soft crooks of her arms, and her breath reminds you of being up in the branches of Charley Bangerter's apple trees.

"Me too," you say. "Is that a violin?"

"It sure is."

"Do they give lessons here?"

"Not private ones. Just band."

"Band?"

"Yeah." Looking at you. "You know."

"Yeah." You looking back. "Band."

"Do you play something?"

"Yeah. Sort of. Piano."

"You can play piano in band."

"It's kind of hard to bring to school."

"They have pianos here. You're being silly."

"Where?"

"There's one in the music room."

"The music room?"

"Yeah. I can show you."

"That's okay. Thanks."

"What's your name?"
"Shake."
"Shake? Like a Dairy Queen?"
"Yeah."
She looks you over smiling.
"It is not," she says. "You're being silly again."
"What's yours?"
"Carla."
"My little brother's name is Karl."
"Oh. Wow. Like the boy way."
"Yeah."
"Now tell me yours."
"Honest. Ask Mr. Kapp."
Through her glasses she studies you again.
"No. I'll just believe you."

The music room. After school that day you look for it like you're on other business, on your way to meet some friend, or talk to some teacher, so that when you find it, you'll look like it doesn't matter, like it's just another room on your way to somewhere else. You finally find it in the new part built on back, at the end of the hallway, just before you go out two glass doors to the baseball and football fields and the armory where they teach gym. You don't go in. Just stand outside, across the hall, and see what you can from there. The floor is layered in big shallow steps of brown linoleum wide enough for chairs and music stands, gray steel chairs like the ones in the cafeteria, music stands like tall black flying spiders with skeleton wings. Cabinets stand along the back wall. Across the room, under the windows, sheet music is layered like shale on long low shelves. A step to the left lets you see toward the front of the room. Cymbals and drums are arranged around a black stool on a low stage where a piano stands off to the side.

You smell the shoe polish smell of the store the first time you were there before Mr. Hinkle was there from out of nowhere. You hear a sound, half whisper and half hum, and when you look up the hall, there's a janitor, skating the whirling pad of a polishing machine back and forth. Panic floods you, here where you don't belong, and for an instant your legs are the jerky uncertain legs again your father caught in his camera when Manny drove Rufus off. He hasn't seen you. You walk the other way, toward the glass doors that will take you outside, where you'll be clear, where you can give yourself to the fierce and eager hunger that wants you to run, run what's left of the hallway, run harder the less of it is left.

CHAPTER 33

"LOOK AT 'EM. They're all as fat as he is."

"Geez, West," says Jasperson. "Take it easy."

"Don't forget," says Doby. "You gotta get your learner's permit from him."

"Then how's plump," says West.

Out back, off the glass door where you hang out after Priesthood Meeting now to watch the cars roll into the parking lot for Sunday School, you watch Brother Clark and his wife and three daughters wrestle themselves out the doors of their dull brown Mercury station wagon, start crossing the lot. Like your father, like all the fathers, Brother Clark takes the half hour break between Priesthood and Sunday School to run home for his family.

"Plump's better," says Doby.

It's late September. The flat underside of a dry gray overcast is butted up against the foothills and extends as far as you can see. You stand there with your buddies watching. Beverly Clark a year older than you are. Her sister Wanda a year younger. Shirley a couple of years behind Wanda. In the flat hush of the light their full round faces are colorless. Brother Clark and his wife fall in behind them.

"You guys ever seen those dolls that fit inside each other?" says Keller.

Doby finally takes the bait. "What dolls?" he says.

"Never mind," says Keller.

You watch the Buick roll through the lot, nose into a stall, your family get out. Your mother's face, already transformed, almost radiant in the flat light with its nervous gloss of smiling sweetness, the scared uncertainty in Molly's, and even from here, even with his bow tie, the teasing meanness gathered in the pinched look of your brother Karl's.

"What?" says Doby.

"Just wait," Keller says. "I'll show you."

It's been nine years since the First Vision. Nothing's been restored. The world is still in its fourteen centuries of apostasy. But it's all about to change. Joseph and Oliver are maybe a month into translating the Book of Mormon. It's tough going. A lot of what they're reading confuses them. One day they come across a passage that talks about baptism by immersion. It stops them cold. They go out to the woods to ask the Lord about it. While they're kneeling there praying, a pillar of light comes down through the trees.

Brother Clark looks at you and your buddies.

"Any of you younger Deacons know who it is?"

Jasperson starts to raise his hand but sneaks it back down.

"John the Baptist. He lays his hands on their heads to give Joseph and Oliver the Aaronic Priesthood. The Aaronic Priesthood gives them the power to baptize. He takes them down to the Susquehanna River and has them baptize each other."

Brother Clark sees Doby's hand in the air and nods.

"What river did you say?" says Doby.

"The Susquehanna."

"Where's that?"

"In Pennsylvania. Close to where Joseph and Oliver lived."

"Have you been there?" says Yenchik.

"No, son. I haven't. Anyway, after they baptized each other, they got out of the water, and on the riverbank there they ordained each other into the Aaronic Priesthood."

Strand raises his hand.

"I thought they already had it. From John the Baptist."

Brother Clark studies Strand long enough to make Strand start looking skittish, like he should have kept his mouth shut, like he's thinking of reaching for his comb.

"John the Baptist conferred the power of the Priesthood on them. He didn't actually ordain them into its ranks. He gave them the power to do that for each other."

Brother Clark clears his throat, reaches up under his chins, straightens the hidden knot of his tie.

"Look at it like this. I can give you the power to drive. Once you pass my course, believe me, you'll have the power to drive, or I'd never pass you. But having the power to drive? That's different from having a license to drive. A license gives you the legal right to exercise that power. See the difference?"

"Yeah," says Strand.

"John the Baptist gave them the power. They gave each other the license to use it." He says it unhurriedly. "That explain it?"

"Yeah."

Even if you were as smart as Strand, you're thinking, you still wouldn't be as smart as Brother Clark.

"Good. The Lower Priesthood's restored. Later that summer, in another pillar of light, the Apostles Peter, James, and John appeared to Joseph and Oliver and gave them the Higher Priesthood of Melchizedek. The power of the Apostles. From Jesus Christ to Peter, James, and John, and from there to Joseph and Oliver. Like I told you boys. That lineage of hands had to be unbroken."

Brother Clark looks back and forth across the room again. Nobody's doing anything but looking back at him.

"Why's it called Melchizedek?" Lilly finally says.

"He was a king and high priest in the Old Testament. Genesis."

"Wasn't Peter the founder of the Catholic Church?" says Strand.

"So they like to think," says Brother Clark. "Any more questions?"

Brother Clark waits, and then inhales, draws himself up, frees himself from the table, expands to half again his bulk, rises from his chair.

"That's it. The Priesthood's restored. The Great Apostasy's finally over."

Chairs creak and squeal while the rest of you get up, go to leave, and then realize that Brother Clark's still standing there behind his table.

"Next week is General Conference," he says. "I want you boys to watch or listen to some of it. Hear your leaders speak."

On Tuesday night, in the chapel for Scouts, Keller slides in next to you, late, things already going. Up at the pulpit Sister Blankenagel is talking about some dance they're having in the gym. Most of the guys, like you, are in uniforms. Some older guys have their merit badge bandoliers across their chests. Keller's got a rumpled paper bag in his lap.

"What's that?"

"I'll show you on the stage. Before we go to Scouts."

The opening service breaks up. The girls head for classes where they're learning how to cook, sew, take care of babies, stay chaste, save themselves for a returned missionary. Classes where, in your craziest most secret dream, they're preparing Susan Lake for you. The guys all head for Scouts. You and West and Doby and Strand and Jasperson and Yenchik follow Keller around the dark side of the gym, away from the big window where some of the girls are gathered in the dazzling light of the kitchen, their babbling hard and shattering as a flock of crazed birds across the cavern of the gym. Keller leads you through the small door up the steps onto the stage. He hits a switch. A small light barely brighter than a match comes on in the back corner. The curtain dulls the babbling from the kitchen to where you can single out voices again, listen for Susan Lake's, while you gather under the frail light around Keller's paper bag. Keller reaches in and brings out a doll the size of a softball, almost as round, wearing this intricately painted foreign-looking red and silver dress, a bump rising out of the top in another smooth ball for her head, a miniature snowman except you can see that she's made of painted wood, her eyes and nose and mouth and rosy cheeks just points of paint, her black bangs painted too where they show from under a painted scarf that grows out of her dress. After your first look Jasperson's breath backs you away from the circle of your buddies.

"This remind you of anyone?" says Keller.

"It's a doll, moron." West backs off too.

Keller grins. He sticks the bag in his armpit, takes the doll in both hands, twists it, and you watch it break around the waist into two shells. The shell with her head is hollow. In the other shell there's another wooden doll, just like the first one, just as round, except that her dress is green and purple, and everything's smaller just enough to fit inside the first one. You take a breath, hold it, and you and West put your heads back in the circle.

"Cool," says Doby.

Keller takes the second doll out of the shell and hands her to Doby. "Go ahead," he says. Doby rolls it around and studies it. Keller fits the first doll back together and stands it on the table. Doby twists the second doll. Sure enough. The grooved wood slips and fractures along a line around the equator of its waist, and when it pulls apart, there's another doll inside it, in a blue and yellow dress.

"My turn," says West. West takes the new doll out of the shell in Doby's hand, breaks it open, and there's another doll, and then it's Yenchik's turn, and then it's yours, and finally Jasperson's, except that the walnut-sized doll Jasperson gets doesn't come apart. Keller's been fitting them back together, lining them up on the table, six of them in all, equally plump, incrementally shorter, more intricate.

"Remind you of anyone now?"

"We gotta get to Scouts," says Jasperson.

Keller takes away the smallest two dolls.

"They haven't had these two yet."

"Who?"

"Start here." He points to the smallest one left on the table. "Shirley."

"You named them?" says West. "What a homo."

Keller points to the next one up. "This here's Wanda."

"I can't believe you named them."

Strand suddenly lets out the loud opening snort of his laugh.

"Holy crap," says Doby.

Keller grins, looks at him, points to the next one up.

"Beverly," Doby says.

"Jesus H. Christ," says West. "The biggest one's their mom."

"Clark's old lady," says Yenchik. "And his fat kids."

And then, as it sinks in what you're looking at, you're laughing so hard you're doubled over, dancing in circles, holding your mouths, choking like you've swallowed someone else's spit. Keller waits until you're just about calm, until you're down to just an occasional hiccup of a high laugh caught like a rising upchuck, and then he stands the smallest two dolls at the end of the row again.

"Old Pear Head's gonna have two more kids," says Keller. "The dolls have spoken."

"Holy frigging shit," says West. "This is too much."

"Brother Clark's a good guy," says Jasperson. "This is mean."

"Then maybe you shouldn't of laughed so hard."

Through the curtain, from the gym, from the kitchen, there's just one voice now, a woman's voice, a teacher's voice, songlike and commanding.

"We gotta go," you say. "We're late for Scouts."

"Man," says Doby. "I can't go to Deacons no more. Sit there and look at him."

"Yeah," says West. "We gotta be careful. He won't give none of us a permit."

CHAPTER 34

THAT SATURDAY you help your father close the yard for winter. There won't be any church tomorrow. The churchhouse will be closed for General Conference. Like hundreds of thousands of people, you're supposed to stay home and watch or listen to the sessions on radio or tv, or go to Temple Square, where thousands of other people from everywhere will pack the Tabernacle and Assembly Hall to hear three days of speeches from the leaders of the Church.

On Saturday, starting at ten, while you help your father, his powerful portable radio never leaves his side. President David O. McKay presides. He introduces one speaker after another. Men whose names you know. Stephen L. Richards. George Q. Morris. Spencer W. Kimball. You barely listen. But you can sense their quiet power and the immensity of the obedient army they command in the low timbre and hypnotizing cadence of their voices. You hear them instruct your father in being humble while he lies on his stomach to clean and shape the dirt around the trunks of his rosebushes one last time. He doesn't talk except to tell you what to do.

It was like this in La Sal, half a year ago last April, the weekend you were packing everything you owned and cleaning the little house of everything that showed your family had ever lived in it. He carried the same radio from room to room wherever he was working. The antenna was long enough to touch the ceiling even when he set the radio on the floor. Sometimes your mother would mock him. Sometimes the great organ would fire up its gold pipes and the Mormon Tabernacle Choir would sing and the little room you happened to be emptying would feel like it was being carried away on the back of a soaring bird as big as the ranch itself.

He watches the afternoon session from the naugahyde couch in the darkened basement recreation room in front of the new tv set, mostly by himself, his face quiet, radiant with bliss, vigilant and anxious as though he's supposed to memorize everything he hears. You join him and listen briefly to Apostle Mark E. Peterson talk about kids who leave the beautiful cleanliness of their religious homes to live alone and unprotected in other cities where temptation and tragedy wait for them. You see Roy and then Molly try to join him before they figure out they might as well be cushions. After the session ends, your father goes into his den, where you hear him fire up his big electric Royal, the machine gun burst of keystrokes, a pause, then another burst when the next thing he wants to say comes out of hiding.

Tension builds like static all afternoon in the dry almost combustible air of the house. It bristles off your mother's hair while she brings the morning wash in off the clothesline and sets up the ironing board. You can hear its electrical hum in her voice when Molly asks her what Papa's doing and she tries to answer her daughter politely through stitched lips. Molly gets it. She takes Maggie to their room. Roy and Karl get it. They stay downstairs where they can hear the irregular clacking of the big Royal through their bedroom wall. Your father doesn't get it. His head's too filled with speeches. He's had too much to memorize.

At supper your mother passes you a bowl of lentil soup. Slices of hot dogs floating like stepping stones in its pebbled surface. When she sits down herself, takes Maggie's spoon in her hand, she passes a crazed smile across your faces, a smile that makes you think of broken glass inside her mouth. Your father says the blessing. In his blessing he acknowledges your mother's hand in what you're about to eat. He doesn't mention the Authorities of the Church. He's getting it. His Amen goes quick around the table.

"So, children," your mother says, meek and weary, as though the tension all afternoon has drained her. "Let's eat. Don't let it get cold."

"Yes," your father says. "Listen to your mother."

"Molly wants to know what you were typing, Harold," your mother says.

You look at Molly. In her face is fear at the way her mother just lied about what she'd really asked.

"Just some letters," your father says.

"Who were the letters to?"

"To different people," your father says. "By golly. Let's just eat."

Your mother passes another smile, wounded this time, around the table. The skins of the lentils give way easily in your teeth. Across the table, Molly has her head down, blowing on her spoon.

"Did you finish the yard, Shakli?"

"Yep. Garage too."

"That is nice." She puts a spoon in Maggie's open mouth. Polish from this afternoon still lines two of your fingernails even though the shoes won't be worn tomorrow.

"I have a surprise in store for you," your father says.

"What?"

"We're going to the stakehouse tonight. They're having a live broadcast of the General Priesthood Session from the Tabernacle. We have to be there before seven."

The stakehouse. Even bigger than the churchhouse. Where the five wards that make up your stake get together every few months for Stake Conference.

"What's a General Priesthood Session?"

"It's like any Priesthood Meeting, except instead of discussing the business of the ward, they discuss the business of the entire Church. The First Presidency presides over it."

"Can I go?" Karl says, from your right.

"You'll have to wait until you're a Priesthood holder."

You look at your mother long enough to see her put a shallow spoon of soup in her mouth and close her lips on the steel.

"How long?" you say.

"Between one and two hours. That's all. But you need to eat. We have to clean up and get dressed."

"Yes, children." Your mother sends another sad smile around, looking for help, then puts her forearms on the table and looks at your father. "Who were you writing letters to, Harold?"

"Nobody, Mother."

"I am your wife, Harold. You can tell me."

"So," your father says. "Let's just enjoy this nice meal."

"You were writing letters to the Church Authorities, weren't you? To tell them how you liked their speeches?"

"By golly, Mother. Let's just eat."

"What makes you think they care about your letters?" she says. "Don't you think they have more important things to read?"

"There's nothing wrong with complimenting someone," he says.

"Yes, Harold," she says. "But you have a wife. You have a family who needs you more than some big shot needs a compliment."

"So, Mother. They're not big shots. Don't call them that in front of the children."

"Stay home tonight, Harold. Please. Stay home and let's just be a family. We can watch something on tv together."

"I'm sorry, Mother. I can't."

"What did you tell them, Harold? Those big shots? Did you tell them about us? Do they take time from their families to write letters to you?"

"By golly, Mother! Can't I have just this one thing! Every six months! This is why we came here!"

"Maybe we shouldn't have," she says, suddenly reprimanding. "Maybe we should have stayed in Switzerland."

"That's nonsense," your father says. "You know it."

Your mother draws back, looks at him like he's punched her, and then turns her face to the rest of you, smiling through her pain like an all-forgiving angel.

"Yes, children. We'll have a nice time tonight. We'll see what's on tv. I can make some popcorn. And we have ice cream with raspberry topping!"

Yenchik's father doesn't go to church. So you ask your father if Yenchik can come along with you. You've never seen so many men and guys and kids like you dressed up. Every one of them a Priesthood holder. Every one of them, to the last Deacon, with more power in one little fingernail than all the armies of the world. You've never been among such vast and concentrated power. You wonder what it's like on Temple Square, in the Tabernacle, where the real heart of all the power is.

In the stakehouse, up on the stand behind the pulpit, all the cushioned seats are taken by the stake leaders, and the bishops and counselors of the wards that make up the stake. Bishop Byrne is there. Around you the field of benches is filled. Next to you is Yenchik, and then West, and next to him his father, who drives around the Intermountain West and sells stuff out of his trunk to drugstores. You smell cologne. Wonder why West would wear it when there aren't any girls around. In every cough in the vast chapel you can sense the power of your father's army. All of them gathered here now, the men, all wearing the armor of their temple garments with the secret sacred buttonholes under their clothes. These are the soldiers when you sing Onward Christian Soldiers. This is the army marching off to war. You've heard them speak before, the men you'll hear tonight, the most powerful men in the Church, men who know the majesty of their enormous power, reverent and humble, as though they stand in awe of having it. The Stake President gets up and welcomes you.

When the speakers come on you're suddenly inside the Tabernacle on Temple Square. You can hear the restless echo of the power rising off the audience there. Then the amplified shuffling of paper and hands from the pulpit of the Tabernacle. Then the wavering voice your father said would be President David O. McKay.

"This is the fifth session of the 127th Semi-Annual Conference of the Church of Jesus Christ of Latter-day Saints. You will be interested to know that these services are being broadcast in the Assembly Hall, in

Barratt Hall, over a public address system, and in addition are being broadcast by direct wire over a public address system to members of the Priesthood assembled in eighty-one other Church buildings in Utah, Idaho, Colorado, New York, Washington, Oregon, Arizona, Wyoming, Nevada, Illinois, New Mexico, Canada, and California."

He announces that the Tabernacle Choir Men's Chorus will do the singing and that Alexander Schreiner will play the big organ and that the opening hymn will be I Know that My Redeemer Lives. You bow your head to the opening prayer from the speakers. And then President David O. McKay is there again to introduce Apostle Mark E. Petersen, who talks about the negative influence of Lucky Strike commercials on the youth of Zion, and says the only way to counteract the influence of their advertising is to advertise right back at them. Yenchik bobs off. You and West nudge his legs to bring him back. The Men's Chorus sings another hymn. This time you're allowed to sing along. You pick up the hymnbook and share it with Yenchik because your father knows all the words. Join your voice to the pipes of the mighty organ, to the voices of the Men's Chorus, the voices of the Tabernacle audience, the voices of the vast army of Priesthood holders who all believe in Joseph Smith and know that every other church is false. I'll go where you want me to go. I'll say what you want me to say. I'll be what you want me to be.

The next speaker is Elder J. Reuben Clark, Second Counselor to the President, a man you remember having the collapsed face of the old bulldog some woman in Rose Park had. Everyone around you listens while they look at the empty pulpit and the unused microphone up on the podium. Deep under the trembling cadence of his quaking voice you can hear the controlled heat of reverent indignation close to anger. Yenchik stays alert this time, his eyes open, his face set, focused on the empty pulpit at the front of the big chapel like Elder J. Reuben Clark is standing there himself. He talks about how nobody has the right to take away a piece of his happiness or anything else of his just because they want a piece of it. How false it is to think that all men are created equal despite what the Declaration of Independence says. How he believes instead in something called spiritual relativity. How the Lord himself has revealed that there never was a time when all spirits were equal. That there never will be such a time. How one will always have more intelligence than the next one. How one will always be more noble. How the Lord has provided different kingdoms and glories for all different kinds of individuals as they come to Earth. How the Priesthood has never been possessed by all individuals.

Yenchik's head is down but only because he's studying his thumbs while J. Reuben Clark goes on about how the Priesthood never was a common endowment. How its lineage has been from father to son. How Cain lost his Priesthood because he made a sacrifice that was unacceptable. How you know the result of what Cain did. How the Lord has always chosen those to whom he wishes to delegate his authority. At the end he warns your father's gathered army not to get off on the theory of the ideology that everyone's alike and that all have equal rights. He tells them that everyone's rights depend on their course before they came here and on their course here since they arrived.

He finally says Amen. He hasn't put things together. Just left them there. From the public address system there's the amplified rustling of papers and then the voices of two men whispering as you imagine them trading places at the Tabernacle pulpit. Yenchik hasn't moved a muscle. Now he leans your way and whispers. "He meant niggers."

"What?"

"He wasn't saying it," Yenchik says. "But that's what he meant."

There's a burst of agitated motion from your father to let you know you're out of line by talking.

"Tell you later," says Yenchik.

Under your butt the bench turns hard as rock. The reverent air gets restless. Men around you shift position. West takes his sunglasses out and rubs them with the end of the first regular tie you've seen him wear. Yenchik goes to bobbing his head again. The last speaker is President David O. McKay. The Prophet. The one man on Earth who talks to God. You can hear how exhausted and frail and white-haired his repeated exposure to God has left him. He talks about how to honor the calling of administering the Sacrament. West ducks his head to try on his sunglasses while even your father looks for position on the rock slab of the wood bench.

On the way out of the stakehouse, crossing the lot toward the Buick, Yenchik tells you the rest of it.

"My dad tells me that anytime they talk about Cain they mean niggers. Or who gets to have the Priesthood and who doesn't. They mean niggers. Or not everybody being equal or having the same intelligence. They mean niggers. Or passing it from father to son. They mean niggers. Cuz if one nigger got it pretty soon they'd all have it cuz they're all related." And then Yenchik says, "It's why my dad don't go to church. When he was in the war, his best buddy was a nigger. My dad watched him get killed."

"Killed? How?"

"He doesn't say. He just says let's leave it there. His best buddy got killed and he had to watch it. All he says is blood's blood and everyone's is red."

In the crowded parking lot your father inches the Buick forward. His tired face shines red in the brakelights of the car ahead. You wonder how he could take that many speeches in one day. Under your butt the upholstery feels like a cloud. In the silence of the ride to Yenchik's you put it together. It isn't hard now that Yenchik's given you the key. Your father drops Yenchik off and pulls the Buick onto the street again.

"What does direct wire mean?" you say.

"It means that a broadcast goes over the telephone wire instead of a big antenna. That way, not just anyone can listen to it."

"Is that because it was a Priesthood Meeting?"

"Yes. Just for Priesthood holders. Otherwise it would have been on television too. Like the general sessions earlier today."

"Was he talking about Negroes?"

"Was who talking about Negroes?"

"J. Reuben Clark."

After a while your father says, "He was talking about all men."

"Was he talking about Negroes when he talked about the Priesthood?"

"Did you hear him say Negroes?"

"No."

"Then maybe you shouldn't put words in his mouth."

"He said Cain."

"He said that Cain's sacrifice was unacceptable to the Lord."

"What did he mean when he said you know the result?"

"We know the result. Cain killed his brother and was cursed."

"But that's who Negroes come from."

"Yes," he says. "That's correct."

At a stop sign your father holds the Buick for the headlights of a coming car and then swings the Buick left.

"I'm just asking what he was talking about."

"He was talking about having to earn the Priesthood. Proving to the Lord that you're worthy." And then he says, "We started doing that in the Spirit World."

"What was he angry about?"

"He wasn't angry. He just has strong convictions." At the top of the long hill your father swings the Buick onto the street where you can see the porchlight of your house.

"Are we supposed to be smarter than Negroes? Is that what he was saying?"

"I don't want you to ever look down on them."

"I don't even know any."

"When you do," your father says.

"Do you know any?" you say.

"No."

When you come from the garage you can see their faces in the darkened recreation room in the watery ghost gray light of the tv. Your mother heads up the stairs in your father's wake. You stay with your brothers and sisters and ride out the storm above you, over your heads, in the kitchen, the storm that makes the ceiling of the recreation room feel like the house has been torn away and left the first floor bare to the weather.

Chapter 35

THAT MONDAY, in the envelope with your check from Chicago, you get a letter telling you to close up Mrs. Harding's yard by Friday. The letter doesn't call it Mrs. Harding's yard. It just calls it the yard. The way she's done with every check they've sent you, the way she opens all the mail that gets delivered to her house, your mother hands it to you opened when you come inside from school, stands there in front of you in the kitchen while you read it.

"Is everything all right, Shakli?"

"Yeah."

"Are they firing you? Did you do something wrong?"

"No. Winter's just coming."

"Are you sure that's all?"

The fretful searching look like you could be lying. Like winter didn't kill things. Like you could go on cutting grass and pulling weeds and rolling her tennis court all winter long if you hadn't done something that got you fired.

"There's nothing left to do," you tell her.

"Why do I never hear you play your trumpet, Shakli?"

This close, out of nowhere, you stand there searching her eyes for what you're supposed to get ready for.

"I don't know."

"Don't you want to play it?"

"Not right now."

"Is it because we made you take it back?"

"No. I just don't feel like it right now."

"But you liked it enough to buy it."

"Yeah."

"Are you thinking of selling it?"

"I don't know."

"Oh, Shakli, why don't you learn how to play? We could play together. I have such nice songs. And I remember what a nice touch you had on the piano!"

This close, her face right there, alive, eager, it scares you, and you have to glance away to shake the thought of Mrs. Harding, what she could have looked like, your mother's age, talking about songs.

"Sure."

"Oh, Shakli! That would make me happy!"

You leave it there. At school, twice a day, without telling them anything, you break away from friends you've made in your classes, friends you walk the halls with, to take a detour past the music room. Sometimes from inside the room you can hear the rattle and thump of a drum, the bleat of a saxophone, the pluck or strum of a guitar. The kids who take band. You get to where you can recognize them anywhere in school. Follow them sometimes. Get to know who their teacher is. Sometimes, after History, you walk down the hall with Carla and the case for her violin.

"We're doing an assembly," she says.

"I know."

"Just before Thanksgiving."

"Yeah. I saw."

The poster in the lobby where you read that they'd be practicing after school on Mondays and Tuesdays and Thursdays. You've been waiting in the library to give them the time you think they need to settle in, tune up their instruments, start practicing for real, before you make your way through the school to the hall where you can hear them.

"I'm playing a solo," she says. "Danny Boy."

"Is that its name?"

"Yes," she says. And when you don't say anything, she says, "You and I should do a duet."

"A what?"

"Duet. Where just two people play. Me violin. You piano."

"I've never done one."

"I don't mean for the assembly. Just for fun sometime."

Home again, opening the garage, taking your bike inside, it's there, in its case against the back wall, the instrument you wanted just for the sound it made so that you could make it too, not anything else, not thinking ahead, not thinking what could happen. If only you could play it somewhere else. Keep it at someone else's house. Not Blackwell's. He'd mess with it. But Doby's or West's or maybe Yenchik's. Then it couldn't make your mother crazy. Then it couldn't hurt your family or set the air inside your house on fire. But then you'd have to tell them that you had it, Doby or West or Yenchik, and from there you'd have to tell them everything. Maybe at school, locked in the music room, like you've seen other kids do theirs. Except that you're not one of them. Some other place. Where you could learn how to play it and nobody would know you had it. You don't know where. And so you leave it there while the way you hold it sometimes creeps into your hands. While the feel of the mouthpiece is sometimes there on your lips like a kiss from a steel girl. While the sound it made, the way it suddenly came free the one time you hit the note right, is the steel bird sound it was in the cattle truck. While it goes from being something you could play to being part of you, the only way it's always been part of you, hidden in its hidden case, part of the house now, like the pipes and wires hidden in the walls.

"So who's Danny?"

"Danny?"

"Yeah. In the song."

"I don't know. Just the boy in the song." She looks at you through the goldfish bowls of her glasses. "You're funny. You thought he was real."

"In the song maybe."

"I think he's dead. Or away from home. Or somebody misses him."

It comes to you, when it does, like what you're doing or thinking about or feeling is this steady flow of water from an open hose, and suddenly an open hand just slices through the water, quick, just once, and then the water's the same again, just this liquid rope again from the end of the open hose, running like it was before, like nothing happened. It comes without you knowing. This hard sharp blinding slice through whatever you're doing or thinking about or feeling. It goes like it was never there. Most all of Mrs. Harding's leaves are down. You clean what's left of them away. Smooth her flowerbeds to where they form long serpentine brown unbroken bellies along her paths. Rake her grass clean to its roots. Rake and roll her tennis court. Roll up the hoses and straighten the sprinklers and tools in her shed. Bring the two rickety doors together to where you can put a stick through the latch to hold them.

CHAPTER 36

"SO JOSEPH and Oliver go back to translating the plates. With the Priesthood they're able to race through the rest of them."

Brother Clark runs his eyes across your faces to let you know that he's come to the end of something, that he's looking for stragglers before going off on something new.

"When they're done," he says, "they're ready. Joseph has everything he needs. God tells him to establish the Church on the sixth of April. Joseph gets together some men he's baptized. They organize it the way Jesus did. A Prophet in his place. A Quorum of Twelve Apostles under him. The ranks and quorums of the Priesthood under them."

When he pauses to run his small eyes back and forth what floods into the sudden silence are Keller's dolls.

"That ended the groundwork. The church was fully restored. But I want to look at where this started. Who did Jesus pick to restore his church?"

Everyone sits there, because it's one of those questions you all know the answer to, one of those questions Brother Clark just asks without looking for an answer.

"Did he pick Albert Einstein? Abraham Lincoln? Thomas Edison? Benjamin Franklin? He had his choice."

He pauses again. Not for an answer but to let you think of a famous man yourself. And what you think instead is holding down this convulsion that wants to move up your throat when Keller's dolls fill the silence again.

"Why not a rich man? A Rockefeller? Someone who could build a cathedral or temple by writing a check? Did he look around Harvard or Yale for an educated man?"

This time you look out the window, for anything you can hook your mind to, anything to keep it from being pulled back into the rising hysteria of Keller's dolls.

"No. He picked a poor uneducated farmboy. Someone clean, pure of heart, an empty vessel, a humble boy who only wanted one thing. The truth."

Brother Clark stops and looks back and forth again. You look at the knees of your pants and start counting the threads.

"That's the way God wants you boys to be. Humble. An empty vessel ready to be filled with the spirit of the Holy Ghost."

Slowly this moaning sound starts coming out of Doby. When you look, he's got his face red, his mouth shut tight against some massive inside pressure like he doesn't know whether to throw up or cry.

"Are you all right, son?"

Doby puts his hand across his mouth and shakes his head.

"Maybe you better head for the restroom. Go ahead."

And then, while Doby's leaving, the sound starts coming out of Yenchik, and then West, who looks like a lizard the way he's got his lips pulled in between his teeth.

"You boys too?"

And it finally gets you too, this welling helpless hysterical bulge from down inside, remembering the shells of Keller's dolls, the vessels of the Clark women, and then you're following West and Yenchik out the door.

A week later, out in back, after Priesthood class, after Brother Clark asks if you're all okay again, you watch cars you know by heart roll like a gathering herd into the parking lot. It's November. All of Charley Bangerter's apples have been picked. But the air is mild from an Indian summer where some of your neighbors have started watering their yards again. The morning sunlight is warm where you stand in its way. West's got on his sunglasses, the lenses this almost blackish green the color of the body of a fly, the frames this thick black shiny plastic.

"I think I got the two Priesthoods figured out," he says.

"How?"

"Remember what Clark said about a driver's license?"

"That whole cop thing?"

"No. How when you get ordained it's like getting one."

"Yeah," you say. "Kind of."

"I do," says Doby.

"Maybe the Aaronic Priesthood's like a learner's permit. And the Melchizedek Priesthood's like when you get your real license."

"Maybe."

"Look at us. We're only allowed to do some of the Priesthood stuff. Like pass the Sacrament. Like with a permit. When you've always gotta have a passenger with a license."

"Yeah," says Doby. "Like we can't baptize anybody yet."

"Like the only passenger you can have is someone with a license," West says. "Someone who can drive himself around."

"Yeah. Kinda useless."

"Hey. Jasperson."

Jasperson moves his shoes and goes on guard.

"Yeah?"

"You believe that stuff about having more power in your finger than the whole world?"

"All I know is what Brother Clark tells us," Jasperson says. "He didn't say finger. He said fingernail."

"Oh," says West. "Now it makes sense. Thanks."

"It doesn't have to make sense," says Jasperson. "You just need to believe it."

"So you're saying you coulda won the whole Civil War with your little fingernail."

"I wouldn't make fun of it," says Jasperson. "You could lose it, you know."

"I'm not making fun of it. I'm just trying to make it make sense."

"You could lose it that way too," says Jasperson.

"If I did," says West, "I'd just steal yours."

"Shit," says Doby. "Is that Clark?"

You look. Sure enough. The shine so gone out of the tired paint that the whole station wagon, where it isn't chrome or glass, looks like it's made out of the brown cloth of an old sofa.

"Yeah."

"I gotta go."

CHAPTER 37

YOU'VE HEARD Manny use the word. Hidalgo too, swearing at sheep that didn't understand what he wanted them to do, at the lame old mangy dog some other sheepherder left behind to lay around the bunkhouse, too tired to herd, too old to care where it vomited or left its bones. Always when they were mad, when their faces went hard, like something at night laid bare for an instant by lightning, so you knew they were swearing. Sometimes in Mexican. "Puta!" Never in church. Never said so calm or logical, like a regular word, like a fact, like you were looking at one in a zoo and the zookeeper pointed her out and told you what she was.

Brother Clark comes in with a couple of books and takes his usual seat at the table he turns into a lunch tray. Out in the empty hallway you can hear Charley Belnap coming, shuffling along, muttering in his high soft astonished voice to the men keeping him going. Brother Clark surveys your faces.

"Okay. Someone had a question some time ago about all the other churches and their so-called authority. Who was that?"

Lilly puts his hand up.

"Okay. This is simple. We know there can only be one true church. When Jesus was here, he didn't establish hundreds of them. He didn't go to these people and say here's a church for you and then those people and say here's one for you. He established one church for everyone. One Church. One Priesthood."

"Yeah," say a couple of guys.

"So out of the hundreds out there today, how do we find the one true church? Easy. We follow the authority. We trace it back. For a long time the Catholic Church was the only church around. It claimed its authority to Christ back through Peter. Let's say for a minute they're right. But how about churches that came along later? The Protestant churches? Where did they get their start? Yes."

"Martin Luther?" says Lilly.

"He was the first. He started his church by breaking with the Catholic Church. Now if the Catholic Church truly had the Priesthood, and Martin Luther walked away from it, what happened to any claim he had to the Priesthood?"

"He lost it," Keller blurts out. Jasperson drops his hand.

"That's right. You don't get to walk away from something, say a police department, and keep the authority it gave you. So right there, Luther broke his lineage back to Christ. Let's say now that the Catholic Church never had the Priesthood in the first place. Where did that leave Martin Luther?"

"He never had a place to get it from," says West.

"So either way, the Lutheran Church can't have the Priesthood, can it?"

"No."

"Well, you can apply that logic to pretty much any Protestant religion. Trace them back and they all go back to a break with the authority of the Catholic Church. Whether that authority was real or not isn't even relevant. Either way, there's not a Protestant religion out there that can claim a line of authority back to Christ and his original church. Understand?"

"Yeah." This time you join in.

"Some of them broke off from one another. Some were just made up. Even those that were made up obviously had a problem with the Catholic Church, or else they would have joined it and saved themselves the trouble. Understand?"

"Yeah."

"So when it comes to the lineage of the Priesthood, we can forget about all those other churches. They're gone. We're only left with two possibilities."

"Us and the Catholics," Keller says, seeing the question coming, cheating Jasperson out of answering again.

"That's right. That's the whole contest. The Mormons and the Catholics."

"What about the Jews?" an older Deacon named Allred asks.

"The Jews are the chosen people, son, but they're lost right now."

"How about Hindus?" Keller says.

"Even more lost than the Jewish people. But let's get back to the real contest. You'd expect the true Church of Jesus Christ to look and act more or less like the original church, right?"

"Yeah."

"Okay. Who's the head of the Catholic Church?"

"The Pope," says Jasperson.

"Did Jesus have a Pope?"

"No."

"How about the guys who work directly under him? The red robes. Cardinals. Did Jesus have cardinals?"

"No."

"What did he have?"

"Apostles," Lilly says. "Twelve of them."

"Like us," Jasperson's quick to say.

"Right. We could go on, picking little differences, but let's get right to what God himself says about the Catholic Church. He calls it the great and abominable church. The Church of the Devil. The great whore that sits upon the waters of the Earth."

Chairs groan as the room comes wide awake. The muscles in your back go tight. You've heard Manny use the word. Hidalgo too. The English word for puta. Brother Clark shrugs.

"I know that's a little strong," he says. "But that's straight from the Lord. I'm not in the business of putting words in his mouth."

He reaches for the leatherbound book on the table.

"Anyone start reading the Book of Mormon yet?" he says.

Jasperson and Lilly and then Keller raise their hands.

"Well, even if you've just started it, you've run into what the Lord thinks, because it comes up early, in the first twenty or so pages, when he reveals the final days of the world to Nephi."

His tongue flicks out to wet a fingertip. And then his big finger leafs with amazing speed through the skin of the pages.

"Here we are. Nephi's account of the revelation." He inhales, inflates himself, and out comes his reading voice. "And it came to pass that he said unto me, look, and behold that great and abominable church, which is the mother of abominations, whose foundation is the Devil."

He glances up, looks back down and reads ahead, to himself, before he starts reading out loud again.

"Next verse. And he said unto me, behold there are save two churches only. The one is the Church of the Lamb of God, and the other is the Church of the Devil. Wherefore, whoso belongeth not to the Church of the Lamb of God belongeth to that great church, which is the mother of abominations. And she is the whore of all the Earth."

This time he looks up longer.

"The Book of Mormon says that?" Yenchik says.

"God says that. To Nephi." He goes back to reading. "Next verse. And it came to pass that I looked and beheld the whore of all the Earth, and she sat upon many waters. And she had dominion over all the

Earth, among all nations, kindreds, tongues, and people."

He closes the book and lays it on the table.

"That language appears again and again in the Book of Mormon. The Lord says the same thing to Joseph Smith in the Doctrine and Covenants. He doesn't come out and name the Catholic Church. But church scholars have confirmed it."

The feeling that it's over spreads around the room.

"Not pleasant, boys, I know. But that's how it is. If those Protestant religions have any authority, it's the authority of the Devil, because they got it from the Catholic Church."

The Indian summer from a week ago is gone. It's cold enough out back that the cars and wagons rolling into the parking lot trail these roiling scraps of vanishing white smoke from their tailpipes. West's got his sunglasses. Everyone's got their hands deep in their pockets. Yenchik's there shivering in his short sleeved shirt. Through your Sunday pants the air around your legs is as cold as standing in creek water deep enough to graze your crotch.

"It really says that?" Keller asks Jasperson.

"I thought you said you read it," Jasperson says.

"Forget that. It really says that whole whore thing?"

"Yeah," Jasperson says, reluctant, knowing he's got a minute of prestige now, wanting it to last. "You heard him read it yourself."

"You even know what a whore is?" says West from behind his sunglasses.

"Me?" says Jasperson.

"Yeah."

"We're on church property," Jasperson says.

"How can a church be a whore?" Yenchik's voice shaking like the rest of him.

"Maybe he means the Pope and the Cardinals."

"Guys can't be whores."

"Maybe the women are," says Doby. "I don't know."

"Nuns can't be whores either."

While your buddies stand there and contemplate the possibility, you tense yourself, get ready for someone to bring up Mrs. Harding.

"They got whores in Nevada," says Yenchik.

"Maybe you shouldn't say that word so much," says Jasperson.

"Why not?" says West. "The Book of Mormon says it. We're just quoting."

"You're showing off."

"You guys know any Catholics?" says Yenchik.

"I don't."

"There's gotta be some at school."

More power than all the power in the world for fourteen hundred years. And that's just in one of your little fingernails. Add in the other one. Add in your other eight and all your toenails. You don't know what that much power means. Neither does Yenchik. But he's got it too. More power than George Washington and Mozart and Shakespeare put together. And that just makes it harder to figure out because it's Yenchik, dopey old Yenchik, who can't keep himself from peeing when his head goes underwater.

For now, along with the other Deacons, you use your power to pass the Sacrament, twice every Sunday, in Sunday School in the morning and then at night again in Sacrament Meeting, to your mother's meditative organ music, under your father's troubled watch from some bench out in the congregation. Two benches are reserved for the Deacons, up front, two side benches, the two right in front of the Sacrament Table, so that when the Priests are done blessing the bread or water, you're there, ready to come forward, take the tray you're handed, head for your assigned benches in the congregation. The benches you're assigned depend on where you end up sitting in the Deacon benches. Sometimes you're smart or lucky enough to end up in the seat that goes to the bench where Susan Lake decided to sit. Sometimes, after a long unlucky streak, you have to negotiate, and sometimes there's nothing else you can do but buy it.

"Trade me seats."

"Why?"

"I need to talk to Strand."

"What about?"

"I just need to talk to him."

"Tell me what first."

"I can't. It's private."

"Then I can't trade."

"Okay. About his bike."

"Liar."

"Okay. A nickel."

"A dime."

"No way. I can talk to him later."

"Suits me."

"Okay. Here. Now trade me."

Sometimes a nickel, sometimes a dime, first the bread, and then the water, in thimble-sized paper cups held in flat chrome trays with teapot handles. When you turn around from the Sacrament Table to head for her bench you've already got the look in place. Locked into your face.

You watch her decide which bite of Wonder Bread to take off your tray. Watch her take a cup of water off your water tray. Feel the tray move in your hand while she works the cup loose from the hole that holds it with her fingertips. Watch her touch it to her lips. See the top of her head, something she only knows by feel herself, where the part in her hair is a thin line of scalp from her forehead back to the whirlpool where her hair turns around and comes forward again. Carry the cup with its paper rim gilded by the light pink imprint of her lipstick back to the Sacrament Table. All the power you want. All the power you've got the guts to use.

CHAPTER 38

THE THURSDAY a week before Thanksgiving, after school, you and Karl put your jackets on and climb into the hills above the sandpit to look for the cave you heard about. The pale yellow stems of the weeds are hard and wiry like the skeletons of birds and fish you used to come across in the fields and creek beds around La Sal.

"Does it have those big icicles?"

"I don't know. Probably not."

"Maybe they were lying."

"No. I see it."

"Where?"

"Right over there. That shadow."

"Oh. Yeah."

And then you're there, in its mouth, just a big rough hole in the hillside, no stone icicles, the floor just the dirt and weeds of the rest of the hill. You wander in to where the sunlight ends. A few feet farther back, in shadow, you can see the collapsing wall where the cave ends too.

"I wonder if Indians lived in here," says Karl.

"Maybe outlaws."

"Maybe they buried their money here."

"Not much of a hideout."

"Let's go back out."

From the mouth of the cave the hillside spills down steeply to the long gouge of the sandpit, to the bare gray orchards, to the dark green yards where the houses start, where the rooftops continue in broken terraces out to the floor of the long gray valley.

"Wow," says Karl. "There's the church."

"There's the circle."

"Where?"

You step in behind him and level your arm across his shoulder like a rifle whose barrel ends at the point of your finger. "There. See? That's the Allers."

"Which one's ours?"

"The one across. With the flat roof."

"Yeah."

You take your arm off his shoulder and step out from behind him.

"This is high," he says.

"Yeah."

"So what did the guy do? When you took your trumpet back?"

"What do you mean?"

"Did he get mad?"

Along the side of his face the sunlight lays the skin so bare the pores have pinpoint shadows. You can see hundreds of tiny white hairs he doesn't know he has.

"Naw."

"I thought stores got mad if you took things back."

"Just if you used them."

"What'd you do with it?"

"Sold it to someone."

"You didn't want it anymore?"

"Naw."

"How come you wanted it anyway?"

"I don't know. It was stupid."

Out across the valley are the railroad tracks along the marshlands where they can't build houses, and then, at the horizon, the long black ragged ridge of Antelope Island out in the Great Salt Lake.

"I want a drum."

"Yeah?"

"Yeah. I hate that stupid piano."

At first the noise is like an insect whirring against a screen or a dead leaf being rubbed on a rock. And then you know. You look down. Next to your shoe, close enough to leave it polished, the long scaled slithering thick hose of its body in the weeds, the autumn-colored chain of diamonds along its rippling back. Every muscle you have goes hard.

"Keep still," you say.

"What?"

"No. Keep still. Play statue. Until I say to move."

"Why?"

"In a minute we're gonna race."

"Down the hill?"

"First one to the sandpit. Just keep still." You can feel yourself start trembling with the effort to keep him there, in place, his own shoes from moving. "I'll say when."

"You'll cheat."

"Okay. Then I'll say when you can say when. Just don't move."

"Okay."

"As soon as I say when, you say go. Okay?"

"Yeah."

You feel him tense up next to you. You glance down in time to see the little cob of the rattle slide past your shoe.

"When."

"Go," he yells, but he's already gone, his hand in yours just long enough for you to get him out of there, airborne, before it can snap its head around and strike, the hill so steep you've sailed thirty or forty feet through air before you touch dirt and kick off again, like giants leaping, like dropping from the sky. Just before the weeds end, at the cliff that falls into the sandpit, the hill turns almost level, and you heel into the dirt, skidding and stumbling, and bring yourself to a stop. Karl goes a couple of steps ahead and then turns back around.

"I won! I knew you'd cheat! I still won!"

"There was a rattler!" In your ears is the pounding surge of your heart. You can't get any breath.

"We were flying!" he says. "Like Superman!"

"There was a rattler up there!"

"A what?" His face goes scared and mean at the same time. "A rattler?"

"Yeah!" You take a breath to slow things down inside you. "Right there! Right next to my shoe!"

"A rattlesnake?"

"That's why I kept telling you to hold still!"

"Holy crap!"

"That's why we raced! To get us out of there!"

"You're lying! You lost! Admit it!"

"I lost! Okay! I'm not lying!"

"You should of told me! I would of bashed its head in!"

"No you wouldn't of! Don't ever say that! Don't ever mess with a rattler!"

"All right! I'm sorry!"

"I mean it!"

"I'm sorry! You don't need to get so mad!" And while his eyes hold their mean defiance you can see from his chin how he's about to cry.

"I'm not mad!" you say. "I'm just scared! God dammit!"

On the Sunday before Thanksgiving Brother Clark comes into class, takes his seat, pulls the table up against his gut.

"What if it's all made up?" he says to Lilly.

"If what's made up?"

"The First Vision. The Golden Plates. The restoration of the Priesthood." He brings the palms of his hands up to his chin like they're holding something, blows at them, and his eyes follow what could be dust or feathers, floating off across your heads. "Poof. All gone. A pack of lies."

"But it's not," says Lilly.

"What if it is?"

"It's not."

Brother Clark looks down, picks at something on the table, looks up again.

"Over the next few years you boys'll be taught many things. The War in Heaven. The Plan of Salvation. The Degrees of Glory. The Law of Eternal Progression. You'll be taught these things until they're part of you as much as your legs and eyeballs."

He looks at Doby and pauses. Doby closes his hand around two marbles he's been rolling in his fingers.

"As you go, you'll see how all the parts of the Gospel fall into place, fit together in one harmonious structure. Here's the problem. Any structure needs a foundation. Something strong to stand on. Anyone know what that is?"

Jasperson's hairtrigger hand lifts an inch or two off his leg but then goes down again like something the wind picked up and dropped.

"The First Vision," says Brother Clark. "Either it happened or didn't. The entire Church rests on that question. The First Vision. True or false. One question. Two possible answers."

He takes a heavy breath and looks out across the room.

"Either Joseph Smith saw God and Jesus Christ that morning or he didn't. If he did it's simple. The Church is true. If he didn't, he's the biggest fraud to ever walk the Earth, and we're in real trouble, because it all becomes a lie. Everything. Even this room we're sitting in built on a lie. And we're wasting our time with all this Priesthood nonsense."

The room goes still. Manny and Hidalgo and the other sheepherders used to joke about Joseph Smith. They called him Jose and made jokes about all his wives. It was okay for them. They weren't Mormon.

"So what have we got that tells us one way or the other?"

"What he said," Jasperson says.

"What's to say he wasn't lying? Any witnesses?"

"God and Jesus."

"Anyone else?"

"The Devil was there," an older Deacon named Wassom says.

"The Devil says it never happened. Let me ask you something. When you boys were ordained into the Priesthood, what gift did you receive?"

"The Holy Ghost."

"Why?"

"So he could help us know the truth."

"That's right. He dwells in each of you. In your bosom where you can feel him burning. There's your witness. What do we call that feeling?"

"A testimony," says Keller.

"Your testimony that the First Vision is true. That's the foundation of the Church. Your testimony."

He moves his eyes off Keller.

"In a few years, I'll see each of you boys behind the wheel of a car. I'll teach you about stop signs, traffic lights, parking, turn signals, speed limits. It'll be all or nothing. You can't pick and choose what suits you. You can't believe in a stop sign and not believe in a speed limit. You have to accept it all, or none of it will work."

Two chairs away you can feel West itching for something that's still almost four years down the road.

"Some of you boys will be going to college. That's where you'll really be tested. You'll have professors introduce you to all kinds of ideas. They'll tell you that Mormonism's just another religion. That Joseph Smith was just a creative guy with a fertile imagination. They'll tell you who the real thinkers were. Aristotle. Socrates. Kant. Hegel. They'll make you feel stupid if you disagree. You'll want to agree just to get along and get that grade. Or maybe their philosophies will just appeal to you. Existentialism. Metaphysics. Agnosticism. Marxism. Cosmology. All the godless stuff men had to make up for over fourteen hundred years."

He stops and contemplates Yenchik. Like he's doing the same thing you are. Trying to see Yenchik in college.

"But that's how the Devil works. He'll have his agents pick away at you. Tell you this or that little thing isn't important. Let it go if you're having trouble accepting it or something better comes along. Soon you've let so much of it go that you've just got pieces left. No harmony. No logic. No testimony. And you're wondering how it happened."

A sharp crack on the linoleum makes everyone jump. "Sorry," says Doby. A marble rolls out onto the open floor. Brother Clark ignores it.

"That's where the Holy Ghost comes in. He's known the Devil a long time. Knows how the Devil works. That's why you need to keep him there. To protect you."

You remember how the hoarse moaning blast of the horn of a train came from out across the long floor of the gray valley. How Karl whipped his head around to look and put his face squarely into the reddening light of the lowering sun. And then a flat hand, held like a blade, knifed through the flow of what you were thinking and feeling and looking at, and for the instant it was there, you were back at the place where the train tracks cut straight across the asphalt of the crumbling road, standing there with your bike, too far from home for suppertime, too far to know you'd never see Mrs. Harding again. And then it was gone. And then you wanted to tell him. The way Mr. Hinkle lied so you could keep the trumpet. How your father fought with your crazy mother about not getting your money back. Where you hid it. There at the edge of the sandpit you wanted to tell him everything. How he could have a drum and maybe you could play together. You remember how you looked at him, his mixed-up half-scared squinting face and his crazed brown hair, nothing but weeds and sky around, and wanted to just keep telling him you were sorry.

CHAPTER 39

YOU SAT THERE waiting all through your father's ordaining prayer. Through the Elders of Israel and the ministering of angels. You tried to close your eyes to keep from looking at the horse's head stitched into the green tie of the man with his stomach in your face. You started getting scared when you felt the ending coming. Your father said Amen. You felt the hands start lifting off your head. Wait, you thought, wait, but they didn't, and then your father's hands came off. It was over. You had to stand up, to men congratulating you, to their hands waiting to shake yours, to their firm grins telling you that you were one of them now. You shook their hands. You grinned back, and thanked them, and held their reassuring eyes, hoping your face had the look of human steel you'd seen Lilly and Jasperson wear, that it was hiding how scared you were. When you got to him your father wasn't grinning. You could shake his hand. You couldn't hold his eyes. He knew. His hands were right there on your head where he would have felt it too if it had happened.

"Congratulations, son," he said.

Men were standing around him waiting to hear him say it. Men slapping him on the back.

"Thanks, Papa."

"Remember who you are now."

"I will."

You went to the bathroom afterward to comb your hair. In the mirror you tried for the look again. It was there. It wasn't much, more like tinfoil, but with enough practice maybe you could turn it into steel. Only your father and you would know. In the bathroom mirror the word hypocrite had came from out of nowhere and then was gone. Just the quick fracture where you could see the typed letters and hear the burst of keystrokes that put them on the paper.

The morning they announce the assembly over the speaker Carla's not in History. You figure they're doing their last rehearsal. After History, in the auditorium, the stage is racked with cafeteria chairs and music stands, a set of drums behind them. From where you sit, back in the dimmed auditorium with Doby, you watch kids play all the instruments Mr. Hinkle played, gold, silver, black, shimmering in the spotlights from high in the ceiling of the stage, the kids you've seen with their cases in the halls. You watch Mr. Marchant, the band teacher, use a baton to lead them. You watch Carla step forward with her violin.

A cleared patch of dirt. A circle of rocks. Clean dry firewood stacked on the kindling of grass and twigs, gradually larger sticks, until you were up to logs, arranged on top like the poles of a teepee, plenty of room for air, the way Manny taught you the summer you spent with him and the sheep in the mountains. You could still remember him saying a fire had to breathe. You built it right. It was ready to burn in your bosom. All it needed was a match. A spark from the Holy Ghost. But the Holy Ghost had come along, looked at you, looked at the fire you'd built, and kept on going.

You've kept it dry for him. He hasn't come back. But now, from back in the dimmed auditorium, you watch Carla step into the spotlight and hear her play a song so lonely and sad and beautiful you never thought it could come from her. And while you sit there listening to the strike and pull of her bow across the strings, you finally feel the flame catch hold in the grass, send its shoots up slowly through the kindling of the twigs, and then into the bigger sticks, and then the logs.

The fourteen year old boy who found a place in the woods. The boy your father would love to have had for a son. After the assembly, the fire inside your chest still warm, you find a place too. Home from school that day you sneak the case out from behind the Christmas boxes, brush the cobwebs off, climb the hill, find a place where you can get on your knees too, not a grove in the woods, but a place in the dirt toward the back of the sandpit, a level place where a couple of banks of bulldozed rubble shield you from the hopper, the steam shovel, the loop of road the trucks have left across the floor. You lay the case on its back in the dirt. You get on your knees not to pray, but to unsnap the latches, lift back the lid, take out the lesson book, and there it is, the way you left it, the bruised and burnished sheen of its brass, the deep shining gold of its pipes, the valve casings, the ivory-tipped plungers for your fingers, the dent in the bell, the tuning slide still set where Mr. Hinkle left it when he tuned it to his big piano. Your knees are cold in the dirt. Underneath your right knee the spike of a tiny rock bites into the bone. You lift the trumpet off its cradle. Small quick halos of steam form on the cold brass around your fingertips. You slip the mouthpiece in, not tight, give it a little twist to lock it, lace your fingers around the cold casings, tuck in your thumb. You remember everything. Middle C. How the flow comes from your lungs. How the hard cup of the mouthpiece feels.

Part 5

The Sandpit

CHAPTER 40

YOUR FIRST TIME there you only got as far as middle C when a pickup truck pulled in and parked and a man got out and started working inside the back of the steam shovel. So you made your way up the hill off the back of the sandpit and looked for a place to keep your trumpet. The place you found was a stand of scrub oak. Inside its brittle tangle of twisted branches, up off the dirt and weeds and coming snow, you broke off branches, made a little shelter with a stick roof, stuffed the branches with black leaves. It looked like a nest when you finished. From farther back it looked like just another snarl of dead collected leaves.

The next afternoon, you use your galoshes to scrape the light overnight snow away to where the dirt is dry, kneel down, open the lesson book. The fingering chart in back shows you how to valve each note. You use two rocks to keep the pages flat. Your gloves are too thick to get your fingers around the casings and the tips too sloppy and loose to work the plungers. Barehanded, you take hold of the cold brass casings, position your fingers on the ivory caps of the plungers, bring the mouthpiece up. Middle C. The valves all open. You blow the note till you can hear it clean. Shy at first, the way the sound splits the silent air and goes racing off around the sandpit, you bring the trumpet down, look around, and then start working up the chart. C sharp. All three down. D. First and third. D sharp. Second and third. E. First and second. It doesn't matter because nothing since C has come out sound. Just dirty air. You try again. Nothing. You let the trumpet down. In your hands, stark gold in the blinding early winter sunlight, it's this thing you never saw for real before.

You turn to the front of the book. Read how low notes need volume and high ones speed. How volume and speed are different for every note. How you change how tight you make your lips and how open you keep your mouth behind them. You turn past the drawing that names the parts of the trumpet to the first exercise. Two notes, C and D, apart and then together. You start with C again. Play it long, long as you can without needing breath, then rest, then play, over and over the way the book says, one long sustained note once you hit the pitch where the sound breaks clear of its bleary uncertain haze and suddenly goes bright and makes the metal vibrate. You try D. Hold the first and last valves down, tighten your lips just slightly and blow just slightly faster, and there it is, the pitch where the metal blazes in your hands again. Then steady and long again until your lungs run almost out of air.

Your fingers are numb when you put the trumpet down. You blow on them, clamp them in your armpits, the ache so bad when the feeling comes back it rocks you back and forth. The metal is ice when you pick up the trumpet again. Two notes. Now that you don't need the book you can get off the dirt, stand up, keep a better lookout. You play them, one and then the other, stop to warm your fingers, play them again, alone and then together, until your lips are finally too numb to hold the mouthpiece and your fingers too gone to feel the valves. By the time you pull the mouthpiece out, close the case, the fire of the sunset along the horizon is down to a few last dying smears in the rags of the clouds in the hard gathering cold of the early stars.

Two notes that are real. Two notes that you own. If you could hold them in your hands, they'd feel round, plump, with the heft of pears or peaches. You put the case back in its shelter and then come down through the snow-crusted weeds of the hillside to the lighted porches and windows of the neighborhood. Inside you, this huge and crazy feeling keeps crashing up against your ribcage the way Rufus would do when you'd first get home from school, this feeling you know you can't bring into the house with you.

In History the next morning, looking at the case on the floor next to Carla's boots, you wonder what it's like inside, how it holds her violin, how the violin looks up close, if her middle C and D sound anything like yours. After class you catch her in the hallway.

"You did really good. At the assembly."

"Are you sure?"

"Yeah."

"It was scary."

"You were scared?"

"I was shaking so bad my violin was shaking."

"I couldn't tell."

"Really?"

"It was really nice. I liked how you played it."

"Wow. Thanks."

"I did."

"You should play next time."

She's talking piano. She doesn't know. You look down at her shoes with the sudden appetite to tell her. How it's a trumpet. How you bought it yourself. But then the questions would start. Questions whose answers have kept you from telling even your buddies that you've got it.

"Yeah. Maybe."

"We could play a duet maybe."

"Except I'm not as good as you."

"We could practice."

"Is a violin hard?"

After the first time past the door of the music room that morning, from Art to Gym, you feel released, the longing gone that's been taking you out of your way to steal a walking look inside. You've got a place too. A place where you take the trumpet out, and look for them, and find them where you left them, nested in that place where your breath and mouth and lips combine to make them, suddenly free and brilliant in the cold December air. C and D. You open the book for the next exercise. Quarter notes. Tu tu tu tu. Notes you need the machine gun of your tongue for. You play C and fire away. The trumpet jams. The sound stops cold. Just forced breath. You try again. Nothing.

You panic. And then think back to Mr. Hinkle. When you imagine him there, his big hands deep in the pockets of his overcoat, his voice is there. Don't try too hard. Don't spit the notes. Keep the flow going. And then you remember the cattle truck. The tall exhaust stack. The flapper on top to keep the rain out. The way it fluttered, the buoyant way it rode the loud black bursting flow of exhaust, the effortless way it touched down light and bounced back up, out of the way again, when Manny hit the gas. You make your lungs and throat and mouth the stack. Your tongue the flapper. Your breath the exhaust. You blow and hold C. Your tongue makes just the quickest touch behind your teeth. It happens. The note breaks. And then keeps playing past the break. You do it again. And again. You warm up your fingers and tackle E, the next note up, and by the time you close the case and put your gloves on, three notes are yours, like arrowheads, like the instruments out of the dashboards of the army trucks in the junkyard across the highway through La Sal.

CHAPTER 41

BISMARCK'S the capital of North Dakota. Two negatives make a positive when you times them. Elias Howe invented the sewing machine. God and Jesus Christ and the Angel Moroni appeared to Joseph Smith. The thought of rejecting the stuff they teach you in Priesthood and Sunday School is weird to where it's stupid. Like the stuff at school, it's stuff you're there to learn, not stuff to argue with or question. And nobody does. Nobody tries to tell you that Mexicans and Indians are brown for some reason other than they're cursed or that the whore who sits upon the waters isn't the Catholic Church. It's just the opposite. Everyone around you keeps telling you how true they know it is.

On the last Sunday of every month, instead of Sacrament Meeting later that night, they hold Fast and Testimony Meeting right after Sunday School. It's the Sunday your father doesn't put on an apron and fry up some eggs and baloney. The Sunday you find him just sitting at the table, no apron, reading the Church News, the Spoken Word on the radio. Nobody's supposed to have breakfast. You're supposed to take the money you didn't spend on breakfast, put it in a brown Fast Offering envelope, and give it to Deacons assigned to collect it.

"That's one cheap breakfast," Keller says, looking down into an envelope.

"You're not supposed to open those," says Jasperson, mad and frantic at the same time.

"There's a dime in here," says Keller. He looks at the rest of you. "A whole dime."

"Whose is it?" says West.

Keller slips the little record card out of the envelope and then slips it back in again.

"The Birds," he says.

"Earl Bird?" you say.

"Yeah," says Keller. "Him and his big gut and his whole family."

The family three houses around the circle from yours. The nasty mud ugly ape of a man who yells at his wife and kids so loud and hard and dirty you can hear him even in winter, all the windows closed, bellowing his head off, teaching you ways to cuss you never knew existed.

"The whole family?" says Jasperson. "Breakfast for a dime?"

"Cheap bastard," says West. "Looks like he eats ten bucks by himself."

"Yeah," says Keller. "He'd probably pass out if he fasted."

"Anybody got Clark's envelope?" says West. "Bet there's a hundred bucks in there. If he's telling the truth."

After Sunday School, in Fast and Testimony Meeting, you hear stomachs all around you growling, smell hunger in the air like the sharp stink of a cold incinerator barrel. You do the Sacrament. In your mouth the piece of Wonder Bread explodes into the best thing you can remember ever tasting. Then, the bread and water over, they bless the babies, the new ones, the ones who were born since the last Fast and Testimony Meeting a month ago, while you and West and Yenchik sit there having thumb fights.

Some men come forward, form a circle in the open space below the pulpit, close to where your mother sits at the organ, her face unbearably angelic as she watches some father bring his baby up the aisle. All the men on the podium, Bishop Byrne, his First and Second Counselors, they're smiling too, even though the baby's usually howling like a banshee out of the pink or light blue blanket it's bundled in.

"Ow," says West. "Let go."

"Say you're sorry," says Yenchik.

"Sorry for what?"

"For being born."

The baby gets put in the circle. The men cradle their hands together underneath it, bob it up and down to get it quiet, and its father uses the power of the Melchizedek Priesthood to give it a name and a blessing. Afterward, the men step back, the circle opens, and the father holds the baby high, usually still howling, to the collective gush of admiration from hundreds of your neighbors.

After the last baby everything goes quiet. Everyone sits and waits for people to start rising from the congregation to bear their testimonies. When they do, one of the Teachers goes running their way with a microphone, laying the long black cord out behind him in the aisle. Doby's got his pocketknife out, pushing the point of its blade into the palm of his hand, seeing how far he can go without going through the skin. Keller reaches over and tries to slam it through.

"Ow! Are you nuts?"

Sometimes people talk about how sick they've been. Sometimes about a scary operation someone in their family had. Medicines and doctors helped, but it was the bedside blessing the Elders came and gave him, rubbing a couple of drops of olive oil into the skin of his temple, that saved his life. Sometimes they start crying, and in the benches for the Deacons, you and Keller and West and Yenchik stop whispering, stop horsing around, just sit there looking at your knees while the speakers mounted in the rafters rain down their amplified heartache and gratitude.

And then they bear their testimony. How they know that Joseph Smith was called by God the Father and Jesus Christ to restore the Church. How they know beyond the shadow of a doubt that the Book of Mormon is the Word of God. Kids get up too. A guy in high school talks about how God helped him win a debate. A little girl testifies how she knows her cat that got run over is in Heaven now with Jesus. Half the time you know they're showing off. The other half you don't know what they think they're proving. Because you believe it too. You have to. Otherwise you'd be a kid in Switzerland.

And then Jasperson gets up, waits for the microphone, starts naming everything he's grateful for. His mother who raised him. His father who taught him right from wrong. His good grades. His health. Brother Rodgers and Brother Clark. And then he bears his testimony. Sitting next to him, your head down, you look at the bagged-out knees of his Sunday pants, the gray cuffs collected around his ankles, the shoes he never shines. On the back of your head, from somewhere behind you in the congregation, you can feel the heat of your father's eyes, wondering why it's Jasperson up there instead of his own son.

"He's so fulla shit he wipes his eyes with toilet paper," says West.

"Yeah," says Keller. "Like he really prays for good grades."

"He was just bragging."

"All he gets in Math are Cs," says Strand. "I've seen his tests."

"What a liar."

"Maybe he oughta do his homework. Instead of just praying about it."

"I got the Holy Ghost too. I just don't go around bragging about it."

"And Rodgers and Clark. God. Like they could even give him a grade."

In Blackwell's basement, in the long family room, one wall is painted to look like you're not in a basement but on some ocean liner like the Queen Elizabeth, on the deck, in the middle of the ocean. Big turquoise waves ripped with white foam run all the way across the bottom of the wall, recede out toward the line of the horizon, meet up with wisps of clouds across a pale blue sky. A white railing runs the whole length of the wall. Out beyond the railing two white seagulls float just out of reach. More seagulls circle in the background. It looks like a warm day.

There's nothing shiplike about the rest of the room. The other walls are paneled in knotty pine and the floor is this light brown peppered tile and the sofa and chairs are stuff you'd find in a farmhouse. You're there because Blackwell called, and your father answered, and you weren't quick enough to come up with a way of getting out of taking the phone. Blackwell said he had something to show you. Now it's on the coffee table in front of you, a National Geographic magazine, open to a photograph of a Negro woman, a bundle on her head, naked from the waist up.

"Nice, huh?" Blackwell says.

"They just walk around like that?"

"Yeah."

"Where?"

"I guess someplace in Africa. I'm gonna find out and move there."

"How do they keep that stuff balanced?"

"On her head?" He looks at you like you're nuts. "That's what you're looking at?"

"Yeah."

"I don't know," he says. "Practice, I guess."

"They gotta have strong necks."

"Necks?" Blackwell says.

She looks young. If she was American she'd probably be in high school. But if she was American she wouldn't be in the National Geographic naked.

"Too bad they're not in color," says Blackwell. "I'd like to see what color her nipples are. I bet they're brown. Dark brown instead of pink."

You could have stayed home for this, you're thinking, the way your father gets the National Geographic too.

"They just walk around like that," you say.

"Yeah. Like that's how she'd go to Safeway."

"They probably don't have Safeways."

"Then maybe church," says Blackwell. "Holy crap. If Scoutmaster Haycock's wife came to church like that."

"You'd have to stay home," you tell him.

"Home?" says Blackwell. "Shit. I'd have to move."

What makes the wall of the ocean weird is that it started snowing on your way here. Tiny stinging icy flakes propelled by a wind you had to lean against to walk. Blackwell puts down the magazine, leans back, looks at the ocean with you. You finally hear him take a long breath in and let it out again. Then he leans forward and starts picking at a fingernail.

"All that Holy Ghost stuff Clark keeps telling us," he says. "You believe it?"

"What stuff?" you say. Wondering if you could get seasick if you stared at the ocean long enough and squinted everything else out of your vision.

"About how he's inside us," he says. "About the unpardonable sin. About being a Son of Perdition."

How the worst sin in the world wasn't murder. It was to deny the Holy Ghost once you felt him in your bosom. It was to say you'd never felt him. It was a sin not even God could forgive. It was enough to make you a Son of Perdition.

"Yeah," you say. "I believe it."

"Him knowing what we're thinking?"

"Yeah?"

"I guess it scares me."

"How come?"

He gives his arms a shrug. "Cuz all I ever think about is tits," he says. "Like Haycock's wife." And then he says, "Sometimes I look at your mom's."

You've watched him do it, right under your father's nose, and your father never seemed to mind, went on laughing at his stupid jokes like Blackwell was the greatest kid he'd seen all month.

"They're pretty big, you know," he says.

"Don't talk about my mom."

"I'm just telling you what the Holy Ghost knows."

"Just shut up about my mom."

"Every time I get a boner, he knows about it. He's right there. He even knows what I get them from. It's like there's this cop inside me. More like a judge. Yeah. And he never says what he's gonna do to me."

"You're supposed to ask him stuff."

"I do. He never says anything." And then he says, "I never even feel him."

You think about telling him. How you never feel him either. How a girl who wears round glasses and plays violin was the one who lit the fire you'd built. How you couldn't deny something you'd never felt. But you can already hear him use what you'd say against you.

"Don't worry about him," you say.

Suddenly Blackwell's voice goes high and watery. When you turn and look his chin and bottom lip are puckered up. "Maybe he's made me a Son of Perdition already," he says, caving in, tears coming. "I don't want to be one. I'm scared."

CHAPTER 42

THE BUNKHOUSE. The long flat porch out front where the sheepherders and ranch hands sat and smoked and talked and Hidalgo sometimes played his battered old red guitar. The butts they threw off the porch out on the dirt. Sometimes you and Jimmy Dennison would rake your fingers through the dirt for them, strip the leftover tobacco into your corncob pipes, head down the long road toward the banked hollow where the creek pooled. You could smell and taste the spit where it had soaked the sweet tobacco. Sometimes, late afternoon and evening, you'd hang out there, sit off the edge of the porch, level with their crusted boots and bare feet, listen to their soft and teasing talk, try to predict where the next circle of spit would suddenly land and sink and leave its dark blot in the dirt. It's your spit now, when the sound starts to gutter, turn ragged, when you open the spit valve, when you watch the same dark blot show up in the cold dirt out in front of your galoshes.

One morning, walking out of History down the hall, Carla wants to know if you know what you're getting for Christmas.

"No."

She turns her face your way and smiles. "Know what you want?"

"Not really."

"Yes you do."

"You know what you're getting?"

"No. I like being surprised."

"You know what you want?"

"Sure."

"What?"

"I can't tell you," she says.

You've got C and D and E where you can play them soon as your lips touch the mouthpiece. Three notes you can work with your tongue, chase back and forth, play simple songs with, send chasing each other around the sandpit. The girl whose round glasses hold portraits of her eyes is wearing a sweater with reindeer and snowflakes across its chest.

"Could I see your violin sometime?"

"My violin?"

"Yeah."

"You've seen it."

"I mean up close."

If she bought it from Mr. Hinkle. If she goes to his store for her music or strings or whatever else a violin needs. If she takes her change from his hand.

She laughs. "There's not much to see. It's just a violin."

"That's okay."

"Maybe you could show me your piano sometime too."

Three notes. Each note with its own equilibrium in the volume and speed of your breath, its own buzz, where the trumpet comes alive with this hard bright sound whose ring you can feel in the metal. And sometimes you feel what Blackwell feels. This fear that you've stolen fire cuts through you. And then this wild certainty that you're doing everything wrong. The long bawl of a train horn comes from the valley across the far ridge of the sandpit. A seagull cries and takes off from the black rim of the hopper. Just this quick fracture in the flow of what you're doing. And then it's gone, and in the cringing doubt it leaves behind, you can't trust anything. Maybe Mr. Hinkle would stand there, shake his head, take his big open hand out of his overcoat pocket and hold it up to stop you, show you, make you start over. You don't know. You don't know how to know.

CHAPTER 43

"COME, CHILDREN, come! It's going to start! Let's not be late!"

The Honeymooners. Your Hit Parade. Red Skelton. Ozzie and Harriet. I Love Lucy. The Lone Ranger. Ed Sullivan. Almost every night your mother rounds you up and heads you down the stairs to the recreation room. If your father hasn't gone back to the office or out on church work after finishing the dishes, turning off his radio on the windowsill, hanging up his apron, he's in his den, and while you and Karl turn the tv on and switch the light off, your mother opens the door on the hard and rapid clacking of his big Royal and brings it to a bothered stop.

"Yes, Mother. What is it."

"Come be with us, Harold. It's I Love Lucy."

"Yes. Just give me another minute."

"Come, Harold. Be with your family. They miss you."

"Yes, Mother. Just another minute."

"Yes, Harold. But hurry! It's starting!"

Karl and Roy bring their pillows and blankets out of their basement bedroom and make beds on the floor like they're camping on linoleum. Molly brings the doll of a baby and holds it like it's real, cradled in her arm where she can look into its glass eyes, while her other arm holds Maggie up against her side. When your father comes in from his den your mother and Molly and Maggie make room for him at the end of the couch. You take a wooden folding chair at the other end. The only light in the room is the light the tv throws, gray and liquid like light through rippled water, where it plays off the laughing faces of your family.

Red Skelton does Clem Kadiddlehopper and Sheriff Deadeye and Freddie the Freeloader. Gisele MacKenzie sings while the Hit Paraders dance. Tonto says Kimo Sabe. Ricky Ricardo calls Lucy crazy. Jackie Gleason yells at Norton. Your mother laughs like a violin. Your father gets laughing so hard he rocks and smacks the armrest. The rest of you laugh too, along with them, because they're laughing, because everything's okay, while your faces all go bright and dark and bright and dark without you knowing it. Deep inside your legs and back is still the embedded cold of the afternoon up in the sandpit, but the light from the tv feels warm, warmer than the sunlight was, warm like a bath, warm like a room with a glowing gas heater, like some motel room where you'll all sleep tonight while the Buick stays parked outside the window and semi trucks roll past out on the highway.

It comes to you, every afternoon after school, the routine, the way you practice. Start by using your breath and hands to get the mouthpiece warm enough to touch your lips to. Then play just the mouthpiece, low to high to low again, this squealing little siren sound like an ambulance for grasshoppers. Then blow the trumpet warm enough to where the spit inside it melts and you can work the valves. Then the long notes, counted off in eight small circling steps you take to break contact with the freezing dirt, then the tongue work, then the two and three and four note drills, then the little melodies from the lesson book. Then what you save for last. The reach up for the next note. At first you can barely catch it. Keep having it turn from sound to squealing air. But you know how it happens now. How it will come your way. F just after Christmas.

"Wow. Look at it. What is it?"

"An arrowhead."

Not your biggest one. But the one that took the most shine when you polished them and looked most like she'd wear it. A streak the rust red color of her hair cuts through the milk white quartz. Your first day back in school, out of traffic under the second floor stairs, she lifts it off the cotton in the little box, trailing its chain of silver, turns it in her fingers.

"Arrowhead?"

"Yeah. A real one. A real Indian made it. See these notches? That's where he tied it to his arrow."

"It's so pretty. Where'd you get it?"

"Where I used to live." And then you say, "You like it?"

"Yes. It's really neat."

"Well, Merry Christmas, then. Try it on."

"Hold this." She hands you the little box, finds the hasp, laces the chain around her neck, hooks it, fixes the way the arrowhead lies on her striped green sweater, looks up at you.

"I didn't get you anything."

From the time you thought of it, and then picked it out and polished it, and then took it to Stark's Jewelry and paid for a silver hook and chain, you were thinking of Susan Lake.

"That's okay. I don't wear necklaces."

"Silly. I didn't mean a necklace."

"You played that Danny Boy song."

"I played that for everybody. Not just you."

You think of telling her. What happened sitting back in the auditorium with Doby. But then, like anyone else you'd tell, you'd have to tell her everything.

"Just show me your violin sometime."

"What's your favorite color?"

Above F the way the notes are valved repeats itself. You play through sunset into dusk when the sharp white trembling points of stars start to pierce the deepening afterglow of turquoise that spans the sky. By then your lips are too numb to play and the cold in your fingers finally too deep to get them warm again. G and then A come your way in early January.

And then, watching Red Skelton do Freddie the Freeloader one night deep in January, you stop laughing, come forward on your chair, let them laugh without you while you sit there staring at his gloves. Gloves with the fingers cut so that his fingertips poke through. Later that night, in the garage, you find what you're looking for. A pair of her gardening gloves in a bucket with her crabgrass digger. Two of the fingertips worn through. She'll need new ones next spring. You sneak them upstairs. You find scissors in a kitchen drawer. At your desk you gnaw the blades through the thick cloth tip of each finger, not as far down as Freddie the Freeloader's, just back to the first knuckle, just enough to where your fingertip pokes through to play the valves. You try them on. Curl your fingers around the casings and over the valves the way they know to hold them. They fit. They work. And then it strikes you. The brown cloth tips on your desk like the hollow heads of mushrooms. Eight of them. You only needed three. The first three fingers on the right hand glove. You think of stitching five of them back on. You pick one up, slip it over a finger, then another one, try to match the scissor marks to the one it came from. You could have thought first. You could have been less eager. You could have labeled them so you could tell which fingers they belonged to.

And it doesn't matter. The next day it snows. In the sandpit, snow comes up over the tops of your galoshes, too deep to scrape away, and so you pack it down instead. The gloves work. Your hands stay warm. The feeling stays in your fingertips. The heat of your breath through the brass keeps them warm. You'll cut the thumbs off too when you get home so they can feel the brass. Around your neck is the purple scarf that Carla knit for you out of special wool that doesn't itch. With the hood of your parka up you play into the soft whirling flurry of the falling snow. In front of your eyes, out past your fingers, on the gold metal of the bell, snowflakes land, crumple and fold into water, trickle off the sides.

CHAPTER 44

FROM LAST FALL, when Brother Rodgers was as brown as Manny, you've watched his tan fade out to where his face and neck and ears and hands are almost white again. You've wondered if that was how it would happen with Manny if he accepted the Gospel. If he'd go white and delightsome slow to give people time to keep getting used to the difference.

"So Joseph starts preaching the news of the restoration. He sends missionaries out. It isn't long before the Lord commands him to move the Saints from New York to Ohio. They move in winter to a town called Kirtland. Converts come in from everywhere. They've left everything they own. Some of them their families. They don't care. They come because of the burning in their bosom. In Kirtland they build their first temple. God and Jesus hand down revelation after revelation. The Law of Tithing. The Word of Wisdom. Joseph puts them in a book called the Doctrine and Covenants. It's a busy time."

You've been looking at Susan Lake and trying to see her brown. Not Mexican brown but Indian brown. The way she sits across the room, attentive and obedient, you can look all you want. Brother Rodgers has her where he wants her. You give her a beaded headband with an Indian feather stuck in back. You turn her dress to buckskin and give her moccasins. You borrow Carla's arrowhead necklace and hang it around her neck.

"The trouble is that Kirtland isn't Zion. Zion's in Missouri, around the town of Independence, a thousand miles away. Saints are called to start to establish Zion there. They get there with next to nothing. But they build a church and consecrate a hill to build another temple on."

Brother Rodgers looks at Yenchik and then at West like he doesn't trust the way they've sat there quiet. Like he's got her hypnotized, Susan Lake turns her head to look, and there she is, her face this sudden brown, not like Manny or even Lupe but just this fake shoe polish brown, before his voice turns her back around and she goes white again.

"Sounds nice and peaceful so far, doesn't it. Well, that all starts to change. Satan doesn't like what he sees. He goes to work on the people who already live in Kirtland and Independence. He makes them unhappy about all these newcomers. Scared of their ways of worship. Angry that one of them calls himself a prophet. And from making them scared, and then angry, Satan finally makes them mean."

Brother Rodgers pauses. He takes a look at Brenda Horn like he doesn't trust the way he's got her either.

"Mobs start coming after the Saints. Houses are burned. Shops and businesses are ransacked. Their leaders keep being arrested. They tar and feather Joseph. Within three years they get run out of Independence. They start another settlement. And then another one. The mobs keep coming. The Governor of Missouri finally has to call on the state militia to protect them. But Joseph learns that the state militia is in cahoots with the mobs. So he puts together his own militia. They do battle at a place called Crooked River. One of the Twelve Apostles is killed, along with one of the soldiers from the state militia. After the battle, the Governor of Missouri puts out an order. Mormons are enemies of the state. They have to be exterminated or forced out of Missouri."

Keller's hand goes up.

"Because they killed a soldier?"

"That was a big part of it."

And now Yenchik raises his hand.

"How come they didn't use the Priesthood?"

"What do you mean?"

"To fight back," says Yenchik. Astounded that Brother Rodgers doesn't get it right away. "To keep from getting kicked around."

"You mean—"

"The Priesthood. The most powerful thing in the world."

"Well," says Brother Rodgers, "I guess they could have. Joseph actually called on God a couple of times to get them out of trouble. A bunch of them are out in the woods one day when an armed mob surrounds them. They're about to be slaughtered. Joseph gets down and prays. All of a sudden it starts raining and hailing to beat the band. The mob runs for cover. By the time it's over, they're not interested in killing any Saints."

"What was another time?" says Doby.

"Oh, gosh. A young Elder who was arrested and held for eight days. One day one of the thugs who's guarding him puts a rifle in his face and tells him to deny Mormonism right there or he'll kill him. The young Elder refuses. So the guy pulls the trigger right in his face. Nothing happens. He checks his rifle. He's had it for twenty years and it's never misfired. He cocks it and pulls the trigger again. Still nothing. Now he's mad. He tries it a third time. Still nothing. So he reloads. Then he pulls the trigger a fourth time."

Brother Rodgers lets it hang there. He smiles to himself, walks toward the window, takes a look outside. You're figuring Yenchik will crack first. But it's Brenda Horn.

"So?" she says.

"The rifle explodes," Brother Rodgers says to the parking lot. "Blows the guy's own head off. Kills him on the spot." He turns back to the class. "So God was there."

"What happened to the Elder?"

"They let him go. Nobody wanted to try to kill him after that."

"So why didn't God do that all the time?"

"Because the Saints weren't out to make enemies. They were out to make converts. They were a peaceful people. Look at what happened in Missouri. All they did was defend themselves and they ended up as enemies of the state. If they'd kept fighting back they'd have had the whole United States Army after them. There would've been nowhere they could go."

"But they could of beat the United States Army with the Priesthood."

"One day that'll happen. The Priesthood will rule the Earth. We'll know when the time comes. Yes, Steve."

"I thought this was Zion," Strand says. "Salt Lake."

"For now. But it's always been Missouri. The Garden of Eden was there. One day we'll all be there. That's where we'll all be gathered."

"Missouri?" says West.

Brother Rodgers puts up his hands. "Missouri. Let's get back to that young Elder. When he had that rifle in his face, did he know it was going to misfire?"

"No."

"All he knew was that he'd be killed if he didn't deny the Church. Why didn't he act to save his life? Why didn't he just lie?"

"Because he'd be a Son of Perdition?"

Brother Rodgers looks at Yenchik surprised. "That's a possibility. In a more positive light, it shows how strong his testimony was. He was ready to lay down his life for it."

"Maybe the guy would've shot him anyway."

"That's possible too. Let's say he denied the Church and the guy pulled the trigger anyway. Do you still think the rifle would've misfired?"

"Maybe."

You wish you'd never tried to make her Indian brown. It was stupid. It left you dirty. You don't know why. Out the narrow window the bare black winter branches let you see through the trees of the orchard to the hill where you keep your trumpet in its patch of scrub oak. You can't make it out from here, which patch of black on the snow of the hillside, but suddenly there's this fiery itch all over you like you're crawling with a thousand burning ants, and all you can do is sit there still and not let it show.

"This rifle hadn't misfired in twenty years. And now it misfires three times. And then it blows up in the guy's face. You don't see God's hand in that?"

"Yeah."

"God was testing that young Elder. The way he tests all of us. Luckily the Elder passed. If he'd failed, I'll bet you dollars to doughnuts that rifle would've worked the way it had for twenty years. Bang!"

CHAPTER 45

THROUGH THE REST of January the afternoon sun is this blinding white off the mounds and flanks and ridges of crusted snow around you. You get a pair of sunglasses. Every day the valves are seized with frozen spit from the afternoon before. Sometimes you feel a tiny crack of ice when you open the spit valve. Nested between the notes you know are the sharps and flats you haven't learned yet. Now you go back for them. Start playing the major and minor scales you can reach while the sunset turns the long hard span of the sky to cold red steel and you know where to look by heart for the first high stars to make their sparse sharp glittering appearance.

Sometimes you see in Carla's attitude and in how she moves this deep internal strictness that has nothing to do with anyone but her. You knew the first time what it was. Her teacher. What she was learning. How she was being corrected. The answers to her questions taking form and turning into steel. In the sandpit winter crosses into February. The questions settle in and make themselves permanent. What you're doing wrong. What will end up buried too deep and permanent to fix. A lesson book can't stop and tell you. That was what a teacher did. That was why Mr. Hinkle took his pencil and wrote The Professor and a number on the cover. The Professor. If you had him for a teacher you could stand there on stage some day in the auditorium. Stand there in the spotlight where Carla stood, your trumpet in your hands, stand there and wait until the auditorium got quiet, until it dawned on them that you weren't going anywhere, until Susan Lake got done gabbing with her friend, and maybe then, from behind you, a drum would start marking the rhythm, a bass guitar would start playing the key, and then you'd raise your trumpet up, gold fire in the light, and close your eyes, and then they'd know.

The little songs in the lesson book are exhausted. Worn thin. Nothing left to them. Songs you've started to ridicule the way you play them. You start playing songs from your head. Radio songs. The Wayward Wind. The Great Pretender. Songs your mother plays. Only Make Believe. Over the Rainbow. A week before Valentine's Day an overcast settles in, gray and low and vast and permanent, and the air loses its numbing bite. Under your galoshes the packed snow starts going soft. Out across the sandpit the mounds and ridges lose their luster. The valves don't freeze. You can play with the hood of your parka down and your sunglasses off. There are no sunsets. Just gray light and then the gradual quiet onset of dark. You keep practicing. At school Carla surprises you with a Valentine's card. A fuzzy bumblebee with a girl's face surrounded by a flock of hearts. It's a day when she's wearing your arrowhead.

"You'll get yours tomorrow," you tell her.

"That's okay." She smiles and shrugs her thin shoulders. "It's just for fun."

"So you'll get one just for fun tomorrow."

"Do you know My Funny Valentine?"

"Is that a song?"

"Yes."

A week later the overcast lifts. Under a blinding sky you practice with your back to a howling wind that freezes everything again, turns the air this bitter cold, the snow around you smooth and hard and blinding like metal painted this brilliant white that brings your sunglasses out again. But high D and E are yours for keeps and the lower notes so natural now you forget what it took to learn them. Forget there was a time you didn't know them. Forget all the questions because this is the only way you know how to answer them. Where you don't question anything.

CHAPTER 46

AFTER THE GOVERNOR'S order it was open season on the Saints. One mob invaded a settlement and massacred close to twenty men and boys. More than eight thousand Saints crossed into Illinois to keep from being exterminated. It was winter. They left almost everything behind. Some didn't have shoes. Blood marked the snow and frozen dirt.

"Brenda."

"How come it's always winter when they have to leave some place?"

"I don't know. Just happened that way."

In Illinois they found land inside a big horseshoe bend in the Mississippi River. Swampland nobody wanted. They figured they were safe. They drained the land and started to build a city. This time it was a city that didn't already belong to someone else. This time they could build it from scratch. The Prophet named it Nauvoo. Hebrew for beautiful place.

"The City Beautiful."

"Sure enough," says Brother Rodgers, and you can tell he's pissed at the way Jasperson just butted in and made him jump.

They mapped out streets and neighborhoods. Built churches and schools and houses. Planted crops and opened shops and started businesses. Set aside the highest ground for another temple. Organized their own government. Made their own laws. Formed a police force and a militia called the Nauvoo Legion. Men were called to leave their homes and wives and families and go on missions across the United States, Canada, England, the Pacific Islands. The Relief Society was organized so women could help the poor and sick. God and Jesus Christ kept handing revelations down. The Temple Ordinances. Baptism for the Dead. Marriage for Eternity. In four years Nauvoo was one of the biggest cities in Illinois. Joseph made himself a general in the Nauvoo Legion.

"In keeping with another revelation, one you'll learn about later, he takes several women as his wives."

"You mean polygamy," says Strand.

Brother Rodgers looks at him cold. "Yes."

"How come we can't learn about it now?" says Strand.

"Because you're not old enough."

"Why not? I know what it means. It's in the dictionary."

"What does the dictionary say?"

"When you've got more than one wife."

"On the surface, that's pretty strange, isn't it."

"It's against the law, too."

"You're right," says Brother Rodgers. He stands up straight. "So let me ask you something. Do you ever make fun of anyone? Someone who's fat? Ugly? Crippled? Poor? Or talks funny. Or dresses strange? Or isn't as smart as you? Or can't catch a ball or run as fast?"

Strand looks at his hands for an answer.

"It's nothing to be ashamed of," says Brother Rodgers. "Not at your age. You're not old enough to see into their hearts. If you were, you'd know that they'd give anything to be better looking, or thinner, or smarter, or more athletic, or not crippled, or have enough money to dress like kids around them. You'd know how much it hurt to have people laugh at you for something you can't do anything about."

Everyone's got their head down except for Jasperson and Julie Quist. If they could all be Susan Lake, you're thinking, all your wives, like Susan Lake in a circle of twenty mirrors, is the only way it makes sense to you.

"But you're young. God doesn't expect you to be that mature yet. Nobody does. So don't sit there like that. It's okay. Heck, I used to be the same way."

Brother Rodgers waits until everyone's head is up again.

"It's the same way with polygamy if you don't understand it. All you know is what the dictionary says."

"It sounds yucky," says Brenda Horn.

"There you go," says Brother Rodgers. "What happened the first time Joseph saw the Golden Plates?"

"He got this big shock," says Jasperson.

"Why?"

"Because all he saw was the gold."

"That's right. He needed to do some spiritual growing up. He could still be influenced by the Devil. Polygamy's the same way. There are people who look at it with an impure heart. Who think it's something dirty. And then there are people who are just too young. Like Joseph was."

Brother Rodgers glances at the girls, finds them looking back at him, looks down at his shoes.

"Polygamy is a doctrine of God. There are sacred reasons for it. Reasons you'll learn when you're older. You'll have to accept that. Don't question it. Don't ever make fun of it."

Keller's hand is in the air. Brother Rodgers finally calls on him.

"My dad says Joseph Smith ran for President of the United States."

"Your dad's right."

"How come he didn't win?"

"He had the Kingdom of God to tend to. He was destined for bigger things than Commander in Chief."

You're thinking Mamie Eisenhower when West just comes out with it.

"What Keller's saying is what if Joseph Smith had got elected. Which of his wives would of been First Lady."

Strand lets out the explosive opening of a laugh. Brother Rodgers whips his head around and glares at West. Everyone shuts up.

"Sorry," says West.

"More than you know," says Brother Rodgers.

CHAPTER 47

THE FIRST WEEK of March the Sunday School Superintendent calls. It's for you. They want you to do a two and a half minute talk. You've known your turn was coming. You've seen Doby do his, and Lilly and Keller, because you can't get your Individual Achievement Award without doing one, and when you turn eighteen you can't get your Duty to God Award unless you've got an Individual Achievement Award for every year since you turned twelve.

At supper, when you tell him, your father already knows, and your mother is breathless when she announces it to your brothers and sisters.

"Your brother is going to stand at the pulpit next week." She beams at you with this open radiance. "My little man," she says. "My little Shakli is becoming a man!"

Doby talked about the Word of Wisdom. Lilly the Law of Tithing. You can't get away with being as boring as they were. After supper, down in his den, the idling motor of his typewriter going and the steel wall of the rumbling furnace quivering as the blower pushes heat up through the house, you ask your father what you should talk about.

"Something you like," he says. "Something that means something to you."

You search his broad and tired face for the answer, then follow his quick helpless glance at the sheet of paper in his typewriter, the start of a letter to Apostle Mark E. Peterson.

"Something religious?" you say.

"Yes," he says. "Of course."

I can only wish I were capable of expressing my gratitude with a fraction of the eloquence you so richly deserve for your constant inspiration.

What you read off the letter by accident makes you look away, at your hands, because it's like seeing him naked.

"Like what?"

"Humility," he says, and when you look back he's your father, dressed again. "Faith. Your testimony. Doing the Lord's work. Sacrificing for others." He takes his hands off his knees and puts them on the armrests of his office chair. "There are many things to choose from."

"Then what?"

"Find an original way to talk about it. Think of some ordinary everyday thing. Then think about the religious message it can have. The best talk always uses a simple illustration. A story or example. Some kind of analogy."

"What's a good analogy for humility?"

"That's easy," he says. "Look around your room. You could use your shoes perhaps."

"Could I use my bike?"

"If you can find where it has a religious message."

"My arrowheads?"

"What would you say about your arrowheads?"

"I don't know."

"Think of some ideas," he says. "Then we can talk about them."

You've already thought of your trumpet. What it could stand for. You've already remembered hypocrite.

"Okay."

The way Brother Clark uses driving. The way Brother Rodgers used the time that he got electrocuted. You rack your brain. Look around your room. Arrowheads. Pencils. Your sketch of Rufus. Your Indian blanket. Susan Lake would laugh if you gave a talk about your blanket. In the garage you look at the rake, the shovel, the hoe, the lawn mower, your bike. Maybe your bike is humility. Maybe the fenders are chastity. Maybe the cans of poison are the evil spirits all around you. At school you look at desks, lockers, chalk sticks, erasers, windows, urinals. Maybe the clean blackboard in History when you first get to class in the morning is like after you get baptized. The cattle truck. Riding Rex around. By Thursday you've got an idea you think you can talk to your father about.

"Remember that engine someone left in the cellar in La Sal?"

"Yes," he says. "Vaguely. There was some trouble about that, wasn't there?"

On the kitchen floor, the rugbeater coming down, your mother's crazy face.

"Remember how old and dirty and rusty it was?"

"I didn't pay much attention to it."

"It was like new on the inside. Everything was clean. There wasn't any rust or anything."

"And?"

"So it wasn't what was on the outside," you say. "It was what was on the inside."

"Okay."

"Like no matter what it looked like, its heart was pure."

Your father looks at you. You see the bright red spider legs of veins where they start at his pupils and reach out across his eyeballs. You don't dare talk or move your face or look away.

"Very good," he says.

"It is?"

"Yes," he says. "We can make a good little talk out of that. It shows how we shouldn't go by appearances."

"I didn't think of that part."

"Now go write it up. Then let me read it, and we'll shape it up and practice it a few times. It can't be longer than two and a half minutes."

"How should I start it?"

"Just like you told me," he says. "With an old engine that someone abandoned in a dark cellar because they thought it was junk. Just because of the way it looked. Think how that applies to people. Then just let the spirit guide you."

It's been there, every afternoon all winter, and now March, the long hoarse cry of a horn from one or another freight train out across the valley. The far ridge of the sandpit has kept you from seeing them. One afternoon you wait for the horn to hunt for the chord it plays. You find C sharp, then E, and then A, and when you hear it again, its long and ragged wail, you play back and forth between them. And then, on another afternoon, a second horn, from another train, and inside the long breath of its rough sound, you find B, then D sharp, then A. You put songs you know to the chords and then the scales that go with them. Learn how to play with them. How to anticipate the engineer who plays them. How it must feel to play in a band. Or a duet with Carla if you brought her to the sandpit.

From the podium, nested down between Bishop Byrne and Superintendent Ostler, what you see as the chapel fills to your mother's organ prelude is every single face, anyone's face you want to look at, there for you to look at. This is what Doby saw. Superintendent Ostler stands up to the pulpit to welcome everyone. The back of his suit is wrinkled and the heels of his black shoes dusty with carpet fuzz. To your left, in the two front benches on the side, you can see the Deacons messing around. Your mother doesn't look up from the organ. When you catch your father's eye out in the congregation his expression doesn't change. They're being watched. They can't show pride. You don't dare look for

Susan Lake. You're being watched too.

The opening prayer. The opening hymn where hundreds of mouths are open out in front of you. Announcements. Everything happening is hooked together and moving past you like a train of railroad cars. And then suddenly the car is you. Your name from the speakers. Superintendent Ostler steps back from the pulpit, smiles your way, and when you get there he pulls the gooseneck of the microphone down to your face, puts his hand on your shoulder to nudge you toward the canted wood slab of the pulpit, then leaves you standing there. Every face on you. All turned up and waiting. Even your mother's face is raised now, to the right just below you, raised and smiling, while you hear the first huge quavering words of your memorized talk.

"Thank you, Shake," says Superintendent Ostler. "That was original, I have to say. You gave all of us something new to think about."

Back in your chair again you drop your head to hide your blazing face. Bishop Byrne moves his big hand off the armrest to pat your knee. It's over. You're still alive. You wish you could leave but you're stuck there, stuck through the Sacrament hymn, through Blackwell bringing you bread and water, through Superintendent Ostler ending the opening service. He shakes your hand. Out in front of you the congregation rises up and floods the aisles. You take the stairs off the podium. Your mother, playing the postlude, gives you this proud adoring smile back across her shoulder. You're still too scared to smile back. Then you're among them, all the faces, all your neighbors, tousling your hair, telling you how good you did.

You father's across the chapel listening to Brother McMaster. He's smiling, smiling big, and when he glances around and sees you, his expression stays the same. It just goes blank for an instant before he goes back to what Brother McMaster's saying. You know. He's on business. He can't acknowledge you. Out of the chapel, in the foyer, your neighbors keep giving you smiles when you happen to look at them. Then West is there when you head down the hall for class.

"You really took an engine apart?"

"Yeah."

"A car engine?"

"More like a tractor engine or something."

"What'd you take it apart with?"

"Some vice grips. A screwdriver."

"You're supposed to use wrenches."

"We didn't have any."

"Was it really like new inside?"

"Yeah."

"The pistons and all that stuff?"
"Yeah."
"Wish I'd been there with you guys."

CHAPTER 48

THROUGH THE FIRST half of March the snow recedes. The yards around the circle come out of winter yellow. In the sandpit, the layers left by different storms pull back, reveal the sandpit floor and its bulldozed banks and cliffs and ridges. Your place comes back, mud first, then hardpack, where you can see your spit again when you blow the trumpet clean. You put away your gloves. Change your parka for your jacket. Through the second half of March the wind blows almost every afternoon. The crushed stiff stems of last year's weeds twitch and shiver. The notes are torn from your trumpet and shredded. Dirt lifts and whistles and whips around you while you work to hold the sound clear, the long notes steady, the beat of a song even. Sometimes the gusts are so fierce and loaded with dirt you have to close your eyes and hold your trumpet up inside your jacket.

"Yes, Brenda."

She's got this shy but kind of tricky smile in her antelope face while she brings her hand back down.

"Did God really say Missouri?"

"What do you mean?" Brother Rodgers says.

"The stuff you read. The stuff God said to Joseph Smith."

"Why?"

"My dad took us to see The Ten Commandments. God had this really big deep voice."

"What are you asking?"

"Because I was trying to picture him saying Missouri with that voice."

"I haven't seen it. But God could have any voice he wants."

"Okay."

"You don't look satisfied."

"It's just strange," she says. "God saying Missouri."

"He says Cincinnati too," says Jasperson. "And Illinois."

"Nashville," says Lilly.

Brother Rodgers just keeps this half-amused smile on Brenda Horn to where she starts to blush. Next to her, Ann Cook puts her head down, fusses with her bracelet.

"Why wouldn't he say Missouri?"

"I didn't say he wouldn't," says Brenda Horn.

"Let me ask you a question. In the movie you saw, did God tell Moses to leave Egypt?"

"Yeah. When all the babies died."

"To leave Egypt, Moses had to part the Red Sea. I hear that they do that in the movie. I hear it's pretty impressive."

"Yeah."

"Okay. God tells Moses to leave Egypt. A few centuries later, he tells Joseph Smith to take the Saints to Missouri."

Brenda Horn looks at Jasperson, but he's got his head down, having a thumb fight with himself.

"What's the difference?" Brother Rodgers asks her.

"What difference?"

"Between God saying Egypt and Missouri."

"Just," she says. And then she says, "I guess because you could get in a car and just drive to Missouri." And then she says, "It's right there."

"God's always talked about real places. Places like Canaan and Jerusalem in the Bible. Places like Zarahemla in the Book of Mormon. In the Doctrine and Covenants, when he talked to the Prophet Joseph, he talked about places like Missouri. He had to. That's what those places were called."

"He just makes it sound like Missouri's a place in the Bible."

"You mean the way he talks."

"Yeah. That old-fashioned language."

"God's always been God. He doesn't change."

"Yeah. I guess."

"Here. Let's try an experiment. I want someone to name me a city. Any city."

Everyone's watching him, thinking what you're thinking, that he's going to pull out another scar or something the minute someone names a city.

"New York," Keller finally says.

"Washington," says Lilly.

"Let's look up New York." Brother Rodgers picks up the Doctrine and Covenants, opens it to the back, turns pages. "Here we go. Okay." Whips back through pages. "Here. This is God telling Joseph to send a bishop named Newel K. Whitney on a mission. Ready, Brenda?"

"Yeah."

"Good." Brother Rodgers raises the book like a preacher. "Nevertheless, let the bishop go unto the city of New York, also to the city of Albany, and also to the city of Boston, and warn the people of those cities with the sound of the Gospel, with a loud voice, of the desolation and utter abolishment which await them if they do reject these things."

He brings the book down to his chest.

"Three big American cities. Cities we could visit right now. Right, Melvin?"

"Yeah," says Yenchik.

"What did it sound like, Brenda?"

"Like the Bible."

"So we hear the voice of God in the Doctrine and Covenants just the way we hear it in the Bible." And now, from the corner by the door, Strand raises his hand.

"You said the Bible was translated."

"That's right."

"So at first the Bible wasn't English."

Good old Strand, you think, the way he sits there quiet all the time, like he's just listening, and then comes out with some crazy thing that just leaves Brother Rodgers cold.

"You're right. In the Bible God spoke Hebrew. Like his prophets did."

"So how could his voice be the same?"

"That shows through the translation, Steve. When God says a word like verily, or rejoice, or abomination, whether it's Hebrew or Swahili, it's the translator's job to put that word in English. Joseph Smith had to do the same thing when he translated the Book of Mormon." Brother Rodgers stops and smiles. "Too bad we're not smart enough to know Hebrew," he says. "Otherwise, God wouldn't have had to learn English."

The end of March the wind lets up. On an afternoon when things are calm you take the family jar of Vaseline and your mother's can of sewing machine oil up the hill. You take the case out of its shelter and find a place to work. You take the trumpet out and then, suddenly overwhelmed, hug it tight to your chest and sit there with your eyes closed, rocking, drawing the long cold loneliness of the winter out of it. You wipe it down with the diaper you stole from Maggie back when winter started. You take your time. Break it down and lay the pieces out on the blue velvet of the case and tackle them one by one. Clean and oil and grease and wipe them down as you put them back together. You look at the case. Spiders have started coming out for spring. You brush their webs away. Where the fake leather was worn away to paper and wood the paper is dust and the wood gray. You rub Vaseline into the paper and wood and the brown leather bands around the ends and then finally into everything.

You play a couple of runs. The valves are slick, light, quick to return, the notes easier to move through. You start your warmup on C. Suddenly, at the point where your lips part, there's this little pulse, and the trumpet jumps up five notes to G. You stop, look at it, test the valves, wonder what you didn't put together right. You try it again. Find you can do it on purpose. Keep going. From C to G, from G to high C, two notes higher to E, another two notes to high G, always with that little pulse, like something the trumpet does to set your lips right. You try other notes. Notes you have to valve in different ways. It works for all of them. You don't know what to do. Just stand there with this scared euphoric feeling like you've reached a place you've never been before, a place that was always there just waiting to be discovered, like the Grand Canyon or the Pacific Ocean, and you don't know what it means or where to go or who to tell.

CHAPTER 49

AT SCHOOL, in your afternoon classes, the teachers start opening the windows. Patches of grass start showing flecks and pools of green in the yellow yards. Buds start turning the branches furry in the orchards. In the sandpit you practice the way you can get the sound to leap until you can make it happen any time. Over two octaves of notes are yours. And all the sharps and flats between them. Soon they'll be opening the sand-pit. Trucks will start pulling under the hopper to be loaded up with dirt. You'll need to find a new place. And then one afternoon it comes to you. April. Almost a year. This is what it was like just before you got here. While you rode up from La Sal in the cattle truck. Where you heard a sound off the radio you didn't know came from this instrument you're holding. How light can taste. How sound can fly.

On the first Saturday in April you help your father open the yard. General Conference is on his portable radio while he lies on his belly again to build little moats for his rosebushes. You think of heading for Doby's or West's, but something keeps you home, something that isn't right, something with the yellow light and menacing calm of a storm from across the desert around the yard and inside the house. Your mother acts like General Conference has never bothered her. In the yard that morning, in her straw sun hat, prowling for crabgrass, your father could be listening to Broadway songs for all the bright excitement in her shaded face. In the kitchen, getting supper ready while you shine everyone's Sunday shoes, the keystrokes of the Royal come up through the floor in explosive bursts she acts like she doesn't hear.

"So, children," she says, at supper, after your father's blessing. "We are in our new home for a whole year now!"

At the head of the table, his spoon in his hand, your father looks lost, like he's still not back from the place where the speeches took and dropped him off. Except for Maggie, clueless in her high chair, the rest of you eat with this guarded alertness in the face of your mother's luminous delight.

"Does anyone miss La Sal?" she says, passing a shining smile around the table.

"I do," says Karl.

"We had a good time there, didn't we, children? All the animals! The little lambs!"

"Yeah," says Karl.

"I miss Rex sometimes," you say.

"Yes, Shakli." She smiles at you with this open adoration you don't know how to trust. "It was wonderful, wasn't it?" And then, as if she's been reminded that she's being childish, her face goes serious. "But we have a better life here, don't we, children?"

That night your father takes you to the stakehouse for the General Priesthood Session again. Last time, six months ago, you left home knowing where your mother stood. This time you're not sure. Last time you sensed the vastness of the army you belonged to. This time you think of the sandpit to keep yourself from drowning in the air your father's army breathes. On the ride home this time you don't ask your father anything. All of the questions are there, at home, and you know that he won't know the answers either.

CHAPTER 50

HER DRESS is this mint green. Her light brown hair is pulled back off her forehead and pinned up off her ears with a white band. Across the room her shoes are white. Spring is incandescent in her skin. A year ago you sat here waiting for Brother Rodgers to call her name. You're still here. Still not any closer. Still where the way she'd smell and look and feel and talk up close are things you have to make up for yourself.

"Susan Lake."

Satan got the Saints chased out of Kirtland. And then Missouri. And now he followed them to the Mississippi River and watched them build the City Beautiful. It was time to go to work again. This time he had more ammunition. A city that called itself the Kingdom of God led by a man with all these wives. Rumors that Mormon raiders came out at night to steal away their daughters. He got nearby towns to fear and hate the Saints. He went to work on people inside the city too.

"Like spies?" says Keller.

"Nope. Regular Saints. But this one's got a weak testimony. That one's got a gripe with Joseph Smith. This one breaks a commandment and doesn't like the punishment. That one gets excommunicated. This one's looking for payback. Satan turns them into bitter enemies and has them spread lies that get people even more riled up. How Joseph is looking to take over Illinois. How from Illinois he's looking to conquer the United States. How he's looking to put polygamy and tithing in the Constitution and looking from there to conquer and rule the world."

Jasperson, to show his disgust, sits there looking dark, shaking his head.

"I know, Johnny. Crazy stuff. But Satan's a smart guy who's been around a while. People get so riled up they go to the Governor of Illinois. Mormons are troublemakers. Joseph Smith's a criminal. A traitor plotting the overthrow of the United States. The Nauvoo Legion's a marauding gang of outlaws. Yes, Melvin."

"Does he want to wipe them out?" says Yenchik. "Like that other guy did?"

"This governor doesn't have the stomach. He comes up with a compromise. Joseph and some other leaders agree to be arrested and stand trial for causing a disturbance. Nothing serious. The Nauvoo Legion has to lay low. He'll see that they're protected. It'll appease people. Joseph turns himself in. But he knows better. I am going . . . Johnny. How does he say he's going?"

"Like a lamb to the slaughter," Jasperson says.

"I knew I could count on you," says Brother Rodgers, smiling, and without even looking, you know the way Jasperson's face is wrestling with not knowing if he's being teased or complimented. "Like a lamb to the slaughter. They put him in the county jail along with his brother Hyrum and some other leaders in a town called Carthage."

This morning, April outside the window, just the early white haze of blossoms on some of the orchard trees, you know where the story ends. It ends where it always ends. Not Brother Rodgers or Strand or even God could change the end or keep the end from coming.

"Anyway," Brother Rodgers says, "people aren't appeased. They're too stirred up to wait for a trial. One June afternoon an armed mob of a few hundred men with painted faces surrounds and storms the jail. They come up the stairs to the second floor and break the door down. Everyone starts shooting. Hyrum tries to block the door and gets shot in the nose and knocked down. He cries I am a dead man! Joseph cries Oh dear brother Hyrum! He jumps to the door and empties a six shooter down the stairs. Then he runs to the window. Two bullets hit him in the back and knock him forward. Another bullet, fired from below, hits him in the chest. He cries Oh Lord my God! He falls two stories to the ground. Someone starts yelling that the Nauvoo Legion's on its way. The mob takes off. The Prophet Joseph lies there dead. He's a martyr now."

Nobody says anything. Brother Rodgers gives you time. Fusses with his books, turns and erases the blackboard even though it's blank, walks over to the window. Sunlight makes his face look glazed where he keeps it shaved. He steps back in front of you again, his face drawn, and asks if anyone has a question. Yenchik's hand goes up slow, almost shy, and for a minute you think it's because he needs to be excused to pee.

"Yes."

Yenchik looks around like he needs permission from someone else to talk.

"How come he had a six shooter if he was in jail?" he finally says.

"One of his disciples brought it in and gave it to him."

"How come they had their faces painted?" says Doby.

"I guess they didn't want to be recognized."

"How come he didn't use the Priesthood?" says Keller.

"For what?"

"To keep from getting killed."

"Yeah," says Doby.

"How would he do that?" says Brother Rodgers.

"I don't know. He could of had God put a curse on the mob."

"Yeah. Like rain. Or fire or something."

"He could of made it rain gas."

"Ethyl," says West.

"He could of made them all have heart attacks. At the same time."

"Or made them all deaf and dumb and blind."

"Or made all their guns misfire and blow their heads off."

"He could of turned 'em all to salt."

"He could of made it so the bullets just bounced off him."

Brother Rodgers stands there grinning with his arms folded. "God could have done all of that." He backs up. When his butt touches the table, he reaches back, sets his knuckles down on it, done grinning. "But he didn't. How come?"

"Jesus didn't do anything either," says Julie Quist. "He let them crucify him."

"That's right, Julie. But Jesus knew he had to. How come Joseph Smith had to die?"

"So he could be a martyr?" Keller says.

"Well, that was the outcome, but not the reason. Let me ask you this. I know you'll know this one. How come God sent us to Earth?"

"To get a body," says Jasperson.

"That's one reason. What's the other one?"

"To be tested," Strand says.

"Tested?"

"Prove how faithful we are."

"That's the only way God can ever know who his true children are. What if Joseph had used the Priesthood to save himself? What if God had saved him? Made him bulletproof or turned the whole mob to salt?"

Brother Rodgers lets you sit there for a minute thinking.

"That would've been pretty impressive. A man with all these bullet holes in his shirt but not a mark on his skin? A jail surrounded by a couple of hundred men made out of salt? Think something like that would've made the newspapers, Steve?"

"Probably."

"Think they would've taken pictures?"

"Yeah."

"Think the whole country would've known about it before long?"

"Probably."

"Think they'd have seen it as a miracle?"

"Yeah."

"There's your answer."

"Answer to what?" Strand finally says.

"To why the Prophet had to let himself be killed."

"Why?" says Doby.

Brother Rodgers looks down at his shoes and comes forward off the table. "What does the Church teach us about signs?" he says. "Signs that prove to us that the Gospel is true?"

"Not to look for them," says Jasperson.

"Why not?"

"Cuz then we'd know for sure."

"Know what?"

"That the Gospel was true."

"Isn't that a good thing? To know the Church is true?"

"Yeah. But then we wouldn't need faith."

"Why not?"

"Because we'd just know. Like we know other stuff."

"So if Joseph Smith had gone around showing off the bullet holes in his shirt, it'd be a pretty good sign he was a real prophet."

"Yeah."

"People would've come from all around the world to see a couple of hundred men made out of salt, right?"

"Yeah."

"It'd be a pretty good sign that the church he founded was true. Right?"

"Yeah."

"So where's the test? Where's the reason God sent us here?"

"There isn't any. We'd just know."

"What would happen to God's plan? To learn who his true children are?"

"There wouldn't need to be one."

"That's right, Johnny. That's why the Angel Moroni had to take the Golden Plates back to Heaven. That's why Joseph had to let a mob of assassins make him a martyr. So he wouldn't show God's hand. So we could be tested. So God's plan could go forward."

CHAPTER 51

MAYBE YOUR father's heard the story too. About the young Elder who had the rifle put in his face and the trigger pulled. Maybe that's why he hasn't said anything about your talk. You haven't passed a test like that Elder did. Haven't shown him you're that brave and faithful. Haven't had that kind of chance. Don't know what you'd do if it came along. After school one afternoon in April, there's the steam shovel, its engine hammering, its bucket lifting its dripping load of dirt out of the cliff, a dump truck waiting underneath the hopper. It's time to move. You climb around the sandpit and up the hill above it to the patch of scrub oak where your trumpet is. You keep climbing. Grasshoppers leap out of the spring green weeds around your shoes. The roar of the sandpit falls away. You go up past the cave. Keep an eye out for rattlers. The place you find is a small ledge, almost a platform, an eroded outcrop of dirt that looks from the scoop in the hill behind it like it just slid out of the hillside.

Your legs burn. Your hair is hot from the sun. You turn around and it takes your breath how much you've climbed, how high you are above the valley, how far you can see across the Great Salt Lake and out across the desert. Below you are the hazed roofs of your neighborhood. You can make out your school. The refinery and the stock yards. The long black line of the railroad tracks.

Soldier Summit in the cattle truck. You haven't seen this far since then. You're scared at first to play. All the questions are back. With all this space your answers aren't good enough. The flight of the first note almost pulls you off the hillside. You plant your shoes, and close your eyes, but the precarious lightness from the hands of your father and his friends is there, and you have to open them again. Nothing has changed. You're still alone. And so you let the questions go. Let yourself play. Let the sound take flight off the hillside, the notes like birds to chase each other out across the valley, and for the first time, when the train comes, you can see it coming, the tiny point of its headlight, the long black snake it pulls through neighborhoods without hurting them, the crossings where you know it has to blow its horn.

They buried Joseph and Hyrum. God called Brigham Young to be the new Prophet. It wasn't long before things around Nauvoo were as hostile as they had ever been. The Saints faced the hard truth that they had to move again. God showed Brigham Young where they were going in a vision. A place out west across the mountains at the edge of a great lake and big desert. They left Nauvoo in winter across the ice of the Mississippi. They looked back from the river and saw the City Beautiful burning in the night.

"Brenda? Got something to say?"

Ann Cook's eyes take a dive into her lap.

"It's always winter," says Brenda Horn.

"Yep. Satan didn't make it easy. Anyway, they get across Iowa. They winter on the shore of the Missouri River. In spring they're off again, across the Great Plains, across the Rockies, and make their way down the mountains through a little canyon. At the mouth of the canyon they stop to get gathered up again. Ahead of them lies a long valley that spreads west toward a great lake. Brigham Young's sick. Bedridden in his wagon. But he lifts his head and takes a look at the view. It's a perfect match to the vision he had from God. Bobby. What were his famous words?"

"This is the place," says West.

Brother Rodgers takes a breath. He got you here. All the way from New York State to the famous words of Brigham Young. The monument at the mouth of Emigration Canyon. You look at Julie Quist so you can look at Susan Lake without looking like you are.

"It looked a lot like Palestine when they got here. Like the Promised Land. Just desert. No vegetation. A big salt water lake just like the Dead Sea. A river that ran up the valley into the lake just like the River Jordan. So they named it the Jordan River. After every other place they tried to settle, this was finally it. This was their Zion."

On your dirt platform high on the side of the hill you learn again to play your way through doubt. Play through the questions you don't have the answers to. You've mastered most all of the radio songs you know and your mother's Broadway songs. You've learned to play around their melodies and make up different ways to end them. You've wondered what kinds of songs the Professor would have you learn. Early in May, you've captured double high C, tamed it from a thin elusive note you could barely hold to a note you can reach anytime you want from anywhere in the octaves below it. You've learned to tell when it's close to supper, when it's time to make your way down the hill, from the cars that come up through the streets of the neighborhood below you, bringing all the fathers home from work.

CHAPTER 52

"COME, SHAKE. Sit down."

"What?"

"We need to talk to you."

From her wounded look and from her voice, pale and sweet and weak like barely sugared lukewarm water, you can tell that whatever it is you probably won't get beat for it. You follow her into the kitchen. Your father's at the table, already out of his work suit and into his regular pants and a short sleeved shirt, reading a piece of mail. Things aren't set for supper but you can smell tomatoes filled with hamburger baking in the oven. Your mother looks at your father. He puts his piece of mail down. Then she looks at you.

"I had a visit today," she says. "From Brother Leatham."

Leatham. The big leather-faced retired man with the thick wavy head of half brown half gray hair who always wears a plaid shirt with the sleeves rolled up and levis and boots and walks like he's in a cowboy movie. The house next door. The last house in the neighborhood before the steep hill starts that goes up to the sandpit. The piece of mail your father's looking at is just a bill.

"Yeah?"

"He saw you, Shakli."

"Saw me what?"

"Up on the hill."

You feel your crotch seize up.

"What hill?"

"Don't play dumb," your father says abruptly.

"He said he started hearing music a few weeks ago. When they could open their windows in the afternoon."

"What music?"

The look in your mother's face deepens into a weak smile of disbelieving grief. Your father's hand starts picking at the corner of the bill.

"He would drive to the sandpit to look," she says. "But the music would always stop."

The big Chrysler Imperial, nosing into the sandpit, idling out into the center, stopping, the door opening, while you watched from your knees from behind the rubble bank.

"Maybe he had the wrong place."

Your father raises his head and looks across the table with this little smile out through the back yard window.

"So yesterday he went again, and took his, oh, how do you say, his spyglasses with him."

"Binoculars," your father says.

"His binoculars," she says.

What he saw. Something catching gold in the glint of the sun. What you looked like when he turned the knob and brought you into focus.

"Yes," your father says. "He had to resort to binoculars to find you."

"He was spying."

"He was looking out for his neighborhood."

"Does he spy on Mama when she plays piano?"

"So! This is his neighborhood! He owns a home here! He has a right to protect it!"

"From what? Music?"

"By golly! He said he liked the music! He wanted to know who it was! Shame on you! He pays you a compliment and you accuse him of spying!"

"He liked it?"

"Yes, Shakli." This liquid sadness comes into her shimmering red eyes. "Why couldn't you stay home and play with me like I asked?"

"I don't know."

"What is so terrible about your mother, Shakli? That you don't want to play with her?"

"I wanted to learn how first."

"I could have helped you learn."

"Do you have any idea how this makes us look?" your father says.

"How what makes you look?"

He laughs. Shakes his head. "Our neighbors see a boy take a trumpet into the hills to play it. A Deacon. A boy they take the Sacrament from. What do you think they think?"

"What?"

"That his parents don't let him play at home. What else could they think? That he goes into the hills to play because he wants to?"

"Why not?"

"Do you see Lee Maxwell up there playing his flute? Or Gene Minette his cello?"

"No."

"Of course you don't. They play at home. They don't make their parents look like monsters to the whole neighborhood."

"I didn't do it to make you look like monsters."

"The Leathams are good people, Shakli. I see them every day. How am I supposed to face them now?"

"You didn't make me. I'll tell them."

"Why didn't you just practice at home?"

"I didn't want to bother anyone."

"Who said it would bother anyone?"

"I didn't want anyone to hear me."

"Why not, Shakli?"

"Papa said I'd be a hypocrite."

"I said what?"

"I'd be a hypocrite if I played in front of anybody."

"What is he saying, Harold?"

"It was in a scripture. You wrote it in my birthday card."

"You didn't, Harold."

"I don't remember."

"You told him he would be a hypocrite?"

"No, Mother. Of course not. It was just a harmless scripture."

"You and your stinking scriptures! Shame on you!"

"So! You're the one who started this! Let's not forget that!"

"I started this?"

"When he brought it home last year! You wouldn't even have it in the house!"

She stares at your father shocked. And then she looks across at you. You watch her face go soft like it's losing all its bones again.

"Yes. You see what I have to live with, Shakli."

"It's the truth!" Your father rocks back hard against his chair. "You don't remember? I had to take him back for a refund!"

"Yes. Now I have no more reason to live."

Your father brings his face around to you. "Where is it now?"

"Where's what?"

"Your trumpet," he says.

"It's someplace," you finally say.

"Bring it home. You can play in the garage. Don't take it out of the house again."

"Yes, Shakli. Bring it home." Suddenly her eyes are clear and she gives you this bright excited smile that scares you more than anything. The smell of her stuffed tomatoes makes you look out the window for air. "We can play together, Shakli! I have beautiful songs to teach you!"

CHAPTER 53

THEY NAMED it Emigration Canyon because it was the canyon the pioneers used to emigrate down the Rockies from. The monument at its mouth marks the place where the pioneers stopped for a look and Brigham Young saw the place God had shown him in his vision. This is the Place Monument.

On a Saturday in May, a week before school lets out for summer, Brother Rodgers and Keller's mother and West's father load you up and take you there. You ride with West and his father and Doby and Yenchik and listen to cowboy music on the radio. The monument crowns a shallow hill up a winding drive from the paved two-lane road that can take you up into Emigration Canyon. Across the road from the monument is the zoo. Hogle Zoo. Down the hill from where the monument stands is Fort Douglas. From there the University. And from there, in the haze, the city, Salt Lake, out across the valley floor under the dead still of the white sky all the way to the black mountains where Kennecott Copper is.

The monument is a set of white stone walls and pillars with bronze sculptures of pioneers and explorers and horses and wagons mounted on the walls and standing on the pillars. The sculptures are weathered green and black but in places, along the forehead of one of the pioneers, on the knees of one of the horses, gold still shows through. A pavilion with stone benches circles the monument. From the center of the monument a white stone pedestal rises maybe fifty feet into the air. Up on top are the statues of three men standing, looking out across the valley, their bronze eyes unable to see the city that inhabits it.

"Who are those guys?" says Yenchik.

"The one in the middle must be Brigham Young," you tell him.

"I thought he was sick when they got here."

"He was."

"I mean in bed."

"Yeah. In his wagon. I heard he had really bad diarrhea."

"Then how come he's standing up?"

"I don't know."

"Maybe he got up for a minute," says Yenchik. "So he could get a good look."

"Maybe."

"Maybe he got up to go to the bathroom."

"Maybe."

West and his father are standing at the edge of the pavilion looking out over the city the way you're doing now. Ann Cook and Brenda Horn are sitting on a bench in their dresses talking. From across the road, from Hogle Zoo, you hear the occasional cry of an animal from its cage. Yenchik hears them too.

"You ever been over there?" he says.

"Yeah."

"You ever see Shasta?"

"The liger? Yeah."

Toward the head of the city you can make out Temple Square from the steady spark of sunlight off the gold of the Angel Moroni on the high steeple of the Temple. Salt Lake. If your father had never heard of Joseph Smith, but had come to America anyway, it would have been to a different city. Chicago. Topeka. Some other American city. There was only one reason to come to the one he did. And everything out in front of you in the haze will be real as long as you believe in Joseph Smith and Brigham Young and everything else they keep teaching you in Priesthood and Sunday School.

"Her dad was a lion and her mom was a tiger," says Yenchik. "That's why she's called a liger. Lion and tiger. Liger. Get it?"

"Yeah."

"She's the only liger in the world."

Next to you, Yenchik stands there squinting out across the city, the low sun grazing the side of his face. You're wondering if your trumpet would end up as long as the Angel Moroni's horn if you took out all the curves and made it straight.

"Remember that secret I kept for you when we got baptized for the dead?"

He whips around. "Why? You tell someone?"

"No. I've got one to tell you back."

"What?"

"If you ever tell anyone, I'll tell yours."

"Okay."

"I play trumpet."

"Trumpet?"

"Yeah."

"What kinda music? Mexican stuff?"

"Jazz."

He looks at you. "Niggers play jazz," he says. "They ain't gonna like that at church."

"Niggers?"

"Yeah. So why's that a secret? You playing trumpet?"

"It just is."

"That's no secret," he says. "That's just something you tell people."

"Yeah. I just told you. But it's still a secret."

"No problem."

It was a test secret. But you can tell it won't go anywhere. The low sun fires the light blue crystals of his pupils and glows orange in his red hair. He turns and squints out across the city again and you can see his eyes the way he looked at you the day Brother Rodgers had his hand clamped over half his face. The way he looked at the floor the day Brother Clark taught you about the sin against the Holy Ghost. Yenchik had made a fire too. You could tell that.

"I got another secret," you say. "One you really gotta keep."

"Better be a real one." Turning to look at you.

"When I got the Priesthood," you say. "When the Holy Ghost was supposed to come and make a burning in my bosom."

"Yeah?"

"He never showed up."

Part 6

Ghosts

CHAPTER 54

YOU HADN'T ridden it just to ride it, just to see where it would take you, since the afternoon you rode it all the way to the tracks where locomotives pulled the slow black snakes of their cars along the floor of the valley. But after your mother and father told you to bring your trumpet home you did. You rolled down the long hill through your neighborhood, holding your breath till you got to Orchard Drive, and then headed north away from the town of Bountiful before you let yourself breathe again. Because you knew when you breathed what your face would do. Lose hold, come unraveled, where people your mother and father knew could see. You held it until nothing rolled past but roadside weeds and cars you didn't know and telephone poles too far from home for Brother Rodgers to climb. And then, still pedaling, you let it go, your breath, your place on the hill, the stuff inside, all the scared and lost and crazy stuff, the aching stuff in your throat, where all you knew for sure about your questions now was that nobody would ever answer them.

You practice after school on the open stall of concrete where your father parks the Buick. You're careful to keep from walking into the spots of oil. You play to the rakes and shovels and to the permanent smell of the engine and to the dust-hazed window that looks at ground level out across the backyard grass. You avoid playing when Roy and Molly get their lessons upstairs. And when your mother plays and sings her Broadway songs you quietly play along so she won't know. From the living room, through the ceiling over your head, her playing and singing have this warbling tremulous sound, like the piano she brought from Switzerland is filled with water.

You've never noticed before how when she sings she doesn't have an accent. How she can sing I've got to love one man till I die and sound American.

"You said you sold it," Karl says.

"So I did."

"There wasn't any rattlesnake either."

"Yeah. There was."

"No there wasn't. That was a lie too. Because you lost."

"There really was."

"You just want the cave to yourself."

"I never went back there. Don't you either."

"You're a liar."

"Call me a liar when you're dead from a rattlesnake bite."

In the sandpit the notes could race around the bowl formed by the cliffs. On the hillside they could skate and dart and fly across the valley. In the garage they come ringing off the walls and ceiling so that the new notes play into the swarming frantic ricochet of the old notes. Like riding Rex in his stall. Like kicking his ribs and trying to make him gallop while his hooves and knees and sides bang up against the boards. You wonder where they go, the notes, when you stop hearing them, when the sound goes out of them. On Saturday, when you sweep the concrete, if they're on the floor, if they're in the dust that lifts behind the sifting black bristles of the pushbroom, if they're like tiny husks, husks too small to see with the naked eye.

She offers you her song books. Showboat. Gershwin. Carousel. Every song could be the one to break her promise. Every note could be the one that out of nowhere snaps her, brings her crashing through the door, her red face clenched, her black hair wild, her rugbeater cocked in her hand. Sometimes you forget. Let yourself do what you did in the sandpit and on the hillside, play not scared of anything, and then you come around, and there's the sudden cut of fear that everything is about to change. But then it's only Roy or Molly coming out to stand there by the door.

"Did you like that?"

"It was pretty."

"Want me to play anything?"

"I don't know."

"What's Mama doing?"

"Reading something."

If I Loved You. Old Man River. Bess You Is My Woman Now. If the next song will ignite some memory. If the next note will be the drop that will make her snap like Chinese water torture. In the garage you know it's suppertime not from the sun but from the groan of the Buick's suspension crossing the hump at the top of the driveway, and then the hot hoarse idle of its blind engine, the ratchet of its parking brake before the garage door opens on its shivering springs and whangs into its cradle. In his suit your father is already headed back up the driveway toward the open driver's door of the Buick. You've stepped back by then, the trumpet in your hand, wishing the thing you've wished this time each night since you came off the hillside, since he started coming home to find you here. Play for him. Ask what he'd like to hear.

"Welcome home, Papa."

CHAPTER 55

"ONLY ONE TREE. The rest of the valley was barren. The dirt hard as rock. Hard enough to break their plows when they tried to till it. But they were determined to make the desert blossom as a rose."

Out the window cars and wagons shimmer in the sunlight. Dirt hard as rock. You think sandstone. The washes and fields of sandstone around La Sal. The whole valley. You wonder how the pioneers made it soft enough to plow. Soft enough to plant grass and make yards and flowerbeds. It would have to be a miracle.

"Once Brigham Young got here, and started to build Zion, the great migration really got started. One wagon train after another. Some of them were so poor they couldn't afford wagons or horses or oxen to pull them. So they built handcarts and pulled them across the plains and mountains. They're called the Handcart Pioneers. There's a monument to them on Temple Square. Here. Pass this around."

He pulls a photograph out of his notebook and hands it to Julie Quist. With spring here, with summer coming, he's turning brown again.

"It was rough going. Husbands watched their wives die and wives watched their husbands die. Mothers watched their babies die. They buried their loved ones along the way. But they never quit. They kept coming. At night they'd gather round a fire, sing hymns, tell stories, dance, pray, give each other the strength to face the coming day. That's how powerful their faith was."

Keller hands you the photograph. The statue is bronze but all of the bronze is black from being old. The blackened statue of the man pulling the blackened statue of the handcart, bent forward, putting his weight into the crossbar and traces where a statue of a horse should have been. The blackened statue of his wife beside him, in a bronze pioneer dress, helping him pull. A covered bundle in the handcart with the blackened statue of a little girl riding in the bundle. In back, bent forward pushing, wearing a bronze hat, the blackened statue of a kid your size. A statue of a family making its way to Utah. A statue you looked at with your father when you moved here. They looked like a Negro family to you then, like the Negroes in the National Geographic, except that they were dressed. You hand the photograph to Yenchik.

"Sacrifice after sacrifice," Brother Rodgers says. "All on faith. You have to wonder. Is my faith that strong? Am I ready to make that kind of sacrifice? Here. Let me see that photo."

Brother Rodgers takes it from Yenchik and holds it up and points to the blackened statue of the kid behind the handcart.

"I want you boys to look at this boy," he says. "Put yourself in his shoes. Helping your mom and dad push a handcart thirteen hundred miles."

Brother Rodgers puts the photograph on the table. Then, for a minute, he looks at his own shoes, and when he looks up again, his face is hard and ledged, his eyes are pointed at the back wall like they're looking through it all the way to Idaho. He lets his breath out and his eyes come down to your faces again.

"Who do you think they did all this for?"

Finally Jasperson's hand goes up.

"Yes, Johnny."

"God?"

"Actually, Johnny, it was for you."

"Yeah," Jasperson says.

"They're gone now. But what they did for us is all around us. You think we owe them anything for that? Brenda?"

Caught off guard, Brenda Horn shrugs, makes her sly smile. "I guess."

"How can we repay them?"

"I don't know. Pay tithing, I guess."

"We can. But not all debts are money, Brenda."

He turns to you and your buddies.

"Here's what you boys can do. Make yourselves worthy of a mission. Come back and marry your sweetheart and start a family. Lead it with the power and wisdom of the Priesthood."

He turns to Julie Quist and Ann Cook and Brenda Horn and Susan Lake.

"Girls," he says, "you can keep yourselves chaste. Grow up to be virtuous young women worthy of entering the Temple with a returned missionary for marriage for time and all eternity. Be obedient to him. He's your key to the Celestial Kingdom. Bear children and raise them to walk in righteousness."

He turns back to face all of you and plants his shoes in the sunlight again.

"That's how we can repay them. Otherwise, we've wasted everything they sacrificed, and they'll know it."

He goes around behind the table, looks down, adjusts his notebook, and when he looks up again, takes a glance at you and looks off at the rest of the class.

"I heard a talk a while ago. Actually a pretty good little talk. About a couple of boys who took an old engine apart."

Some faces turn your way. Brother Rodgers comes out from behind the table.

"Just an old engine. All rusty and dirty. Not much use. But these two boys were curious. They had to see what was inside it. What made it work."

More faces. Your stomach starts to feel wild and cold and like it doesn't have a bottom.

"When they got inside they were pretty amazed. It looked brand new. A whole lot different from the way the outside looked."

"That was you," Yenchik whispers.

"Well, they learned a pretty good lesson. They learned that you can't judge things by the way they look. They were smart enough to see that about people, too."

Brother Rodgers looks down and back up again. This time he doesn't look at you at all.

"That's where the talk ended. But let's take it from there. See if there's another lesson we can learn. What do you think happened to that engine?"

This time nobody's looking at you.

"Did they put it back together? Get it running?"

You and Jimmy dividing up the parts. Each one of you getting a piston.

"Maybe it was junk," Brother Rodgers says. "Maybe it had some life in it. Maybe someone could still have used it. We'll never know. What we do know," he says, "is that it ended up ruined. In pieces. Just to satisfy the curiosity of a couple of boys."

It was already ruined. Everything was busted off. Where it had pipes and tubes their ends were cut and pinched. Where the carburetor went there was just a round hole choked with rusty mud and spiderwebs.

"Your testimony's like that engine," he says. "Full of mysteries inside. Lots of questions you'd like answers to. Things you'd like to know for sure. Things you're curious about."

He picks up the photograph and points to the blackened statue of the kid behind the handcart. "This boy here," he says. "What if he'd told his mom and dad he had some questions, and wasn't going anywhere until he had the answers?"

You sit there looking at the knees of his brown pants.

"I'm sure that the pioneers had reason to wonder what they were doing and why. Especially when they had to bury a loved one. Imagine burying your mom. But they held their faith. They didn't need some sign. They didn't need Joseph Smith to be bulletproof. If they'd needed that, they'd never have started their journey, and we wouldn't be here."

You don't know where to look, at your hands or your knees or the floor or the table legs or someone's shoes, because you're here, in front of Susan Lake and everyone, in your bow tie and sport coat, in your polished shoes.

"Curiosity," he says. "And doubt. They're like a wrench and a screwdriver when it comes to your testimony. Satan wants you to use those tools to take it apart. He knows you'd destroy it in the process."

"So we're not supposed to be curious," says Strand.

"Sure. But curious about the right things. As long as you keep your curiosity out of Satan's hands and let it be guided by the Holy Ghost."

"What do you mean the right things?"

"Like I said. Let the Holy Ghost tell you. Sometimes it's not about being smart. It's about being humble enough to know that God's smarter than you are."

"So what about Shake?" says Yenchik.

"What about him?"

"You saying he shouldn't of taken the engine apart?" says Yenchik.

"All I'm saying is that he missed the real lesson of his story. Some things have to be taken on faith. Look at this boy. He pushed this handcart thirteen hundred miles. He didn't need to take it apart to see how it worked."

"He's a statue," you say.

Brother Rodgers turns his face on you, hard as quartz rock, rock you can tell you fractured, and you try hard to hide the hate and fear all mixed together in this crazy wild cold inside you.

"What's that supposed to mean?" he finally says.

"That kid's not real. He's just a statue."

"He's a symbol," says Brother Rodgers. "A symbol for a lot of kids."

"Maybe the engine was a symbol too."

"For what?"

"For how a heart could be pure."

"It was just an engine. An engine doesn't have a heart. Only people and animals have hearts. That's what you should have talked about."

"You can't take people and animals apart without them dying."

"That's the point. You have to have faith."

"A statue of a handcart kid doesn't have a heart. But he gets to be a symbol. Maybe the real kid was a jerk. Maybe he didn't even have a testimony."

"You're skating on thin ice now."

"You weren't even there."

"Where?"

"In the cellar."

"I didn't need to be."

"Yeah you did. So you'd know. It was already ruined. It didn't even have a carburetor."

"That wasn't my point."

"You don't know anything about my testimony, either."

"Whoa. I never said anything about your testimony."

"You said I didn't have one."

"No I didn't." He looks away at the rest of the class. "Any of you hear me say that Shake didn't have a testimony?"

His question makes you crazier.

"Maybe you don't have one."

"What did you say?"

"Maybe you take things apart too."

"If I do, it's to fix them, and I'd watch myself if I were you."

He just stands there and you finally look down, and there his shoes are, thick and black and wrinkled in the sunlight, the dust in the leather creases like frail threads of white fire.

CHAPTER 56

SCHOOL LETS OUT. On the last day, out in the hall after History, Carla reaches out her hand, her right hand, the hand that strikes and cuts the bow across the strings. It's hot and moist and small and fierce in your hand.

"Well, be good, Shake Tauffler. Behave yourself this summer."

"You be good too. Carla Ogilvy."

"Keep practicing."

She doesn't know. The fire her playing ended up lighting. The sand-pit because of the strike and pull of her bow. You could tell her now, standing there, but you don't know how.

"You too."

"Oh, my mom'll make sure of that."

"Yeah."

Suddenly her eyes go wide and flood the lenses of her glasses.

"I never showed you my violin," she says.

"Show me in eighth grade."

"Okay. When we do that duet."

You've figured out how you'll do it. You'll have learned Danny Boy. And you'll surprise her the way she likes surprises. That way it won't have been a lie. That way you were just kidding her.

"Okay," you tell her.

"Okay," she says. She lowers her eyes to your chest. Looks up and smiles. "See you then."

"I knew Rodgers could be a prick sometimes," says West. "I just never knew he could be an asshole. The crap he said about you taking that engine apart."

"Yeah," says Doby. "That wasn't called for."

On the way home the last day, the air clear and the sun bright after a morning cloudburst and then a long rain that kept you from riding your bike, pockets and trails of fog still lying in the deep ruts of the mountains, some of the gutters and sidewalks still puddled, you and Doby and West use the shoulder of the street to stay off the mud of the busted sidewalk. Keller's there too because he just showed up and you couldn't think of a way to ditch him quick enough.

"It's a free country," says Keller.

"What does that mean?" says West.

"It's his class. He can say anything he wants."

"Anyone invite this dork to walk home with us?" says West.

"Not me," says Doby.

"Me either," you say.

You get to the little cinderblock store called Cottage Market with the asphalt yard. Doby needs a tube of Brylcreem. Keller cruises through an issue of Escapade looking for boobs. West sticks a copy of Hot Rod magazine down the sleeve of his jacket while the old man at the register gives Doby his change and slips his Brylcreem into a little paper bag. You're just out the door when a rust-colored Jeep comes banging into the paved yard and gets jerked to a stop. Four guys come catapulting off the sides, big guys, guys in Bountiful High School letter jackets, red and gray, laughing, bopping toward the door that just swung shut behind you.

"Hey, kids," one guy says. Two other guys nod. On their jackets you've already spotted the pins that mean they're football players. The last guy turns and comes ambling over to where you've stopped to watch them pull in. To be this close to guys who could be famous.

"What you kids up to?" he says, grinning, looking back and forth. He's got a red flattop and a big face raw with zits and teeth so jutted out you wonder if he can close his mouth enough to touch his lips together.

"Just hanging out," West says, trying to keep his own voice easy, but you can hear how he's looked at the guy's eyes and seen the same cold trouble there that you have.

"Just hanging out, huh?"

"Yeah," says Doby. "Just walking home."

"Yeah," says Keller. "What's the big deal?"

You can feel Doby and West wince too. The other three guys come over. The tallest one's got a skinny face, a nose where you can look up into his nostrils, this wavy Everly Brothers hair that rises off his forehead. The shortest one's got shoulders and this solid build, short black hair so thick it looks like fur, a furry line of a beard that comes down around the bottom of his face like a chinstrap, ringing his face in fur like a gorilla's. The last guy makes you think of your dentist, Dr. Belnap, just a friendly-looking guy you'd see in church. Keller starts walking. The dentist guy takes an easy step and herds him back. Then the four of you are circled where the only thing you know for sure is that things from here on out will just happen.

"Doing some shopping first?" says the guy with the Everly Brothers hair.

"Yeah," you say.

"What'd ya buy?"

"Nothing."

"Yeah? Then what'd ya steal?"

"Nothing."

"This one did." The redheaded guy nods at Doby's hand. "What'd ya buy, kid?"

"Just—"

The guy snaps out his hand, snatches the little bag, pulls out Doby's Brylcreem tube.

"Hey," he says. "Brylcreem."

He drops the bag and puts the tube up in the air. Doby's scared face follows the tube up and then back down again where the redheaded guy holds it out in front of him.

"You paid for this, didn't ya."

"Yeah," says Doby.

"Know how I can tell?"

"No."

"Because if you'd of stole it, it wouldn't of come in a bag, would it?"

"No."

"You wouldn't swipe something and then ask for a bag for it, would ya."

"No."

"Naw. You're not that stupid."

"I don't swipe stuff."

"Naw," says the redheaded guy. "You're too smart for that. I'm pretty smart too."

"Yeah."

"Tell me how smart I am."

"You're smart."

"Tell me I'm really smart."

You watch the redheaded guy. His grin keeps flickering toward being mean like his eyes. A scar off his forehead cuts one of his eyebrows in half. Doby's chin starts losing hold, dimpling up, quivering.

"You're really smart," you say. "Now give it back."

The redheaded guy turns and fixes this look on you that makes your guts churn. Whiteheads pepper his ravaged skin in the sunlight.

"What'd you say, twerp?"

"He didn't do anything to you."

"Sorenson. Come on."

It's the gorilla guy. You watch him move, shift his weight, but all the redheaded guy does is turn back to Doby.

"Your buddy says I should give this back to you. You want it?"

"Yeah."

"Yeah what?"

"Please."

"First you gotta sing the song."

"What song?"

"The Brylcreem song."

"The Brylcreem song?"

"Yeah. You're a smart kid. You know it."

"The one on the radio?"

"That's the one."

"You want me to sing it?"

"You want your stuff back?"

Doby looks at you and then at West. His fancy hair, all the work he's put into training it, has never had much to do with his face. Now it just sits up there like some little animal. He looks back at the tube where the redheaded guy is holding it.

"Brylcreem, a little dab'll do ya," he sings, but the words come out warbling, in big hard backward swallows, like hiccups underwater. "Brylcreem, you'll look so debonair."

And then he just stands there while the redheaded guy lets him figure out for himself that he's not finished.

"Brylcreem, the gals'll all pursue ya, they'll love to run their fingers through your hair."

"That's good." The redheaded guy slaps Doby on the shoulder hard enough to make him take a step. "Whaddaya say, guys? Give the kid a hand."

The dentist guy and the guy with the Everly Brothers hair do a couple of slow motion claps. Doby's scared enough to let this little smile out.

"Come on, Sorenson." It's the gorilla guy. "Let's go."

"Sure. Here you go, kid."

The redheaded guy puts the tube out to Doby. Doby reaches for it. The guy pulls it back an inch, lets it drop, raises his leg, and when his shoe comes down, the crimp along the bottom of the tube blows out, and white cream spurts in one big blob out on the asphalt.

"There ya go, kid," he says. "How's that for a little dab'll do ya."

You've never seen so much Brylcreem all at once. Never seen it in sunlight. Flat, with its bottom blown open, the tube looks like a gutted fish, a fish that was gutted through its mouth. The dentist guy and the guy with the Everly Brothers hair are snorting like hogs. Even the gorilla guy laughs. But the redheaded guy just stands there, done grinning, just looking mean, his mouth in a tight snarl around his teeth. Doby starts crying for real. The redheaded guy turns to you.

"Your turn next time, twerp."

They head for the door into the store. The guy with the Everly Brothers hair knocks your books out of your arm. You give them time to get occupied inside. And then you scoop up all the Brylcreem you can in both your hands, run for the Jeep, reach up over the hood, lay Brylcreem in broad circular smears across the windshield, the passenger side and then the driver's side, wipe your hands on the driver's seat, snatch up your books, and then the four of you are running.

"You probably shouldn't of done that," West says, quiet, breathing hard.

You stay off the streets. Run stumbling through people's yards and the weeds and slick dirt of open fields still muddy from the rain. Run with your books tucked like footballs up under your arms. Dogs bark. A fat man with a shovel hollers when you go tearing through his dead garden. Back behind you, through the neighborhoods and fields, you can hear them bellow, the engine catch and roar, the gears clank, the tires howl. You get honked at crossing Orchard Drive. Keep going through yards on the other side and into the ridges and hollows and flats of a field of bulldozed dirt where new houses are being built. You can hear them shouting. You duck behind a rubble bank and watch them go cruising past. The redheaded guy in the passenger seat is looking so hard he's hanging off the Jeep, the guy with the Everly Brothers hair driving, the gorilla guy and dentist guy on the bench in back, looking around, riding high and close together like they would in some parade.

"There! Hey! Stop!"

From behind the rubble bank you glance around. Keller's up and running the other way. They've seen him. The Jeep comes jumping up over the gutter, gunning out onto the bulldozed field, swerving, throwing mud, the guy driving the only guy still in it, the other three out front, running your way, charging hard in their letter jackets, keeping their arms in tight and their heads level the way football players run, bounding like deer over bulldozed ridges. You and Doby and West take off after Keller, but you already know you're running on principle, not really to get away, because they're football players, and chasing guys down and tackling them is what they do. It's just a matter of time before you hear one of them behind you, before your jacket yanks you backward, before your books go flying out ahead of you, before you get hauled back to the Jeep.

It's the dentist guy who gets you. The guy with the Everly Brothers hair gets West. He's got West by one hand and West's Hot Rod magazine rolled up in his other one. The gorilla guy gets Doby. The redheaded guy's got Keller by the ear.

"Which one of you little fucks did this?" The guy with the Everly Brothers hair looks crazy. "I said who did this? Tell me or I'll fucking kill every one of you!"

And before you get a chance to put together how to say it, there's Keller, stepping up and doing it for you.

"He did," he says, his arm up, pointed at you, his head cocked sideways because the redheaded guy's still got his ear. "I told him not to." His voice shakes like a tin roof about to let go in the wind. The redheaded guy takes hold of Keller's other ear, starts lifting him off the ground. Keller howls and grabs the guy's wrists to take his weight off his ears.

"Lookit what I got me," says the redheaded guy. "A little snitch."

"Owww! Stop!"

"Rat out your buddy like that? Think that's cool?"

"I'm sorry!" Keller howls. "I'm sorry!"

The guy with the Everly Brothers hair is there. He's got your hands. You watch his hair. When he looks back up his face is so close you can make out the tiny holes where his eyelashes come out of his eyelids.

"You little twerp motherfucker," he says quietly.

"It was my idea," you hear West say. "Leave him alone."

"I'll clean it off," you say. "No big deal."

"Yeah," he finally says. "With your fucking tongue."

He ducks, puts his shoulder into your stomach, picks you up, turns around and throws you on your back across the hood of the Jeep. The dentist guy is around the other side to catch you. They get you on your knees, on the hood, the windshield in your face, hands clamped around your arms and legs. Their strength is absolute. On the windshield are bug scars, streaked arcs of dirt, gouts and smears of Brylcreem you can smell from how hard and fast you're breathing.

"Leave him alone!" you hear West yell. "Chickenshit bastards!"

"Lick it off, twerp," says the guy with the Everly Brothers hair.

"Up yours."

The redheaded guy jumps up behind you, grabs your head, jams your face into the slick sweet mess on the windshield. Through the smeared glass you can see Keller running, reckless across the field, heading for the street for everything he's worth.

"Lick it off, you little fuck."

"Up yours."

One hand lets go of your head just long enough to cuff it hard enough to set off lightning in your eyes.

"Lick the fuckin windshield."

"Up yours."

The redheaded guy drags your face like a rag back and forth across the glass. You taste Brylcreem. You hear Doby bawling harder.

"Okay!" you yell. "Just let go!"

"Lick, you little cocksucker!"

"I will! Just let go of my head!"

"Up yours, kid. Start licking."

"I can't unless you let my head go!"

"Let him go." It's the dentist guy. "We got him."

The redheaded guy lets up. His hands lift back, hesitate like your head's some kind of grenade, then let go all the way. They've still got your arms and legs. But you've got enough play, enough to bring your head back, lower it, ram it hard as you can into the glass. You know how it breaks from watching Danny Archuleta do it. This rubbery shatter where the glass turns into this spider web of a million cracks and the cracks grab your hair when your head comes back off the glass.

"You fucking little shit!"

"The little bastard!"

They throw you off the hood. When you hit the dirt they pick you up, cuff you around, kick you back and forth, keep you on your feet, kick you again when you lose balance or stumble or lunge away. You keep your face covered. Someone kicks you in the leg and sends you to your knees. Someone picks you up and kicks you in the back and sends you lurching into someone else's legs. Someone shoves you back. Someone cracks you hard enough in the head to knock your hands off your face. West breaks away and comes charging in swinging before he's down in the mud and then back in the grip of the gorilla guy. The guy with the Everly Brothers hair takes you by your jacket and slugs you twice in the face. The shock turns the soles of your feet to ice. He slugs you in the stomach. You fold over, go to your knees, try to get your breath back. You hear West calling them chickenshit fuckers. Doby howling loud for them to stop. The redheaded guy steps in, pulls you up, steadies you, and you watch him cock his arm back, and all you care about is breathing.

"Hey." The gorilla guy catches his arm, pulls him around. "He's a fucking kid."

You go to your knees. Try to swallow air. From their shoes you can tell they're standing toe to toe, the redheaded guy and the gorilla guy, staring each other down. West's shoes come in, kicking, and you can tell he's swinging for all he's worth. You raise your head. The gorilla guy gets him in a bear hug.

"You chickenshit bastards!" says West. "Let me go!"

"Here." The gorilla guy passes West to the dentist guy and comes back to the redheaded guy. Dizzy, trying to breathe, you look down again.

"You were about to slug a kid," the gorilla guy says.

"He just busted the fucking windshield," the redheaded guy says.

"He's bleeding. You fucking jerk. He's hurt. Let the fuck up."

The gorilla guy comes over, squats down, puts his face right into yours. "You okay, kid?" he says. You watch his eyes skate across your face. "Jesus." He looks down at your mouth. "You can't breathe." You shake your head. He looks around. The guy with the Everly Brothers hair is looking at his windshield. The gorilla guy gets up. Nobody says anything. The gorilla guy gets to the Jeep and stops.

"Motherfucker," he says.

The guy with the Everly Brothers hair jumps, spins around, finds the gorilla guy right there, jumps again when he sees how close he is.

"What the fuck's with you?" he shouts.

"You slugged a kid." The gorilla guy says it calm. Then shifts his weight. "Split his lip. Knocked his wind out."

"Yeah? Well, he left all his fucking hair in my windshield, too."

"You slugged a kid. How the fuck you think that's gonna look."

"Like you're gonna tell."

"Motherfucker."

"Yeah? Well, motherfucker yourself."

The gorilla guy hits him so quick you don't see it. Just the way all his hair explodes like a cheerleader's pompom up and off his head, twice, once when the gorilla guy hits him, again when the back of his head cracks the steel frame of the windshield. His face amazed, the guy with the Everly Brothers hair steps back, puts his hand to his mouth.

"Get us outta here," the gorilla guy says. "Let's go." He walks around the guy with the Everly Brothers hair to the back of the Jeep.

"Tell me how the fuck to see where I'm going," says the guy with the Everly Brothers hair. The gorilla guy stops, squints into the sun.

"Lay the fucking windshield down," he says. "If you're worried about the wind messing up your sacred fucking hair, you can wipe my ass with it. Wear your goddamn helmet."

"You don't need to have a shit hemorrhage."

You try to keep the shivering deep inside your bones from showing while they open the buckles that hold the windshield up and swing the frame down slow onto the hood. Splinters and crumbs of glass rain out across the metal. Doby walks off. When you turn around again they're in the Jeep. The engine starts, the gears grind and clank into place, and then it swings around, skidding and spitting mud, heading toward the street. The gorilla guy's in back with the dentist guy, shoulder to shoulder, and when the Jeep swerves and bounces and drops off the curb onto asphalt, the two of them move together, back and forth, up and down, puppets being made to dance, passenger dolls on swivel hooks in the back of a toy Jeep.

"Chickenshit bastards!" West yells.

Seeing them move like that you're dizzy and sick again. Watching them hunker forward in one motion when the guy with the Everly Brothers hair, all four wheels on asphalt, guns the engine, finds second, guns it again. The shivering in your bones has spread to where you're shivering all over, your whole body, your voice too, this shivering sound like you've just come from freezing cold into a warm house, and it feels good just to shiver, like sneezing, like peeing when you've had to hold it in too long.

"How bad is it?" West has his hand on your shoulder.

"You tell me." Slurred and shivering.

"Think you can get up?"

"In a minute."

And then Doby's back. He's got all your books. His eyes take in your face.

"Holy crap," he says. "Holy crap."

You take a look at the books he's holding.

"I left Keller's. I kicked the crap out of 'em. They're all muddy and ripped to shit."

Big Doby. Maybe he's never been hurt. Doesn't know that it turns out okay. You're just glad he's there, your big aircraft carrier buddy, you coming in for a landing with your fuselage and rudder shot to pieces and only one of your wheels down, West coming in with you, mud in his hair, all down his face.

"Can you walk?" says Doby.

"Probably. Yeah."

You start off slow. Doby carries your books. West walks close to your side.

"Use my shoulder if you need to."

"I'm okay."

"Keller," he says. "He gets us into it and then takes off."

"What a rat," says Doby.

"Adopted piece of shit," says West.

The more you walk the more you learn how to do it without it hurting. By the time you get to your neighborhood you know how to breathe without feeling the spike of pain in your side. At the corner where West has to break away for his house you stop. He looks you over again. From the way he does, the way he's quiet, you remember the way he studied the Gullwing that afternoon in Mrs. Harding's garage.

"You gonna be okay?" he says.

"Yeah. I just wanna stop at Doby's. See what I look like."

"It's gonna scare you," says Doby.

"I just wanna see."

"You can come to my house," says West.

"Doby's is on the way home."

"Okay." West looks up the street. "Call me later."

"Holy cow."

"I told you."

"That's me."

You watch your face move when you talk, feel how crusted and stiff your skin is when it moves, how your mouth feels like you've been to the dentist, and it's the only way you know for sure that what you're looking at in the mirror in Doby's basement bathroom is you. There's blood glued in with mud in your hair. Some still red and shiny where it's mixed with smears of Brylcreem. One side of your upper lip is blown up like a bulge in an inner tube, and there's more blood, down from your nose into your mouth, dried blood just inside your lips, in crusted lines out to the corners. Your eyes look back at you, eyes you've always had, except like they're looking at you out of someone else's face, because the face you're looking at should hurt a thousand times more than it does.

"I can't go home like this."

Doby looking too. Over your shoulder behind you in the mirror.

"Yeah," he says.

"Good Lord."

And then it's his mother's face there too, and then her in the little bathroom, in her apron, nudging Doby aside, turning you around, taking a good look. She takes you upstairs, puts you in a kitchen chair, runs a big steel bowl full of water, sets it on the table, pulls another chair in front of you, sits down, cleans your face and hair and hands with a soapy washcloth and then a hot one, pulls your lips back to get the blood off down inside them, burns the cuts in your lip and forehead when she dabs them with rubbing alcohol. Doby tells her everything that happened, from when he bought the tube of Brylcreem to when he went back and got your books and carried them home for you. He leaves out the swear words and West filching the magazine and the way he had to sing the Brylcreem song. When his mother hears about the windshield, she fetches a magnifying glass and a pair of tweezers, tells Doby to bring a lamp from the living room, take the shade off, plug it in, and hold the bulb next to your head. You feel its heat. Feel the tweezers scrape and scratch and dig when they hit a piece of glass. She drops the chips in a little tin saucer next to her elbow on the table. Right in front of you is her lined, loose-skinned throat, the hollow of skin up underneath her jaw. Intricate little cords of muscles ripple across her collar bones while she works her arms and fingers. Doby's going back over parts of the story, remembering new things, telling old things again just to tell them.

"Hold the lamp still, George," she says. "Bring it closer."

The heat from the bulb stronger.

"Those boys are hoodlums," she says. "They should be in jail."

"Should we call the cops?" says Doby.

"That's up to Shake. Ask me, they already got their comeuppance, driving around with a broken windshield. You want to call the police, sweetie?"

"That's okay."

"Well, we could tell Lloyd Wacker, and probably get them kicked off the team."

"Lloyd Wacker?" says Doby. "From church?"

"The high school football coach. Those boys don't have any business on the team. Being treated like heroes." She drops another chip of glass into the saucer, so tiny you can't hear it land, and says, "You're the hero. A foolish one, taking them on, but a pretty brave kid."

"I did a good job kicking Keller's books to pieces," Doby says.

"Books are school property," his mother says. And then you remember she's a third grade teacher. "You shouldn't destroy them."

"Shake destroyed a windshield," Doby says.

From the way the muscles tense and the skin moves underneath his mother's jaw you can tell she's smiling.

"I just got mad," says Doby.

And then, after nobody says anything, he says, "Thanks for sticking up for me."

"That's okay."

"George. Hold the magnifying glass for me."

You can feel her fingers stretch the skin on your head apart from different directions. You wonder how she can see them, what she looks for, chips of glass so tiny they don't make noise when they hit the tin saucer, the way mosquitoes land. Then her fingers are gone.

"That looks like it. Put the lamp down, George. Go get the mercurochrome. And that blue box of gauze and the tape."

Doby comes back. His mother unscrews the cap off the mercurochrome bottle, draws out the fuzzy dark red dripping ball on the wire stick, wipes it on the neck of the bottle. You clench up for the sting.

"It's okay, honey," she says. "Relax. This doesn't burn."

She dabs it on your head. All you feel is the wet. And then you wonder if it's as good as the stuff your mother has, the stuff that stings, if it's as strong, if you can trust it the way you can your mother's stuff.

"Now get me the scissors."

Doby hands them to her. She unrolls and cuts off a length of gauze, folds it, puts it on your forehead, cuts a couple of pieces of white tape, stretches and tapes the gauze in place.

"That takes care of that. Where else are you hurt, honey?"

"Nowhere."

"George said they kicked you. He had to carry your books home."

"My knee." And then you say, "My legs a little."

"Okay. Stand up. Drop your pants. Keep your undies up."

You shoot Doby a question with your face. His face shoots back the answer. Places in your legs hurt when you stand up and push your pants down.

"Oh my."

Doby's mother turns you around, pokes her finger into your legs here and there, and a couple of times it hurts enough to make you pull away.

"I'm sorry, sweetie. They kicked you good. You're bruising up already. You'll have them for a while. But nothing time won't heal. Nothing broken. Let's get the mud brushed out of your hair and clothes and get you combed up. Then I'll call your mom and we'll get you home."

CHAPTER 57

YOUR MOTHER waits till after she's smiled and waved to Doby's mother out in her Bel Air and gets the front door closed. Then she goes nuts. Wants to know what makes you think you can come into her house like this. Wants you out. Brings out the rugbeater. Chases you out the back door and slams it so hard the kitchen window quivers. From the bottom of the porch steps you hear the lock turn. You don't know where to go. Back to Doby's. Over to West's. Even Blackwell's. Places that make sense. But that would just make things crazier. Roy, then Molly, look at you out the kitchen window, then disappear. The door gets torn open. Your mother screams at you to get out of the yard and slams it shut again.

You go across the field and down into the orchard. The ladders folded, the bushel baskets stacked, the branches bare of anything to pick, you find a place to hide and try to sort things out. Later, you hear your name, your father calling from the back porch. Dusk and then finally the gathering of dark in the branches draw you up from the orchard back across the field to the edge of your yard. Through the lighted kitchen window across the grass your family's having supper. Kidneys and gravy and mashed potatoes the way their forks look. Round slices like different sized coins except thicker that give to your teeth like soft disintegrating rubber while the dense flavor explodes across your tongue. Karl telling everyone that kidneys are where pee comes from. With his back to the window his head looks like a vase or bowl your mother keeps on the windowsill. How easy they'd be to kill. It scares you to suddenly know. It scares you so bad your throat hurts.

The kitchen finally empties except for your father. You watch him take off his watch and wash and rinse the dishes and clean the kitchen and hit the light switch on his way out. When the back of the house goes black there's suddenly the sky, still and ambient and pale with starlight, soaring and huge and all around you. Fear you don't understand makes you want to cry. Sometime later the kitchen window is sudden light again. It's your father. The back porch light comes on, the door comes open, and when he steps outside he calls your name into the dark.

You come forward into the yard where the light can reach you. He tells you to come in. Sits you at the table while he goes to get your mother. In your head you can see what you look like through the window from the dark at the back of the yard. From the stairwell to the basement you can hear the shallow rattle of laughter from the tv down in the recreation room. From the hall you can hear the arguing murmur of your mother answering your father. Everything around you in the heavy penetrating leftover smell of kidneys is familiar. But something's gone, something permanent, like heat in winter. You touch your upper lip. The fat part with the small hard stubborn knot inside it.

And then, ahead of your father, she comes in, sits down across from you, the same pale green dress she was wearing the last time you saw her, except now she gives you this smile, this sweet weary version of her church smile. And then your father sits down too, takes his watch out of his pocket, puts it on his wrist, looks at it, then at you.

"So," he says. "Tell us how this happened."

"I saved your plate for you, Shakli. Let me heat it up for you."

Glancing at her. "I'm not hungry."

"You have to eat, Shakli."

"So, Mother," your father says. "He said he isn't hungry."

"Yes, Harold."

"Now go ahead. And keep it brief. I don't have long."

And so you do. Sit there and tell it the way Doby did, just not as long, not repeating parts, leaving out the swear words, putting in the Brylcreem song and Doby bawling. You mostly leave Keller out. Just that he was there. When you're done, your throat is tight and strained from telling it, from wanting them to see it like Doby's mother did.

Your mother doesn't take her weary smiling look off you. Your father spends the whole time studying his hands, his face heavy, his eyes hooded by his eyelids. He doesn't look at you until you're done. By then you've remembered Mr. Hinkle and what he taught you not to do, not strain, play from your lungs, but where your lungs come up it feels like a fist is gathered in your throat.

"Was there anyone involved that we know," he says.

"The high school guys?"

"Anyone who might have seen this."

"No."

"Nobody from the ward."

"No." And then you say, "Just Doby and West and Keller."

"And Sister Doby," says your mother.

"Did you know them?" your father says. "The boys from high school?"

"No."

"Did they know you?"

"No."

"You're positive. We're not going to get any phone calls."

"No."

"What did you do to provoke them?"

"We were just walking home."

"You must have done something, Shakli," your mother says. "They wouldn't pick on you for no reason."

"We were just walking home."

"There had to be something," your father says. "Who are you to them?"

"Nothing. Nobody. They just came up to us."

"Why didn't you walk away?"

"They wouldn't let us."

"Didn't they eventually go inside the store?"

"Yeah."

"Wouldn't that have been the time to walk away?"

"They made Doby cry. They mashed his Brylcreem."

"Why was that your business?"

"He's my friend. They made him sing. They made him bawl. I just stuck up for him."

"He didn't stick up for himself?"

"No."

"He's twice your size. Why would he need you to stick up for him?"

"I don't know."

"Did he ask you to stick up for him?"

"He didn't have to."

"You decided on your own to mix in?"

"He's my friend."

"But tell me. Did your friend come home in such sorry shape that his mother couldn't even let him in the house?"

"It wasn't him. It was me." And then you say, "His mom fixed me up."

"Yes, Shakli," your mother says. "You had no right to bother her."

"Is your friend at home right now with a bandage on his head?"

"No."

"Do your friend's clothes have to be washed? Do his pants have to be fixed?"

"No."

"Did your friend spend the night wandering around outside?"

"No."

"No. He sat down to a nice calm supper with his family. He didn't let a tube of Brylcreem bring trouble into his home and upset his whole family."

"I told you. He was too scared."

"How do you know?" your father says. "Maybe he was smarter than you. Or maybe he remembered what the Gospel teaches. To turn the other cheek."

"Yeah," you say. "Maybe that's why he was bawling."

"Don't talk like that to me."

"Then don't say he's smarter than me."

"Don't tell me what I can say."

"Don't call me stupid."

"I didn't. Don't put words in my mouth."

"You said Doby was smarter than me."

"That's different."

"He was glad I did what I did. He said thanks."

"I'd be glad too," your father says, "if I had someone else to fight my battles."

"His mom was too. She was glad they got paid back."

"I'm sure she was," your father says. "It isn't her mess to clean up."

The scratch of the tweezers, the heat of the light bulb, the feel of her searching fingers.

"She called them hoodlums. She said they belonged in jail. She wanted Brother Wacker to kick them off the football team."

"Oh, Harold." Your mother puts her hand against her cheek like something there like a tooth just started hurting. "It just gets worse."

"Nobody is going to say a word to Brother Wacker," your father tells her. He looks back at you. "Four boys should get kicked off the football team," he says. He slowly shakes his head. His mouth spreads open in this small admiring smile but his eyes go mean and you can hear his back teeth going. "All because of you. By golly. You're an important man for your age. You're a big deal."

"Doby's mom said I was a hero."

"Surely she was joking."

"You weren't there."

"I think I know Sister Doby better than you do. Now lower your voice."

"She said I was brave too. Why can't you say that?"

He laughs, loud, rough, abrupt. "Brave," he says. "Now I know she was joking." He goes serious. "You think what you did was brave? Let me tell you. Your friends were the brave ones. They did the hard thing.

Stand there and take it. Let it pass. Not make it worse. That's what it is to be brave."

"Yes, Shakli," your mother says. "They made a sucker out of you."

The trumpet the first time home. The fist in your throat gives way to the same hot dirty charge of hate and panic.

"I'm not a sucker!"

"Yes, Shakli. You are."

"No I'm not!"

And now her standing, hulking over you across the table, her wounded weary smile gone like so much powder, her face raw and clenched and red and snarling.

"You are a sucker!"

"You don't even know what a sucker is!"

"I know that you are one!"

"Sit down, Mother." He sounds tired. "Sit down and shut up."

She reaches back for her chair without taking her eyes off you. "Yah," she says, ominous but harmless, like lightning and thunder past you and going the other way. "Yah."

"And you keep your voice down," your father says.

"You always help people. That doesn't make you a sucker."

"No," he says. "Because I don't get beat up for it."

"So what would you of done?"

"Well, by golly, for one, you could have bought him a new tube of Brylcreem."

"That's nuts. That's plain crazy."

"How much was it? Less than a dollar? You want to compare that to a windshield? Well, by golly, maybe one day you can try paying for a windshield."

"Maybe they should of thought of that."

"Thought of what?"

"If a tube of Brylcreem was worth getting their windshield busted."

"You still don't see the error in what you did."

"What have we done, Shakli? Aren't we good to you? Why do you keep hurting us?"

"So, Mother."

"I didn't do it to hurt you. Don't say that."

"Then why did you go to Sister Doby? You know, Shakli, you have a mother of your own. It's a slap in the face to me."

"I wanted to know what I looked like. She was just there by accident."

"Where was your friend Keller while this was going on?" your father says.

"Don't call him my friend."

"Why suddenly isn't he your friend?"

"He just isn't." And then you say, "He told on me."

"So what did he do wrong? He told the truth. Should he have let them think it was him?"

"It was my job to tell them. And then he just took off."

"Why should he have stayed around? He had nothing to do with it."

"He is a good boy, Shakli. He has good parents."

"Then maybe you should of had him instead."

You watch your father go on guard. "What do you mean?" he says.

"If you wanted an adopted chickenshit for a kid."

Across the table your mother lets out a cry. Your father just stares at you.

"So that's the kind of example you set for your brothers and sisters. One that comes home beat up. One that says terrible things like that to his good mother."

"Yeah? Who's my example supposed to be? You?"

The phone goes off on the wall behind him. He's off his chair with the receiver snatched off the hook before the second ring.

"Hello," he says. You watch his face do its mutation into his church face, his voice into his church voice, grinning like whoever called can see him the way they can hear him.

"Yes, Art. Fine, thanks. What can I do for you?"

Your mother watches him, nervous but with her own smile in place, as if the First Counselor can somehow see her too. It makes you want to cry to watch them. "Don't mention it, Art," your father finally says. "No. It's fine. I'll be there shortly." And then he hangs up.

"So," he says. Turned back to the table but standing. "Are we finished here?"

"Tell me where you will be shortly, Harold."

"I have to go to the ward," he says. "They need my help."

"It's late, Harold. Stay at home with your family."

"I'm sorry, Mother. They have no one else who can do this."

"Please, Harold. Let's just be a family tonight for once."

"I was supposed to go to the office anyway tonight, Mother. I told you that at supper. Don't you remember? What's the difference if I go to the office or to the ward?"

"No, Harold. I don't remember." And then she looks at you. "Did you hear your father say he had to go back to the office?"

"He wasn't even here for supper, Mother. You don't remember that either. But I told you. This shouldn't come as a surprise."

"No, Harold." Her voice like someone died and her face with this gentle resignation like she's at their funeral. "Nothing comes as a surprise any more to your wife."

"Not in front of your son," he says. "This isn't his business."

"Your children have a right to know how little their father cares for them."

"Now I've heard enough," he says. "I have to go."

"Yah. Go. Your son is right. You are a sucker. A sucker for the church."

"So! I am not a sucker! I have an obligation!"

"Yah! To everyone but your family!"

"I have to leave now! I won't take this!"

"Then I am leaving too!"

And suddenly she's up, on her way out of the kitchen, and your father moves in front of her to stop her, but he's awkward, like someone with arms but no hands at the ends of them.

"Let me by!" Her voice fierce now and her arms quick and her hands like lunatic birds all over his chest and face. "Don't touch me!"

He goes back easy. And then she's down the stairs, and you can hear the door to the garage, and then, through the floor, things being banged around, then quiet, then the door back, feet quick on the stairs. She's got a suitcase. The suitcase she filled in La Sal and emptied when you moved here. She heads into the living room.

"Children!" she calls. "Children! Come! Your mother has to leave now!"

From the doorway of the kitchen you watch your father talk to her. Ask her where she'll go this time of night. How she'll get there. Who'll take her in. How she'll eat. What she'll wear. She ignores him. Just keeps calling for the children, looking for them to wander in, first Molly and Maggie, then Karl, Roy behind him, until everyone's there in the living room.

"Your mother is leaving, children," she announces, gently and wearily, and reaches down to stroke Maggie's head. "She has had enough. She can't take it any more."

"Take what?" says Karl.

"It doesn't matter. I have to leave now."

With his thumb in his mouth Roy quietly starts crying. Molly's crying too.

"Please don't go, Mama. I'm sorry."

"Yes, sweetheart. Don't worry. Your father will find someone to wash your sheets and nightgowns. Your mother is tired."

"Stay home, Mama." Karl trying to pry the handle of the suitcase out of her hand. All her kids around her now. Your father standing back.

"Who will support you? How do you plan to get there? Tell me!"

Your mother ignoring him, moving toward the door, impeded by the herd the five of you make around her, Karl still wrestling for the suitcase.

"It's too late to start worrying about me," she says.

"Go then! Go out and learn how good you have it! Karl! Let go!"

Karl letting go, backing away shy, holding his hand like it's been burned.

"Please stay." You trying to be the example. "We'll be better."

"Don't worry, children. Someone will look after you. Your mother just has to go now."

CHAPTER 58

YOU TRAIL her out of the house, the five of you, down off the dark porch, Molly and Roy and Maggie not sure of anything, Karl on his own, going out front. Ahead in the moonlight, your mother is the shadow of a woman with a suitcase going down the walk past the shadows of your father's roses, out into the circle, up and around the Allers' house, along the street where the pavement goes level. Karl waits, and when you get to him with Molly and Roy and Maggie, he's scared, his legs uncertain.

"Where's she gonna go?" he says, the way mean and scared always go together for him.

"I don't know."

"Maybe to the store first," he says. "For stuff to put in the suitcase."

"They're closed."

"What happened to your head?"

"I got in a fight."

"Who with?"

"Nobody."

"Tell me."

You hear an engine, and the pavement around your feet gets bright and your shoes and legs light up, and then the Buick is there, next to you, the passenger door open, your father leaning across the seat from the steering wheel. The dome light in the roof puts his big ridged face in Halloween relief.

"Get in. No, Molly. Just your brother."

"Why?"

"We have to bring your mother home."

Down the street the headlights reach your mother, walking hard, the heels of her shoes, her calves, the back of her dress, the suitcase in her hand, past the Allreds, halfway to the corner where the street turns and goes down the long hill all the way to Orchard Drive. Your father pulls even with her to where she's not in the headlights but walking along just out your window.

"Open the door," he tells you.

You push the heavy door out into the street and put up your foot to hold it there. Pain cuts through your leg and ribs. The dome light comes on and shows you the color of her pale dress, the street, the gravel embedded in the asphalt moving past below the metal threshold of the door.

"Mother," your father says. "Please get in. Don't be ridiculous."

She keeps walking, looking straight ahead, as if she has a destination.

"Mother. Please. Where will you go this time of night?"

"I have places." Without turning her head.

"Your place is at home. With your family."

"No. It is over."

"Now come. Your family needs you. Let's end this spectacle."

"Yah. That's too bad. Now it is finally what I need."

"You can have it, Mother. Whatever you need."

"I need a husband."

"I am only trying to do my best for this family."

"Your family means nothing to you."

"And what do they mean to you? Putting them through this charade in front of the whole neighborhood!"

"Yah! You'll see what a charade it is!"

And then they're both quiet, like they've been reprimanded, your mother walking, the big Buick idling forward.

"I'll stay home more often," your father finally says. "Is that what you need?"

Past her, back from the street in the moonlight, the yards, the houses of your neighbors, the Bradshaws, the Hansens, the Becks, curtains drawn across the living room windows, tv sets going behind them, the gray flickering light in the curtains like quiet lightning going off deep inside the clouds of their rooms.

"Talk to her," your father says.

"Please come home, Mama."

Her looking straight ahead like you never said a word.

"Try again," your father says. "Promise her something."

"What?"

"I don't know. That you'll make her life easier."

You sit there, your foot holding the heavy door, heat from the idling engine welling up from underneath the Buick, waiting till she's past the house where Blackwell lives before you try again.

"We'll behave better, Mama." And then, "We'll help you more."

"It isn't you, Shakli," she says, but she keeps walking, looking straight ahead, and you look at the chrome button that opens the glove compartment door, your face on fire.

"By golly, Mother." Your father's voice is like a bark from next to you. "I'll stay home. I promise. Just come home with us."

Her slowing down and stopping. Your father working the brake pedal. And then her just standing there, looking ahead still, and the Buick stopped too with the headlights blazing and the engine idling, in front of the house where the Brockbanks live, the corner house where you turn to go down the long hill to school and into town.

"Call them back," she says. "Tell them you can't come tonight."

"I can't do that, Mother. Don't ask the impossible."

"Then it is over. To hell with you. You and your church."

She starts walking again.

"Okay. I will. Just come home. Please. I beg you."

And then she stops, and stands there, still looking straight ahead, and then she turns her face and looks at you.

"If I come home, Shakli, will you eat your supper?"

"So tell her yes," you hear your father whisper, hard and quick, when you've sat there too long thinking, thinking about eating the way your throat and stomach feel.

"Sure," you say.

"I made kidneys. With gravy and mashed potatoes."

The slight upturn of excitement in her voice has the hint of a quickening melody.

"Answer her," your father says.

"Sounds good."

"We'll make it warm again," she says.

"Okay."

"I can put your kidneys in a pan with a little gravy with the lid on to make them nice and warm and tender again."

"Okay."

"You were my first born."

"I know."

And then she turns, toward the Buick, opens the door behind you, and talks to your father across the back of your head.

"I am only doing this for the sake of the children."

You hear the suitcase bang through the door and then skitter a couple of times across the back seat. Feel the Buick take her weight when she gets in, settles herself, slams the door.

"Go now," your father says. "See to your brothers and sisters. See that they get home."

"Okay."

"They're right behind us."

You get out. The asphalt feels good through your shoes. Heat from underneath the Buick wells around your ankles. You bring the door against its latch. Nudge it to where it catches. The inside of the Buick goes black. You look back and see them, gathered on the street back from the rear of the Buick, Roy and Molly and Karl and Maggie, this loose cluster, their faces red from the dull burn of the brakelights, red ghosts, kids out trick or treating except for masks and candy bags. Maggie's arm is up where Molly has her by the hand. Roy his thumb in his mouth. Karl standing there. The red goes out and their faces dark as your father guns the Buick, swings it deep into the corner to turn around, and this time it's the slash of the headlights, blinding them, backing them out of the way, turning their scared faces blazing white before they go dark again when the Buick goes past. When you reach your brothers and sisters they're already moving, following the luminous river of the street, trusting the pale gray asphalt.

"You guys okay?"

"Maybe she's just going back to fill up the suitcase."

"No. She's gonna stay."

"How do you know?"

"I just know."

Ahead of you, where you can make out the black shape of your house, the garage door is dark and the porchlight on. Your father putting the empty suitcase back in its place in the garage. Your mother in the kitchen pulling out a frying pan. You at the kitchen table, just you, trying to find a way to eat what your mother warmed up for you the way your throat and stomach feel, knowing you'll have to clean your plate to keep her home, knowing what you'll look like to someone watching from the dark out back, out by the barrel where you burn trash off the edge of the yard.

CHAPTER 59

IN THE MORNING your legs and ribs and back hurt worse than they did yesterday. In the bathroom mirror you take off the bandage Doby's mother taped to your forehead. Where she painted it the skin is this almost neon red. Scabs of deeper red show the cuts and scratches you couldn't see yesterday. There's a blue and yellow streak in the skin below your eye. A cut in your chin that probably came from a ring. One side of your lip is puffed up like a mouse in the body of a snake. You flush off your face, wet and comb your hair, brush your teeth. The cut inside your lip is raw from the way the kidneys and gravy last night kept burning it. You were stupid to let your mouth get hit. Everything else is okay. The way it should be. What you did yesterday to earn it.

You tell your mother not to touch your face or cook you breakfast. You top off the tank on the Briggs & Stratton and hook the catcher on back. Flat crates of baby petunias are positioned along the flowerbeds where your father's on his knees, on a board, his radio going wild with violins, half a crate already set in limp rows in the dark soil. Around the circle his neighbors are getting their yards going. Hellos get hollered back and forth. Saturday morning, everything okay, last night gone the way water closes over the hole a diver leaves, the way air closes on the jagged gash that lightning cuts through it. Just your face. The evidence of your face and the hole where the bottom of your stomach used to be.

You cut both yards. The spring grass is lush and fierce and wet with dark green pungent juice. Dunes form from the clippings you dump in the field. Sweat burns the cuts and scratches in your forehead while you work. When you're done you ask your father what else he needs. He pushes himself to his feet. His hands are black. His face is red and vexed and sweaty and he looks at you surprised until he remembers why you look the way you do.

"Nothing," he says. "That's all."

The number's too faded to read but you don't need to read it. You've had it memorized so long you can close your eyes and see it fresh like Mr. Hinkle wrote it. Downstairs, in your father's den, you pick up the phone on his desk and dial. While the phone rings in your ear, you go up and down the alphabet of his flip-up directory, looking at names he's written under C and K and N.

"Hello?"

His voice on the phone. His voice like a thief inside your house. And then you don't know what his name is. Just the Professor.

"Who's calling?"

And then you wish you had a different name. Like Bill or Jimmy. One you wouldn't have to explain to him. A name from your father's directory. Nelson. Nordquist. Niederhauser.

"Shake," you say. "Shake Tauffler."

At Priesthood Meeting the next morning your father's friends give you the usual handshake and the usual grin of human steel while their eyes skate up and down your face. Some of them wince and then try to ignore what you look like. Others make lame tough guy jokes. It hurts your lips but you match them grin for grin. Across the roiling deep-voiced racket of the chapel you can see your father working while he talks to one or another brother. Brother Brockbank slaps him on the back. When you break for class, Jasperson and Lilly show up with their faces on, like this is just another Sunday. You've got yours on too.

Brother Clark takes a look at you just a second longer than usual before kicking off his lesson. You don't much listen. Just watch him. Wonder if he knows them, the jocks in the Jeep, if he taught them how to drive and signed their permits. And after class you're all outside, Doby and Yenchik and Strand and Lilly and Jasperson, West in his sunglasses. Blackwell for once. Keller too, bright-eyed, like all of this is news to him.

"You look like you got smacked with a shovel," says Yenchik.

"What happened?" says Blackwell.

"Four high school jocks," says Doby. "Football."

"You were playing football?" says Jasperson.

"We got in a fight with them," says Doby.

"Who?"

"Him and West and me."

"How come you guys don't look like him?" says Strand.

"He took them on," says Doby. And then, while your father's friends come out the glass doors, while the fellow soldiers of his army head for the parking lot to go home and fetch their families for Sunday School, Doby tells the story. He leaves Keller out.

"Brylcreem," says Lilly, smiling.

"With your head?" says Yenchik.

Doby looks hard at Keller. "You should of stuck around," he says. "After you started it."

"I didn't start anything," says Keller.

"Well, I hate to disagree, but you did," says Doby.

"You're full of it," says Keller, trying to organize his suddenly crazy freckled face around a laugh that comes out like a bark.

"And then ratted Shake out," says Doby. "And then took off."

They're all looking at Keller now.

"You ratted on Shake?" says Yenchik.

"Why not?" says Keller. "He's the one who did it."

"And then took off?"

"I wasn't gonna wait there like some stupid shit for it to be my turn," he says.

"A stupid shit's better than a chickenshit," says Yenchik.

"Had to save that pretty face, huh," says Blackwell.

"Least I didn't stand there bawling like a baby," Keller says, looking at Doby now.

"I stuck around," says Doby. "I got him home."

"Keller," says West. "You need to shut the fuck up."

"You shut the fuck up," says Keller.

"I'm telling you," says West. "You need to shut up."

Keller stares at West like he's seeing him for the first time. And then he darts his rabbit eyes back and forth across all of you.

"I thought you guys were my friends," he finally says.

Strand is working the patch on the back of his head with his tiny comb. "Takes one to be one," he says.

"You ever go back for your books?" says Doby.

"Screw all you guys," says Keller. He wheels around, bumps into Blackwell, goes back through the glass doors.

"Good riddance," says Lilly.

"West," says Yenchik. "Loan Shake your shades so he can hide that shiner."

"I don't need to hide it," you say.

"Here," says West. "Take 'em."

Things turn this charcoal green when you put them on, the faces of your buddies emerald ghosts, the old scared feeling of being a kid in Switzerland instead of being here.

"You busted a windshield with your head," says Yenchik, starting to grin.

"Just the driver's side."

"You coulda used the Priesthood," says Yenchik. "Instead of your head."

"You keep joking about the Priesthood, you're gonna lose it."

You look at Jasperson. His short sleeved shirt limp and dingy in the sunlight. His brown hair plastered down and parted crooked. In the human steel of his face the unbearable responsibility for everything Brother Rodgers and Brother Clark keep teaching you.

"There's your old man," says Blackwell.

The Buick noses into a parking stall. Your family climbs out. Maggie in a white dress that shows her chubby knees. Karl with a bow tie clipped to the collar of his shirt as if making him look like a present could take the scared mean look from Friday off his mouth. Your mother in a red dress. Her lips greased red. Molly wearing braids around the infusion of shame and retreat in her face for having wet her bed. Roy with his hair combed slick as though a comb could rid his face of its open bewilderment. Everyone's shoes shined. Everyone ready.

You pass the Sacrament to your mother's organ music. You can feel your father caged in the congregation somewhere. Lloyd Wacker is out there too. You pass shreds of Wonder Bread and paper thimbles of water to faces that turn your way wherever you turn your own. Your face. Little kids stare up at you. Mothers look at you alarmed but it's Sunday School and there's nothing they can do. Your mouth hurts. The scabs on your forehead itch. The clean defiant feel. In class, from across the room, the girls stare like you're incapable of staring back. Susan Lake's mouth comes partway open, and her eyes go big, and then when they go soft again they're like medicine, like a warm wet washcloth drawing all the hurt and itching out, like magic hands that can touch and heal anything they look at.

Brother Rodgers comes in, reads through his roll book, closes it, looks up and across the boy's side of the class.

"Anyone know where Keller is?"

He waits for an answer. Then he stands up and looks at you hard with his chrome blue eyes while you remember the way he came after you for ruining an engine.

"I hear you took on some real bullies," he says.

"High school football players," he says, when you don't say anything. "Four of them."

"Yeah."

"Because of what they did to your friend."

And then he just keeps looking while you sit there, getting nervous, wondering where he plans on taking you, what he's got in store for you when he gets you there.

"You've been the talk of the ward all morning," he says.

Here it comes, you think, in front of Susan Lake again.

"Don't look down, Shake. I'm talking to you."

And there are his eyes again, where you left them, gentle and stern.

"Your dad should be real proud."

You search his unsmiling face. And then you look down just long enough to ride out the punishing lash of his sarcasm before you look up again.

"I told him that this morning," he says.

"What?"

"How proud he should be." And then he says, "A few of the brethren did."

Your face catches fire. You look down at your hands without seeing them.

"I'm serious. I couldn't be any prouder. And I'm just your Sunday School teacher."

CHAPTER 60

BY MONDAY morning most of the neon has faded off your forehead. Your eye still looks the same and there's still a hard small knot in your lip but the puffy look is gone. In the garage you take your trumpet out. It hurts at first, your lip stretched tight across the hard bowl of the mouthpiece, but that afternoon you're on your bike.

His house is down on Second East, two streets up from Main Street, in the older part of town where the trees are bigger, where there are sidewalks, where the sidewalks are square plates of old cement, heaved up and cracked in places next to trees, and your trumpet case teeters and skids in the wire basket bracketed to the handlebars. His small house is dark red brick with a heavy green roof that shadows the deep porch across the front. Two windows in the roof have their own small roofs built over them. A blue Pontiac stands in the driveway off the side. A small sprinkler sends a sparkling bloom of water into the warm still air. Along the front of the porch are flowerbeds, not the petunias your father and his neighbors plant, more like the flowers Mrs. Harding had.

You swing off your bike and bump it up the steps to the porch and lean it against the low brick wall in front of the steel frame of a porch swing with its cushions gone. The shaded air feels cool. There's a mat in front of the door made of black rubber ribs. There's no doorbell. Just a screen door with a black handle, a faded black tin mailbox, a label with a handprinted name. Donald Selby. The screen door rattles when you knock. You hear the knob turn. Watch the screen pulse inward when the door behind it pulls back. See the ghost of a hand come forward and reach for the handle to the screen. You want it to be his wife or kid because suddenly you're not ready. Air comes out the door, the smell of air, old like sanding varnish off used wood. And then it's not his wife or kid.

"You must be Shake."

This face. This old guy's face. These gray eyes and this calm and alert and quiet strictness in the webbed and crosshatched lines in the skin around them. This broad flat solid face built like an Indian's face except it's white, lined and soft and settled in, the lines not fresh and raw like your father's but quiet, like ancient lines in sandstone, like whatever put them there was a thousand years ago, white where the finely ridged skin of his forehead crosses what used to be a hairline into the polished skin of his scalp. The white hair left on the sides is short, his beard cut close, like short white grass, around the whole bottom of his face and up into the ledged plates of his cheeks. His lips in this unparted calm expectant smile that makes his eyes and the rest of his face look like they could be friendly too. You're not sure. You don't know. It's all you see. All you see of what he thinks of you while his eyes take in the way your own face looks.

"Yes," you say. And wait for him to make a joke out of your name.

"Well," he says. "I'm Mr. Selby. Come in."

He's not tall. Not lanky like Mr. Hinkle. Built more like your father, but not as restless, the way he stands back slightly on his heels like that's where he's comfortable. He's wearing this short sleeved shirt, plaid, tiny red and yellow squares with thin green lines, and a blue tie with a bright green parrot painted on it. Maybe you should have dressed up too, clipped your bow tie on, put on your corduroys like him.

"Is my bike okay there?"

"Where?"

"Over there."

When he turns his head to look where you're pointing, he moves with this easy precision, not more than he has to move to see it.

"What do you mean okay?" he says.

"Just parked there."

"Oh," he says. "No. It's fine."

You stand there. He can't look at you and tell. The questions you've come here with. The chafed piece of wood in front of your shoes where his house starts. Where all the answers are.

"Come in," he says, reaching for your shoulder, standing back to give you room to go ahead. "Let's see what you've got."

CHAPTER 61

THE ROOM where he gives lessons is the living room of his house. A short upright piano stands against the back wall. On the piano there's the same pyramid-shaped metronome your mother has on hers. In the wall to the right there's a brick fireplace. The bricks along the top are licked black, you realize, from fire. A window on either side of the chimney looks out on his Pontiac. Shelves filled with sheet music and record albums run below the windows. There's an old desk along the front wall, its top even with the sill of the front window, a teacher's desk, a desk with drawers. A staircase with a banister goes up the wall to the left to rooms upstairs.

And from where you stand, just inside the front door, there are private things you know you're probably not supposed to notice. A coffee mug. A small bowl of steel marbles. A ring of splayed keys on his desk. A little grizzly bear statue and a little frame with an army medal on the rock shelf of his fireplace. A model fighter plane hung from the silver nut that holds the wavy glass bowl for the ceiling light in place. The way everything feels old, worn in, here for a long time, long enough to settle in with all the other things around it.

"Go on in," he says behind you. "I need to finish a conversation. I'll be back. Just make yourself at home."

He goes through the door out to the kitchen where you can see the spindled back of a chair, the edge of a metal table, a refrigerator with a round top flanked by light green cupboards, a light blue linoleum floor. You step into the center of the room. The polished floor is bare. The only things upholstered are the mushroom seat of the piano stool and the squashed brown cushion of his desk chair.

A gray cat with sleepy yellow eyes looks down on you through two spindled railings from the stairs. But the wall below the stairs has already caught your attention. It's covered with photographs in frames. You go closer. Musicians. Musicians with saxophones and trombones and pianos and drums and guitars. Most of them are autographed. You don't try to read what they say. Most of them are men. Most of them are Negro.

"I see you found my gallery."

You can't stop looking. Some of them with thin sharp moustaches. Others with goatees. Some with frizzy hair and some with their hair slicked back in shiny waves. Some on stage with microphones with their faces gleaming in the lights. Some with the standup violins you were stupid enough to think were for giants. Fierce faces. Some look kind. All different. The face of the Negro girl in Blackwell's National Geographic. The speech you heard in the stakehouse whose jigsaw puzzle pieces Yenchik told you how to put together. Yenchik saying nigger and you not saying anything because you knew he didn't mean it bad. You can't stop looking. It cuts through you, this flash behind your eyes like nothing afterward will be the same, and then it's gone, and nobody's noticed anything.

"Who are they?" you say.

"This one," Mr. Selby says, pointing to a young Negro playing a long saxophone. "Erik Dolphy. One heck of an improviser. Full of surprises. Nobody can touch him on flute."

"He plays flute?"

"Oh, yes."

And then he starts pointing at photographs, giving you names, names you try to memorize like the names of the dead men you were baptized for.

"Ornette Coleman. Totally free improvisation. Charlie Parker. Yardbird. King of bebop. Clifford Brown. Beautiful trumpet player. He died just a year ago in a car accident. Tragic. Only twenty-five. Let's see. Sonny Rollins. Another great sax player. Oscar Peterson. Ron Carter. Here we go. Errol Garner. You know the song Misty?"

"Yes."

"He wrote it. But you must know this gentleman."

An older elegant looking Negro with a sad smile and heavily bagged gentle eyes wearing a white tuxedo and tie at a piano.

"No."

"That's Duke Ellington. The Duke. He wrote some astonishing songs. I'm sure you've heard them."

"Do you know him?" you say.

"I worked with him once," he says.

"Do you know all of them?"

"Most of them," he says.

"I know this one."

"Louis Armstrong."

"I saw him on tv."

"Okay," he says. "It's time to see what you can do. Let's get that trumpet out."

He has you open the case on one of the low shelves next to his fireplace. He has you step out into the room. He asks if you need the music stand. You ask what he wants you to play.

"Anything. Just to see where we are."

"Scales?"

"If you know them," he says, standing back against the fireplace.

Before now, nowhere except for the sandpit, the place up the hill, the garage. Now in this new place, in the middle of this living room that isn't one, you bring your trumpet up, hit the first note, the sound so quick and loud and ringing that you stop.

"What's wrong?"

"I didn't know it would be that loud. Sorry."

"Don't worry. I want you to play for all you're worth."

And so you run your trumpet through a couple of scales the way you've figured how to play them.

"Okay." He folds his arms. "What else have we got?"

"Songs?"

"Let's hear one."

Before now, never for anyone, except for your brothers and sisters when they came wandering into the garage. Now for this man you called, the Professor, wearing a tie like it's someone else's house and he's just visiting, back against the fireplace, where the little grizzly bear looks out across his shoulder. I Loves You Porgy.

"Sorry."

For a couple of botched notes not far into the song that make your face burn.

"Don't be nervous," he says. "Take your time. Close your eyes. Breathe. You'll get it."

And so you close your eyes and go back to where you were when you figured out the notes and learned the song you'd heard your mother play. Your place up on the hill above the sandpit. How keeping them closed you can stand there underneath his model airplane and play the song all the way through. You open them and let your trumpet down.

"You're not exactly a beginner, are you," he finally says.

"I know all the stuff in that book."

You pointing to the book where you left it next to your case on the shelf. Him turning his head to look.

"Okay," he says. "How about your range?"

"I can play all the notes in the back of the book."

"Oh. You mean the fingering chart."

"Yeah. Should I show you?"

"Let's just hear them."

Starting from the bottom, the big fat notes you have to flood with air, then going up, narrowing and speeding up the flow, catching a quick pull of air at high C, then following the C scale up another octave.

"G above double C," he says, after you bring your trumpet down. "How long have you been playing?"

"Since after Thanksgiving."

"So six months." A little smile where his beard and moustache make a clearing for his mouth. A change of light in his eyes. He rubs his beard. You don't know how he means six months. You look at the floor to keep from seeing the little grizzly bear across his shoulder.

"Why don't you blow the water out before we go on."

"Okay. I'll be right back."

"From where?"

"Outside."

"Hold on." He goes to his desk, takes a folded white handkerchief out of a drawer, shakes it open, hands it to you. "Use this."

You stand there afterward, not knowing what to do with his handkerchief, wet with your spit now.

"It's yours," he says. "Just keep it in your back pocket, where it's handy. Let's hear how your tongue is."

The two machine guns Mr. Hinkle taught you. The exhaust stack of the cattle truck. Your breath the black smoke, your tongue the flapper, light, just a quick slice through the running flow of air. After you've done them both he puts his hand up.

"What else can you show me?"

Songs left to pick from. Someone to Watch over Me. Over the Rainbow. It Ain't Necessarily So. And the trick where you keep the valves the same, start with the low note, then just barely tighten down your lips, blow just a beat faster, and there's that tiny pulse where the trumpet skips up on its own, a rock across a pond, five notes, four notes, two notes, up across two octaves. Your lip has started hurting, the cut deep down inside it, but you've kept going.

"Harmonics," he says afterward.

"Harmonics?"

"Yes." He goes over and picks up your book, looks at the stiff streaked weatherbeaten cover where his name and number used to be, turns through its warped pages.

"You didn't know that," he says. And then absently turns another couple of pages. "Well. I'm glad your teacher left me something."

He closes your book, flaps it slowly against his other hand like a stiff rag out of a dry washbucket, puts it down, stands there by the shelf in front of the window to his driveway, looks at you. In his gray eyes you can see him thinking about asking you who your teacher was. You want to run your tongue across the cut inside your lip because it burns and tastes like blood but you hold still. Don't move. Because then you'd have to either lie or tell him everything. The mouthpiece so cold it burned. The valves iced up with spit. Always the wild feeling that no matter how good you thought it sounded, you were doing everything wrong, and that maybe it didn't matter anyway, because you'd always be the only one around to hear it.

"Six months," him finally saying. "I don't know what he did to get you there that fast. But I'll tell you, he gave us a heck of a head start on the rest of it."

"I want to know what I'm doing wrong."

"Don't worry. I'll let you know when that happens."

"I mean now."

He just looks at you. And then he turns around, squats down, pulls a thick book out of a shelf, gets up again, comes over to where you're standing, holds the book where both of you can see the cover. Arban's Complete Conservatory Method for Trumpet.

"Here. Take a look. Let me hold your trumpet."

Fat, hefty, most of its hundreds of pages dense with notes, exercises where crowded notes race crazily in steps and ladders and sawtoothed runs up and down the lines of the treble cleft. You look at the cover again.

"Is this someone? Arban?"

"He was a music professor at the Paris Conservatory, oh, a hundred years ago now. His book is still the standard. It's to trumpet players what the Bible is to preachers. Once you master it, you can call yourself a trumpet player with the best of them."

"The whole thing?"

"Well, hopefully, right to the end," he says. "I know. It looks tough all at once. But look at it the way you do a phone book. You don't open it thinking you've got to call every number in it. Just one at a time. Don't worry. We'll work through it together."

The mouthpiece cold. The way the stars came out. Most of all the questions. You look up from the book in your hands.

"You'll be my teacher?"

Holding your trumpet, looking at you, the skin between his eyebrows tensing into a hundred tiny intricate lines.

"I'll teach you everything I know," he finally says. And he nods toward the wall below the stairs where all the photographs are. "And then I'll teach you everything they know."

Part 7

The Scoutmaster's Wife

CHAPTER 62

THE WAY he heard you play. Afterward, the ring of your notes still infused the air of the room, like what happens after rain, like they'd left everything bright and fresh and shimmering. And then that sudden cut through everything the way it was. It was when Mr. Selby stood there and just looked at you when you asked if he'd be your teacher and the skin between his eyebrows tensed into a hundred tiny intricate lines. In the choiring of those lines you thought you saw surprise. Maybe other stuff. And maybe something else. The wild inkling of the possibility that he might be thinking you were good.

Pride had knifed through you. And then, when it was gone, and everything was supposed to just go on like it had never happened, this cry from down inside, for your father, to be there, to be proud too, to say okay, to come with you. This time, after that knifing cut was gone and everything was just supposed to go on happening, nothing was the same. Nothing had anything to do with him. You were going where you'd never been. You were on your own. You were scared. Maybe you didn't belong here. It didn't matter. Nothing would be the same.

After he tells you what he'll teach you he asks how old you are. Almost thirteen. And then what you know about jazz. Nothing. If you've heard much of it. The line on the truck radio. What Mr. Hinkle played in his store. Maybe some of the music you heard from the music room. But what you heard from the music room didn't have that sound like it could fly. So you tell him maybe. He throws some names at you to see if you know them. Blues. All you can think of is sad. Swing. All you know is that he doesn't mean a regular swing. Bebop. You've heard of bop. Improvisation. Intervals. Diminished. Augmented. Modulation. Chord progression. Resolution. No. No. No. He tells you not to worry. They're just names. You'll get to them. He wants to know if you've ever played with anyone. You know he doesn't mean train horns or your mother. Not really, you tell him.

"You don't take band," he says, not like a question, more like the answer he expects.

"No."

"Okay," he finally says. "Let's talk business. How does Tuesday afternoon sound?"

"For lessons?"

"Yes. Say two o'clock. Are you free then?"

"Sure."

"Okay. This is Monday. We'll skip tomorrow. We'll wait a week to get started."

"Wait?"

"Your lip's hurt," he says. "It needs to heal."

How he could tell. If blood has come up where he can see it. If it's on your mouthpiece.

"Okay."

"I don't want you to play at all before next Tuesday. You'll tear it up. We'll call that your first lesson. A lesson in patience. In fact, if you don't mind, you might leave your trumpet here till then. Just in case you're tempted."

"Here?"

"It'll be safe."

"I didn't mean that."

"Are you worried you'll forget how to play?"

"No."

"We need to let your lip heal. Next week we'll get you started on those exercises."

"Okay."

"Have any jazz records?"

"No."

"A record player?"

"Yes."

"Does it play albums? Big records?"

"Yes."

"What you're going to do this week is listen. I'll loan you a couple of albums. I want you to listen and listen and listen. All you can."

"Okay."

"So I'll have your trumpet and you'll have my albums. Collateral."

You don't understand the word but you tell him okay.

"Now. Tell me what happened to your face."

Almost a year ago your father brought home a big radio and record player cabinet and set it up in the living room. The portable record player he used in La Sal to play Rigoletto and his other operas was left the way he packed it, bundled in an old sheet tied with string, and shelved in the new garage. It's yours now. That afternoon you set it up on the workbench and find a plug and look at the albums Mr. Selby sent you home with. Clifford Brown with Strings. The Genius of Charlie Parker. In the photographs on their cardboard album jackets both men are Negro. But Clifford Brown is playing a trumpet in flame red light. And among the songs listed in white letters in the stark black shadow of his trumpet's open bell are songs you know already. Laura. Blue Moon. Can't Help Lovin That Man.

Violins play an introduction. You keep it low. The needle is old and the sound from the small speaker thin and scratchy and remote. And then it startles you to hear it, when the needle suddenly sets free the first clear notes of Laura, when they suddenly break free of the violins and soar off on their own, that steel bird sound again. Startles you because this time you know what you have to do to make it. Because you can look at Clifford Brown's fingers laced around the casings and holding the valves in what could be an F, look at his lips stretched tight across the mouthpiece, and know what you look like, playing the same thing. Like Clifford Brown took your trumpet out of your hands and said this is how you do it. This is how you play this big shot thing called jazz. And nothing will ever be the way it was before again.

CHAPTER 63

IN JULY, your face healed, not much left but the story, they pack all of you into station wagons, you and your buddies and the older scouts and now some younger ones, and head you north through Wyoming toward a town called Pinedale for a week of camping on Fremont Lake. All your tents and sleeping bags and stoves and other gear make the ride in the back of Brother Kieffer's pickup truck. Brother Kieffer's one of the men who help Scoutmaster Haycock out with the scouts. Hitched to the back of his pickup truck is Brother Swenson's motor boat. Brother Swenson's another one of the men who help Scoutmaster Haycock out. You make the ride in Brother Reid's big station wagon. He's another one. And another one is Earl Bird. He makes the ride in Brother Kieffer's pickup.

The men cook. You spend the days fishing and swimming and hiking and doing scout stuff and water skiing behind Brother Swenson's boat. The nights around a campfire roasting wieners and marshmallows and singing and listening to stories. You start and end each day with prayer. You share a tent with West and Yenchik. One night, out of your tent and in the dark in the woods to take a pee, you hear them talking over the high night breeze in the pines, one voice quiet, trying to coax the other voice more quiet too.

"He's a good man."

"Not saying he's not. Just kisses too much ass for my taste."

"There's no need to talk like that."

Through the trunks of the trees, they're in silhouette, standing with their backs to you in the low red glow of the campfire they're letting die. From their voices, from the way the sides of their faces gleam where the dying light just grazes them, you know them. Scoutmaster Haycock and Earl Bird. You finish peeing and put your pud back in your underpants.

"You're telling me you haven't seen it," says Earl Bird.

"I'm saying he's a good man."

"I want to spit on him sometimes. Just to see if he'll get mad. Or just stand there with that ass kissing grin and thank me."

"Come on, Earl," Scoutmaster Haycock says.

" 'It's good to see you, by golly. What can I do to help you?' "

And then you recognize that a third man has joined the conversation. Your father. His voice. His accent. His way of talking. Only it isn't him. It's Earl Bird making fun of him. Your stomach goes cold.

"Take it easy," says Scoutmaster Haycock. "He can't help his accent."

"Maybe that's part of it," says Bird. "That kraut accent. Still makes me think of being over there."

Big bad Earl Bird. The big beefy baggy hulking guy with a thick brown crewcut down into his forehead and a head like a bull and this leathery face and these dull mean eyes when he doesn't think anyone important's looking. A tank mechanic in World War II in France. The little dark-haired French wife Nicky he brought home with him. A bus mechanic until three of his fingers got mashed and had to be amputated. Barber college after his fingers healed. Hairdos now at Grant's Hair Styling, where his French wife Nicky works, where she got him a job. Their house three houses away around the bottom of the circle. Her always out puttering in her flowerbeds. Him always with this surly sullen look like the war's not over yet, like living with Nicky keeps making him think he's still in France, this warning look like you'd better not mess with him, the way he must have looked at Germans. Swear words combined in elaborate ways you've never heard before when he yells at Nicky and his kids. Nicky with sunglasses or red eyes sometimes when you wheel your bike around the bottom of the circle and she looks up from the flowerbed around her mailbox. This far from home. Mocking your father.

"He's Swiss," Scoutmaster Haycock says. "Not German."

"I just wonder why we need a foreigner teaching us Adult Gospel."

"He's a fine teacher. He puts a lot into his lessons."

"You know what I'm saying, Ron."

"No, Earl, I don't. You married a foreigner. Your own wife's got an accent."

"You seen him at church. Toadying up to people. Makes me sick. Bet if I slugged him, he'd stand there shaking like a leaf, bleeding, then thank me."

"Why would you slug him?"

"By golly, Earl." Bird doing your father again. "That was quite a punch, by golly. Look. I'm even bleeding."

Bird laughs like he just told himself a dirty joke. Scoutmaster Haycock pokes a stick at the fire, raises a geyser of sparks, like he's there all by himself, and then tosses the stick across the fire out into the dark. "Listen," he says. "I'm tired. I've got a kid who just found out he's adopted. I need to sit up with him. Let's call it quits."

The kid who just found out he was adopted was Keller. It was after supper. You and your buddies and some older scouts were hanging out on some boulders down by the lake. An older scout named Huber just came out with it. Keller was doing what he did best, pissing someone off, and it was Huber, and Huber finally said it.

"Hey. At least I'm not adopted."

"Me either," Keller said.

And Huber just stared at him. And then said, "Shit, Keller. I'm really sorry."

And then, from Huber's face, from his apology, from the way nobody else said anything, Keller knew that it was true, screeched, and took off running, hollering for Scoutmaster Haycock.

"Shit," said Yenchik.

"I thought he knew," said Huber. "I feel like crap."

"I thought he did too," said West.

"Me too," said an older scout.

"I guess we all did," said Lilly.

"How come we all knew," says West, "but he didn't?"

"His dad and mom shoulda told him."

"This is a shit way to find out. Without his dad around."

"Explains why he doesn't have an English accent like his dad."

"Explains a lot," says West.

"Take it easy," says Lilly. "He just found out."

And now Scoutmaster Haycock is telling Bird the same thing. Take it easy. He's a good man. He can't help his accent.

"Ever hear the empty veenie story?" Bird saying.

"Empty what?"

"His old lady."

"Elizabeth?"

"Yeah." And laughs dirty again. "Please may I have an empty veenie. You must of heard that one. It made the rounds."

It's your mother's voice this time.

"I don't think so," Scoutmaster Haycock says.

"The ward barbecue last year. Beck's doing hot dogs. I'm next to him passing out corn on the cob. She comes up with her paper plate and asks Beck for an empty weenie. Please may I have an empty veenie? That's what she says. He asks her what she means. Just an empty veenie, she says. Beck hands her a bun with nothing in it. That's not it. She wants just the opposite. Just the wiener without the bun. He finally gets it." Bird laughs again. "I near peed my pants. Please may I have an empty veenie."

"Your wife's got an accent, right?" Scoutmaster Haycock says, his voice dark. "French?"

You watch Bird look at him slow. And then down into the embers.

"I'll get the fire out," he finally says.

You were there, right behind her, while Brother Beck used tongs to place a wiener on her white plate, while Bird used tongs to fish a corn cob out of his pot for you. If she moved ahead and kept her smile innocent but knew. Could feel Bird mocking her like fire on her back. Scoutmaster Haycock walks out of reach of the firelight. You sneak back to your tent and lie sleepless in your bag. Your father being slugged. You hate Bird. You wonder if he's right, if your father would stand there bleeding and compliment him, and you hate him more. Hate him so bad it scares you. Because there's still your mother to hate him for. Because maybe this is what your father meant when he talked about a train station in the middle of nowhere with danger all around you in the dark.

In the morning Brother Reid drives Keller home. By then you're not scared. You've got it figured out. You can't beat Bird up. You can't tell him what you heard in front of other scouts. They might say he's right. Because like Keller, not knowing he was adopted, your father may be the only man who doesn't know what he comes across like. Forget your mother. So all you can do with Bird is dog him. Let him know you're there the way you did the man with the bulldozer from the edge of Mrs. Harding's yard. Dog him the next two days, and on the day you leave, and they need a volunteer to ride in the pickup truck because they've lost a station wagon, it's you who makes the ride home between Bird and Brother Kieffer.

CHAPTER 64

CRICKETS. They came in hordes. The Saints had been in the valley less than a year. That winter they'd started plowing and planting crops. Wheat and corn and garden vegetables. Beans, squash, cucumbers, melons. Then, when everything began to sprout and grow, huge black crickets came from out of nowhere and started eating everything. They came by the millions, thousands of tons of them, so many you could hear them eating, their munching a shrill and shrieking chorus. The Saints tried killing them with hoes and rakes and shovels. They set fires to their fields. Finally, overwhelmed and in despair, they fell to their knees in their ruined fields and prayed.

That was when the seagulls came, from the Great Salt Lake, out of the west from the desert, thousands of them, a roiling cloud that blotted out the sun, darkened the sky, swooped down on the fields, and started eating crickets. They ate until they filled their bellies. Then they flew to some creek or to the Jordan River where they got a drink and threw up everything they'd eaten. Then they came back and filled their bellies again, and went back and threw up again, over and over, and when all the crickets were gone the seagulls left the way they'd come.

The Saints named it the Miracle of the Gulls. They built the Seagull Monument on Temple Square. They surrounded the monument with a shallow pool whose turquoise water sparkles copper from the field of pennies on the bottom. They made the seagull the Utah State Bird. They made it illegal to kill one.

Sometimes they visit the circle, wheel high overhead, touch down on the asphalt, tuck in their wings, hop around like pecking chickens. Your mother lets you take the heels off her loaves of Wonder Bread, tear pieces off, toss them out to where the seagulls come swooping down for them, like you're passing them the Sacrament. Blackwell tells you he knew a guy who would take his fishing pole, wad bread around the hook, cast the line into the street, let a seagull come down and take and swallow it and fly away again. One afternoon a seagull drops a long white spiraling line that gleams in the sun like a silver necklace, and Molly goes running out into the circle to get it.

Later that afternoon your father comes home in a brand new Chevy station wagon with a turquoise body and a white roof. He leaves it in the driveway. From inside the garage, you hear an engine, not the Buick, hear it die, wonder who it is before you go outside. Brother Leatham comes ambling down across your yard. Woody Stone comes across the circle on his long loose skinny legs, strips off his gardening gloves, bends over the fender, puts his head under the hood while the fingers of his gloves look like they're trying to climb out the back pocket of his dark green pants. Earl Bird's rat Mercury sits in his driveway. You watch his house till Woody Stone goes back across the circle. You call West.

"Did he get a V8?" he wants to know.

"Yeah."

"Your dad? You sure?"

"I looked. Eight spark plugs."

"That's cool. Stick or automatic?"

"Automatic."

"That's all my dad buys too."

After supper your father takes you out to Pace's Dairy Ann. Riding in back, you don't sink into the fat cloth couch that was the back seat of the Buick, but sit up straight instead, like church, almost level with your mother, your head there in the passenger window when the station wagon moves in a long reflected ripple across the windows of the stores. Karl goes after Molly for chasing out into the circle to catch the falling spiral of a necklace sparkling in the sunlight.

"No," your mother says. "She didn't."

"Yeah. I saw her. She went running out to get it."

"What did you think it was, sweetheart?" From the front seat your mother half turns her head to look at Molly next to you.

"A necklace," you say.

"A necklace?" Your mother looks at your father with this nasty scolding shade of ridicule in her smile. "What would a seagull do with a necklace?"

"It looked like a necklace," you say.

"It looked like seagull crap," says Karl.

"So!" your father says.

Earlier that afternoon you watched her. Everything was there in her face. How stupid you could tell she knew she'd made herself look when she made her way back from chasing what she thought was a necklace.

In her face, between her obedient braids where shame withered the way she wanted to look like nothing happened, like there had never been the mistaken anticipation of finding a necklace, like trying to smile for a photograph with a spoon of vinegar in her mouth too punishing to swallow, her skinny legs unsure the way yours were in the dust of Manny's pickup truck in the face of your father's camera.

Karl wants chocolate. Molly wants strawberry. Roy wants chocolate too, until Karl calls him a copycat, and then vanilla, like your mother gets for her and Maggie. You get black cherry. You eat your cones in the parking lot in front. Molly walks across the line from the shade of the building into the light of the sunset and stands out by the sidewalk in her braids and ribbons and little dress, licking her cone, while cars and trucks drive past her out on Main Street. There's this loose nervous fear in your back and legs. This fear like the time she walked too close to the edge of the sandstone hill your father sometimes used to stop and let you play on. This fear like that afternoon, when she came to the garage, stood there while you finished the scale you were playing, then asked if you could play Jesus Wants Me for a Sunbeam.

Down the next block, across the street, the windows of Hinkle Music are glazed this fiery red. In your head you can see the sunset stain the long wood floor while Mr. Hinkle reaches up and dusts the bassoon up on the wall behind the counter. You've done your part. Not gone back. Shame keeps you back in the shade. You want to go out, take Molly by the hand, bring her back too, but the chance is there that he might come out and look up the street and see you. Soon she turns around and comes back on her own, squinting, blind, her legs uncertain again, looking into the furnace blaze of the sunset for where the rest of you are standing. Then it's time to go.

"No, children. No ice cream in the car."

"I'm not done."

"Me either."

"Take another lick. Then we have to go."

"Two licks."

"I can bite mine. Look."

"So. Hurry. I have things to do."

"What should I do with it?"

"Here. Let me have it."

On the ride home that night from Pace's Dairy Ann you wonder what Mr. Hinkle would think if you told him you were finally seeing the Professor. If it would make a difference. By the time you're home you've decided to tell your father and mother before they hear it from someone else. At the dining room table they're going through the papers for their Chevy V8 station wagon.

"I've got a trumpet teacher."

"Yes, Shakli." Your mother takes on that unfocused look where her eyes and mouth seem to float in the pool of her face. "Who is it?"

"Mr. Selby." And then you say, "He's a professor at the university."

"Brigham Young?" you father's quick to say.

"The University of Utah."

"But how do you go to the university, Shakli?"

"I don't. I go to his house."

"Ah," she says. "You go to his house." And her face goes lost as she looks to your father.

"Where does he live?" your father says.

"On Second East."

"Is he LDS?"

"I don't think so. He's from New York."

"And we're from Switzerland," your father says. "It means nothing where you're from."

"He's not Mormon."

"Oh, Shakli."

"You couldn't find a teacher who was?"

"I didn't look."

"Why would a university professor take the time to teach you?"

His rough face waiting for an answer. With his brand new Chevy station wagon waiting to see what you have. Looking at him you try not to hear Earl Bird's dirty imitation.

"I pay him to."

And then, watching him work through different answers to get to the right one, you wish you could tell him about Earl Bird. Not so he'd do anything. Just so he'd know enough to look out for himself.

"If he's a professor," he finally says, "that's what you should call him. Not Mr. Selby. Pay him some respect too."

The Buick's just gone. You don't know where. All your father says is that he traded it in. Just the stains left by its engine on the concrete where you practice. Just the sharp thorny feel of crumbs on your fingertips when you stuck them down into the crack between the bench and the backrest, fishing for coins.

CHAPTER 65

OVER THE COURSE of the summer you turn thirteen. Keep spending Sunday mornings listening to Brother Clark and Brother Rodgers. Keep working Old Man Tuttle's fields and then, when the trees come due, start on Charley Bangerter's orchards. Keep coming home from work to the closed garage where you listen to the records Mr. Selby sends you home with. One Friday, when you're done working and Old Man Tuttle pays you, you ride into town, spend money on a piece of leather the size of a towel, some lacing, two buckles that come with rivets. That night and when you've got time on Saturday you get to work. Cut the leather to size. Leave a border. Mark rows of holes. Take a hammer and nail and punch the marks through. Fold the leather over. Weave the lacing through the holes. Cut two belts from the leather that's left, rivet the buckles into the ends, punch holes in the other ends, cut slits in the back of the pouch, run the belts through them. By Saturday afternoon you're done. A pouch with a flap for a lid and belts to strap it to your back. You slip one of your father's records inside, strap it on, not tight but loose to keep the curve of your back from bending Mr. Selby's records, take a test ride.

Roy catches you when you roll back down the driveway into the garage. He's got his new trike on its side. He gets up off his knees, holding a screwdriver, while you put your bike on its kickstand.

"What're you doing?" you say.

"How did you get your fenders off?" he says.

"You want yours off too?"

"Yeah."

"Okay."

"Will you show me how to race?" he says.

"Race?"

"Out in the field. Like you."

You haven't done the field since last summer sometime. But now you remember looking back across it to your house. Finding Roy standing there at the edge of the yard next to the incinerator. Barely as tall as the barrel. Not much bigger than a fire hydrant, and about as motionless, just standing there watching you and Blackwell go hurling around the track where weeds have started taking over.

"Sure."

"Good."

You slip the straps off your arms and lay the pouch across the string-tied canvas rolls of a couple of sleeping bags on a shelf.

"What's that?"

"Just a pouch." You grab the crescent wrench and pliers off the nails they're hanging from the shelf to the side of the workbench.

"What's it for?"

"Just for work. Don't tell anybody."

"Okay."

"I'll put your fenders back on if you do."

"Are you a mailman?"

"Naw."

You take him out to the field and have him follow you around while you try to make out the old track in the weeds. Once you've got it down, you take him around again, and then again to crush the weeds more, give him a clearer path to follow, help him remember it. When you can watch him ride it once on his own, still wobbling but starting to grin, you let him go, head back inside, make the call for Sunday shoes, lay newspaper out on the kitchen table, break out the wooden box with all the brushes and socks and flat little cans of polish. You get a rack for the back of your bike and work out how to lash your trumpet case to ride snug behind the seat using clothesline rope from the bundle your father keeps rolled and tied on a nail. On Tuesdays you head for Mr. Selby's house.

Your lesson starts as soon as you're inside. Warm up your lips. Then the mouthpiece. When you buzz just your bare lips, he does his too, along with you, tells you to watch the way he's doing his while his gray eyes watch the way you're doing yours. Guides you up, high as you can go, this thin sharp zinging line like a kite string burning through your fingers, then down, down low, where you're flooding air into the mouthpiece, big and slow, the sound fat and round where it wants to come welling back into your mouth and down into your lungs again.

Then finally the trumpet. He opens the piano. Hits and holds B flat, like Mr. Hinkle did, like you've done, while you blow middle C and move the tuning slide until the two sounds come together to a single sound, like railroad tracks in the distance just before they vanish. You work on scales and intervals and arpeggios. In front of the music stand, the Arban book open, you play through the exercises he circled a week ago. You work on attack. Duration. Pitch and quality. He does everything with you. Stands right there next to you and plays along. Sometimes his gray cat Theo wanders in and rubs your leg and goes shambling off to another room or the kitchen. When you're done with last week's exercises, Mr. Selby rifles pages back and forth, stops and ponders, checks off a new set, shows you how to play them. And then you work on a song. Work on it in pieces, on phrasing it, on learning where it will let you grab more air without interrupting it.

He tells you to never eat or drink before you play because what you put in your mouth will end up in your trumpet. But after every lesson he brings a bottle of milk and a couple of glasses and a plate of homemade cookies from the kitchen, slides the wooden typewriter tray out from the front of his desk, sets things down, sits in his wooden swivel chair, pours the milk, has you roll the piano stool across the floor and sit across the other side of the tray from him. Oatmeal and raisin. Chocolate chip. Peanut butter. Brownies. Sometimes they're fresh because you can smell them when you walk in for your lesson. Sometimes they're still warm.

He tells you early on how important it is to play with musicians. You've heard it too, what you've been doing wrong, from the records he's been loaning you, how they play in time and rhythm, how they harmonize, how they take turns, step forward to solo and then drop back for someone else. Alone in the closed garage, the record player going on the workbench, listening to them play off each other, you've heard it too. How all you've done is play alone. You've gone and thought you needed to play hard and fast and all the time because the music would stall and die if you didn't.

"So tell me again why you're not taking band."

"I don't know."

"That's not a reason."

"I wanted to wait till I knew how to play."

"You didn't think you were good enough."

"I guess. Maybe."

"Did your teacher tell you that?"

"No."

"Did he tell you how important it was to play with other musicians?"

"No."

"A trumpet's a band instrument. Not like a piano or guitar. He didn't tell you that?"

"No."

"I've never asked," he says, "but do you mind telling me who he was?"

You look at him knowing how things are about to change. And while you sit there wondering how they will, you finally feel your face go hot because you can see that he's had the time to figure it out on his own.

"You never had a teacher," he says.

"I didn't want another one."

"I'm your first one."

"Yes."

"The first day you came here. All of that was on your own."

"I had a book."

"Never a teacher."

"No."

"Never played with anyone."

"No."

And then you're thinking except for you. He does this little smile and lets it go. Without looking away, he slides his hand across his desk, dips his fingers into the little bowl of steel marbles, fiddles with them like they're balls of hard candy and he can't decide if he wants one or not.

"Okay," he says. "But down the road we'll get you in some bands."

"We will?"

"The ones you've been taking home."

"The records?"

"Sure. We'll start playing with them. Sitting in."

This open door. This door you were waiting to have him close. Instead, he's bringing you inside, through this open door into this place where all the musicians from his records play. You and your trumpet and Mr. Selby. Playing with them. One of them.

"You look scared," he says.

"I'm not scared."

"If you don't think you're good enough for band class," he says, "these guys will eat you for lunch. You should be scared."

"I guess," you say. "Maybe."

"I'm kidding," he says. "It's a good crowd. They're good guys. They'll like you. But they won't wait for you."

So far he's told you just to listen. He hasn't let you play along. Even with your trumpet there, in your hand, you haven't wanted to. There's been way too much to listen to. Too much to imagine when you've taken what you're hearing and tried to see and smell and taste and feel it too. And so you've been happy to listen, and on the live records, after a solo or at the end when people clap and sometimes sigh or quietly yell, you can feel the room, and that's all you've cared about.

Now he wants you to play with them. Just start off light. He puts an album on his record player on the shelf next to his fireplace to show you. Just come up alongside, close enough to the band to brush them, play a note or two, then let them go again. Just let them know you're there. Start on the ballads because they're not as fast as some of the crazy bebop stuff. Listen to the way they play behind each other's solos. Just the stroke of a note or phrase for color. Don't try to keep up at first. Don't try to play along just yet. Stay out of the way for now. Just the brush of your own sound in there now and then. Try some hit tunes too. Your own records. Moonlight Gambler. Peggy Sue.

CHAPTER 66

THE DAY he tells you he's going to teach you about tones and intervals the wind is howling on the ride down. When he answers the door his tie is pink. Green and blue fish swim back and forth across it while wind slaps the walls of his house, rattles the windows, has the fighter plane doing this lazy rotation from the motion of the ceiling down through the lamp and the string it hangs from. It's your first lesson in what he calls jazz theory. He starts with the difference between notes and tones. How a note on its own is just a note. How a tone is what a note becomes when you put other notes around it. Like a scale or a melody. How a note can take on different tones depending on the melody or phrase or scale it's in.

"Like a letter of the alphabet when you put it in different words," he says. "Are you with me?"

"No."

"Okay. The letter A. It's just a letter. But in different words it takes on different sounds. Cat. Cage. Caught. Same letter. Different sounds. If the letter A was a note, those sounds would be its tones."

"Can you show me?"

"Sure. Come here."

You follow him to the piano, where he sits down, pushes the lid back, reaches up and whacks the A key.

"Your basic A," he says. "Okay?"

"Yeah."

"Now I'll play two scales. Listen to the A each time. Not to the pitch. But to the motion of the sound. Listen for the difference."

He plays up the scale from D. And then up the scale from B flat. He stops on the A both times. How in the first scale it sounds like it could end there. In the second scale how much it wants to keep on going.

"Hear that?"

"Yes."

"That's the difference between a fifth tone and a seventh tone. Same note. Two different tones. Cat and cage."

Wind smacks the side of the house. Something in the kitchen makes this quick sharp little rattle. Theo comes scampering through the door past your shoes. Mr. Selby looks up at you.

"Okay. Now we'll have some fun. Take your horn and play an A. Hold it. While you're doing that, I'll play through some different chords. Listen to your note. Listen to it change."

You bring your trumpet up, set your lips, punch the first two valves down, play and hold the A while Mr. Selby starts playing chords, big fat chords, both hands going now. You hear it. A changing river, moving under your single note, deep with a changing current, pulling and skating your note along, changing the way it sounds and moves and even feels without you doing anything. Mr. Selby finally stops. You bring the trumpet down. Stand there staring.

"How many notes did you play?" he says.

"One."

"How many tones?"

"I don't know."

"You're wondering what all this means."

"No." And then you say, "Sort of."

And so he tells you. Starting with steps. How the notes of a scale go up or down in a pattern of half steps and whole steps. How the pattern's the same for all of the major scales. How there's a pattern too for each of the three different kinds of minor scales. How starting with the root tone, the steps add up to intervals, intervals called seconds, thirds, fourths, fifths, sixths, sevenths. How tones are numbered that way. By their intervals. By how many steps away from the root tone they are. From scale to scale, with notes, their letters always change, but when you look at them as tones, when you number instead of letter them, their numbers always stay the same.

"No matter what scale you're in," he says. "A third is a third. It always has the sound of a third. A third in F will always have the tonal quality of a third in B flat. That goes for a fourth, a fifth, on up the line. With me so far?"

What you came here for. Another open door where you didn't know there was one, with something on the other side to grab, take back home, practice till it's yours, too deep and secret to have anyone take away.

"Sort of."

"Don't worry. You'll get it. Okay. Let's take chords. And chord progressions."

How there are patterns of intervals for all of the major and minor chords. How the chords are numbered too. How when you link chords together in patterns, by their numbers, you end up with progressions. How the chords when they move through a song will always sound the same no matter what key you play the song in. Just like the intervals they're patterned on.

By the time he's done, he's played some chord arrangements in different places on the keyboard, counted them out, shown you how they work while you've stood there, watching his flat hands and thick fingers move without thinking back and forth across the keys.

"You know this song?" he says.

For a minute you listen. And then you hear it. The cry for the melody where the melody should be.

"I Loves You Porgy."

"You played that your first time here."

"I know."

"What was missing just now?"

"The melody."

"Get your trumpet ready. Play me the first few notes."

You bring the trumpet up, punch down the first valve, play the opening note and then the next four while he cocks his ear up, listening.

"Okay. Key of F. Let's see here." You watch his hands hover, fish for keys, play some trial chords. And then you're hearing the song in a higher key than the one he played it in before. "Okay," he says. "Got it. Let's go. Let me play an intro before you come in."

And while you play you watch his hands and think a couple of musicians. As long as you can keep doing this.

"Good. I was your rhythm section. Your bass line, your tempo, your changes. Your trumpet was the melody. The right hand. But you need that left hand. A band to play with."

"I know."

"Yes," he says. "And you know what will happen?"

"What?"

"I'm your singer. I tell you I can't sing that song in F. The key's too low. I need it a step up. In G. What are you gonna do?"

"That's what happens?"

He laughs. "That always happens. And you need to be ready. Singers can be fussy. Let's try it again. Take it up a step. Key of G this time. Let me play the intro again. Ready?"

"Yeah."

You open the melody this time on G. And suddenly you don't know where the next note is. Or the next note up from there. Just fish for notes that all sound wrong, and fish again while Mr. Selby pulls ahead, and then you're so far behind what Mr. Selby's doing it's like chasing a train down tracks on legs that keep going out from under you. You finally just stop. Mr. Selby too. Looks up at you, where you're standing, not knowing it was possible to feel this stupid.

"What happened?" he says.

"I got lost."

"You only know the melody by its notes. That's how you play it in your head. I loves you Porgy. F A C E G."

You watch him play them.

"Okay."

"It's okay to learn it that way. But when you keep it that way you're always stuck in that one key."

"Okay."

"Now look at them as intervals. I loves you Porgy. First third fifth seventh ninth."

Watching him play the same notes again.

"And when I go to the key of G the same thing. Different notes. G B D F sharp A. But the same intervals and tones. First third fifth seventh ninth. See how that works?"

And now this door. Where you stand there staring. This door to this sudden place where you're free of notes. Of having to use them to play. Of the key they're printed in. Of their names. Of the way their dots are caught in the bars of the clefts of sheet music. This place where the bars of the clefts are suddenly gone and the black dots are free to be tones instead. Free to go anywhere. Free to fly. Free to catch the wind outside. The sound you heard in the cattle truck. Close enough to where you can almost reach it. Close enough to be possible.

"Okay."

"You learn a melody by its tones," he says. "Then you can play it from anywhere."

"Okay."

"That's when you'll know a song. When someone can call out a key and you're there. You won't care where."

He pulls the black lid back over the keyboard. You back away to give him room to get up off the stool the way he sat down on it, his back straight, his body rising like the thick steel trunk of a car hoist, straight up off his legs, like he gets up off his desk chair. He nudges the stool back into place with his knee and turns to you.

"I want you to work out the melody to I Loves You Porgy in every key. Start with your lowest. Then work your way up. All the way up the octave."

"Okay."

"That's thirteen different keys," he says. "Not just eight."

"Okay."

"I still want you to play your scales and your Arban pieces. But I want you to think tones and intervals when you do. Forget what the notes are called."

"Okay."

"Next week we'll learn how to read chord symbols and lead sheets."

"Cool."

"And we've still got blues scales. And modal scales." He gives his head a slow shake and smiles down at his open hand. "It makes me hungry just thinking about it. I could use a cookie or two or three. How about you?"

"Sure."

CHAPTER 67

SONGS YOU thought you knew. If I Loved You. Over the Rainbow. Someone to Watch over Me. Songs now that he helps you take apart and understand and then put back together again. Stormy Weather. Laura. Don't Get Around Much Anymore. Songs whose chords he'll sit down and play on his black piano while you start playing scales and arpeggios across the shifting surface of their moving current.

For the scales and exercises he tells you to use a metronome. You borrow your mother's. The little wood pyramid with the little door you pull off to get to the swinging blade inside. You set it on the workbench, wind it up, use the sliding weight to set the tempo of the blade, play to its hard regulated clack. He tells you to always start out slow and practice till your notes are sure and your changes sharp and clean. And then take the tempo up. And then have fun with it. Listen to hear the beat on two and four instead of one and three. Play with it. Anticipate it. Come to it late. Play all around it. And always come back to it.

"We'll call it your drummer for now," he says, and smiles, and then says, "Till you decide on a human one."

In the deep part of summer, when nothing by way of weather comes in across the vacant sky and nothing interrupts the sun once it clears the foothills in the morning, the heat in the afternoon in the closed garage thins out the air to where you can't hold notes as long. Can't run up and down a scale as many times while the metronome keeps clacking. Sweat burns your eyes and tickles where it runs into your ears. You take the bandana Lupe gave you, tie it in a band around your head, and later, when you hear the springs of the Chevy wagon cross the hump at the top of the driveway, take it off and roll it out and drape it over the handles of the lawn mower to dry.

He teaches you to play your scales around the circle of fifths. Start with the C scale. Then up a major fifth to the G scale. Then back a perfect fourth for the D scale. Up another major fifth to play the A scale, back a perfect fourth to E, up a major fifth to B, until you've done all thirteen keys, until you've circled back to C. As you go each scale picks up another flat. When you get halfway, the flats convert to sharps, and each scale drops a sharp on the way to C again.

You've watched. "What's it for?"

"Chord progressions. Changes. You'll hear the relationship between them. The way one will move into the other."

"I did. I heard it."

"We'll go over it. This is how you'll play your scales from now on."

Through summer into fall, lesson after lesson, you get used to the way he talks, to the deliberate way he moves, not slow or stiff, but like he's planned out every move ahead of time, practiced it, made it precise. The way he holds his trumpet. The way he smiles. Just enough. Afterward, on his piano stool at his desk, timid at first to have the full attention of a man without the shield of a lesson, shy about picking up another cookie, you come to get to know him.

How he was born in New York City, in 1900, in January, so that once he's had his birthday, he's the same age as the year is. How in 1901 he was one and in 1913 as old as you are now. How his mother and father had him study classical piano. How in 1917, when he was seventeen, he ran away and joined the Army, and they sent him to Europe to fight in World War I. How in France, when his company learned he knew music, made him their company bugler. How he loved the bugle. How one of his soldier buddies found a trumpet one day in a bombed farmhouse and brought it back for him. How he brought the trumpet home, to New York, when he was discharged, and how his mother and father sent him to a conservatory to study it for real. How the conservatory was where he learned about Professor Arban. How he eventually started playing with the symphony. How one night, in a speakeasy, he sat there and heard real jazz and blues for the first time, got hooked for good, and quit the symphony.

Sometimes he stops talking and sits there smiling for a minute, not in secret or even in your direction, just at a place on his desk or at the cookie he's holding.

"So you've got a real head start on me," he says once.

"How?"

"I didn't get to know our friend Professor Arban till I was almost twenty."

"What's a speakeasy?"

"Just a night club. You know, drinks, music, dancing. It's what they were called during Prohibition. A place where you could get a drink."

You remember Prohibition from Mr. Kapp in History. When it was illegal to drink. Bootleggers, gangsters, the FBI. When the whole United States had to obey the Word of Wisdom. At least the liquor part. Starting in 1920 when Mr. Selby was twenty.

"How come they were called that?"

"You had to, well, speak easy. Be quiet about it. Not let the police know."

"What did they look like? On the inside?"

"Oh, about like any club, I'd say. A bar with some stools, a stage maybe, dance floor, tables and booths, dim lighting. Some were fancier than others."

"Did people get drunk?"

"Let's say they enjoyed themselves."

That fall, the air in the garage cool again to where the air in your lungs can last, you start eighth grade. Sometimes you walk, with Yenchik, West, Doby, Jasperson, Keller, if you meet or catch up with them in the morning when the neighborhood spills its kids down off the hill to their different schools. Mostly you're on your bike. Everyone's there again. Everything's the same, except in a different room, or at a different time of day, the periods shuffled. English instead of History for home room. Susan Lake has Geography the period before you do, in the same room, from Mr. Ball, and sometimes you get there in time to see her leave, and sometimes you wonder which desk is hers, and that's as close as you come to having a class with her. And Carla's in your Biology class this time around, in the afternoon, and she shows up with her violin case.

"So what did you do all summer?"

She's different, maybe her hair just longer, her face less round, you don't know, standing there waiting for the teacher to show up.

"Just messed around," you say. "What'd you do?"

"We had to bury Oscar."

"Who's Oscar?"

"My dog." And then she says, "He got killed in Yellowstone."

"How?"

"He chased a bear and it got mad."

"Wow. I'm sorry."

"It's okay. He was old and sick a lot. So did you sign up for band?"

"Naw."

"You're different." Tilting her searching face to the side. "What did you do?"

"I don't know."

Mr. Selby changes your lesson from two o'clock on Tuesday to Thursday after school. On Thursday morning, you rope your case to the rack, ride to school early to get there and not have Carla or the other kids with cases see you bring yours in, keep it in your locker for the day, then rope it back on after school and pedal through the quiet old neighborhoods off the back of Main Street to his house.

Old Man Tuttle's rows of beans and peas are picked clean for the season. You pick cherries and peaches and apricots and apples in Charley Bangerter's orchards. You've been handing your father ten percent of what you're paid for tithing and putting the rest away for lesson money for the winter. On Thursday, on your ride to Mr. Selby's house, old men have started standing in their yards with rakes, tending smoldering little piles of burning leaves.

Clifford Brown. Louis Armstrong. Charlie Parker. Coleman Hawkins. Dexter Gordon. Your heroes. You've listened to them for weeks in the closed garage, again and again, until you were there inside the songs with them, hearing the play of the melody against the bass, the deep changing moving river of the chords. You've raised your trumpet and brushed in your own sound here and there, let them know you're there, almost one of them, except that most all of them are Negro, and your face and arms and hands will never be that brown, or your hair that black and fiercely curled. You'll always be different. You've known that. Always be a white kid. And then, late that fall, Mr. Selby sends you home with a record by a trumpet player named Chet Baker. In the photograph on the cover, he's young, white, a face that says leave him alone, his brown hair long and thick and loose and glossy, the way you can make your own hair look.

CHAPTER 68

HE TEACHES you the patterns for all the diminished and augmented scales and their chords. You chase them too around the circle of fifths. He teaches you the patterns for all their inversions where you don't have to always play them from their root positions but starting from their thirds or fifths or sevenths. Because you can only play a single note at a time, you can't play chords the harmonic way a piano can, but you can string them out, play them as arpeggios, arpeggios that draw the progressions out as melodies. The circle of fifths is the beginning of understanding how the chords move. The intervals like a single language on which all the patterns are based. The patterns are dialects that all use the same base intervals. It doesn't matter if you have a testimony. It doesn't matter if you believe in Joseph Smith. What Mr. Selby teaches you is the way it is no matter what.

And he teaches you the patterns all the blues scales use. You love the way they sound. Defiant, outlaw scales almost, but outlaws just for the fun of being outlaws, like if scales could be rascals, this would be them. By your next lesson you know them well enough to blow through all of them. Mr. Selby's grinning when you finish, while you clear the pipes, blow spit out the valve into the handkerchief he gave you.

"Wow. You had a good week."

You lower the trumpet, tuck the wad of the handkerchief back in your pocket, can't help from grinning yourself. "They're fun."

"Okay," he says. "Let's talk jazz."

How a note can only make sense, can only take on tone, when it's moving. How to mean anything it has to come from somewhere and be going somewhere. How it's defined by where it came from and where it's going. He's wearing a yellow tie without a pattern, just all yellow, a black shirt, and his gray eyes look at you with their usual steady scrutiny.

"Understand?" he says.

"Yeah." Still calming down, still doing a hundred miles an hour, still riding the rascal scales you sent tearing around the room. "Kind of."

And when he smiles his cheeks go up and the skin goes creased around his eyes. "Let's use the piano," he says. "It's easier to see what we're doing. Sit down."

He slides the lid back off the keys and stands next to you.

"Play B above middle C," he says.

Long oval rings are worn into the pale ivory, like the grain in a flat stick of wood, and the key surprises you how easy it goes down.

"What do you hear?"

"B," you say, not knowing what he's after.

"That's right," he says. "Just a B. No way to know where it's coming from or where it's going."

"No."

"You might as well play an F or a D for all the difference it makes."

"Yeah."

"Now play the C scale up to the B. Then hold the B."

You run the scale to the B. This time you hear it. The unfinished sound of a seventh, the pull toward the next note, the high C, the end of the scale, the note it started on an octave higher.

"What do you hear this time?"

"A seventh." You've been here before. You're still not sure what he's after.

"How it's not finished," he says.

"Okay."

"That B has motion now. It's come from a place that makes it a seventh. And it wants to go somewhere. It wants to go all the way."

You turn on the stool, look up past his bearded throat to where his gray eyes look down on you.

"A seventh always does," you say.

"Let's talk about that."

How the key of a song is its home tone. How the other tones in a song all come from that sense of home. How through all the other tones all through the song the feeling for home is always there, where home is, the feeling that the song will have to get back there before it can end. How you can always hear it in a song no matter how far away from home you take it. No matter how long you keep it away.

"Home is two places. First, it's a place to get away from. A song doesn't start till it leaves home. Goes out and has an adventure. Second, it's a place to get back to. Where we live."

"Okay."

"That seventh you just played. Where did it want to go?"

"Home?"

"Some tones want to go home. The seventh is a real homebody. We'll call those tones the go home tones. Other tones can't wait to get out the door and never come home again. We'll call those the stay out tones. And there are tones that are pretty stable where they are. They kind of wait to be told what to do. Like a third or a fifth. You never know what a fifth is thinking. Maybe it wants to stay out. Maybe not. It usually leaves it up to the next tone. Play the root and the fifth. Hold it. And then the seventh."

When you play the C and then the G it just sits there. You hold it and play the B and there it is, the immediate longing for home, and for just a second, from the dark edge of the back yard, you see your family through the kitchen window.

"Hear that?" he says. "How the fifth wasn't sure where it was going till the seventh came along?"

"Yeah."

"Okay. Every tone in every scale will have its own relationship to its home tone. One or another way. The sharped and flatted tones too."

"Okay."

He tells you how the tones will play between pulling a song away from home and pulling it home again. How this play between the stay out tones and the go home tones is what gives a song its tension. You've heard it. It's just never made you think of home.

"It's called modality. This tension. This tug of war between the stay out tones and the go home tones."

"Modality?"

"Right."

"Modality."

Mr. Selby smiling. "You say that like I'm going to test you."

"Sorry."

"Don't be. Okay. I've got three more intervals for you."

And he shows you the ninth, the eleventh, the thirteenth.

"They're the real stay out tones. Especially the ninth. Eventually they resolve, but in the meantime, they're all about taking a song away and getting it lost. All about dissonance and mystery. Hear that?"

"Yeah."

"Add them to your arpeggios. To the chord progressions you've learned. You'll hear it. The dissonance and tension. Try flatting and sharping them. Once you can hear their quality, listen to the records for the ways they're used."

"Okay."

He tells you how sometimes during a song its key can change and take the song to a totally different home. Sometimes just for a while, like a borrowed home, like visiting a friend or a relative, before it heads back to the home it started from. And sometimes for good.

"Like moving," you say.

"Yes. Just like moving."

There's a name too when the key changes and the song either visits or moves to another home. Mr. Selby calls it modulation. This time you only say it once.

"That's it."

He tells you how all a song's adventure happens while it's out. How the farther away you take it, the longer you keep it out, the more adventure you give it. He calls the adventure improvisation.

"Improvisation."

"Yes," he says. "That's where you set yourself apart. Let people know who you are."

"Okay."

"Just always know the way back," he says. "The audience counts on that."

"Yeah."

He tells you how sometimes right in the middle of an adventure you'll get thirsty, or need the bathroom, so you'll come home long enough for a drink, or to pee, and then take off to finish your adventure before you come home for good. How you can do that with a song too. Bring it home in the middle and then take off with it again.

"It's called resolution. A song resolves when you bring it home. Whether you do it in the middle briefly or at the end for good."

"Resolution. Okay."

"Think you got everything?"

You look at the keys. All the intricate logic between and underneath them.

"I don't know."

"Don't worry. You've had a crash course in the basics. We're going to be going over everything again. Again and again."

"Okay."

"And another thing. What matters just as much as anything is what you feel. More than these things we can name."

"Okay."

"I like your new hair style."

"Thanks."

Long enough to where you can comb it back in fenders past your ears and down into your neck some. Droop it over your forehead like it's accidental. Give it some shine with Brylcreem. You don't tell him about Chet Baker. But your face goes red and you wonder if he's guessed.

"I like it. Hip. I remember when I could used to do that."

"But you're lucky. You got a beard."

He laughs. "Don't be fooled," he says. "A beard's nothing but a consolation prize."

CHAPTER 69

RESOLUTION. Modality. Modulation. How the things you can do on the trumpet are named. Note. Tone. Two words, the same four letters, two of the letters switched, the only difference you can find. Pedal. Sometimes just to outrun the neighborhood where you know all the streets and the people who live in just about every house. To outrun the town of Bountiful. To outrun all the things whose names you know. What the roads are named. What the towns are named when you go through them. What the people are named who live in the houses you pass. Pedal. Pedal to where you're clean of names. The names of the towns connected by the names of the roads that go through them. The names of the roads connected all the way back to Bountiful. From there to the names of the streets of your neighborhood. From there to the street your house is on. From there to your own name. From your name to the way your father wants you to be a god someday. From there to the way he stood there, holding the doorknob, probably thinking it would never happen now, because what he was standing there watching was you, just you, without the name he gave you, the way you are when you play trumpet.

Outrun all the names. Know only from the gray and yellow mountains that run along the valley how to get back home. Know from where the sun is in the sky out toward the desert when it's time to start heading back. Know from how tired your legs are getting when you need to turn around and pick up the trail of all the names home. Tone. Note. Two names joined in a single puzzle. You turn them around and around, wondering where they unlock, where they fall apart, where you can finally tell how they're different.

"It's your hair," says Carla. "That's what you changed."

"I know My Funny Valentine," you tell her.

As you go into winter your buddies have things to say about it too, your Chet Baker hair, not knowing who Chet Baker is, you not telling them. West wants to know if you're going greaser. Doby tries to give you pointers on training it. Keller's almost totally used to being adopted by now. He tells you get sunglasses. Nobody comes around and says they figured out who you swiped your hair from. Susan Lake doesn't let you know one way or another that she's noticed anything. A cow pie on your head. A rattlesnake around your neck. What it would take.

And going into winter you've come to know him more, this man with his white beard and tie, who brings out cookies and milk and tells you things about himself like it's just you and Doby or Blackwell or West talking. How he learned to play jazz and blues once he quit the symphony, got together a small band, started playing what they called hot jazz in speakeasy after speakeasy too. How he got restless and started hooking up with the big bands, doing some of their arranging, traveling the country with them. How World War II came along in 1942, when he was forty-two, and most of the guys in the bands enlisted and went away to fight. How he signed up again. This time he wasn't the bugler for a combat company in France because he couldn't be in combat. There was a piece of metal in his chest, close to his heart, shrapnel from a grenade in France in World War I the first time he was in the Army. How he spent the war playing for soldiers instead of being a soldier himself, in army bands with his trumpet, in battlefields in Europe and at army posts and hospitals in the United States.

"You were in both wars?"

"A bunch of us were."

"Is it still there? The metal?"

"Oh, sure. It always will be. It's like old Theo now. Old and grouchy. We've learned to live with each other."

"How?"

"I just have to remember it's there. Be careful how I move. Don't surprise it."

Sitting there, at his desk, where he can look at you or past you at his fireplace or out his picture window, at the handlebars and seat of your bike, at the street. You on his piano stool. The typewriter tray between you. One fig newton left, a quart bottle with the milk mostly gone, your empty glasses. Sunlight through the picture window comes off the gleaming snow from a storm this morning. Where it reflects off his polished desk it underlights his face.

"So it's always there."

"It is," he says. "But back to you. What about band this spring?"

"I don't think so."

"Boy." He sits back. Just looks at you with this little smile you've come to know means he's working you over in his head. "How come?" he says mildly.

Your place in the sandpit. It was just the way it started. It was how it was.

"I'm still not ready."

"Okay then," he says. "We'll have to use the bands we have. You must have some hit records. Rock and roll. Radio stuff."

"Yeah."

"Pick a couple of songs you like. Listen to them for how they do the things we've talked about. Not by what they're named but how they feel. Then jump in. I don't mean just add a note or a phrase here and there the way you've been doing. I mean jump right in. Take the song over. Take it away from them for a while. Then bring it back."

You look through your records and pick a slow one. To Know Him Is To Love Him by the Teddy Bears. Put it on and listen. And play it, and listen and play it again, until you're inside it, almost one of the Teddy Bears, hearing the play of the melody against the bass, the deep changing moving river of the chords. In a week you're back in his living room with records of your own. In the presence of the musicians watching from their framed photographs, their albums racked along the long shelves, you feel like a little kid with your choices. Moonlight Gambler. Peggy Sue. Get a Job. Wake Up Little Suzy. All I Have to Do is Dream. He nods. Names the singers after you name the songs. Frankie Lane. Buddy Holly. The Silhouettes. The Everly Brothers. It amazes you that he knows them the way you and your buddies do. That he's a man and knows them.

"I don't have any jazz records," you say.

"No," he says. "They're good. The main thing is you got to know them."

"Yeah."

Playing them on the record player, finding all the notes of their melodies, setting your tuning slide to their pitch and the metronome to their tempos, practicing till you could roll too, till you had the same relentless motion, and then you were playing, playing with the Teddy Bears, with Buddy Holly and the Crickets, with the Silhouettes, with the Everly Brothers.

"So which one's first?"

When you're done, and he's lifted the needle off the record, his calm gray eyes are steady while tiny muscles flicker in the skin around his eyes.

"What aren't you telling me?" he says.

"Nothing."

"This isn't your first time at this."

"No," you finally say.

"You've been doing this with my records too."

You remember the first time. It was the first album Mr. Selby sent you home with. Clifford Brown. The song Blue Moon. A week later, when you got your trumpet back from Mr. Selby, how after listening a couple of times you thought you could hear what the song was doing. And then had to jump in. Pick up your trumpet, find the first note, set the tuning slide to the record, start the needle, go. Then look for the second note and have the song keep going, out suddenly from under you, like you weren't there, like you mattered as much to the song as you would to a moving train. There you were, kicked off, looking for notes on the side of the roadbed while the song kept rolling. How powerless you were to slow it down and have it wait for you. You could get behind on the metronome and still catch up. This was different. It scared you, but you loved it, the way it showed you up, gave you something to chase down.

"Yeah." This flicker in your stomach that you should have maybe lied. "I have."

"I knew I had you right."

"You did?"

He studies you. And then he says, "Here's what you do. First you copy. Get to where you can copy the way Dizzy or Clifford or somebody plays a song or solo. Where you know exactly what they're doing and how they're doing it. Where you can only hear one instrument. And, from there, once you know them enough to do that, learn from them by finding how and where you're different. Where you pull away from them. Where your instruments separate again. Understand?"

"Yes."

"First copy. Then learn."

"Okay."

"Okay. I've got something I keep meaning to give you. It's called a mute. To keep from bothering the neighbors." He crosses the room to the corner where some cone shaped silver cans are gathered at the end of the long shelf. Your mother, you're thinking, where at supper sometimes she talks in her singsong mocking way about the crazy noise from the garage, tells everyone around the table she can't take much more of it. Where your father sits there eating, his face red and ridged and rough, and finally starts going after you for not picking a violin or flute, an instrument that would let your mother have her peace of mind. Mr. Selby comes back with one of the cone-shaped silver cans in his hand. "Here. You'll like the sound too. Let's give it a try."

Sometimes when you're practicing, if you're not playing when it happens, you can hear the groan of the wagon's springs from inside the garage as it angles across the hump of the curb outside at the top of the driveway, and the quietly idling engine coasting closer down the driveway toward the door. You have time to run over then and open it for him, move out of the blazing path of the headlights, have him just roll the wagon into the garage where the headlights pick up the still swinging blade of the metronome on the bench. Sometimes you don't hear the wagon. Just the latch rods being twisted back, and then the springs shriek and light and outside air come flooding in across the concrete floor like the rising door is an irrigation gate, and all you're left with is to stand there squinting in the white fury of the headlights with your trumpet down. He's seen it too, your new Chet Baker hair, not knowing who Chet Baker is, not knowing you didn't steal it from Billy Hess or some other kid he'd rather have than you.

"Hi, Papa."

"Hello, son."

His silhouette in the headlights in his overcoat as he gives the door its last push up into its cradle. The cut of the hunger to show him what you can do. This time with the silver mute that Mr. Selby gave you lodged inside the bell.

"Welcome home."

But he's already turned his back, headed up the driveway for the driver's door again, left the front of the wagon clear to where the smoking headlights and the rush of fresh cold outside air make the floor feel like you're standing in the middle of a night road somewhere.

Sometimes you use the mute to take out some of the steel and give a song a breezy carefree kind of sound. Sometimes to keep from bringing your mother down the stairs. The night you brought it home you took it to bed with you, the lamp on your nightstand on to let you study it, every silver curve, the cork strip that held it in place in the bell, the dent that mated it to the dent your trumpet has, the worn label where you could still read Harmon on the crossbar of the big red H, the little silver cup on the end of the silver tube that slid in and out through the center to change the sound. Remembering how it sounded at Mr. Selby's house, Mr. Selby grinning like there was no tomorrow while you played along with the Teddy Bears, Buddy Holly and the Crickets, the Silhouettes, him picking up his trumpet to play along with you, to show you how far from home you really can take Peggy Sue.

CHAPTER 70

ON AN AFTERNOON in early April a brief but crazy blizzard blows monster flakes past the windows of your last class. By the time you're pedaling home with Doby the roads are almost dry except where long thin blades of snow let go and float down off the wires and wet rags drift down off the branches of the trees. You're bucking the skewed concrete shelves of the busted sidewalk along Orchard Drive. Doby's riding behind you on his big bike.

"Holy crap. It's them."

You've seen it coming too. Heard it first. Felt the tingling itch up your neck and the back of your head when you first heard the distant engine, the engine you heard last year, back in the fall, through the houses and yards and trees, cruising the streets, Brylcreem on your hands, you and West and Doby running. You hear a tire skid behind you, turn, and see Doby, standing on his pedals, going hard up the driveway of the little brick house you're passing. You turn back. The same Jeep. Two heads behind the windshield. Everly Brothers hair on the driver's side, puffed out and flailing, red hair on the passenger side, low sun in their faces, big teeth, music going. The same letter jackets. The gorilla guy in back behind the Everly Brothers hair. The dentist guy next to him. His head turned your way. Doesn't recognize you. Just part of the scenery. The taste of Brylcreem. Your father taking everything you'd done apart to show you how you'd done it wrong. The motherfuckers.

You're already stopped. Your hand comes off the handgrip and your arm goes up. Your finger's already there, stuck up high, locked in position, as long and hard to miss as you can make it. You keep it aimed their way. They come even. You watch the dentist guy take your finger in and his face go into shock. Up front, the redheaded guy just barely catches you, then whips his head around to see what's up.

"Hey!" Leaning around. Grabbing the side of the Jeep. "That kid just fingered us! Hey! You're dead, kid! You little fucker! Hey! Turn around! Turn this thing around, man!"

You keep your finger up. Let it turn and follow the Jeep as it cruises past. Let them all get a look. Give the gorilla guy time to turn around and take one. All three of them are yelling. The Jeep keeps going. And then the message gets to the guy with the Everly Brothers hair. The Jeep gets yanked around so hard its inside wheels are pulled right off the street. And then it just rolls up, the whole Jeep, onto its passenger side, does a crazy little shimmying skid while the guys come catapulting off, and then goes over all the way, down in a hard and dirty crash on the asphalt, upside down, flat as a brick on the street, the wheels in the air still going.

You take your arm down. Three of them. You count again. Just three. Picking themselves up off the asphalt, staggering around out in the middle of the street. Just three. The bottom goes out of your stomach.

"Holy crap. Holy crap. Holy crap. Holy crap." Doby, his voice all high and wobbly, next to you, back from his run up the driveway.

"How many guys you see?"

He takes a minute to count and then count again the way you did. "Three. Holy crap. Holy crap. There's only three. Holy crap. Oh god."

"Yeah."

"Holy crap. He's underneath. He's dead. He's all mashed. Holy crap. Oh god."

The guy with the Everly Brothers hair bent over, hands on his knees, his head drooped down between his shoulders like he's watching ants fight. The dentist guy up and limping back to the Jeep. The gorilla guy getting down on his hands and knees, face to the asphalt, looking under the passenger side, jumping back up, crouching down and groping for a hold along the side to lift it. The dentist guy doing the same thing. Both of them yelling deep and raw and savage.

"One! Two! Heave! One! Two! Heave!"

Football practice. The redheaded guy dead. Back and forth where it's real and then it's too terrible and amazing to be real and then it's too hard and cold and crazy not to be. Like a shock wave has seized the gray street and the houses and yards and trees and sky and taken anything that feels familiar out of them and left everything with the cold bleak look and smell of iron without being iron.

"Let's get outta here," says Doby.

The guy with the Everly Brothers hair stumbles over to the Jeep, crouches down and gets hold too, starts yelling. A white pickup truck coming from the other way slows down and stops. The man driving jumps out, comes running around, grabs the tailgate of the Jeep, starts lifting with nobody telling him what's going on. In the bed of his truck a big brown dog starts woofing. The Jeep comes inches off the ground. The gorilla guy gets down, reaches underneath, gets hold of something, pulls. A shoe. Then a leg. Then another shoe. This time just a shoe. Your stomach goes cold at the wild chance that there's a foot inside it, chopped off, like one of those wooden feet your father puts in his shoes to keep them from curling up. The gorilla guy reaches under the Jeep again. This time he brings out a sock, a white sock, but there's a foot in it now, and an ankle, and from there the start of a leg. The gorilla guy gets up and scuttles back to where he can grab both ankles, and while the dentist guy starts this groaning holler from the strain of holding up the Jeep, the rest of the redheaded guy comes out from underneath, on his back, his letter jacket bunched up under his arms and around his shoulders, his white belly naked where his shirt got pulled up too.

"They're gonna see us. We gotta go."

It's been there for you too, the whole time, this nervous feeling that all it would take is for one of them to turn around, happen to look back, catch you standing there, or just remember where this started and why it happened when all they were doing was just out riding around on parade in their letter jackets. There's a woman standing on the shallow porch of the house right there where everything is going on. Old and fat in a yellow bag of a dress just watching everything.

"I gotta see," you tell Doby.

And so does Doby. While the redheaded guy's red head comes out and his arms pull clear. While they let the Jeep down with a collective groaning expulsion of breath. While the man with the pickup truck goes running toward the house right there, doesn't see the woman standing on the porch until he's on her, stops and almost trips, tells her something, and she turns around and goes inside. While the high school guys leave the redheaded guy lying there where the gorilla guy stopped pulling him and let his ankles go, on his back, one shoe and one sock, his arms and legs out, someone making a snow angel on the asphalt, not moving. Then his arms move and his head comes an inch off the asphalt and goes back down. And then he rolls over, slow, in stages, taking his time, and then just lies there on his naked belly for a minute, and then hunches up his butt and gets a knee beneath him, and then the other knee, and then he brings himself up on his elbows, and then just stays there, on his knees and elbows, his head down, his letter jacket and shirt bunched up around his shoulders, his back bare. And then the other guys are groaning and the man with the pickup truck is turning hard and walking away like he's all of a sudden mad at something.

"Holy crap," Doby says. "He's puking."

He's okay, the redheaded guy, just puking up all the nasty crap inside him, puking everything up through the hole of his big rock ugly teeth that he can't even get his mouth around. How's that for a little dab'll do ya. Just saying it in your head you can hear the high and wobbling and half-scared way it would sound if you said it out loud.

"Come on," says Doby. "We gotta go."

Two other cars stopped at the curb now with their doors left open. Three cars coming the other way just sitting in the street. Six guys lined up along the passenger side, counting the three high school guys, crouched down, taking hold, and now the Jeep comes up, up on its side while the redheaded guy still hangs there drooling on the asphalt on his hands and knees, and the windshield comes with it, the glass half gone, the frame all bent and twisted crazy like a hanger, dangling from a single hinge. And then the Jeep goes over hard, hard on its wheels again, this hard bounding slam that whips the frame of the windshield and snaps the other hinge and sends it flying across the street in this jangling skid when it hits the asphalt. The woman in the yellow dress is out on her porch again.

Slowly the cold iron hold on the street and the houses and yards and trees and sky lets go. They haven't looked your way yet. It's getting now to where they will. Where they'll think back to how this started. Just riding along. And then a kid on a bike with his finger up. And then all they'll need to do is look back up the street.

"Okay," you tell Doby. You leave slow to not draw attention. To be two kids who stopped to watch, like everyone else, and when there wasn't much to watch remembered they were heading home and started heading home again.

CHAPTER 71

JOURNEY. Over the winter he wore a sweater vest over his shirt and tie and left his sleeves rolled down and buttoned. Sometimes he made hot chocolate so that when you rode or walked home afterward there was this reservoir of heat inside you. Crumbs caught in his whiskers while you went on learning who he was and where he'd been and come from. How he came home from the war a second time. Soon afterward, still in the 1940s, when he was still in his forties too, how all the big bands started breaking up. How it started getting hard to make a living playing in New York. How he remembered Salt Lake from going through it on his trips across the country. How the climate and the notion of living where the Rocky Mountains met the Great American Desert suited him. How a couple of his buddies had made the move already. How he moved in 1948 when he was forty-eight and bought this house and opened up his studio and started teaching classical and jazz. How he teaches trumpet and music theory and composition now in the Music Building at the University of Utah. How with all the traveling he did he never married. How he sees the musicians on his wall and his students as his family. Them and his cat Theo. How he has what he calls a following, smiling when he says it like it's a stupid word to use, members of the Utah Symphony, because they love jazz, because they like his record albums, because they like his stories. Stories about bands. About the musicians who played in them. About the places they played.

Stories he tells you. Where sometimes he'll go to the wall where the photographs hang, take one down with both his hands in the practiced deliberate way you now know the reason for, bring it back to his chair. Most of them are dressed up, tuxedos and gowns, like Mrs. Harding and the Negro men in your photograph, holding a smiling pose for the camera, but your favorites are the ones where they don't look like they know or care they're being photographed, where they're just in their regular clothes in a room somewhere with music stands and folding chairs and ash trays and their instruments, just caught in the act of playing, looking at music, talking, the way you and Mr. Selby do. Sometimes when your father gets home without you knowing, and the door lifts and there you are in the headlights with your trumpet, you feel like that's what you look like, one of them, like headlights are flashbulbs, like your father could frame what he photographs and you could tell him it was a trumpet player named Chet Baker.

Spring breaks for good in April when you can tell in your bones and from the confidence in the way the grass and leaves and flowers start taking off that it isn't going to snow again. In the Saturday morning momentum that comes out of hibernation in the houses around the circle and by Saturday afternoon has left the yards shaved and the edges scored to the white roots and the flowerbeds bruised where they've been picked clean of any blemished leaves and petals. In this fierce resolute sense of battle all around the circle against the reckless way things keep wanting to grow. You join in. Two months ahead, in June, your fourteenth birthday, your ordination to the rank of Teacher. Journey. All around you. Molly's crushed and helpless face in the brutal sunlight under the screeching and wheeling of seagulls overhead. Swinging the mower around and seeing Roy where he stands bashfully off the edge of the house with his baby blanket looking all the way across the yard at you while the Briggs & Stratton engine hammers in your ears and the curved blades throw their steady green pungent rain of grass into the catcher.

"There's an old Clark Terry story your bike reminds me of," Mr. Selby says. "You remember him. That Swahili album."

You can see it out the picture window, leaned against the low front wall of his porch, where you've always parked it. The leather pouch for his albums hangs off the handlebars. The rope you use to lash the case in place is bunched and coiled on the rack behind the seat.

"Yeah," you say. "Slow Boat."

He turns his face back from the window smiling.

"He always worked as a kid. He'd have a couple of paper routes, pinboy in a bowling alley, anything. It was the Depression. He was probably your age. He was always supposed to hand the money over to his dad. But he saved some back and bought a bike. A few bucks down and then something like a buck a month. His dad was furious. He pretty much said that now that he had a bike he could just keep riding it. And that's what he did. He just kept riding. He never went home from then on."

How far he rode that first time. How long he kept on riding. Where he ended up and then where he rode from there. How far and long you could ride if you didn't have to save half your legs to get back home on.

"Did he have a trumpet then?"

"Hmmm. Good question. I'm not sure when he started."

Journey. The way you've sat here, Thursday after Thursday, on his piano stool, the centers of your lips numb and fuzzy from the lesson, busting with things you wish you could ask him. Why he always wears a tie. If he ever played on Mrs. Harding's tennis court. What it feels like when a grenade goes off. What his mother and father did when he brought his trumpet home from France. If they were mad. And the big one. How good you are if you're good. How you stand up to other kids with trumpets. How much more you've got to prove before you're one of them.

You don't ask. Or tell him much about yourself. You tell him about not taking band but not about Carla or her violin. About the garage but not about the sandpit. About coming from Switzerland but not about coming from La Sal. About hearing a trumpet on the radio but not about Manny or Hidalgo or Mr. Hinkle. Or Joseph Smith or Susan Lake. Or how a tube of Brylcreem looks turned inside out in the sunlight. Or the Holy Ghost, how he's there, your own piece of shrapnel, next to your own heart, and how you have to be careful too, not about the way you move, but about the things you think and do. Not about your mother leaving home with a suitcase full of air. Or the air horns and the chords they play when the long trains crawl north along the shoreline. Or the way you ride your bike too, to outrun things, like Clark Terry when he was a kid. Or the way the Jeep rolled over the second time you saw it and you saw the shoe and thought at first there was still a foot inside it.

You and Doby don't talk about the Jeep either, until late in May, one day in the school cafeteria. Old women with gray hair bagged in spidery nets stand behind big steel pots. Noise ricochets off the pale green cinderblock walls. Teachers wander up and down the rows of tables looking back and forth like people in a store not sure of what they're shopping for. You sit across from Doby eating beans and hot dogs gray from having sat in water.

"I wish we could tell West," says Doby.

"We should. He'd be okay."

"You know him and cars."

"He wouldn't care."

"You going with that redhead with the violin?"

"Going with her? No. We're just pals. Lab partners in Biology. We cut up this baby pig yesterday."

"Real romantic."

"Yeah. I can still smell formaldehyde."

"West's going with that Tracy somebody."

"Yeah. Mayfield."

"Remember what Clark told us? About how much power you've got in your finger?"

"What about it?"

"You rolled over a Jeep with yours."

"That's sacrilegious."

"No. You proved it."

"Clark said your little finger."

"Same difference."

"He didn't even say little finger. He said little fingernail."

"I know. Same idea, though."

"You're full of it."

"Think about it," says Doby, whispering hard, leaning out across his plate of beans and hot dogs on his elbows to get his big face close to yours. "They're going down the road and you give them the finger. And the Jeep goes rolling over."

"He turned too hard."

"I mean what made it happen."

"Him turning too hard."

"No. You. If you hadn't of fingered them, he wouldn't of turned, period."

"They started it. You're gonna get bean juice on your shirt."

Doby looks down, moves his elbows, pulls up his shirt, leans back off his plate some. "No. They would of just kept going."

"They started it."

"Yeah. But you finished it. With your finger." He looks quick from side to side and leans in close again. "With the Priesthood, man."

"I just got them mad."

"You turned over a whole Jeep full of assholes," says Doby.

"Maybe I oughta get a holster for it," you say.

"Yeah," says Doby. "A little scabbard."

"Yeah," you say. "A scabbard. That's what I meant."

Resolution. Modulation. Inversions. Voicings. Changes, progressions, substitutions. The Arban exercises. He's kept his word. All winter he's taken you through them, again and again, the structures and movements of jazz that rule the thirty notes of your range to where you own them and can drop their names, to where you don't remember what you were like your first time here. He's answered every question you've ever had the guts to ask him. Your new strength and certainty. You've felt it grow and settle in. He spends most of each lesson at his piano now to play the shifting currents of the changes underneath the surface you skate and skip your trumpet lines across.

Sometimes you stand side by side or face to face, calling and responding, testing each other with longer and tougher and crazier lines. But from your first time here you've never taken this for granted. This place, what happens here, the way you come to this house and have the door open, the way he's here to tell you come on in, the way Theo rubs his arched side along your leg. Never trusted it when you've let yourself feel like you belong here. Always watched yourself for questions you could ask that he could only answer by asking you to leave. Leave and just keep riding. It could always change from what it was. It could be as quick and easy as some rule you didn't know was there. And so every Thursday is its own Thursday. Not the Thursday between the last Thursday and the next Thursday. Just the Thursday that could be the last one.

CHAPTER 72

"IT'S CALLED a nipple?"

"Yeah."

"And it just screws in?"

"Yeah. Right where the muffler goes."

An hour ago, maybe two, you rode down from your neighborhood, you and Blackwell, through town and then across the highway, and then you found the rutted two-lane road out west across the valley to where the tracks cut straight through the rubbled dirt and asphalt and kept on going in either direction. Two years almost and the crossing still looked the same except it was earlier in the day and Blackwell was there.

This time you turned and followed the tracks where they ran along the top of a straight dike of oil-stained dirt and gravel across the brine-white marshlands along the Great Salt Lake. Rode between the rails on the black ties and rust-colored gravel. Got to this place out here where there wasn't a house or building or road within a couple of miles and where you could see someone coming long before they could see you, especially a train, and decided this was the place. Where you'd do it. Where you'd lay the stuff in your pockets out along the shiny backs of the tracks and wait.

You've been here long enough now to be used to things around you. The sharp smell of the black oil the gravel of the roadbed is stained with. The stiff needles of dead weeds and the points of rock in the bank of rough sand across from the roadbed where you've smoothed and shaped out places to sit and lie back. The quiet lazy buildup of afternoon heat between brushes of light spring wind. The calls of marsh birds and sometimes their startling break out of nowhere. The distance of everything. You've already tried to pick out your houses way across the valley where the roofs of your neighborhood creep up through the orchards into the foothills hazed green with new weeds. The church-house was easy. The two steep slabs of its roof like one of those big chalets in one of your father's calendars from Switzerland. The needle of the thin steeple up from the orchards.

"It must be pretty loud," says Blackwell. "Just a pipe."

"Yeah."

How West souped up the engine of his father's power mower with a six inch piece of pipe called a nipple. You fold the dry straw of a dead weed in half and then in half again. Blackwell's moving. Soon as school is out next week to Albuquerque. His father's new job. You never saw it happening like this, where he'd move, where all you had to do to get out of being his friend was wait. Blackwell shifts his butt, looking for more comfort, then starts smiling.

"What?"

"They really call them nipples."

"That's what West said."

"I wonder how come." He rolls to one side, reaches back, pulls a rock out from under his butt.

You saying, "Beats me."

"They don't look like nipples."

"Nope."

You flip the weed you've folded off toward the roadbed. Watch it spring open as it leaves your fingers like an insect taking off.

"Bet they don't feel like nipples either," he says.

"Guess not," you say, thinking how in Albuquerque he'll be saying nipples too, every chance he gets.

"Haycock could tell us for sure," he says.

The Scoutmaster's wife. You think right then that if Blackwell writes you letters he'll be asking how her boobs are doing. On top of the roadbed, lined up along the shiny backs of the two rails, the reasons you pedaled down here. Pennies. Paper clips from your father's desk. Nails and washers and screws Blackwell found in the cabinet in his garage. You gave Blackwell his choice of rail because he's moving. He took the near one. Your stuff is lined up on the far one. Neither one of you knows what the wheels of a train will do to it.

"That train's never coming," he says.

"Yeah it is. It comes every afternoon."

"You made it up. Just to get me down here."

"No. I swear."

Blackwell gets up and walks to his bike where it lies in the dirt off the roadbed next to yours. He picks it up, swings it upside down, sets it on its seat and handlebars, starts turning the pedals. There's a playing card clipped with a clothespin to the frame of the back wheel, its edge faced into the spokes, so that when he rides the card barks like an engine. The card is shot, half torn away, the sound ragged and slurred when Blackwell cranks the pedal and gets the spokes going. He unclips it, throws it in the dirt, takes a new card out of the pocket of his shirt, clips it where the old one was, cranks the pedals again. The sound this time is sharp and quick and clean like it's supposed to be. He lays his bike back down, takes a step up the roadbed, looks down the tracks, comes back and sits in the sand again. He doesn't know about the horns. The way you figured out the notes and used to play along with them.

"You got any hairs yet?" he says.

Everyone's had hairs for a while now. At least that's what they've said. Everybody's voice has started changing, cracking, doing harmonics, going low out of nowhere, skipping back up again.

"A couple," you tell Blackwell.

"When'd you get the first one?"

"I don't know. Sometime."

"How come you didn't tell me?"

"I forgot."

"You didn't forget." And then he says, "Bet you told Doby."

What you've done is lie. Like maybe some of your buddies have. Check yourself every day or two and then lie. Keep things out of sight in gym while more and more guys have started parading their pubies around the locker room. Lie till a couple of weeks ago when you finally woke up and had one. In the meantime Keller and West and Jasperson got peach fuzz and Doby's getting real whiskers. He had you run the backs of your fingers up his cheek where you could feel them.

"I forgot to tell him too."

"You jack off yet?"

You sit there. Pull another dead weed with its withered string of a root out of the dirt between your shoes.

"If you got hairs, you're ready to."

You've heard other guys talk about it and gone along like you've known what they were saying. Blackwell won't be around to tell them you didn't. That he finally had to show you. He doesn't even have anyone to tell.

"Okay," you say.

He gets up and pulls his pants down off the tops of his legs to where his shorts are showing. Then he pulls his shorts down over them. You sit there staring at his pud and in the sunlight all the reddish hair around it, red like a clown wig, and then you realize you're staring and yank your eyes away.

"Get your pants down," he says.

Nobody he could tell. In your head you go through everybody possible. Nobody he could write a letter to from down in Albuquerque.

"Out here?"

"Yeah. That train's never coming."

And so you rock back on your shoulders and raise your butt off the sand and get your pants down too. He's sitting down again and then laying back against the bank of dirt.

"Just start doing this to it," he says.

You take a look. Look off when you see his pud start growing. And after a couple of minutes start feeling your own pud getting fat and hard like in the morning.

"Feel anything?" he says.

Thinking back to La Sal. You and Jimmy Dennison doing this to horses to get their puds to come out long and dangling to where you could shoot rocks at them with slingshots from the fence.

"Just a boner."

"Keep doing it."

"What's supposed to happen?"

"Just keep going."

"How long?"

"Think about tits."

"I still don't feel anything."

"Big ones. Haycock's old lady."

You close your eyes. Think hard. Picture them right there in front of you. You can't keep from looking back up, at her face, at her friendly hawk-nosed face, smiling like you're there just to say hello to her.

"They gotta be naked."

"I know. I'm not stupid."

You listen to Blackwell starting to breathe funny.

"Feel anything yet?" he says.

"A little I think."

"Touch 'em. Play with 'em."

"They're big. That's for sure."

And then Blackwell starts breathing hard and tensing up. And then his shoulders and back are coming off the dirt and he's making this sound like he's being slugged. And then he just goes limp and lies there. You go back to work. What you're doing feels good. You were even wondering if you were done. Now you know you're not. Blackwell gets his shorts and pants back up. He catches a grasshopper and starts picking off its legs.

"How much longer?" you say.

"Just keep going."

And then before long you can hear it. The distant hammering throb of the big diesels. The faint ringing whistle and ringing squeal of metal coming from the tracks where your stuff is. Then the familiar long wail of the horns.

"Holy shit," Blackwell says. "That's it."

And then you're up, pulling your shorts up over your boner, your pants up over your shorts, doing your belt and pulling up your zipper, but your boner pops out through the slit and the zipper catches the end of it. Pain shoots down your legs into your knees. There's blood on the end when you push it back inside. Blackwell scrabbles up the roadbed to take a look at his stuff on the rail. He crawls back down the gravel on his belly. You join him where your eyes are level with the tracks. Flatten down on the sharp black rocks of the roadbed. Look back along the tracks to where they take this broad long sweeping bend and then disappear into silver air. Look and wait for the train.

Its headlight first. This blazing yellow swiveling eye out of this gathered haze of heat and smoke. Then out of the haze the trembling shape of the locomotive, small and square and black, the black head of an iron snake pulling the long black line of its cars around the bend behind it, hovering just off the tracks in this shimmer of silver light above the roadbed. The hammer of the diesels in your legs and stomach and hands and the gravel of the roadbed now. The whistle and squeal of metal coming from the track in front of you more alive now, more charged, like electricity almost.

You raise up and take a quick look across Blackwell's track to your own. All your stuff is there. The sudden fear that maybe the nails and pennies could derail the locomotive. You look back down the track. You can see it for real now. Its white and yellow face the size of a truck. Mean black stripes like warpaint across its nose below the roving eye of its headlight. And then the size of a house, rocking slightly, black heat coming off its roof and turning the air this haze of quivering liquid.

Down in your shorts the sting in your pud is crazy, but you don't dare move, just keep lying there, flat against the roadbed, the gravel trembling under your hands, keep holding on in the hammering thunder and wind of the diesels. And then suddenly the horns. The first blast makes you jump and jam your mouth into the rocks. And then blast after blast after blast the way you never heard in the sandpit. And then just this long constant blare. You look up high for the windshield. Search through the pale sky mirrored on the glass for the engineer. You can make out the hat and then the head and then the face and then the mouth. A face yelling. A face made out of rage. A face looking down on you and yelling. Yelling where you can't hear what it's yelling for the blaring of the horns and the furious hammer of the diesels and the clatter and shriek of the wheels in the track and the quaking roadbed. A face where all its yelling and rage are meant for you. You look back down and the big yellow blade of the locomotive comes hurtling past and power and noise and wind and dirt explode around you. Your pennies and nails and paper clips go jumping like crickets and grasshoppers into the air below the dizzy rush of the undercarriage. The hammer of the diesels and the blaring of the horns go down in pitch as they go past and then keep going. And then the horns stop and there's just the rolling and groaning and shrieking clatter of all the wheels of all the endless cars.

It could go through your house if your house was on a railroad track. Break it open from the front door through to the back door and just keep going. You could sit at your desk and watch car after car go rolling shrieking through your house. You lie there next to Blackwell waiting. Waiting for the last car. Finally the fields across the tracks and the valley and the foothills where you live and the sky are there again. The noise falls off. The quiver goes out of the roadbed. The tracks go quiet. Your mouth hurts where you jammed it into the rocks. You taste salt and oil. Blackwell takes his arms off his head and looks around. The side of his face is dimpled red from the gravel. Down the track the caboose is this rocking toy house with a back porch. You reach for your crotch to relieve the burning in your pud. Blackwell's on his feet. And then you're there too, with Blackwell, scrambling up the roadbed, looking for your stuff in the oil and rust of the gravel and ties and spikes along your rail. Not knowing what you're looking for because you don't know what it looks like now.

"Hey!" Blackwell coming toward you holding something. "Look!"

A thin oblong copper wafer when he gets to you and holds it up where you can see it. Smooth as a spoon. Wiped clean.

"Wow."

"This used to be a fucking penny!"

"What was on it? Remember?"

"I think it was Lincoln." Blackwell turns it over like it could be written on the other side. "Shit. Was it Lincoln?"

"I don't know."

"You got a real penny left?"

"I used 'em all."

"Me too. We can find out later. I gotta find my other stuff."

The first thing you find is a flattened strip of smooth silver metal maybe four inches long. It looks like a sword. What used to be a nail. You holler for Blackwell. He comes running. You go hunting again. Looking for the glint of your own pennies, paper clips, screws, washers, stuck between the rocks, under the spikes, in the gravel down off the roadbed, not knowing what they are at first, standing there amazed when you get it figured out.

At home you find a real penny. One that still has a face on it. Sure enough. Abraham Lincoln. You look close at the side of his head where it's carved into the copper. His beard. The way his hair is combed. His ear and nose. The side of his pulled-down mouth. His tie. Everything tiny and intricate. A grasshopper's eye was bigger than Lincoln's eye. Someone had to carve it. You wonder how. If they had to use a magnifying glass. Blackwell sitting there picking the legs off a grasshopper while you worked on your boner wondering what was supposed to happen. When it would happen to you where you'd come rising up off the dirt and start sounding like someone was slugging you. Abraham Lincoln waiting in the meantime. Just waiting there, on the rail in the sunlight, for the wheel of the locomotive to come along. The Lincoln Memorial on the other side. Under the lamp on your desk you look at the things you got the train to smash. Toy swords for toy soldiers you don't have. Paper clips almost as thin as tinfoil and the flattened wires fused together. A penny wiped clean of Lincoln's face. The face there instead of the engineer. In the smooth spooned surface of the copper the hat and the face and the yelling mouth and the teeth of the engineer. Tiny and intricate. Heads or tails. It doesn't matter any more to Lincoln.

CHAPTER 73

EVERY SUNDAY morning for the last two years you've counted on Brother Rodgers walking into this room. You know all his shoes and ties. When he's about to get his hair cut. The way it makes his face look bigger when he does. You've watched him bless two of his babies in the chapel. Watched his dark brown summer face go white and turn into his winter face two times. Now, the end of May, you're watching his winter face go brown again, turn back into his summer face, the face he had when you started coming here two years ago. It's not that you're tired of him. Just maybe too used to him. The man who taught you everything from the First Vision to the Golden Plates to the Miracle of the Gulls. And then kept going. Lately he's taught you about the Millennium and the First and Second Resurrections. And lately it's started to feel like you've been marooned on an island with him too long.

Lately he's acted sometimes like he's had it too. Like he's tired of his ties and shoes even when they're new. Tired of his hair growing. Tired of coming up with new ways to keep Yenchik from sleeping, the girls from watching him with their faces blank and their eyes the stone blind eyes of statues, West and Doby and Keller from picking on each other. Jasperson and Lilly too. Tired of having to call on them when their hairtrigger hands go up. Like he wished he could rattle them into being real. Drop them off a telephone pole just to see if they'd be human by the time they hit the ground. He's always had it with Strand. Sometimes, if you were looking when he came walking in, you could catch this small fugitive wince in Brother Rodgers' face when he glanced at the class on his way to the little table. Just this quick wince that it was still you and Doby and West and Ann Cook and Susan Lake and Julie Quist and Brenda Horn and Strand.

And now it's over. You've known for two weeks that all of you are moving on from the man who showed you his scars from when he was electrocuted. On this bright late spring Sunday morning, the morning of the last time you'll hear what he has to teach you, there's a cake on the table. White frosting all hairy with shredded coconut. Fat cords of pink frosting in a circle around the wobbly strings of the words "Thank You Your Class" on the coconut frosting on top. Paper plates, plastic forks, napkins, a silver kitchen knife. The grocery bag everything came in folded on Julie Quist's lap like a paper purse. Brenda Horn looking like bringing Brother Rodgers a thank you cake is the dumbest thing in the world anyone could do. A flower missing. Blue on Yenchik's teeth. You thinking ahead, to frosting, to Susan Lake, using the point of her napkin to dab it off her lips.

Brother Rodgers comes into the room, sees his cake, and stands there with his back to you where you're looking at the vent in the back of his sport coat, the bag where his wallet hangs in the back pocket of his shiny brown pants.

"Wow."

He turns around. Sees the bag in Julie Quist's lap, sees her dip her eyes down, her face go pink, so that when he looks at the rest of you, he already knows who brought it.

"What's the occasion?" he says.

Everyone sits there staring like maybe the man who wrestled Yenchik and tried to keep him from praying in the Sacred Grove is fooling around again.

"Your last day," Strand finally says.

"I plumb forgot," Brother Rodgers says, and you can tell from the way his face goes soft that he did. "I'm so sorry. Boy. This is special. I'm really touched. Thank you, Julie."

Brenda Horn sits there looking like she can't stand herself. Brother Rodgers looks at the cake some more and then at Yenchik.

"And thanks for testing it for me, Melvin."

"West made it," says Doby.

"I did not," West says, trying to reach around Keller to slug Doby, Keller trying to block him, but everyone's laughing, even Julie Quist, even Strand, even Brother Rodgers, even Susan Lake, surprising you with her white teeth, letting you imagine them smudged pink and blue and sugary with frosting.

"We'll save this for later," Brother Rodgers says. And then he sets the books he's always brought but hardly ever used next to the cake, turns to face you, spreads his arms open.

"Welcome to the Telestial Kingdom!"

Everyone jumps back hard. Chairs groan. Ann Cook barely catches her little gold purse on its way off her lap.

"Nice to have you here!"

He stands there grinning big, grinning as big as his voice, this ringing shriek off the walls of the little room.

"Chip! Ever imagine a place could be this beautiful? Look at these flowers!"

He reaches out his arms and hands like he's holding and looking at a basketball or a skull.

"Amazing! Big as pumpkins, but light as a feather! All the colors of the rainbow! And the fragrance! Just smell 'em!"

He brings whatever he's holding up to his face, draws breath through his nose, closes his eyes in ecstasy.

"Ever smell anything so good? Here."

He hands what he's holding off to Julie Quist. She looks at him like he's nuts but brings her own hands up and takes it.

"Smell it!" he says. "Go on! Pass it around! And these apples and peaches! Ever seen such big peaches?"

He reaches up, plucks one off like there's one of Charley Bangerter's peach trees in the room, takes a big pretend bite, stands there chewing.

"Mmmmm. Sweeter than honey. Always fresh. Always ripe. Just pick 'em right off the tree, don't even have to wash 'em, never have to worry about biting into a worm! But if you did, you wouldn't mind, because the worms here taste like licorice, or butterscotch, or whatever you'd like 'em to! Here, Johnny, have yourself a bite!"

Brother Rodgers makes like he's lobbing it. Jasperson brings up his hands like he's fielding it, like he's bringing down a softball, while Julie Quist just sits there with her hands still cupped, holding her big imaginary flower, because Brenda Horn wouldn't take it from her when she tried to pass it on.

"Talking about worms, George, you like to fish? Well, if you didn't, you will now! See that lake out there?"

Brother Rodgers extends his arm toward the window. Everybody looks before they remember it's just a parking lot where the dazzling blades and spears of sunlight aren't coming off water but off the polished bodies of all the cars and wagons.

"You don't even need a pole! Just walk up to the water, spot yourself a nice one, and it'll jump right out into your hands! Oops!" he says, acting like he's fumbling a loose football he was tossed through the closed window. "There we go! Ever seen a more scrumptious looking fish?" Holding it up. "You don't even have to cook it! Eat it right off the bone!" Bringing it up to his mouth like a big slice of watermelon, taking a deep bite, the girls squealing, twisting away from looking at it, Julie Quist forgetting about the flower. "Here, Ann, try it!"

Brother Rodgers tossing it her way, Ann Cook screaming, skidding her chair backward, grabbing her purse, brushing off her legs like crazy like it's landed in her lap.

"Hey! What's that sneaking up behind you there, Susan? A big lion?"

Susan Lake twisting around and up off her chair, moving faster than you've ever seen her move, the guys laughing, stupid and rough with their voices changing.

"Ah, don't be scared, Susan. He just wants you to pet him is all. Him and his little lamb buddy there."

Susan Lake nesting back down, straightening her dress, you not looking.

"But here's the best part," Brother Rodgers says, quiet now, hands flat together, fingers pointed up just underneath his chin. "You're done shoveling snow. Done mowing grass. Done with school, with work, with chores. Done with everything you ever didn't want to do. None of that up here. No death, no pain. No hunger, no thirst. Ever again. No getting old, either. You've got your brand new immortal body!"

Looking around the room again.

"Nice place, isn't it? They say that if people really got a look at it, they'd commit suicide just to get here!"

And now he's pausing, looking serious, sweeping his lighthouse head back and forth.

"You know why you're here, don't you."

Nobody says anything.

"You know this is the lowest kingdom. Well, you're here for the same reasons all these other people are. Because you wouldn't accept the gospel. Or keep high moral standards. Or live a decent life in other ways. Or you're a liar, a thief, a murderer, a hypocrite, a false prophet." And now he's grinning again. Spreading out his arms. "But that doesn't matter, does it! Because look at this place! It's great! What more could you want?"

And now he looks at Yenchik.

"What's wrong there, Melvin? Why the sad face?"

You look at Yenchik too, try to see where he's looking sad, instead of just dopey and surprised.

"I think I know," Brother Rodgers says. "You're looking for Jesus, right? All your life you heard you'd be spending eternity with him. Well, I'm sorry, but he doesn't come down here. Or Heavenly Father. But you didn't care about that on earth, so why care about it now? Hey! Just have a peach! Or a fish! It'll cheer you up in no time!"

"I do too care," Yenchik says.

Brother Rodgers ignoring him, already looking at Ann Cook, her shifting in her chair and looking down.

"Ann. You're looking for someone too, right? Let me guess. Your dad. Your mom. Well, sorry, but you don't have a dad or mom anymore. There aren't any families here. No sisters or brothers. But heck. You didn't love them that much anyway, did you?"

"Yes I did," Ann Cook saying. "I mean I do."

"Well, I hate to differ, Ann. If you'd truly loved them, you wouldn't be here. You'd have worked harder on earth to make sure you could spend eternity with them."

Leaving Ann Cook alone, swiveling his head, stopping when it gets to West.

"Bobby. They've got the wildest cars you've ever seen in here, cars that can go a thousand miles an hour, all chopped, channeled, lowered, leaded, raked, frenched, metalflake paint, candy apple red, seats all diamond stitched, spinners like you've never seen! Neatest thing is, no grease, no dirt, no mess! No tools either! All you gotta do is look at your car and think of what you want and it happens! No paying for gas! Just look at the tank and it's full of ethyl! So what's the sad look for?"

West just sitting there looking amazed because Brother Rodgers knows this stuff about rodding up cars.

"I get it," Brother Rodgers saying. "As neat as the cars here are, you're wondering how much neater they've gotta be in the two higher kingdoms. And let me tell you, they're a whole lot neater. All this futuristic stuff! But then you've had your shot at life. This is what you've earned. So now you're thinking if you'd only lived a little better, you'd get to see those other cars, maybe have one. But what really kills you is that Johnny or Julie could be driving a car a whole lot neater. Someone who never knew the difference between lakers and appletons."

Brother Rodgers wanders over to the window where the skin of his face where he shaves goes slick and shiny in the light. He looks across the faces in the room again.

"Any questions before we move on to the next kingdom?"

Yenchik raising his hand.

"Melvin."

"Is there gravity?"

"Gravity?"

"Yeah. In the Telestial Kingdom."

"You got me there," Brother Rodgers saying. "But I'd say yes. Sure. In some heavenly form like everything else."

"It'd be weird," says Yenchik, "not having gravity."

"Can people fly there?" Keller jumping in and asking.

"I wouldn't call it fly. You'll be able to move at will and cover great distances with just a thought."

"Can you go around the universe?"

"I don't know. But I can tell you where you can't go. Upstairs. The two higher kingdoms. The Terrestrial and the Celestial. Not even to visit. So if you know somebody up there, well, you just gotta wait till they decide to come visit you. Anyway, we need to move on. Ready?"

He goes out the door and closes it just long enough to open it and come back in.

"Hey there! Welcome to the Terrestrial Kingdom!" He stands there shaking his head slow with all this reverent wonder. "This place. I can't describe it. Compared to where we've been, this is like the brightness of the full moon compared to the dimness of the stars."

Everyone watching him look around, sweeping his head back and forth like he's outside, in some huge place like Zion's National Park.

"Wow. It's almost too hard to look at it's so beautiful. Look at these cars here. Don't even need tires. Just cruise along just off the ground. Wow! You see that one just take off? Straight up! I was wondering why it had tailfins! Brenda, look at those waterfalls, full of colors, so tall you can't even see where they start. And the music the water's making! What a place! Look! There's Jesus down for a visit! Hurry! Let's go! He doesn't come here that often, and he never stays for long! Wow, Julie, it's like Fabian, stopping in to sign some autographs! We gotta catch him!"

Brother Rodgers pausing long enough to let Julie Quist get over her reaction and then her embarrassed blush and everyone laugh some. Then going serious again.

"How did you end up here? Three ways. First is this. You reject the gospel on Earth, but then once you die, you get a second chance to hear it in the Spirit World, and this time you say okay. Then the Holy Ghost arranges for someone here on Earth to be baptized for you."

The man who took you to the basement of the Temple to get baptized for the dead takes a look around.

"Another way. You had the chance to accept the gospel on Earth and in the Spirit World and rejected it both times. Usually that would land you in the Telestial Kingdom. But you were a good person. You did good things. You sheltered the poor. You found cures for diseases. You helped the sick. Or you just lived a virtuous life and Jesus could see in your heart that you were good. That you'd just been blinded by the craftiness of men."

"So is that where Gandhi is?" Brenda Horn says.

"You know who Gandhi is?"

"We learned about him in History."

"Well, that all depends on Gandhi. He may well have already accepted the gospel. In the Spirit World."

"Does that mean he can go to the Celestial Kingdom?"

"That depends on how valiant he is. But we're not there yet. We're still down here in the Terrestrial Kingdom. And we're down to the last reason for ending up here." Sliding his hands into the pockets of his sport coat. "This is the one that applies to you. Ready?"

"What is it?" Doby finally saying.

"Okay. You're here because you're Mormon."

He looks around for how it settles in on you.

"That's what's got you puzzled. That's why you don't look happy. Being Mormon, you were banking on the Celestial Kingdom. Am I right there? Melvin?"

Yenchik's head comes up off his chest like an apple you let go of underwater.

"That's why you're all so mopey-faced. Too sad to even eat. Just ignore all this fantastic food. Walk right past these beautiful flowers here without even seeing 'em."

"Yeah."

Brother Rodgers smiles. "Well, I guess just being Mormon isn't good enough. Otherwise you'd be upstairs. So let's look deeper. Let's say you minded your parents but in your heart you never really honored them. You just minded them to keep from being grounded. You loved your little brothers and sisters but griped about helping them with their homework. Didn't take them along when you went places with your friends. Whined when you had to babysit them."

He ambles around to the back of the table where he looks like a man who baked the cake in front of him and brought it to a bake sale.

"You always went to church except when something better came along. Baseball, fishing, a matinee, swimming. You only paid your tithing after you took care of everything else. So you were short sometimes. And you took a church job just so you could brag about having one."

Looking down for just a minute at his cake. Maybe too close to talking about Jasperson and Lilly and needing to catch himself.

"So you were a Mormon. But you were a lukewarm one. That's why you're here."

Susan Lake raising her head and looking across the room at the window, not to see anything, just to keep from looking at Brother Rodgers.

"You probably loved your family more than someone down there in the Telestial Kingdom. But not enough to want to spend eternity with them. Because there aren't any families here, either. Sure, you might run into your dad, but he's just another guy now. And your mom, she's just this lady you know. You can't even call her your mom. That's all gone."

The room quiet. Doby finally raising his hand.

"Yes, George."

"What am I supposed to call her?"

"Your mom? What's her name?"

"Jenny."

"Then that's what you call her."

"Jenny?"

Brother Rodgers shrugs. "You could always give her a nickname if you wanted. Bobby, your mom's Eva, right? Susan, Iris? Brenda, Karen? Johnny, can you see yourself calling your mom Betty?"

"No."

"Your dad Lamar?"

"No."

"Then let's get outta here! Next stop, the Celestial Kingdom!"

Chapter 74

BROTHER RODGERS stands there looking at his goodbye cake. And then he brings his hands up, rubs them together, and for a minute you think he's contemplating digging into it right there. But then he looks over and says, "Julie. How many layers in this wonderful cake?"

"Three?"

"Perfect." He's smiling now. "Do you mind if we pretend it's heaven?"

"No. I guess not."

You can see her nervous. Maybe thinking she should have done a better job. Maybe made the flowers bigger.

"Good. Mind if I cut myself a slice?"

"It's banana," she says. "And coconut. I mean the inside's banana."

"Okay. Perfect." And the man who came after you for taking an engine apart centers the point of the knife, brings down the blade, takes it through the cake, does it again, then works the wedge out, takes a plastic fork to push it off the knife and set it standing on a paper plate. Three layers, each the same rich light yellow, stacked, held together like soft bricks with bands of white frosting. White and pink frosting slathered down the back, thick coconut frosting on top, a big blue flower cut through its velvet heart.

"Wow," he says. You smell banana. "It looks scrumptious, Julie. Take a look. All of you. Like a slice of heaven. A cross section. Three degrees of glory. I don't know, Julie. It just looks so tempting I'm not sure I can wait till the lesson's over."

Julie Quist going pink again. Everyone else laughing. Even Brenda Horn but it looks like it's killing her.

"Okay. Which layer here looks yummiest?" He points the blade of the knife, all smeared and hairy now with cake and frosting, at the bottom layer. "This one?"

"No," says Yenchik.

"This one?" Moving the knife point up to the middle layer.

"No," says Yenchik. "The top one."

"This one?" Bringing the knife point up again. "Up here where all the good stuff is? The coconut and frosting?"

"Yeah."

Brenda Horn muttering to Ann Cook.

"What's that, Brenda?"

"Nothing."

"No. Tell us."

"If you like frosting, I guess."

"Not a big frosting fan, huh."

Brenda Horn shrugging. "It depends."

"Well, then I guess Melvin wouldn't mind trading you his middle or bottom layer for your top layer. Right, Melvin?"

"Sure. Yeah. I'll trade."

Brother Rodgers goes serious. "But first, Brenda, let's take a look at what you're trading away." He uses the knife to touch the two bottom layers again. "We've been to the Telestial and Terrestrial Kingdoms. But here." Moving the knife point up again. "Here's the real deal. The Celestial Kingdom. This is where the good stuff is. This is where we achieve true exaltation."

He pulls the dirty knife away from the cake, sets it down, stands himself up against the blackboard, and there's his lighthouse head, maybe for the last time, roving back and forth.

"Unfortunately, we can't really visit the Celestial Kingdom. We're still mortal. We're not pure enough to handle it. It's where God the Father lives. His glory is so great we'd be blinded in an instant. Maybe killed. Comparing it to these two kingdoms is like comparing the brightness of the sun to the brightness of the moon. You can stare at the moon all night long. You look at the sun too long and your eyes turn into raisins. Pow! Right in their sockets."

Strand raising his hand. Brother Rodgers looking at him, thinking what you're thinking, that it's his last day, and he has to deal with Strand till the bitter end.

"Yes, Steve."

"Joseph Smith was mortal."

"Yes?"

"He didn't go blind or die when he saw God."

Brother Rodgers looking at Strand for a minute.

"God had to shield Joseph from his full glory to do what needed to be done. He couldn't restore the gospel to a blind boy. Joseph needed his eyes to translate the Book of Mormon."

"How about sunglasses?" Yenchik says.

"They'd have to be strong. Anyway, since we can't go in, let's say this is a waiting room. You can't see inside. But you can get the feel. Put your hand up here," he says, and puts his hand up flat against the wall next to the blackboard. "Right on the other side of this wall is the glory of the Celestial Kingdom. You can feel it humming just a little."

"Is it thick?" Doby says. "Like a bomb shelter?"

"It doesn't need to be thick. It's made out of material we don't have here on Earth."

Brother Rodgers comes around the front of the table and spreads out his hands like the painting of Jesus doing the Sermon on the Mount.

"So here we are. The highest degree of glory. The home of our Heavenly Father and Jesus Christ. The reason you're here is obvious. You earned it. You were valiant in all things. You kept your heart pure. You knew that any talent or ability you were blessed with was a gift from God. And so you put it all into furthering his work."

An engine coughing to life outside, a powerful one, being raced, shivering the window a couple of times before idling down, taking the load of the clutch. Brother Rodgers looks down, waits till the sound gets to the street and goes, before he looks up again.

"Here's the main reason you're here," he says. "You passed the one true test of faith. You never questioned things. You left the thinking to the leaders of the Church. You knew when they spoke that the thinking had been done and the questions answered. You knew that if you didn't get an answer it was because you didn't need one. You knew that God would answer everything in the fullness of time."

He turns to the wall next to the blackboard again, puts the side of his head up close to it like he's listening, nods his head, this little smile going.

"Bobby. I can hear your mom and dad. They're waiting. Yours too, Brenda." He brings his head off the wall. "Eager to have you back in the family. Except now," he says, "it's your family for eternity. Immortal. Nobody can ever take it away from you."

He comes around to the front of the table again, slow, to give everyone time. Your father. How he brought you all the way from Switzerland so you wouldn't have to call him Harold and your mother Elizabeth. Everywhere you've lived a train station. So you wouldn't have to live in different houses, different neighborhoods, in different towns or cities.

"That goes for all of you," Brother Rodgers says. "Here in the Celestial Kingdom you'll always be a family."

Brother Rodgers takes a long deep breath and lets it out slow. His face goes soft, and then this flicker of something like doubt or longing quivers in the skin around his eyes and mouth, and then he's looking down, and his face is resolute but soft again when he looks back up.

"I want you kids to know that I love each and every one of you."

Everyone sits there. At the front of the room the man who said you were a hero in front of Susan Lake looks at his hand and moves his fingers like he's making sure they work.

"We love you too," Yenchik finally says.

Brother Rodgers looks at Yenchik surprised. Then he brings up his arm, takes hold of his wristwatch like it's a coin, reads what it says. The room goes restless. You know what's coming. This is ending. This is like it will be when he gets to the last telephone pole he'll have to climb. Maybe they'll have a cake waiting when he comes down. He lets his watch go, lets his arm back down, looks up again. For a minute his face screws up like he's got a big sneeze coming. But then it doesn't. It just leaves his face hard and fierce and anxious.

"I need to talk to you in earnest now. Heart to heart. If you never remember anything else I've taught you, that's fine, as long as you always remember what I'm about to say. Deal?"

"Yeah," some of you going.

"You kids." Looking at you some more, then grinning like he can't help it, shaking his head. "You kids." Wandering over to the window, standing there looking out at the parking lot, and then at the orchard up behind the lot and from there the foothills. The lines that fan from the end of his narrowed eye across the skin of his temple are ledged like they're cut through shale. He turns and follows his brown shoes back to the table. He doesn't look up till he's standing behind it. Like he has to wonder what he's done here. If he's done it good enough.

"You know the changes you're going through. Boys, you're becoming men. Girls, you're blossoming into young ladies. You're both experiencing all kinds of feelings. You won't understand them right away. Just that here they are, these new feelings, and here you are, confused, even scared maybe, not sure what's happening."

Suddenly a soft knock on the window, the crying chirp of a bird, everyone jumping, even Brother Rodgers, then going on, a little smear of powder on the glass.

"But Satan's real sure. He knows that this is the time of your life where he's got his best shot at you. In a few short years, that shot will be gone. You'll be stronger, smarter, getting married, starting a family, pretty much out of his reach. So the next few years are it. And he'll try every trick he's got up his big red ugly sleeve to get you."

All the girls except Julie Quist are looking hard into their laps.

"What's happening to your bodies, you boys too, is that God is preparing them for the greatest of all his blessings. He's preparing them right now to bear his spirit children. To be their earthly parents. To give them the mortal bodies they need for their own salvation. Satan wants us to forget that purpose and just pursue the pleasure."

And now you and all the guys except Strand and Yenchik are looking down.

"That's why God gave us the law of chastity. Here's why it's so important. You can always correct a lie. Pay for that pack of gum you swiped. The thing with your chastity is that once it's gone it's gone. You can't bring it back any more than you can bring someone you've murdered back to life to say I'm sorry. You can feel all the remorse you want but it won't restore your virtue. You can pretty much forget about a temple marriage. You know what that means. Just take a look at Julie's cake here."

Heads come up slow.

"If there's anything I pray for, anything I want, it's to see all of you here in the highest kingdom. Forget these two down here. You're better than that."

There are voices and footsteps out in the hall now, a clamoring river of grownups and kids, released and happy and on the move. Julie Quist looks down at the folded grocery bag in her lap, pulls a wrinkle out of it, smoothes it over. Brother Rodgers lets his face go gentle, gentle and grave, where all the ridges and lines and shelves of skin dissolve and go soft like mud.

"That's it. I'm done. Now let's have some of this delicious cake." He picks up the knife, pulls away the napkin where it comes up with the blade, turns to Julie Quist, holds out the knife to her, handle first. "You mind doing the honors?"

"Is there time?" she says startled.

"Sure. We've got a couple of minutes before your folks send in the rescue squad."

Julie Quist gets off her chair, lays the folded grocery bag on the seat, takes the knife, and then just stands there, the knife ready but the blade unsure.

"I'll take this one," Brother Rodgers says. "Come on, kids. Get yourselves one."

He picks up a fork, tips the wedge of cake he's used for the Three Degrees of Glory on its side, cuts himself a big bite, puts it in his mouth. All of you get up.

"Banana. Delicious." Crumbs puff out on the breath of his muffled voice. His lips grope out to catch them but they're gone. And then he notices Julie Quist still standing there and stops and wipes his chin with his wrist.

"What's the matter?"

"I don't know. It feels like there's a spell on it or something."

"There's no spell, Julie. It's just a cake."

And then all of you stop. Because Brother Rodgers is standing there, just holding his plate and fork, because Julie Quist is standing there not doing anything, just crying, not out loud, not obvious, just her cheeks and chin wet, just her face.

CHAPTER 75

"YOU STILL like surprises?"

"More than ever, " says Carla. "Why?"

"I've got one for you."

"You do? What?"

"Can you stay after school the last day?"

"The last day? Next Wednesday?"

"Yeah. They're letting us out early."

"Yeah. How long?"

"Not long. Like half an hour. Can you bring your violin?"

"We're doing that duet?"

"Kind of. Not quite."

You've waited a few days to let your pud heal up before you take another run at finding out what happens. That night you try again. What Blackwell said and what you watched him do. Imagine the Scoutmaster's wife. Get yourself a boner, in the dark, the door closed, your father at the office, everyone else in bed. The Scoutmaster's wife just stands there, friendly and oblivious, with her boobs out. They're huge. Bigger than they ever looked when she was dressed. And they don't have nipples. You try to make them up. Take her black eyes and her hawk nose and her thin lips and try to make her some. They won't go right. They come out tiny. But you keep going. Maybe the way Blackwell started breathing hard. Maybe the way he tensed up off the dirt in a way you'd never seen. Maybe because he's moving to Albuquerque. Whatever it is. You just keep going wherever this will take you.

A long time later headlights play across the ceiling. And then you hear the Chevy stop in the driveway, the door open, the garage door come up into the ceiling down under your bed. You keep going. Try to get the Scoutmaster's wife to stop looking at you friendly while you keep trying to make her nipples. It's too late. Your father's home. You get her dressed. In the green turtleneck sweater you've seen her wear to church. You hear your father turn the Chevy off, nudge its door closed, keep the springs quiet when he brings the garage door down, come in through the basement door, come quiet up the stairs, while you make the astonishing discovery that with her turtleneck sweater on you can touch them. It doesn't matter if she's looking at you friendly. She can keep her high plume of black hair. Her glasses on. You run your hand up the warm round curve of dark green mohair wool. Feel the way that if you stopped, and squeezed, or just pushed, it would give and then come back again.

You hear your father sneak the refrigerator door open. Something starts happening. In the backs of your legs, deep inside your back, this force starts gathering, hot and raw and itching and insistent, this new impossibly powerful gathering force. Under her sweater they're big and soft and real, and then suddenly they're gone, out of the way of this stupendous force, gathered and moving now from everywhere inside you toward your hand and what it's doing. You cry out, just once, and then catch yourself while it comes roaring through you, while sudden light from the hall floods your bedspread, while you look, while you strain to keep your eyeballs from exploding, while you can't stop, while you see your father standing there with the doorknob in his hand.

"Is everything all right?"

"Yes."

The word comes out in this tight convulsive moan like a cough you try to hold back while someone in church is praying. He just keeps standing there. While it just keeps happening. While you know there's nothing you could do to stop it. While it finally starts to let up and then recede and leave you here and you don't know where it came from or where it will go from here. And then, slow and deliberate, the way you heard him open and close the driver's door, the garage door, the basement door, the refrigerator door, he backs into the hall and closes the door to your room again, and whatever it was has taken the rush of its stupendous force and moved on without slowing down and left you here, the middle of nowhere, where in the quiet again you can start to hear the murmuring cries of animals in the dark around you.

The last day of eighth grade, for the first time, you take your trumpet to school, and when they let school out at noon, for the first time carry your case through the halls. She's waiting on the broad stone porch, off to the side, out of the path of the clamoring avalanche of kids spilling out the front doors into the sunlight across the front yard on their way home for the summer. She has her own case with her. She's wearing a light yellow sweater with sleeves that come just past her elbows and a black skirt. It's the first time you've seen her with her hair up where you can see her neck and how it rises up into her jawline and its tendons reach up behind her ears. In the sun her skin has never looked this white. Her lipstick is pink and the round frames of her glasses black. Silver teardrops hang off hooks in the lobes of her ears. She's wearing your arrowhead.

"What's in there?" she says.

"Your surprise."

"What is it?" she says. "A little circus piano?"

"Where do you want to do this?"

The skin between her eyebrows draws tight. She looks back and forth. There's a dark mole just below her ear.

"I know. Come on."

You follow her around the side of the school. At the racks where your own bike stands with its front wheel through two bars, kids are dumping the stuff they've emptied out of their lockers into their handlebar baskets, opening their combination locks. You follow her around the back of the school past the armory. Kids are hitting and fielding balls on the baseball fields. By now you've got it, where you're going, and so you beat her to the two glass doors, open one, let her in. At the other end of the hallway you can make out a janitor getting his polishing machine plugged in and padded. She opens the door. You follow her in and close it.

The music room. Your first time inside. It hasn't mattered for a long time. Just a room where kids sit in gray steel folding chairs in front of music stands on the tiered floor and play their instruments. Cymbals and drums still stand on the shallow stage around a stool.

"There," Carla says, nodding at the upright on the stage. "You can use a real piano."

You don't say anything. Just cross the floor and lay your case on the long shelf that runs under the windows. You can hear the latches snap as she opens her case. By the time she turns around you're standing there.

"A trumpet?"

She comes up close. You bring it up where she can look at it. The smell of strawberry comes off her hair while she slowly runs her finger the length of a long bruise in the brass. And then she backs away and takes a longer look.

"Wow. It really suits you."

"It does?"

"I never could see a piano. I don't know. I don't see you sitting still. A piano just felt too heavy. Like it would hold you down. A trumpet's so perfect."

"I'm glad. Thanks."

"I should've known. That nervous little sideways tease your smile's always got."

Then, before you can think of anything else, she holds her violin out by its neck.

"Here it is. You always wanted to see it."

You hand her your trumpet. For the music it makes you never thought a violin could be this light and small and frail and simple. The black pad for her jaw. Four simple strings arched off the thin black neck her fingertips keep polished. The tuning knobs. You turn it over in your hands and back again. Dark stains and the healed scars of nicks and scratches in the bowed wood let you know it isn't new.

"It was my grandmother's," she says. "Where's yours from? It looks old too."

"Some jazz musician."

"You bought it like this?"

"Yeah."

She looks up. "Is that what you play? Jazz?"

"Yeah."

"My teacher says the older the better. Maybe that works for trumpets too."

"Yeah." You trade instruments back. "So you ready for that duet?"

"Sure. What are we doing?"

"Danny Boy?"

"Danny Boy? It's not really a duet."

"I'll show you."

You watch her nest the violin below her jaw against her neck. The strike and pull of the bow is raw while she tunes the strings. When she's done tuning you tune the trumpet to her violin. You let her take the lead. Face to face across the floor of the music room you watch her play the lonely yearning line of the melody. She watches you while she plays it. Where there are rests, where there's space, you bring the trumpet up, come in soft, brush up alongside the melody, lay down some color, some tension, some harmony, some dissonance, take off again. You take her only gradually off the path of the melody she knows and the stepping stones of its notes across the moving current of the silent chords. At the end of the song she brings down her violin.

"Keep going," you say. "This is where it gets fun."

She doesn't smile. Crosses the room and lays her bow and violin on the long shelf. When she glances back at you across her shoulder her glasses are this flash of outside light through the window. She takes them off and sets them down and comes back to where you're standing. It's the first time you've seen her eyes bare.

"I never liked the color of my hair," she says.

And suddenly reaches up and kisses you. And takes your trumpet out of your hand and carries it across the room and lays it down next to her violin and then comes back and this time kisses you for real.

Part 8

Stallions

CHAPTER 76

"EARL BIRD?"

"Yeah. Friggin' Bird."

"The hairdresser guy?"

"Yeah."

"Holy shit. I mean crap."

"How do you know?" you say.

"My mom found out," says West.

"How?"

"She's a hairdresser. She talks to his wife."

"You're sure."

"Yeah. Wait and see."

In the Sacrament Room up behind the podium in the front wall of the chapel, under the organ pipes, it's Keller and West and Doby and you. Keller and West are getting the Sacrament ready for Sunday School. They've already turned fourteen and been made Teachers. Doing the Sacrament is their job. Doby and you, still Deacons, are there just to be there. Earl Bird. Where Brother Rodgers used to be. For a minute in the little room there's silence, just water running, the clink of trays, your mother's organ music from the pipes up overhead.

"He's a mean prick." Keller laying out slices of Wonder Bread.

"How mean could he be, doing old ladies' hair?" West passing a water tray back and forth under the running tap.

"Maybe that's why he's always pissed."

"He's been pissed since he lost his fingers and couldn't work on buses any more."

You can still hear him do your father's accent and then laugh like he'd told a dirty joke. Wait for Scoutmaster Haycock to laugh too. You feel bad for ever messing with Scoutmaster Haycock's wife. Keller takes a tray from West and wipes down the steel around the paper cups.

"He does dead people's hair too," Doby says.

"What?" says West.

"Yeah. Like at Union Mortuary."

"Friggin' dead people?" says West.

"Yeah. For their funerals. He shaves 'em too. If they're men."

"They're friggin' dead."

"Their whiskers keep growing."

"Yeah," says Keller. "I heard that. Their toenails too."

"That's not all," says Doby. "He talks to 'em while he does their hair."

"About what? They're dead."

"I dunno. Guess the same stuff he does his customers. The live ones. Weather and stuff. You know."

"They're friggin' dead," says West.

"I know they're dead, numbnuts," Doby says. "That's why they're in the mortuary."

West opens a cupboard, pulls two washed and folded tablecloths off the shelf, hands them to you. "Here," he says. "Go lay these out. We'll bring the trays."

"I'd never let him near my hair," says Doby.

At church he doesn't act like the nasty thug he really is. Just tough, tough and friendly, tough like he's the bodyguard for the congregation, friendly but with reservation. You've seen him talk to older ladies almost like he's flirting. Get them to giggle, turn their faces aside with this fake look of shock, wave off what he's saying to them with the long fingers of their bird-boned hands. You've wondered if they're his customers. If he just did their hair yesterday morning.

You'd never let him near your hair either. None of you would. You can tell that from the way all of you go quiet when he walks in and sets down his books and looks around. Like he's looking at your hair. Wondering where all of you go. If he can tell just by looking how you and West and Doby go to Morry's. He hitches up his pants. Tucks the front of his shirt down inside them. He's got a smile going, a small one, but it's dull the way his eyes are.

"For those of you who don't know me," he says, "I'm Brother Bird. I'm your teacher. It looks like we're stuck together. Everyone okay with that?"

Everyone's got their head down, looking up from under their forehead, like sneaking a look at someone while they're praying.

"Okay?"

This time everyone answers. You're noticing his earlobes. Big and long and meaty and tough enough probably to hang cinderblocks off of.

"Good. I want to lay down some rules. First, no arguing. If you've got a question, that's one thing, but if you're here to argue with what

I've got to teach you, guess again. You're here to listen and learn."

You wonder how Strand, sitting in back, is taking being told he can't argue, while Bird takes a look at Yenchik.

"Second, no horseplay. That goes for you girls too. Don't come in here expecting to joke around, or show off, or any other nonsense. You know better. If you don't, you know where the door is, and you can tell the Bishop why you're not in class."

And then he's looking at Yenchik again.

"Third, pay attention. Eyes on me. I catch anyone looking out the window, or nodding off, I'll have you tell me what I just said. And you better know. We got too much ground to cover to have to cover anything twice."

And then he's looking at Yenchik for good.

"Here," he says. Raising his right hand, holding it up and turning it like a vase, wagging the stumps for his three amputated fingers like stems where three flower heads used to be. "Take a good look."

"Sorry," says Yenchik.

"No. Let's get this out of the way. Here. Everybody." He walks to where the girls are and holds out his hand like it's holding something he wants to give them. The girls push back against their chairs and screw their faces up but keep their eyes glued to the way his stumps are wagging. And then the guys. All of you lean forward for a better look. Jasperson studies it like an assignment, like something he was told to do, like the twitching heart of a gutted frog in biology. You look long enough to see the crossed scars across the tops where they folded the skin to give them smooth new gift-wrapped ends. You can hear and smell him breathing. He goes back to the front of the room again.

"Okay. Fourth rule. I'm not gonna pretty things up for you. Not gonna make you feel all warm and mushy. Not gonna tell you any bedtime stories about how good boys and girls behave. You've had a bellyful of that. The gospel's serious. Life's serious. I'm gonna give it to you straight. Everybody got that?"

Everyone lets him know they did.

"How about you back there?"

"Sure," says Strand.

Bird's eyebrows go up just a flick. Maybe surprised that Strand has a deeper voice than he does now.

"Okay. Today you're gonna learn about keeping the Sabbath holy."

CHAPTER 77

A BROOMSTICK, a big nail driven straight into the end, then the wood chiseled and whittled and sanded to a long smooth point, the head of the nail filed off and sharpened to a point too, like the lead of a pencil, something Blackwell could sharpen over and over. Bands of green and red and blue and yellow yarn wound tight and glued in stripes around the stick. A handgrip in the center made out of a long leather cord wrapped tight and knotted in place and oiled and rubbed. Feathers the one thing missing. In La Sal, when they shot buzzards and hawks, you had all the feathers you wanted. Here all you've got are seagulls.

"Wow," he says.

He forgot all about it. That deal you made in the field two years ago before you got the Priesthood. He looks it over, touches the point with the pad of his thumb, wraps his hand around the coiled leather cord of the handgrip, hefts it back and forth, runs his finger across his initials. You show him where he can sharpen it. Out in his back yard you show him how to spin it when he tosses it to keep it going straight. And you show him where the feathers go, tell him how to tie them on, if he finds any down in Albuquerque when he moves there.

"Is this like the one you had?"

"Yeah. Except it's better."

"You ever kill anything with yours?"

"A couple of snakes. Once I got a trout."

"I bet this could kill a mountain lion or a bear."

"Maybe. You'd have to get it right in the heart. Or through its eyeball to its brain."

He looks at you. He's thinking his part of the deal.

"You try it again?"

"Yeah."

"Did it work?"

"Yeah," you say.

He gives you this big grin. Eager to know that he's even for the spear.

"Feels good, doesn't it?"

You look at the white rubber toes of your sneakers where grass has scuffed them green.

"Yeah."

Blackwell holds the spear up high and does this war dance in a circle on the grass.

"Were you scared?" he says.

"Yeah."

"Yeah," he says. "Me too." And then he says, "Did anything come out?"

"Like what?"

"Me neither at first. It will. You just gotta keep doing it."

"What's supposed to come out?"

"Keep doing it."

He doesn't have to tell you much. Just where it comes from. Why it feels the way it does. What it's called and what it means. What you're supposed to do next. Now that you've felt it. Now that you know what to do to feel it again. What he was thinking while he stood there with the doorknob in his hand.

Is everything all right.

And after that he never said anything. Never sat you down and told you, with the meticulous logic of taking apart an arithmetic problem like a watch, what you did wrong and why you were wrong when you did it. Just kept it to himself. When he's idled the Chevy wagon into the garage and caught you standing there to the side. On Sunday morning, in the kitchen, his suit on underneath his apron. And so you don't know. You lying there in bed. What was in his face lost in the silhouette of his head. Your bedspread and face in the light where it came around him from the hall. The little tent your other hand was holding up. The bed shaking. You trying to keep your face from blowing open. He must have known. He had to. It was crazy not to think he did. Why he kept standing there. To make sure you got to the end okay. To see if you had any questions afterward. If he knew you couldn't stop. If he knew you didn't know what was happening. If he knew how you wanted to hide what was happening but felt like you didn't even have skin to hide inside of. If his face looked like he'd had it. Like it was something he expected. Or if he was just watching and wanted you to know it.

Yes. No. Yes.

You don't know. You don't know anything. You ask the questions a thousand times, and when you get to the end of them you're where you always are, at the cold edge of a sudden cliff like Dead Horse Point, where the level ground with its red dirt and its warm calm sagebrush just suddenly drops away, thousands of feet down through open sky, where the air comes whistling and moaning up the vertical sandstone face of the cliff and plays in little circles all around you, where your father is the cliff, where the stark sudden vault of so much open space makes you stand there hot and cold together for how vast and still and bottomless it is, and the next step you take is where your father is waiting to answer everything.

One of the last things Blackwell tells you is that Bishop Byrne will want to know if you've done it. School's just out. From the small slope along the top of his yard, you've been watching three men bring things out of Blackwell's house, off the porch, down the walk to the street, up this long ramp with the quaking flex of a diving board, into the dark open back of the trailer of the moving van. Inside the trailer another man wraps the furniture in big gray quilts. He works back toward the back door as Blackwell's house goes empty. Sometimes the men stop, stand around and smoke in the shade of the trailer, pass around the water hose, drink, bend forward and run water over their heads, like the men who emptied out Mrs. Harding's house. One of the men is a Negro. In the shade of the trailer, his white cigarette is crisp against his dark face, and in the sun, the beads of water in his hair make a sparkling cap of a thousand diamonds.

"He's gonna ask?"

"Yeah."

"When?"

"When you do your interview for Teacher."

After your birthday a couple of weeks away. When you turn fourteen.

"How do you know?"

"He asked me if I did."

"What'd you tell him?"

"No."

"You just fibbed?"

The Negro man comes up the driveway carrying Blackwell's bike up.

"I'm a Teacher, ain't I?" says Blackwell.

You figure maybe because Bishop Byrne could take one look at Blackwell and know he needed to be asked.

"I didn't know you had a ping pong table."

"Yeah. We just never had room for it."

"What makes you think he'll ask me?"

"He asks everybody. He has to. It's a rule."

Your buddies who turned fourteen already. Moved on to being Teachers. You know what they all told Bishop Byrne when he asked. Otherwise they'd still be Deacons. But if they had to fib like Blackwell did. You figure Lilly and Jasperson told the truth. Keller and West must have fibbed. Strand you can't say. You take a glance at Blackwell's eyes. If Bishop Byrne could see Scoutmaster Haycock's wife back there. If Blackwell's version of her has nipples.

"You think he believed you?"

"Byrne? He had to."

"Why?"

"Because nobody ever saw me do it. He never had any proof."

Blackwell heaving and bucking like a trout on the bank of dirt across from the roadbed where the tracks ran. You not knowing then what was going on.

"He's pretty easy to fool, anyway. Don't worry about it."

And then Blackwell's gone. And your father sets up your interview with Bishop Byrne for the day after you turn fourteen. Tuesday. Six-thirty. Half an hour before Scouts. When he asks you the question, when you lie, when you try to keep him from seeing the Scoutmaster's wife, you'll be wearing your scout uniform. You promise yourself you'll stop a week before the interview. That way you can kind of tell the truth. Tell him no and mean the week you haven't done it for. Just hope he doesn't ask how long it's been. Doesn't ask you if you've ever done it. Doesn't say Scout's Honor. Or that your father won't have told him.

Sometimes it's the crazy stuff that makes you go. Stuff that leaves your stomach raw and your throat sore and this itching fire going in your skin. Where the air in the house and garage is this charged electric smoke you can't get any breath from. Where your head feels like forty seagulls are screeching around inside it looking for bread. Other times it's just the stuff you can't make sense of. The stuff you're always getting wrong. Stuff you need to think about yourself, answer your own way, stuff you can't understand till you get away from the way your father answers things. Ride. Out of the choking calm of the neighborhood with nothing going but its sprinklers. Keep riding like Clark Terry when he was a kid. Out where you don't know anyone and nobody knows you. Just keep on riding till you've outrun everyone. Till anyone who's chasing you has to stop, double over with a side cramp, gasp for air like there's not enough in the universe, let you go. Till it's just you. You and your bike and the road and asphalt and gravel and dirt, right there, in front of you, where it always is, where it will always be. You. Just you and as long as you crank the pedals how you keep on going.

CHAPTER 78

IF YOU THINK of it as something holy. Like Brother Rodgers said. Like your pud belongs to God. On the Tuesday a week ahead of your interview, in bed after Scouts that night, you look ahead to answering the question across your promise to go seven days without doing it. You do everything you can to keep the door closed on the Scoutmaster's wife. To keep from reaching down. Pin your hands behind your head. In your armpits. Under your pillow. But they're hands. They get loose. Getting loose is what they're good at. You don't have any extra hands to hold them down, and even if you did, they'd have to be held down too. You fold them under your chin and pray through the ceiling to God to help you resist the Devil. And then tell the Devil to go to hell. And then feel stupid for telling the Devil to go where he already is. And then lie there and name all the states. And then form your hands the way they hold your trumpet and finger through some exercises. And then try to count all the peas you've ever picked for Old Man Tuttle. And then count the days until the interview, and recognize that seven days in front of next Tuesday, a week away, doesn't technically start until tomorrow. Wednesday. And there she comes. Out of the dark of the doorway. The Scoutmaster's wife in her mohair sweater.

On Wednesday afternoon Molly comes home from the churchhouse with a paper doll of an angel she made in her Primary class. Home from weeding Old Man Tuttle's rows, you're at the kitchen table, reading the little story jokes in the Reader's Digest before heading downstairs to practice. Your mother's across the kitchen, behind the counter, making stuffed tomatoes, when Molly walks in and holds up her paper doll.

"Look what I made."

"Yes. That's nice. An angel."

The fretting sound in your mother's accent while she uses a knife to slice the cap off a big tomato and a spoon to hollow out its insides into a big steel bowl.

"It's my guardian angel."

"Yes. One day you will have one."

"Don't I have one now?"

"No, sweetheart. You have to earn one. You can't expect one just to be given to you."

"When will I earn one?"

"Maybe when you stop wetting the bed." Gutting another tomato. "We have to wait and see."

"Do you have one?"

"Of course. How do you think I am able to raise five children?"

Your mother makes a quick little joking cry of a laugh. Scoops browned hamburger meat into the gutted tomatoes she's laid out in rows on a baking tray while Molly watches.

"Does Papa?"

"Of course."

"My friends all have guardian angels."

"Then that is because they deserve them."

Molly looks down at her angel. You wait for her to give your mother the opening for her famous line. They just don't know you like we do. Daring your mother to say it. Your head hot and your back bristling and your arms itching. Molly looks back up.

"When I get one, will it look like this?"

"Now you are being silly. How should I know what your guardian angel will look like?"

Your mother puts the caps back on the stuffed tomatoes, picks up the steel bowl, runs the seeded red slurry of their insides into the tray around them for sauce.

"You've already got a real one," you say. "That's like a photograph of her."

"Yah, Shakli. That is nice, to contradict your mother."

You ignore her. "We'll tape her to your headboard. Where she can look over you."

"Yah, Shakli. Maybe you should go practice now."

"I need to help Molly first."

On Wednesday night, the seventh ahead of your interview, the kick-off day, the day you can't afford to lose, you have to get out of bed to keep from doing it. Turn on your desk light, try doing some reading, then try drawing. Faces. Hot rods. Boats. Fighter jets. Faces again, wrinkled old droop-eyed faces wasted by age, while your hand keeps wanting to draw just the two full curves of her mohair sweater. You hear the Chevy wagon coast into the circle. The idling engine enter the open garage below you. Exhaust rises up the front of the house through your open window. He's seen your light. Sure enough, after the refrigerator door, his careful footsteps down the hall, the door behind you opens, and there he is, hand on the knob again.

"Is everything all right?"

This time you've got your pants on, your hands out in the open, nothing going on.

"Yeah."

"What are you still doing up?"

"I couldn't sleep."

"Well, give it another try. We need to shut the house down for the night."

"Okay."

He stands there and waits for you to turn out the desk light, get down to your underpants again, slip into bed.

"Did you say your prayers?"

"Yeah. A long time ago."

"Good night, then. Pleasant dreams."

"Good night, Papa."

"Remember who you are."

"I will."

You lie there in the dark. Through the sound of crickets you can hear the door open and close to the bedroom where your mother's been asleep, your mother fret in this sleepy questioning voice about the time, the bed take your father's weight. Remember who you are. Somewhere out there a car horn honks. And then drowns in the sound of crickets. And then you give in to sleep yourself before your hands know sleep was even coming.

The next day, wearing a gold tie decorated with blue and white flowers tucked down the neck of his sweater vest, the smell of fresh-baked oatmeal cookies from the kitchen, smiling the way he always does when something good is coming, Mr. Selby starts to teach you modal scales. Names like dorian and phrygian and mixolydian. Scales that are modes inside the regular major and minor scales. Scales you can run on your trumpet over the same long chord without it changing. Scales that can come unleashed from the changes underneath them while the changes themselves can move in sudden unexpected ways. You've heard it on his albums. You didn't know what you were hearing. You didn't know there was more. You didn't know it was named or had this logic.

"Here's the fun part. Instead of straight ahead, you play to the right, or left, or off at some crazy angle, whatever you'd like, as long as somewhere down the road you can make it make sense. You're not tied to the changes. You don't have to make it back in time for them. You can stay out longer. Take it farther out."

In bed that night, when the Scoutmaster's wife comes looking, you're way too charged to care. In the haven of your house you fall asleep to running all the dorian scales of all the keys.

CHAPTER 79

THE NEXT AFTERNOON, home again from Old Man Tuttle's, the house has the hushed kind of lull that means your mother's napping. You'll use your mute the way you always do. You're washing up, getting a tumbler of water, eager to get downstairs when Karl comes into the kitchen.

"They're tearing down Harding's house," he says.

He stands there waiting while you drain the tumbler.

"Liar," you say.

"Go see for yourself," he says. His face too mean and eager to be lying.

"You seen it?"

"Yeah." And then he says, "Want me to show you?"

You've stayed away since it was sold around two years ago by the high-heeled woman with the white Chrysler, sold and then left to sit there, the yard that had paid for your trumpet left to go wild and shaggy with weeds and then finally dead, windows to go cracked and busted out. The last time you saw it, long gray weathered scabs of toilet paper were stuck to the roof where rolls had been lobbed across the house the night before last Halloween, still clinging like abandoned insect nests high in the branches of the trees.

There's a loose crowd out in the street. Mothers and kids. Long sawhorses holding them back. Men in overalls and helmets milling around. Up on the rise of Mrs. Harding's front yard, the steam shovel you heard while you were running up the hill, the dirty hammering bawl of the engine. Black smoke coughs out of its stack and settles in the dirty haze of gray around it. The front of the second floor is open. The roof gone. The walls and floors ripped and splintered back. The rooms half gone. What's left of them exposed to daylight. Rose-colored walls in one. Light blue walls in the next. Sunlight sparkles in the beads of a chandelier about to fall from a busted edge of a ceiling. A bathtub dangles half off the ragged cliff of a bathroom floor. It amazes you how the rest of the house, the untouched lower floor of the front of the house, the windows and the long porch, can look so calm. Like the steers they shot and strung up at the ranch just hung there calm while they were gutted and skinned.

"Look!" someone yells. "Another swing!"

You watch the cab of the steam shovel swing the long extended yellow arm of the bucket away from the house, stop, then swing back hard on the sudden howl of the engine. Watch the bucket smash through the lower corner of the second floor and keep going, keep ripping through the front wall, wood and brick and dust exploding in its wake. The bathtub lets go. Tips off the edge of the floor, hangs for a second on the grip of a pipe, then slides down the front of the house like a shiny white boat off a waterfall before it hits nose first, sinks over in the wreckage on its side, while kids around you scream and holler.

That night, your mother and father off to a Utah Symphony concert, the kids downstairs watching tv, you look for the photograph Lupe gave you, find it on your closet shelf under a box for a model of a battleship, sit down at your desk, turn on your desk light. The last time you saw it was when you brought it home. Hidden more than a year on the shelf has made it new again. Lupe coming out to the yard, standing there, handing it to you, the house behind her emptied and scrubbed, the porch where Mrs. Harding used to stand while you washed your face in her bowl and dried it with her towel. You're there again. Only this time it's the woman in the photograph. She's standing there on boards so real you can see the grayed wood through the worn white paint. The four Negro men are standing there with her. You've got your trumpet. They want you to play with them on her tennis court while she sings. You know the song when they ask. You tape the photograph to the wall above your chest of drawers next to your drawing of Rufus.

All morning Saturday, while you work the yard, dump trucks with squealing brakes keep rolling down the hill, easing around the corner past the circle, rumbling away down the street the way Manny and Hidalgo took the cattle truck, dust shaking loose off the wreckage their beds are loaded with. Sometimes seagulls follow them, swoop down, get spooked, veer off again. When the trucks aren't running you can hear the bulldozer. When the truck with the steam shovel on its long flat sagging bed comes easing down the hill and past the circle you stop sweeping the gutter long enough to watch it round the corner past the house you still call Blackwell's house. Sometime that afternoon, you bring Molly into your room, pick her up where she can get a close look at the photograph.

"She's your guardian angel?"

"Yeah."

"She's a real one."

"So is yours. Don't listen to Mama."

"I mean a real person."

"Not now. Now she's an angel. Like yours."

Waking Sunday morning, the Mormon Tabernacle Choir coming from your father's radio in the kitchen, it doesn't matter. You've added two more nights to your obedience to the law of chastity. To your power to look at Bishop Byrne and tell him no on Tuesday when he asks. Two nights where you could let your hands go anywhere they felt like going. Where your room was this reservoir of quiet assurance that everything made sense. Wherc streams and rivers went back and forth with other reservoirs where everything held its place, made sense where it belonged, where the Scoutmaster's wife stayed home and fixed dinner for Scoutmaster Haycock, where Mr. Selby put out a bowl of night milk for Theo, where Mrs. Harding was smiling because she knew about your trumpet now. If you pass your interview Tuesday then this morning will be your last class from Brother Clark. You hear the crack of an egg on the lip of a pan, jump out of bed, and you're washed and dressed and your hair Chet Baker combed in time to watch your father slip breakfast onto your plate.

CHAPTER 80

HOME THAT AFTERNOON from Sunday School you put together a new blue bike for Roy. Out in the circle, while your father runs his camera, you hold his seat while your kid brother goes round in wobbling rings, scares himself when he jackknifes or almost tips the bike, breaks out helpless with this shy grin when he starts to catch on. Back in the house there's the smell of a Sunday roast out of the oven. Maggie helping Molly set the dining room table. Back in your room you spot your father's scotch tape holder on your desk from a couple of nights ago. Hoping he hasn't needed it, hasn't had to look for it without finding it, you grab it and head for the door to run it back downstairs.

"Come, children!" Your mother's cry like it's Christmas. "Let's eat!"

It stops you cold, the blank place on the wall next to the drawing, gets your head racing when you look again. If you took it down. If it fell. You look behind the chest. In the closet, on the closet shelf, in the drawers, under the stuff on your desk, behind your nightstand, under the bed. Everywhere again. And then you're down to nothing, just turning wild circles on the rug, knowing that it never fell, that it wasn't you who took it down, or Karl, or Molly. On the tiny piece of tape still stuck to the wall, you can tell where a fingernail nibbled at it, then let it go.

"Papa says to come eat."

Roy in the doorway. You follow him to the dining room. From the head of the table your father looks at you. Your mother looks up from her chair to his right. The brown shingles of a sliced roast on a big pink platter. A steel bowl of mashed potatoes. Corn. Gravy. Biscuits. A steel pitcher you know holds apple juice. Steel tumblers, china plates, knives and forks, napkins where Molly and Maggie laid everything out. Roy gets on his chair. Your mother's raised face is like it is at church, at the organ, angelic and obedient, like she's looking at Sister Lake the chorister.

"Yes, Shakli." Her church voice too, inviting and polite, like you're a kid from someone else's family. "Now we can eat, children."

"Where'd my picture go?"

You watch this tight little shock of hurt go through her angel smile, firm up the sweetness, while she looks away quick, across the table at Roy.

"Sit down," your father says. "We've had to let your mother's wonderful cooking get cold enough."

And so you sit there while your father's long blessing takes its usual journey around the world. Sit there with your eyes shut to keep them from looking at food, your breathing to where you won't draw the smell of the roast too deep into your lungs, your hands locked hard together, noise in your head to drown your father out. You feel the eyes of your trapped family opening around you, the way yours usually do, trading looks across the table at each other, going closed again. You're ready when everyone says Amen.

"Where'd my picture go?"

From across the table your mother looks back at you with this faraway smile, like you're barely there, like you're in some dream she's having.

"Yes, Shakli." She turns and looks at your father like he's in the same dream. "Help me, Harold."

Your father takes his fork, stabs hard into the roast to get two slices, hoists them back to his plate.

"Where'd it go?" you say.

"We had to get rid of it," he says.

"When?"

"This morning," your mother says. "When Molly showed it to me."

You look across at Molly, her face down, blind with the shame of taking your mother into your room, too innocent with everything she learned in Sunday School to know what would happen. You look back at your mother. Close your throat down hard on this flood of sudden fury. Lock eyes with her.

"What'd you do? Take it down in front of her?"

"So," your father says. "Calm down. Let's get the food going. Roy. Take a biscuit. Karl. Take some potatoes. Let's get going, by golly."

"Did you?"

"Of course," she says. "She had to know."

"What did she have to know?"

"Keep your voice down," your father says. "Take some roast, Mother."

"The truth." Ignoring your father too. "That we don't tolerate that kind of thing."

"What truth? What thing?"

"You know. Don't make me say it in front of the children."

"Know what? What'd you tell her?"

"Calm down," your father says. "I won't say it again. Molly. Take some potatoes. Give your sister some."

"How could you do that, Shakli. Tell your little sister that woman was your guardian angel. What is wrong with you?"

"What'd you do with it?"

"It's gone. It's where it belongs."

"Where?"

"We tore it up."

Your father uses the back of the ladle to hollow out a crater in his mound of mashed potatoes for the gravy.

"You tore it up?"

"And threw it out. Now take some potatoes. Mother, pass me the gravy, please."

"Where?" Fit and tape the pieces back together. "Where'd you throw it?"

He floods his mashed potato crater with gravy and runs another couple of spoons across his roast.

"It's gone. That's all you need to know."

"Where?"

"Lower your voice."

"Tell me where!"

"In the incinerator! There! Are you happy now?"

"Are you crazy? You burned it?"

"So! Try to calm yourself! Put some food on your plate!"

"You burned it?"

"Shakli, look at me. Please."

Your mother's veined piano-playing hand snakes its reaching fingers through the bowls and the platters across the tablecloth. You follow her arm up to her face, find the same reaching worry waiting for you there.

"We just can't have that in our house. It broke my heart to see it there."

"What broke your heart?"

"You know, Shakli."

"What? Mrs. Harding? The Negroes? What?"

"Should I spell it out for you? The way she was dressed? Half naked? That look that she had in her face? All those men around her?"

"She was a singer! That was her band!"

"Yah. Is that why you want to play the trumpet? To be in a band like that? So you can be around those women?"

"So! That's enough! Can't we just have dinner!"

Through your father's first muffled bark, through him moving the food in his mouth out of the way, through him saying the rest of it, you stare at her, the fierce bright blazing hate in her eyes, all the tortured wires drawn tight behind her skin, her lips stitched tight on the dirty snarl of her voice, like she's never been your mother, you her kid.

"Why didn't you tell us? We would never have let you go to work for her! Now I have to wonder what were you doing there all day!"

"I did her yard!"

"Yah! The yard of a tramp!"

"She wasn't a tramp! She was a singer!"

"A real singer doesn't have to go around half naked!"

"You don't know crap about her!"

"Yah! We know enough! We know you! Hanging her picture on your wall where you can stare at her! Pfui! Shame on you!"

"I didn't hang it there for that!"

"You think we don't know you? Shame on you! Pfui!"

"Shame on you! You crazy witch!"

"That's it!" The shock of your father's big fists makes all the china and steel on the table jump. "So! Leave the table!"

You back your chair away, get up, up from the prepared stillness of the table and everything waiting on the tablecloth, from the waiting stillness of your family, this crazy feeling of tearing yourself out of this photograph you don't belong in, this family ready for Sunday dinner, food going cold as long as you keep standing there, half behind Roy, the top of his head, this crazy idea that you'd barely have to move your hands and he'd be a Deacon, this crazy need to get away, this crazy need to stay, this crazy need to look at your father and find what you need in his face.

"Wait in your room," he says. "We need to talk."

You look at Molly, her head lowered, her hair pulled back tight from the white line where it's parted to feed the tight weaves of her braids.

"You didn't do anything wrong," you tell her. "Don't feel bad. Don't worry. It would of happened anyway."

CHAPTER 81

YOU'RE IN your room just long enough to grab your trumpet case and the sock you keep your mute in. Downstairs, you throw the garage door up on the sudden sunlight of the driveway, bang it so hard into its overhead frame it leaves the springs whanging. Across the circle Woody Stone's got the hood up on his Plymouth. He dips his head and cranes it around your way. In her yard, Nicky Bird looks up too, from her knees at the flowerbed around her mailbox. You loop the piece of belt through the basket on your handlebars and buckle the sock with the mute in place. Grab the rope and start lashing the case to the rack. Try to control your hands at tying knots you know by heart.

"What are you doing?"

Your father, out toward the open door, mostly this shadow cut out of the hard sunlight of the driveway behind him. You know from his voice that he's already checked the circle, seen Woody Stone and Nicky Bird, waved if he caught them looking his way.

"Going."

"Come. Come back in. Let's finish this inside." He's heading across the garage, reaching for the strap that pulls the door back down.

"Don't touch the door."

"What did you say?"

"I'll yell my head off."

And then he stands there, his arm raised, the strap in his hand, looking out across the circle like he's there just to see what's going on around it.

"I mean it. I will."

You watch him let the strap go. You go back to the knot you were tying.

"Let's be reasonable," he says. "Let's handle this like men."

Your hands the way they're racing everywhere. You stop them for a second, take charge of them, go back to the knot again.

"She wasn't a tramp."

"Nobody said that."

"You heard her."

"You know your mother. You know she didn't mean it. Sometimes we have to take what she says with a grain of salt."

"She meant it."

"Nobody thinks she was a tramp. I'm sure she was a decent woman. But you have to look at her appearance, by golly. You have to look at the way she appeared to your mother."

You give up on the knot, pull it apart, start it over.

"Did you even see it?"

"The photograph? Yes. She showed it to me."

"When?"

"When we got home from Sunday School."

Her showing him while he was changing into what he's wearing now. Him standing there looking.

"Did you think it was dirty too?"

"I could see where it would make someone like your mother think that way."

"Why didn't you tell her?"

"Tell her what?"

"That she was wrong?"

You look up. He looks back at you and then away. You watch his face work for a minute. You go back to the knot in your hands.

"That's not the point. It's that the picture led her to think that way. By golly. Don't you know that we have to avoid even the appearance of evil?"

"Is that why I hung it up?"

"How should I know why you hung it up? I can't read your mind."

Suddenly you're crying, not out loud, just these tears, blurring what your hands are doing, coming off your face, splatters you hope your father can't see on the trumpet case. You get the last knot tied. Take your bandana and tie it around your head.

"Come now," he says. "We'll apologize to your mother. Everybody will settle down and enjoy a nice meal. She has your favorite dessert. Ice cream with raspberry topping."

"Apologize? For what?"

"You can't call your mother a witch."

"I need to go."

"She hasn't had an easy life. You need to understand her."

"I do."

"Did you know she only had one dress in high school?"

"No."

"Every night she would wash it in the kitchen sink. And iron it in the morning. She didn't go to just any school. She earned a scholarship to the top school in Basel. All the other students were rich. They hated her. She was poor and got the best grades in the school. She was beautiful and kind. They ridiculed her. She took it like something she deserved."

She doesn't know Carla. She never will. It makes you shiver all over again.

"In the end it didn't matter. Her father got sick. Cancer of the stomach. When he died she was seventeen. She had to leave school and work in a shop to help her family pay the bills. She had to give up everything. And she makes those sacrifices for her family now."

The steel yoke of the handlebars, the basket, the gym sock with your mute inside it buckled to the wires. There's just his voice, a voice without a face, a radio voice, out of nowhere.

"Did you know her then?" you say.

"Yes."

"What color was her dress?"

"Her dress?"

"The one she had. Her only dress."

You stand there looking down. So hungry to leave you could leave your skin behind if you could take it off.

"It doesn't matter," he finally says. "That isn't the point."

The grind and catch of an engine being started, revved twice, left to coast down again, a door slamming, and when you take a quick look up, Woody Stone leaning on his fender, looking down into the open hole under the raised hood of his Plymouth.

"Was it pink?"

"Her dress? I don't remember. What I'm trying to say is that she has suffered enough. By golly. Why do you think I'm always trying to make her feel special?"

The tribute he writes to her on his typewriter every Mother's Day, and every August for her birthday, and then reads to all of you at the supper table. The loving wife and mother.

"I feel bad for her," you finally say.

"A week from now you'll be a Teacher. You'll be called upon to be a peacemaker. This is an opportunity to show that you can do it."

You start toward the door. He steps half in front of you. Grabs the basket. Woody Stone and Nicky Bird out in the circle make him clumsy.

"Let go."

You look at his face. The way the lines are raised in red congested ridges that make him look half wild. Across the circle, Woody Stone slams down his hood, stands back wiping his hands while he looks his

Plymouth over.

"Don't do something you'll regret."

"I won't. Just let go."

"On one condition. That you're back in time for Sacrament Meeting."

"Okay."

"And tomorrow's your birthday. Let's not do anything to spoil it."

"Let go."

CHAPTER 82

PEDAL. OUTRUN the tears to where all that's left of them are the dry tight shriveled lines you can feel in the skin from your eyes back to your ears. Outrun what your mother said. The stranger in her voice and the way she looked at you. The sound that won't stop coming up from down inside your chest. The way your throat and stomach hurt. Outrun air to turn it into wind. Wind that can make Mrs. Harding clean again. Make her like she was. Outrun your face.

You don't care. The Holy Ghost can go to hell. Between then and your interview you do it every chance you get. That night in bed after Sacrament Meeting. The next morning, waking up to having turned fourteen, after your father leaves for work. That afternoon when you get home from Old Man Tuttle's fields. That night after you've had your family celebrate your birthday. The next morning. The next afternoon. You see so much of the Scoutmaster's wife you feel like you're going steady.

That night, after supper, half an hour early, you put on your uniform, head down through the orchard, find Bishop Byrne in his office down the quiet hallway of the churchhouse.

"Hi."

"Hello, son. Come on in. Sit down."

Three armchairs made out of wood stand on the carpet in front of his desk. You go for the closest one. He motions you to the middle one. You watch him take a piece of paper and put it in front of him with hands like the roots of trees from how big their knuckles are. On the top curve of one of his big ears there's a drop of light green paint from doing someone's house that day.

You've never seen him in a short sleeved shirt. Never seen how big and rough his arms are. How they match his face. What you always feel is his kindness. Kindness he spreads like a quiet pool of calming shade for the congregation. Like his strength and his kindness are fused. Like he's taken all the strength in his arms and hands and face and put it into making his kindness big and powerful. The way other men take their strength and put it into being mean. Like Earl Bird. On the wall behind him the curtains are closed. The late afternoon sun is this glowing honey-colored circle in the cloth. Its light gives the office the feel of a gold aquarium.

If you've fondled yourself. That's how Blackwell said he would ask you.

He wants to know what you've been doing. How school went. How your mother is. He tells you how much he likes to sit on the podium listening to her play. How much he enjoys the lessons your father gives in Sunday School. How modest they both are.

"Okay," he says. "I need to ask some questions. Knowing how your folks have brought you up, I'm sure I could answer them myself, but I'm supposed to ask you anyway."

If you've paid your tithing. Yes. Kept the Word of Wisdom. Yes. Been to all your meetings. Yes. Except for the Sunday in March when you were sick. Paid fast offerings. Yes. Lived all the commandments. Yes. Been obedient and helpful to your folks. Yes. Set a good example for your brothers and sisters. Yes. Worked on your testimony. Yes. Kept your thoughts clean.

"Yes."

"Haven't had any thoughts you wouldn't want your folks to know about."

Your answers have to be quick.

"Not really. No."

Your neckerchief tickles your ear but you keep from moving. Keep your eyes on his. Stay ready for the big one. But he gives you this smile, slow and easy and kind, and then breaks away his eyes, looks down, draws his hands off the paper, picks up a pen, writes something down.

"Okay," he says, putting the pen down. "No sense wasting more time on things I already know."

You stare at him. Where the question went. If he's saving it for last.

"I guess you're looking forward to being ordained a Teacher," he says.

"Sure."

"The next big step," he says. "Your folks must be proud."

"Yes."

"Okay. Let's talk about your new duties. Have you learned what they'll be?"

"Yes."

"Why don't you share what you know with me. Then we'll fill in any holes."

You start with the jobs you've seen your buddies do. Get the sacrament ready. Usher at the meetings. You move on to the ones you're not too sure about. The ones where your buddies don't look too sure themselves. Watch over the church. See that there's no iniquity or hardness or backbiting or evil speaking. Help the members do their duties. Be a peacemaker.

"Very good," says Bishop Byrne. "Think you got them all?"

The list your father stuck in your birthday card. Anything you missed.

"When people get up to bear their testimonies, bring them the microphone."

He smiles at his desk and brings his hands together on his stomach.

"Any you don't understand?"

"Not really."

"Well, let's go over them anyway. Just to make sure we're seeing things man to man. What does it mean to watch over the church? See that there's no iniquity or hardness?"

"Make sure everything's okay," you say. "Make sure everyone's reverent." And then you say, "Make sure nobody talks bad about anyone."

"I'm counting on you to help me do that," he says. "Okay. How about helping the members do their duties?"

"Help them keep the commandments."

"That's what you'll be doing when you go ward teaching. Visit your assigned families, find out where they may be having trouble, pray with them. You'll be our eyes and ears for those families. Let us know how they're doing. If there's anything we can do to help them."

How it used to be Brother Jeppson and Billy Hess. How Brother Larsen and Tall Paul Peterson come to your house now. How the house feels like church the way your father and mother act. How Brother Larsen asks if everything's okay. How your father and mother are always quick to tell him yes. How everyone kneels around the coffee table afterward and Brother Larson prays and you're kneeling there next to Tall Paul Peterson, a high school basketball star, wondering what he's making of the look he's had inside your family. How they leave and soon the house is just your house again.

"I'll remember," you say.

"Okay. How about the calling to be a peacekeeper? A calming influence? Do you understand that one?"

"Yeah. I do."

"I know this sounds like a lot of responsibility. Don't worry. The Lord won't ask more of you than you're capable of. And you know where to find me."

"Okay."

"Any questions?"

"No."

This expanding feeling in your chest. This feeling of warm expanding light in the clearing in your chest. If this is it. Where the Holy Ghost decides you're good enough. If this is what they mean. Noise has started coming in this clattering ricochet down the hallway. Your buddies, here for Scouts, looking for you. You don't want to leave. You want to stay here, in his office, in this field of gold light from the glow the sun burns in the curtain, this immersion in his kindness, and make the feeling last, not long, just long enough to give you time to trust it. But Bishop Byrne rocks forward, hauls himself off his chair, reaches his big right hand across the desk.

"You go home tonight and tell your folks the good news. Tell your dad he's got himself a Teacher to ordain this coming Sunday."

For the next four days there's wind. No weather, just the sky this steady baked-out blue, this hot wind off the desert, loaded with dirt that tastes like salt and turns your teeth to chalk and your snot gritty and crusts up your bandana where your sweat dries. Sand comes howling off the sandpit on the moaning wind. Your mother keeps the windows closed. The rooms turn into furnished ovens. The garage door shakes and slaps inside its frame. Sand forms lines of tiny dunes along the crack where the door meets the concrete.

For the next four days all you care about is getting to your trumpet lesson. Make sure he's there. Make sure the piece of shrapnel has stayed where it is and hasn't turned a razor's edge toward a chamber of his heart. On the ride to his house the wind is hot. Hard gusts, gusts like someone's ripped them out of dirt and thrown them at you, want to pull you off your bike. There's no steam shovel in his yard.

"I like the bandana," he says, closing the door, muting the rough howling sift of the wind, smiling and calm like there's all the time in the world.

"It's how I practice."

Everything in his living room the same. Just this different more crazy feel. Where tomorrow or the day after the room could be bare. The fighter plane gone. The medals. Squares on the wall where his photographs were. A steam shovel in the front yard with the fist of its bucket cocked back and raised for its first swing. Mr. Selby just this man who came from somewhere and could just as easy go somewhere else.

"This wind must be tough on a bike."

"It was okay."

You stand there looking back at him. France. New York. Other cities all across the country. All the places where he's had his face. Where his skin has been weathered this soft and lined and sometimes thin and fragile way by everything he's told you he's seen and done and everything you've imagined. Where everyone he's come across and known and taught and played with is there in his gray eyes, deep in the back of them but still visible, in the clear and even way they look at you, and you're just a kid, trying like crazy to keep your face from losing hold, your eyes from looking off, him from knowing anything you haven't told him.

You're done with Brother Clark. Last week was it. The gang still left was down to you and Yenchik and Doby. You sat in back with them and wondered how it was for the man who'll be teaching you to drive. The merry-go-round of his class. Your buddies who turned fourteen and then left, one by one, the same way new kids, just turned twelve, just ordained Deacons, kept showing up. Brother Clark would take a long blank steady look at them the first day they were there and then not pay them much attention. He may have looked at them that way to memorize which lesson they came in on, which painted animal they were starting on, so he'd know which one they'd have to end on. Every kid had to have every lesson at least once. Every kid had to ride every painted animal. Maybe Brother Clark was used to it because it was the way his job was, teaching high school kids to drive, kids who kept coming when they had their birthdays, just kept showing up all eager in their school clothes, stupid to stop signs and speedometers, things he would never be done explaining. For Brother Rodgers it was always the same group of kids. At the end it was Julie Quist's banana and coconut cake. For Brother Clark it was kids who just kept passing through on their way to becoming gods.

You took the chance to say goodbye to him in case you passed your interview.

"Thanks for being my teacher."

You shook the loaf of his massive hand across the little table. Looked up at his bland face and felt bad for Keller's painted dolls that fit inside each other. Felt bad for losing him.

"You're welcome. Hope I taught you something."

On Sunday morning, at the churchhouse, for the second time, your father and five of his friends take you down the hall into a classroom, close the door, move chairs back, leave one chair standing in the middle of the floor. Your father moves into place behind it, moves his arm the sweeping way a barber would, his hand out, letting you know to sit down, and when you do, his friends move in around you.

Chapter 83

IN BUT not of the world. You've heard it before. The first part was easy. You had to be in the world. You couldn't help it. Here you were. What you've never understood is why you can't be of the world. You look at your hands and they're like other people's hands. Sing along with Elvis like any other kid. Have your mother do laundry with Tide like women on tv. On vacation in California you stood on the beach and watched the sun go down and heard the other families there cheer like the sunset was their baseball team. You wondered why they were of the world, of the ocean and the way it put the sun out, of the slow enormous blaze of nothing but the sky, and why you couldn't stand there and feel like you were of the ocean and the sunset too. You've learned since then what they mean. You're of the Kingdom of God. You're supposed to stand apart from the other people in the world. But it still feels like a cracked riddle. A division problem with a weird remainder. Because everything you are is of the world. The stuff you eat that turns into your skin and hair and fingernails. Why you were somehow a visitor from the Kingdom of God when all the other families on the beach were there just to watch the sunset too.

And now Bird stands there in his bagged-out suit and thinks he can tell you the difference. His dull gaze has turned the room bleak. The walls dingy from air that feels like it's been breathed too many times. He doesn't ask questions. He'll answer them but mostly he just talks. You've wondered if this is what he talks like when he's talking to the dead. Like he doesn't expect to be heard or even seen. Like he could do anything he wanted. Pick a booger. Pee on the floor.

"Go to school. Do your homework. Cut the grass. Fight for your country. Brush your teeth. All that stuff is in the world. It's stuff you have to do. Of the world, that's something else. You think you're smart enough to have everything your way. Live like you don't owe anyone.

Like a heathen. Like an animal that doesn't have the sense to know the only reason it's being fed is to be butchered. That's being of the world. Just doing stuff you choose to."

It doesn't suit him any more than his suit does, talking like this, like he's behind a pulpit, working his face like he's eating something he's never tried before.

"Brigham Young made it easy. Believe in Jesus Christ and Joseph Smith, you're of God. Don't believe in Jesus Christ and Joseph Smith, you're of the world. An antichrist."

And now he stops and looks past everyone to where Brother Rodgers used to look when Strand raised his hand. The room perks up.

"Yeah," says Bird.

"That doesn't make sense," says Strand.

The way Bird's eyes go mean you can tell he's not behind a pulpit any more.

"What?"

"Being an antichrist if you don't believe in Joseph Smith."

"Meaning what?"

"You said if you don't believe in Jesus Christ and Joseph Smith, you're an antichrist."

"I know what I said."

"What if you don't believe in Joseph Smith but you believe in Jesus Christ?"

And now Bird just looks at Strand.

"You can't do that," he says.

"Lots of people do," says Strand.

"They're kidding themselves. If they don't accept Joseph Smith, then they're denying Jesus Christ."

"How come?"

"Because they're a package. You want to tell me you can believe in God without believing in Jesus Christ?"

"The Jews do."

"The Jews are lost."

"So they're of the world," Strand says.

"Until they catch on to Jesus Christ, and then to Joseph Smith, yeah."

"Okay."

"You got anything else?"

"Nope."

Bird steps back, takes air again, looks at the rest of the class. And then shoots one last hard look at Strand before he looks at the class for good.

"Okay. We got that straight? In the world and of the world?"

Nobody says anything.

"Let me spell it out for you. Of the world. You got murder. Greed. Lust. Adultery. Drinking. Smoking. Stealing. Swearing. Pretty much everything we got a commandment against. And anyone who's not Mormon."

"Windowpeeking," says Keller.

"Prostitution," says Yenchik. And when Brenda Horn gives him a nasty look, he hurries up and says, "They got 'em in Wendover."

"How would you know?" she says.

"Okay," Bird says. "Got the idea now?"

Everyone says yeah. And then he's looking right at you.

"I didn't hear you."

"I didn't say anything."

"And why's that?"

"Because I don't get it. Not all the way."

Cautious laughter ripples across the room.

"I just can't get away from you, can I."

And then, without waiting to hear what you've got, he turns to the class. "This kid. All I hear is his trumpet. Gotta keep my windows closed. Even on hot days. Everyone on the circle's sick of it. It'd be different if he was any good." He turns back to you. "You been paying attention?"

"Yes."

"Tell me what I just said."

"You said it'd be different if I was any good."

The heat in your ears is so fierce you wonder if Susan Lake can see them blazing.

"I mean before that."

"You asked if we got the idea."

Bird can't help but smile before the dull look moves back in around his eyes.

"So what don't you get?"

"The in the world stuff," you say. "Like school. Grass. Fighting for your country. It's of the world too."

"Try me again."

"It's in and of the world. There's no difference."

Bird goes to the window, folds his arms, leans against the frame. The light from outside makes the side of his face look like a leather statue of an angry general.

"You ever ride a bus?" he says.

"Yeah."

"So when you ride a bus, what are you? A seat? A window? A handrail? A tire?"

"Just a kid. Riding the bus."

He pitches his weight off the window frame. "So you're not a part of the bus. Right?"

"No."

"You're just in the bus. You're not of the bus."

"Yeah."

"Just a passenger."

"That's what I don't get."

"What?"

"The other people in the bus. They're just passengers too."

"What's your point?"

"Like Catholics and Protestants. They're not of the bus either. They're just in the bus too. Like me."

"Try me again."

"They're just like us," says Lilly. "Passengers. There's no difference."

"I got that much."

And then Strand has his hand up.

"Yeah."

"What if an antichrist gets on the bus?"

Bird freezes. "That's pretty stupid," he finally says.

"Why?" says Strand.

"Just take my word for it."

"Okay," says Strand. "People can be of the world but they can't be of the bus. That's what you're calling stupid."

Bird looks at Strand again like he's trying to see him in some place he understands, some battlefield in France, a chair in Grant's Hair Styling.

"You're not real spiritual, are you," he says to Strand.

Across the room Julie Quist's hand goes in the air.

"Think you can come in here and play games," says Bird.

Julie Quist's hand goes higher. Bird finally turns to her.

"Yeah."

"Is it like when you say that someone's out of this world? Like Fabian?"

"No. Jasperson."

"Maybe the people of the bus are people who always ride it," says Jasperson.

"Yeah," says Doby. "Instead of just once in a while."

"Yeah," says Keller. "People who don't have cars. Bus people."

"I got it," says Lilly. "If you were born on the bus and rode it till you died you'd be of the bus."

"Where would you go to the bathroom?"

"It'd have to be a Greyhound. They've got bathrooms."

"Yeah. But they're stinky from all the Indian vomit."

"Indian vomit?"

"That's what my dad says. He rides one down to Price sometimes. He says there's always some drunk Indian in the bathroom with vomit all over him."

"Hey," Bird says. "All of you."

"You've never been on a Greyhound."

"Have too. With my parents."

"Hey. You kids stop now."

You hear the voice you've heard from inside his house. You watch him take his suit coat by the lapels and look hard at the floor for a minute.

"So where were we?" he finally says. "Everyone understand? Susan?"

To just be able to call on her like that. To have the power to hear her voice any time you wanted to.

"I thought I did," she says. "Now I'm not sure."

CHAPTER 84

EARL BIRD. First your father and mother. Behind their backs. And now you. To your face. Walking home from Scouts on Tuesday night it comes up again.

"I still don't get that bus deal," says Keller.

"Maybe we're on our own bus," says Doby. "A special bus."

"Yeah. Like a charter bus."

"What's a charter bus?" says Yenchik.

"When you got enough people to get a bus all by yourself."

"You all gotta go to the same place, though," says Keller.

"Yeah. And all get on and off at the same time."

Mr. Selby, you're thinking, telling you about riding buses around the country with one or another band. If they were charter buses. Or buses they owned. If the Negroes he rode them with were of the buses they rode.

"Bird used to fix buses. He's gotta know what he's talking about."

"Who you kidding. He gives dead people haircuts."

"Strand sure made him look stupid."

"Yeah. Like he'd been shot for a minute."

"Remember when he showed us his fingers?" says Keller.

"Yeah?"

"I was trying to see his spirit fingers."

"His spirit fingers?"

"Yeah. You know. Where his real fingers stop and his spirit fingers keep going. His spirit knuckles and fingernails."

"I never thought of that."

"That's a lotta power."

"God, Doby. You and your finger power."

"I'm just saying what they told us."

"What's he got against you, anyway?"

"Beats me," you say.

Why he lied. When you were brought down off the hill and had to start using the garage you went to every house around the circle to ask if your playing was too loud or bothered them. Sister Hohlman. Sister Woodard. Sister Stone. Sister Leatham. Sister Aller. Nicky Bird. None of them were bothered or said it was too loud. None of them could hear it from inside their houses. You told them if it ever bothered them to let you know. No one ever has.

That Saturday afternoon, doing Sunday shoes, at the other end of the table your father's been reading the Deseret News and using a spoon to carve crescents out of a slice of cantaloupe. He's been here before while you've polished. This is different. Intervals where he hasn't been carving or chewing or turning another page. Where all he's done is raise his head and you could feel him study you.

"So," he finally says. "How are those shoes coming?"

"Last ones."

"The rest are done?"

"Yeah. Just need to brush these."

You pick up your mother's left shoe and start whisking a brush across the toe.

"How's your job coming?"

"Okay."

"Sometime next week we need to go ward teaching to the Midgleys," he says. "How does Wednesday look?"

"Okay."

"Then I'll call them."

You get up to set your family's shoes on the floor in front of the washing machine.

"Wait. Sit down again, please."

Across the table your father looks down at his forearm for a second, picks at his wrist, looks back up.

"Your Sunday School teacher had a talk with me."

"Bird?"

"Brother Bird. Yes."

And now you know why your father doesn't look mad. Why his face just looks grim and sad and tired. You've messed with the church somehow.

"What about?"

"About you. What else?"

"What about me?"

"He said you were a troublemaker."

"How?"

"He wasn't specific. He just said you went out of your way to ruin his lesson."

You run through what happened in class. Bird stopping the lesson to come after you. To make you look like crap in front of Susan Lake.

"I didn't. Honest."

"Maybe you've forgotten. Think back."

"I didn't ruin anything. I just had a question."

"About what?"

"About being of the world."

"Why would he call you a troublemaker for having a question?"

"I don't know. Other kids didn't understand either."

"Surely he knows the difference between an honest question and a troublemaker."

"I didn't make trouble."

"I don't want that kid of yours tearing up my class again. That's what he told me. Word for word."

You stare at him. Quoting Bird with his Swiss accent. The accent you heard Bird mock at the campfire.

"I didn't tear up his class."

"So you're telling me he made the whole thing up."

"I don't know what he did. I didn't make trouble."

"Then who did?"

"Nobody. Everybody. He said this thing about a bus—"

"Did he go to any of the other parents?"

"I don't know."

"So he just looked around the classroom and singled you out."

"I didn't make trouble. I swear."

"So you think I should believe you instead of him."

"Yeah. He's a lying bastard."

"So! Watch your language!"

"He lied. He doesn't like me."

"Why wouldn't he like you? Why would he care one way or the other?"

You look hard into your father's vexed face. Eyes that look hard as marbles. Want him to believe you so bad your throat aches. Wish you could tell him. How Bird mocked him. How Bird called him an ass kisser. How Bird mocked his wife. So he'd know enough to hate Bird too.

"He's just a mean bastard."

"So! I won't say it again!"

"You hear the way he swears. At his wife and kids."

"Bishop Byrne called him to teach Sunday School. You think Bishop Byrne would call a mean bastard to teach the gospel?"

"Bishop Byrne doesn't hear him call his wife a frog whore."

And now you watch his face change like his brain's been slapped inside his head. Just go thoughtful. Look down at his forearm again and clear his throat.

"What didn't you understand?" he says. "What was this question?"

"About not being of the world."

"What in particular?"

"How other people are of the world. But we're not."

"What did he say?"

"He started talking about this bus."

"What bus?"

"Just a bus. How if you rode it, you were just in it. Not of it, like the seats and windows. Just a passenger."

"That sounds reasonable. What's so difficult?"

"The other passengers. The ones who aren't Mormon. How they're supposed to be of the bus the way they're of the world."

You hold his gaze and watch him think.

"Yes. I can see where that could be confusing."

"That's all I was asking. So was everybody else."

"Obviously their questions didn't get his attention like yours did."

"It was just a question."

"Okay. We can settle that later. First let's figure out this problem you're having."

He catches you looking to his left and turns around himself to see Molly standing there, holding one of her dolls, its head as bald as an apricot, scabbed with patches of dried glue. Karl. Somewhere in this house he's got its hair. Somewhere you could find him and in a second take the mean victory off his nasty face. Molly holds the doll up.

"Not right now, sweetheart," he says. You can see from the change in her face the way his tenderness is dwarfed by his impatience. "I'm having a talk with your older brother."

"Okay."

"I'll fix it," you say.

She folds her baldheaded doll back in her arms. The back of her little dress is gathered by a huge bow, the same fabric, an enormous limp-winged butterfly. Your father pulls a fold out of the sleeve of his shirt. He looks at you again. There's the biting stink of shoe polish high inside your nose.

"Now where were we?"

"Riding a bus."

"Your mother and I moved here so that you could grow up as a priesthood holder in the heart of Zion. And everything is still a joke. Now I see what Brother Bird was talking about."

"I wasn't joking."

"When a bus breaks down," he says, "who repairs it?"

You see Bird standing there, holding his wrist, howling swear words like a crybaby, staring at the mashed ends of fingers he's seen for the last time.

"A bus mechanic."

"And how is a bus mechanic different from a seat or a window of the bus?"

"He's not of the bus. He just fixes it."

"How is he different from a passenger?"

"The same way."

"Yes. You can't expect a seat or a window or even a passenger to repair a bus."

"Okay."

"We're here to fix the world," he says. "That's why you're going on a mission when the time comes. But we can't be of this world if we're expected to fix it."

"Okay."

"So you can't be of the world if your purpose in life is to fix the world. Understand?"

"Yeah," you say. "We're like world mechanics."

"Unless, of course, you choose to be."

"Be what? Of the world? Why?"

"Asking too many questions. Arguing with your teachers. Making fun of what they teach you. Don't ask me why you would do those things."

For the last few minutes your mother's been in the kitchen, in the part across the counter where the stove and the sink are, picking up the big steel pot of lentils she started soaking earlier, pouring them into the strainer in the sink, rinsing them with the little sprinkler.

"So, Harold," she says, abruptly enough to make your father jump. "He's just a boy. He's not your Sunday School class."

"I have an opportunity to teach him something. Isn't that my job?"

"Does he know what Brother Bird told you?"

"Yes, Mother. Can't you leave anything to me?"

And now you get this feel from them, from their muted serious humble way of talking, that they're scared. You look from one of them to the other.

"What?"

Your father pushes back his chair, gets to his feet, his face red again.

"Clean up your shoeshine equipment," he says. "Wash up. Someone is waiting for us."

CHAPTER 85

ON THE way to Grant's Hair Styling you stare out the windshield and into the wind of the open passenger window without seeing anything the way it was or like you were ever here. Cars come the other way and sunlight flares white as sparklers off their chrome and paint and glass. In the passenger seat your stomach hurts, hurts bad, this raw and hollow hurt like you've cried hard for a long time or done a thousand situps. Your father's voice from the driver's seat the only thing familiar.

"This is how to make things right. The best way to show Brother Bird that there are no hard feelings. The way to start out fresh again on the right foot."

Your father swings the wagon onto Main Street. You pass the mortuary where Bird cuts dead people's hair. A Texaco station. People going in and coming out of shops along the sidewalks. And then past Morry's Barber Shop. He's in there, good old Morry, cutting hair, in there behind his Hair Today Gone to Morry's sign in the window, but all you can see is the weaving turquoise image of the wagon pass across the glass, your head in the passenger window, the head of a kid who was never here.

Your father noses the wagon into an open stall across the street from Grant's in front of a store called Mode O' Day. Plaster models hold out their tireless arms in smiling lipstick poses and look back at you from low platforms behind the big shadowed picture windows. Your father hands you a dollar bill. You take it. Look at George Washington. His hairdo, long and white and curled, like it would look if he went to Grant's Hair Styling.

"I've got my own money," you say.

"This is my treat."

You've already said hello to the way your buddies will razz you. To all the funny looks when you and Doby stand there ushering people through the door into the chapel. To making up a story when Mr. Selby asks what happened. You've already said goodbye to your Chet Baker hair and to Susan Lake and any chance you probably ever had with her.

"You know what he's gonna do."

"He'll do exactly what you tell him to."

"No he won't."

"He's a professional. He has to."

Wanting to tell him the truth about Bird so bad your throat hurts all over again.

"No he doesn't."

"What?" You can hear the ridicule rise into his voice. "Do you think he's going to give you a bad haircut on purpose? To get even for something?"

"No."

"You need to think more highly of people."

You get out, put the dollar bill in your pocket while you wait for cars, cross the street in the wash of hot exhaust. Through the glass door the air is cool. Sharp and sweet with the smells West's mother has in her beauty shop in West's garage. Barber chairs line a long wall in front of mirrors ringed with bulbs like lighted tennis balls. Most of them are occupied by older women while younger women stand behind them working. Along the wall in back are naugahyde chairs with big space helmets like the one West's mother has. In chairs under two of the helmets, like passengers on a rocketship, two old women read magazines like going to Mars is something they do all the time.

You look for Bird. You see his wife Nicky, halfway back, rolling light pink curlers out of the cords of an old woman's ghost blue hair. The voices are like music, the music of glass, a creek of sparkling glass and spangled water. A woman with this huge tumble of dark red hair and broad hips, dressed in a dark blue church dress and high-heeled shoes, comes from around a corner. She walks your way in this heavy prance that looks like it hurts her somewhere. Before she gets to you, she's already smiling, this big red gleaming lipstick smile, a wire hook tucked up behind one of her side teeth like your mother has for her one false tooth.

"Well, hello, young man. Do we have your mother here?"

"I'm here to see Mr. Bird."

"What's your name? I'll tell him he's got a visitor."

"I'm here for a haircut."

"A haircut? Oh. Is he expecting you?"

"Yeah. At four o'clock."

"Well, he's ready. Come with me."

And you follow her back, into another room of barber chairs and mirrors, not as many, and there he is, in the barber chair back in the corner, wearing the white smock Morry wears, looking at a magazine. Somewhere along the way, following this woman on the black sticks of her high heels through this place, your stomach stopped hurting.

"Earl?"

You watch him bring his head up from the magazine, use the mirror to see who called him, look at you, then roll around to get up off the chair.

"This young man says he has an appointment for a haircut."

"Thanks, Ginny. Yeah. Come here, Tauffler. Sit down."

You can feel the heat his body left in the naugahyde through your pants and shirt and in the armrests. He slips the magazine into a shelf below his barber stand. You can't see the name. Just a photograph of a woman's face with a short blonde hairdo that fits her like a shower cap.

You look past the scissors and other steel tools and bottles and curlers on his stand, past the drinking glass with some silver money in the bottom, straight ahead, at your face in the mirror, while he throws a light blue barber bib around you, brings it around your neck and clips it. Watch your head and shoulders bump higher up into the mirror each time he jacks the chair up. Keep your eyes on your face. Don't look at the dark chocolate brown of your Chet Baker hair. Just your face. You can see his head up there, the bulk of his body in his smock, his heavy arms, while he looks at his row of scissors, picks up a pair, arranges the rest of them.

"So how's that trumpet?"

"Fine."

"Heard you playing some bebop the other afternoon. Sounded like Charlie Parker."

"Yeah."

"I know who he is. Bird. That's what they call him. Like me."

"Bird's his nickname," you say. Remembering the story Mr. Selby told you. How Charlie Parker picked a dead chicken off the road and had it cooked and ate it. How chickens were called yardbirds. How people called him Yardbird after that and then just shortened it to Bird. He goes around behind you. In the mirror his arms and body are just this background where your head rides. Your face like something he's wearing on his chest.

"So what'll it be today?"

And this is it. Mr. Hinkle. Mrs. Harding. You bring them in. Surround yourself with them. Mr. Selby. Charlie Parker. See them in the mirror with you. You've already said goodbye to the comb in your back pocket. You've already worked out Carla. School on the other side of summer is more than two months away. You'll have it all back by then. She'll never have to see. You'll never have to tell her. There won't be any photographs. You'll make sure.

"A mousie," you say.

"Mousie?" Bird looks at you in the mirror. You don't look back. "What's that?"

"A crewcut. Like a mouse has."

"A crewcut? You sure? This great head of hair?"

"Yeah."

Your eyes stay on your face while he touches your hair, sees how long it is, how it's cut, while you try not to pull away.

"I could do something real sharp with all this hair."

"That's okay."

"I mean it," he says.

"That's okay. I wanna try something different."

"You could do that with a new style."

"I wanna go from scratch."

"You're sure."

"Yeah."

"Sorry. You came in here for a real haircut. That's what you're gonna leave with."

Mr. Hinkle talking to your father. Lupe coming out to look for you to bring you lemonade.

"I can't."

"Why not?"

"I told my dad I was gonna get a mousie. To go with my brothers. He said good. He's out in the car."

"You thought about how you're gonna look?"

"Yeah." And then you say, "I'm gonna look like my brothers."

Without looking right at him, you can watch him wait, then go dull and mean, then come around, put down the scissors, take his electric clippers off their hook, start picking through different sized attachments.

"How short you wanna go."

You look at the attachment he's holding and then at the other ones lying on his stand.

"That one on the end."

"This one. You're sure."

"Yeah."

"You got it, kid."

Look back at yourself in the mirror while he snaps the attachment onto the blade of the shears, tosses the cord loose, comes back behind you again, starts the humming buzz of the motor and the steel blades going. It's time. It's here. Think dead. Just a dead kid in a mortuary getting a haircut. Think fuck you to brace yourself when he takes hold of your head with his good hand, bends you forward, starts up the back of your neck with the sharp buzzing rake of the attachment. Think fuck you while he turns your head to the left and right and then bends it down and runs the clippers up behind your ears and neck and shaves your duck's ass off. Think fuck you when he brings your head back up to where you can look at your face again. See your fenders go and remember how the dirty winter wool would gather and tumble ahead of the moving shears when Manny or Hidalgo or another Mexican held down a bleating sheep in the spring out at the pens to harvest it. Think of the pale pink wrinkled skin where it was shorn. Think how pathetic and skinny and lost they looked when they got let go, ran off a ways, stood there blinking. Think fuck you just a dead kid when you feel the rake of the clippers start up your forehead in his big stump-fingered hand, see hair start coming down across your face, see it collect in slivers and chips of silk spun chocolate on your bib. Think Mr. Hinkle. Think Mrs. Harding. Think Lupe. The sandpit in winter. Modulation and resolution and chord progression. Mr. Selby's cookies. Cold milk. Your trumpet in the garage. Your bike and the pouch you made for bringing home his records. How weird your ears look. How round the top of your head is. Molly's doll when she brought it into the kitchen bald. How white your scalp is through the raw fuzz of your mousie. How what you are is finally down to what they can't take away from you. What's left that they can't get their hands on. Think fuck you while Bird takes the attachment off the clippers, grabs the top of your head again, rolls it back and forth to trim things up around the edges.

Neither of you talk for the couple of minutes it takes. Bird blows the head of the clippers off, hangs them back on their hook, takes your bib off, and there you are in your shirt again, the one with all the horse heads, the one you picked when your father said to wear something besides a teeshirt.

You forgot about the razor Morry always used to clean your neck up. Now Bird picks up his, snaps out the blade, takes his smooth wide leather strop, pulls it tight, whisks the blade back and forth. A little chrome machine like Morry has churns out a rolling gob of foam into his open hand. You look at your face again while he dabs it out along the hairline of your neck and up behind your ears, warm, moist, fresh on your skin. Look at your face while you feel the quick little scuffs he does with the razor, feel his thumb wipe foam out of the way ahead of it, feel the sudden catch of the blade and then the sting.

"Ow." Wishing you hadn't said it.

"Just a little snag," he says. "We'll fix it up."

Wiping down the blade with a small towel on another hook. Taking another towel and wiping down your neck. Taking a little pencil and touching up the cut. Taking a brush, sprinkling white powder into the bristles from a canister, dusting the back of your neck.

"Okay," he says. "One mousie to go."

Picking up a hand mirror. Bringing it around behind you, holding it to where you can see where Morry used to show you how cool he'd made your duck's ass look.

"Looks good," you say. Think fuck you. Think back to the last time you saw how the back of your skull was shaped. When your father used to cut your hair back in La Sal.

"Glad to hear it," Bird says. His voice as dull as his eyes now when you look at his face in the mirror. "Nothing like a satisfied customer."

Outside again, your father's change in your hand where the redheaded woman put it, waiting to cross the street where the back of the Chevy wagon is angled out into the traffic, the back of your father's head through the rear window, you feel the sudden unusual heat up into your naked neck, behind your ears, in your scalp where your fenders were. Standing there, this shudder goes through you, this hard convulsion, this reflex to shake off his hands. Your father looks up from the book on the steering wheel when you pull the door closed. For a minute he sits there looking. Sunlight reflected off the hood underlights his face and gives its heavy skin the sheen of turquoise. You let him look while you look through the windshield at the plaster models in the windows of Mode O' Day, in their wigs, with their eyes that never blink. And then you can't look at them either.

And for the first time, before he says anything, you wonder where he goes to get his own hair cut, combed straight back in dark waves off his forehead, what he tells his barber, what they talk about.

"By golly," he says. "I haven't seen you in a crewcut since La Sal."

"Yeah."

A woman in a striped green summer dress comes out of Mode O' Day, smiling, still riding high on having said goodbye to people, bringing two big white shopping bags out the door with her. She glances at you and your father behind the windshield and heads down the sidewalk on high-heeled shoes, her bags swinging, the muscles flexing in her calves where the seams of her nylons run up them.

"You should be proud of yourself," he finally says. "You did what was right. I know it was hard. You handled it like a man."

"Thanks." And then you say, "Here's your change."

He doesn't take it. After a minute, you close your hand, put it back on your leg.

"I was sitting here doing some reading. About the importance of setting goals, and following the example of men who have achieved them."

You don't say anything. Let your eyes down to the silver button on the door of the glove compartment.

"Have you paid any thought to your future?"

You've been here before. Where your father wants to hear that you want to be a teacher, an engineer, a businessman, a doctor, anything but a trumpet player, something else you can use to make yourself an instrument of the Lord.

"Not a lot."

"What you want to do with your life?"

"Finish school. Go on a mission."

"How about after that?"

"Not really."

The sun through the windshield is hot on your chest through your horsehead shirt.

"How about idols? Men you admire?"

"Yeah."

"Who?"

His fierce black face. His white hot eyes. His hair short. The shape of his head like yours now. On the covers of some of Mr. Selby's albums. You've listened to his records and looked at his pictures and seen in his long dark fingers the same instrument you were holding. Seen the mouthpiece up against his lips and known what his tongue was doing. It was when Mr. Selby started to teach you the modal stuff. After you'd learned the swing and bebop stuff. Because you couldn't have gone straight to the way he played. Because you needed to know how he got there or you'd never know what he did and never understand what made him do it. And then Mr. Selby took a photograph out of a scrapbook and gave it to you.

In the photograph he was sitting on a chair, holding his horn on his knee, studying something, probably a chart, on a music stand in front of him. In his dark face and fierce eyes was the gathered and silent and focused rage you've seen in pictures of Beethoven's face. Except that in his dark face it was clean and gleaming. In the foreground the corner of a grand piano. A double ribbon of smoke curling in from the right, above the corner of the piano, from a cigarette in an ashtray just off the edge of the photograph. You could tell from the paper and from the writing on back that it was a photograph Mr. Selby cut out of a magazine. You gave the photograph back to Mr. Selby and asked him to keep it for you for now.

"You don't know him," you tell your father.

"Who is he?"

"His name's Miles Davis."

"No, you're right. I don't know him. What does he do?"

"He plays trumpet."

You've been here before too. Where your father has wanted to know how many Mormon trumpet players there are. Where he's treated the concept of a Mormon trumpet player like it was impossible.

"And where does this . . . what did you say . . . this trumpet player live?"

"I don't know. New York maybe."

"What's his religion?"

"I don't know."

And then your father doesn't say anything. You don't look at him. Just sit there with the slivers of hair in your collar starting to itch your neck. Feel this thick and angry and congested sadness coming from him. Like he's worked and slaved at putting something like a bike together for the fiftieth time, read the instructions over and over and tried to follow them, gone out and spent his money on the right wrenches, and the seat and the handlebars and pedals still fall off when he turns it over and sets it on its wheels. Or the bike goes sideways when he tries to ride it. You've got all your parts. All your arms and legs and fingers. But somehow he just can't put you together right, this bike he's building for God, and somehow it's because of you that he'll never get it right. Because there's something wrong with the steel, or with the way it was engineered, something so deep it can't be fixed.

In his silence you finally sneak a look at him. He's still got his book on the steering wheel, closed now, and he's looking straight ahead out through the windshield, like you're going somewhere, like what's in front of you could be a highway. The sheen of turquoise off the hood makes his quiet face look almost wild. And there's a tear. Under his eye, just off his nose, high on the skin of his cheek. One tear. You look away. You try to turn it into a drop of sweat instead. But you can't. The rest of his face is dry. Just the single crystal of the one tear with the tint of turquoise in the light it holds. Your stomach hurts again. You sit there, your head naked to the feel of the heat and air and noise of Main Street, smelling the powder Bird dusted your neck with, not knowing what to do with your hands except leave them the way they are, on your legs where you can look at them.

CHAPTER 86

PEDAL. Pedal until you've outrun things to think about. Until you've outrun thinking period. Because God always knows when you're thinking. It's how he keeps track of you. It's the way he knows where you are and how to find you. When your head's going. Like a telephone ringing, or an Indian stepping on a twig, or a submarine making noise underwater with a destroyer listening up above, or sneezing while you're hiding. So the way to get away from God is not to think. Not of anything. Shut off your head. But not on purpose. Because when you do it on purpose you have to think about doing it, and to God it's like shining a searchlight down on your back, like a loudspeaker going off. So shutting off your head is something that just has to happen, on its own, without you knowing it's going to, without you noticing when it does.

Just pedal. Just be what you are right now, this pedaling kid, like the handlebars are just handlebars, like the seat, the tires, the dirt, the sharp knuckles of the stones, the burst and suck of wind off a passing car, the chasing dust, the side of the road where sometimes there are sunflowers. Just this kid pedaling. Past a guy at a gas station wiping the windshield of a white car while the woman driving it watches his rag and a black hose runs gas through its open taillight into its tank. Past a song on a radio coming from a garage with its door open and a man moving around inside back where it's dark. Past an old lady making her way along the roadside carrying two paper grocery bags from somewhere to somewhere else. Just a kid pedaling. Past a man in a suit on the porch of a house with a boxy-looking suitcase. When you've pedaled far enough, gone long enough without caring what anything is named, you're free. Free to think again, about your own stuff, about stuff you know God won't be looking for.

They get it out of you, Doby and West and Keller, the next morning, in the Sacrament Room up under the organ pipes, after they've looked at your head enough to laugh, then run out of ways to tell you what a dipshit dork you look like.

"You told him you wanted a mousie?"

"Yeah."

"How come a mousie?" says West.

"You're an idiot, West," says Doby.

"Why?"

"Why? Because you can't chop up a mousie," Doby says. "You can't ruin it. Jeez."

"Oh. Yeah."

"Bird's an asshole," says Keller.

"Forget it."

"God," says Doby. "Those creepy fingers. Doing dead people. Touching your head."

"I didn't look."

"My dad would've told him go kiss my ass," says West.

You stop what you're doing, running the smooth clear liquid rope of tap water into a row of little cups, and try to picture your father saying that to Bird. His Swiss accent. Yes, Earl. Yes. I understand. I'll tell you what you can do. You can go kiss my ass.

"We oughta get him," Doby says.

"Let the air out of his tires."

"Yeah," says West. "Take his hubcaps."

"Windowpeek on his old lady," says Keller.

"She's French," says Doby. "She's probably all hairy."

"No." You tilt the tray to even out the water levels in the little cups, then hand the tray to Doby, waiting with a towel. "Leave him alone."

"We gotta pay him back."

"No. I got to."

"How?"

"I'll figure it out."

"When?"

"You'll know."

"You gonna tell us?"

"Depends on what it is."

Everyone works on preparing the Sacrament in the little room where even your mother's organ music sounds different with all your hair gone. Keller hands you another water tray whose holes he's stuffed with little paper cups.

"You ask Bird what he says to dead people?"

West laying slices of Wonder Bread on the shallow chrome beds of the bread trays. You hand the dripping tray to Doby.

"Yeah."

"You did? Jeez. Did he get mad?"

"Nope."

"What'd he say?"

"He said he swears his head off at 'em. Just stands there and cuts their hair and calls 'em every dirty word he can think of. Or make up."

It takes a minute. And then Doby slams the tray down on the table, sending water flying, doubles over like he's throwing up, and then him and Keller and West can't stop laughing, this crazy stumbling dance to your mother's organ music going.

It starts coming back. All you need to do is wait, wait while you learn not to look at your shadow, the melon-round shadow of your head, the way the shadows of your ears sprout off the sides like mushrooms. You sit there that first Sunday, your head still raw from the afternoon before, and let Susan Lake stare all she wants. On Thursday when you go to Mr. Selby's you've got your smile in place when the screen door opens and his eyebrows rise and a frown goes quick like the shadow of a sparrow across his face.

"Whoa," he says. "That's a brand new look."

Your ears go hot but you hold your smile in place.

"Yep."

"What's the occasion?"

"Just something new."

"Sure you're not trying to look like me?"

"I just want to play like you."

Wait. All you need to do while Bird starts showing up for Sunday School in a brand new suit, a gray one, soft and sleek, a suit a gray-haired president of a bank would wear, a suit that fits him better than his old one did but looks more borrowed now than ever, makes his head look more than ever like the ravaged head of a mangy bull. While you wait you watch him while he stands up there, Sunday after Sunday, and gets used to thinking he got away with everything. With what he said to you in front of Susan Lake. With thinking that out of all the kids in class he knew enough to pick the one whose father wouldn't tell him to kiss his ass. With thinking he'd never have to think about you again. With thinking a banker's suit could give him a banker's head and regular ears and maybe even his fingers back. With thinking he's got you and Doby and West and Keller and Jasperson and Yenchik and Lilly and all the girls and even Strand fooled with his big religious voice, his borrowed voice, the voice he wears the same dull angry borrowed way he wears his brand new suit.

Wait. When you hear that Bird won't be going on this year's scout trip you decide to stay home and watch for him and practice. Practice through summer in the closed garage. And somewhere along the way this stuff that Blackwell said was jizz starts coming out. And somewhere else along the way you figure out the bus thing for yourself. How you're in the world to people who don't know you. Who like you but don't know anything inside you. Brother Rodgers. Brother Clark. Bishop Byrne. Scoutmaster Haycock. Superintendent Ostler. The men and women who drift through the chapel door while you usher them in, your jaw fixed, your smile fierce as you can make it, your handshake firm when someone reaches out to test it. And how you're of the world to people who like you even when they know the stuff inside you. Know the stuff you do and why you do it. Blackwell and West and Doby and Keller and Yenchik and even Jasperson and Lilly. Like you're a band of Negro kids who got on the bus together, at the same time, going the same way, and everyone else who was already on the bus, already going somewhere, was just a stranger. Your father's and mother's friends. All strangers who could look at you while you headed down the aisle and think they somehow knew you and could maybe even like you but would always just be strangers. It was you and your buddies and Carla and even Mr. Selby and then it was everyone else. It wasn't the bus. The bus had nothing to do with it except that all of you were on it, and maybe Earl Bird was driving it, was sitting there in the driver's seat when you put your nickel in his box.

Another nickel, Tauffler.

Sorry.

Nice try.

And from there you figure that nobody really knows you except in pieces. Blackwell came closest. Him and Carla. But not even Blackwell and Carla knew about the sandpit. How spit would freeze the valves. How snowflakes wrinkled quick to water when they touched the heat your breath left in the brass. How you had to work your knees loose slow because the cold had locked them. What Mrs. Harding looked like when she sang with a band of Negro men. The sugared sunlight the ice cubes in Lupe's lemonade could capture for you to swallow down.

Toward fall your hair comes back to where you can start to work Chet Baker's fenders into it again. And then you recognize, in the mirror, that fenders are for cars, that your ears aren't wheels, and that what you like instead is what you had a few weeks back, this pelt, short and thick, this dusty chocolate, long enough to comb but not enough to have to, long enough to get messed with by the wind but not to where you'd need Brylcreem to hold it down. You have Morry start cutting it that way. You feel his soft gut brush against your shoulder while he tries to get you to tell him who your secret girlfriend is and you start to lose, under his hands, the feel of Bird's fingers when you look at them in Sunday School. Wait. While Morry trims it back to where all your hair is new, to where everything old is cut away, everything you had when you walked out of Grant's Hair Styling that afternoon, anything Bird ever touched, anything he ever breathed on, or anything he ever knew or could ever remember about your hair.

You take ninth grade, your high school freshman year, where you took seventh grade and eighth. Bountiful High School isn't big enough to take ninth graders from your school and all the other junior highs of the towns around Bountiful that don't have high schools of their own. Everyone's there but shuffled around again. This time your home room class is Math. This time you have to look for her because she's not in any of your classes. It's been since you played Danny Boy with her in the music room. Where she said what she did about the color of her hair. Where you could taste the smell of peaches in the high and heavy branches of Charley Bangerter's orchard when you kissed her back. And afterward the hum of the polishing machine outside and its glancing thump against the door that made her pull away and fix her hair and sweater. You stood there warm and dizzy everywhere. As she pulled away, you wanted to follow her, the way water follows something that moves through it, the way dust followed the tailgate of Manny's pickup.

"I can't see you this summer," she said. Her glasses in place. Her eyes back to round.

"Why?"

"My dad got a job in Saudi Arabia. He's taking us. I'll be back for ninth grade though."

"Saudi Arabia?"

"Yeah. My mom's mad. She can't drink liquor there."

You look everywhere. Where her locker was last year. The music room. The halls. The kids with the instrument cases. Why she said what she did about her hair. You finally ask the woman in the office.

"Carla Ogilvy. Yes. She moved."

She doesn't say it mean, just flat and toneless, like something you could have read, like the way a frog can look at you and let out a croak and then just keep on looking.

"I know. But she came back."

"No. I'm afraid not. They ended up going somewhere else. They sent for her records."

Through fall and into winter, in the closed garage, Roy comes in sometimes and stands there listening in his brown cloth jacket.

"How come you're smiling? What's so funny?"

"No fingers." He takes a hand out of his pocket to point to your gloves.

"Nope."

"How come?"

"I can't play with the fingers. Just like you couldn't play piano with them."

"Hobo gloves," he says.

"Yeah," you say. "That's what they are."

"Like Freddy Freeloader."

"Yep."

You take the arm off the record to keep the next Bill Evans tune from playing.

"Can I have some?" he says.

"Why? Do your hands get cold when you practice?"

The sudden collapse into shame in his round face lets you know you've just asked him a question your father would ask.

"No."

"You can have these when your hands get bigger. Okay?"

"Can I play piano with them?"

"Sure you can."

"When will my hands get bigger?"

"I'll make you some now."

Wait. To where you almost forget you're waiting. And while you wait you set the needle on Mr. Selby's albums and fill the closed garage with musicians. Louis Armstrong and Coleman Hawkins, Dizzy Gillespie and Lester Young, Sonny Rollins and Thelonius Monk, Count Basie and Oscar Peterson, Art Tatum and John Coltrane, Billie Holiday and Bill Evans, Art Blakey and Miles Davis, most all of them Negroes, in this closed garage in this circle of houses in this foothill neighborhood, this closed garage with its rakes and shovels and hoes hung on the wall, the smell of old exhaust and gasoline, dust burning off the top of the raw hot light bulb in the ceiling. The notes of the melodies fall like husks away from all the tones inside them, so that you play without music, so that you play from simple charts, so that you play from nothing, so that you play from what the albums play. Sometimes there's applause when someone ends a solo and the other players join back in. Sometimes there's Carla. Sometimes her violin. Sometimes she stays. And sometimes it just cuts through you where she's there, in History again, and while she's there it's real enough to smell the hot dust rising off the hissing radiators. Winter lets go. Roy starts showing up in one of the little sweaters you remember you or Karl wearing.

CHAPTER 87

AND THEN one morning the lesson Earl Bird kicks off is on sheep and the shepherds who tend them. Bird. Bird in his bank president's suit. Bird with the head of a bull. Bird telling you the difference.

"Being a sheep means having faith in Jesus Christ. Hearing his voice. Doing what he tells you. Looking at him as your shepherd. Being a member of his flock."

And after he looks across the room, and can't find anyone who wants to pick a fight with him, he keeps going.

"Okay. A shepherd. That's where you turn around and do for other people what Jesus does for you. Help him care for his flock. Feed his sheep. That's why you boys go ward teaching every month. Those families, they're sheep you've been called to take care of. That's why you boys and some of you girls are going on missions."

Bird looks around again. You know what West is wondering. Out of the girls in the class which girls Bird means. Which ones won't be married by twenty-one. Which ones will be old maids by then, their lives over, nothing left to do but go on missions.

"You're not being asked to do anything Jesus doesn't do," says Bird. "He's a sheep and shepherd too. That's why he's called the Lamb of God. And the Good Shepherd."

Bird gives one of his stump fingers a lick and turns a page of his lesson book.

"Okay. Free agency. That's where God gave us the freedom to choose between right and wrong. We're here to be tested to see if we'll use it the way we're supposed to. We need to spend any more time on that? Yeah. You."

"If we're being tested," Strand says, "how is it free agency?"

"You can either pass or flunk. That's your choice."

"That's not a choice."

"That's what being tested is."

"Yeah. But it's not a choice. Not a free agency choice. You get punished if you choose the wrong thing."

"That's life," says Bird.

"A choice is a hamburger or a hot dog," says Strand.

"Yeah?"

"You can choose either one. It doesn't matter. You don't get punished for choosing the wrong one. There isn't a wrong one."

Bird gets that hard dull gray look where he thinks he's being screwed with. It makes you sick. You know he won't go after Strand. Because Strand doesn't care. Because his father's in the Air Force. A fighter pilot at Hill Field. A father who'd tell Bird the stump-fingered hairdresser to kiss his ass in a millionth of a second.

"You think that's funny," Bird says. "A hamburger or a hot dog."

"Okay," Strand says. "Then a Chevy or a Ford."

You watch Bird's big gray gathered face freeze suddenly like he's just been smacked in the head with a hammer. You take a look at Strand but his face is blank. Just this cool look back at Bird like all he did was say what day it was.

"I'll tell you something," Bird says. "God don't care if you drive a Chevy or a Ford or eat a hot dog or a hamburger. God knows we got a war on. A few of us against the world and the hosts of Satan. You're supposed to be a soldier. But you wanna be a comedian instead."

And then it's here. Your hand goes up like it's been waiting on its own. Bird brings his gray face and his dull eyes around to you.

"Yeah," he says.

"How come sheep?" you say.

He gives you this look where he can't put you together with anything he knows.

"How come sheep?" he says.

"Why not stallions?"

"Why not stallions?"

"Yeah. How come we can't be stallions?"

Still looking. Like your question's something you actually want him to answer.

"Because the gospel tells us that we're sheep."

"Sheep are dumb."

"Sheep are obedient."

"So are stallions when you break them."

"Sheep don't think they're Charlie Parker."

This time it's like Popeye with a can of spinach. This time it just makes you tough with the way you hate him.

"Neither do stallions."

"Sheep can be herded," he says. "They get lost."

"Stallions can too."

"Sheep are what Jesus Christ says we are. You got that?"

"Sheep are cowards."

And now you get that look full on where you can see what his French wife Nicky and his kids must see. Points of mean red light inside his dull eyes.

"You want me to talk to your dad again?"

It's like tossing you another can of spinach. To where hate makes you feel like you could take and tear off his ugly head and send it flying down the hallway like a leather medicine ball. From across the room you can sense Susan Lake's attention, this eager fear inside it, this eager big-eyed Olive Oyl fear.

"We're supposed to fight this big war. Against Satan. Sheep can't fight a war."

"You think you can tell me what a war's like."

"I know what sheep are like. I lived on a ranch. They're stupid. You can sneak right up behind one and cut off its nuts and it won't even know it."

And now it's here. The real Bird, rising up, naked inside his borrowed-looking shirt and suit and tie, naked inside his borrowed-sounding big religious voice. The Bird you hear through the closed windows of his house. No father here to make him reconsider. Just you. Just you like it's just his wife Nicky and his kids. You can feel the panic start to come off Julie Quist. When it shows itself you know she'll start to cry again. Next to you, Yenchik comes to attention, and West and Doby and Keller start getting it. It's here. Its time has come.

"I'd like to be a peacock," Julie Quist blurts out. Bird whips his head her way. She jumps and her purse goes coasting off her lap.

"I wanna be a rabbit," says Keller.

"If we're stallions," says Doby, "Jesus could be a cowboy instead of a stupid shepherd."

"Cats don't get lost. Let's be cats."

Brenda Horn. Your one guess for an old maid with nothing left to do at twenty-one but go knocking on doors for two years somewhere.

"How about alligators?" Yenchik says.

"We could all be different animals," Doby says. "Then Jesus could be a zookeeper."

And then West.

"How about zebras?"

"Lions!"

And then Susan Lake.

"How about giraffes?"

"Wolves!"

"Eagles!"

"Elephants!"

Bird's head has been whipping around like Rufus trying to snatch a scared housefly off a door screen. Now suddenly it jerks to a wild bug-eyed stop.

"Awright! Christ cocksucker! All you kids! Just shut the fuck up! Judast motherfucking priest!"

Part 9

The Cries of Animals

CHAPTER 88

NOBODY KNOWS you the first time you pedal to Bountiful High School with your trumpet case lashed to the rack behind your seat, ride around the vast parking lot behind the sprawling colossal modern building all made of bricks and windows looking for a place to lock your bike up, and find a steel railing off a dock down by the garbage bins. Nobody knows you the first time you walk down the hall with your case and then walk into the band room.

Nobody knows you were never one of them.

You pick a chair with a vacant chair on either side and set your case on end on the floor between your legs. A brown-haired girl in a blue dress takes the chair next to you and puts what looks like a flute case in her lap. You don't remember her. You figure she's here from one of the other junior highs that feed tenth graders to this place. By the time the bell rings there's a kid with a guitar case on your other side and you're one of maybe seventy kids on folding chairs in tiers that rise toward the back of the big room. Your hands leave sweat on your case. There's a music stand in front of you. You've counted eight other trumpets. Down in front, at a desk to the side of a low stage, the teacher is this scrawny big-boned man in a short sleeved white shirt with a skinny plain black tie, thin but wild black hair, black-rimmed glasses, knuckled hands so big they look like they could reach two octaves on a keyboard, a jawbone shaded this emerald black with whiskers. His name's on the blackboard behind him. Hannibal Frank. He calls roll from his desk. Names come out of him in the deep bursts of a big dog woofing. He doesn't look up unless he doesn't get an answer. Orval Kershaw. And then he looks up mad and calls it out again. Kathy Mann. Everyone's eager to say they're here.

"Shake Tauffler."

"Here."

And for the first time when someone answers, Mr. Frank looks up, and you know what's coming.

"Where?"

"Here." You put up your hand and wait for his glasses to find you.

"Shake?"

"Yes?"

"What's your real name?"

"Shake. Tauffler."

Your whole head blazes in the crossfire of every set of eyeballs in the room. The girl with the flute case and the short kid on the other side both have their faces turned your way like the closing sides of a vise. Sweat breaks out of your armpits and darts in crooked lines down across your ribs.

"Your real name's Shake."

"Yes."

"It's not a nickname. Like Sparky or something."

"No. It's real."

"Like this," he says, and shakes his head back and forth a couple of times. You hear giggling. The mutter of a couple of guys laughing.

"What on earth," he says. "Shake it is," he says, and then keeps going. Darrell Talmadge. Here. Russell Tolman. Here. Susan Walkowiak. Here. He gets up from his desk. You didn't figure how tall he'd be and how long his arms were.

"Okay. Those of you with reed instruments, I want you to get your reeds wet while I say a couple of things."

You hear the snaps of instrument cases. Here and there, kids take their reeds out, start working them like popsicle sticks.

"First thing. You're not here to learn how to play an instrument. You're here to learn how to play together. Keep time. Keep up. You never play an entire composition yourself. I don't care if it's a symphony or love song. You play parts. You'll learn how to read a score. When to come in, play your part, get out of the way again."

He takes a minute to look around the room while the lights in the ceiling play across his glasses.

"Second thing. You're not here to show off. You're not here to be a star. You're here to make me look good. Because when I look good, the school looks good, and that's good for everybody. You'll all be performing. Playing an assembly or two. Your folks will be here. And you'll sound good for them. Okay," he says, and walks across the stage to the piano. "You reed players should be ready. All of you, get your instruments out. Here's C. Tune up."

The note rings out, over and over, steady as a metronome, while chairs creak, cases snap open, tubas and oboes and flutes and trombones and guitars and saxophones and other horns come out, all the instruments on Mr. Hinkle's wall, and the room fills with the jangled and honking and chirping racket of an orchestral jungle, and for the first time, bringing your trumpet up, blowing soft, adjusting the tuning slide, listening for the sweet center of that repeating piano note where it vanishes inside the note you're blowing, you're one of them. The notes of other instruments start to fall with more certainty into formation, start finding Mr. Frank's note, until the room is the steady blare of an almost single note. He finally stops hitting the key, brings up his hand, moves to the music stand on the stage where he picks up a white baton.

"Okay," he says. "A C scale. Like this." He raps the baton on the edge of the music stand. "One. Two. Three. Four. Steady. Twice up twice down. Okay. On one."

All the time you waited, and then when you went in, you knew you'd pay a price. For baiting Bird. For saying nuts in Sunday School, in front of girls, and meaning real nuts, not hazelnuts or walnuts but sheep nuts, nuts that you and Jimmy Dennison used to fire at one another with slingshots when the sheepherders castrated the lambs in spring. And you knew you'd be on your own when everything took on motion afterward. When the kids in class went home and told their parents, when their parents called Superintendent Ostler, when the Bishop and the Superintendent turned around and called in Bird, and then when you were called in too, into the office, the Bishop behind his desk, the Superintendent in the corner chair. You wondered who told them what you'd said about cutting nuts off sheep. You knew they wouldn't tell you who, but you knew that someone had, because it was the only thing they asked you, if you'd said the dirty word for testicles.

"You mean nuts?"

You'd already looked for the way you'd felt the last time you were in his office. It wasn't there. You knew you could say the word again because you knew when the feeling wasn't there that you were on your own.

And Superintendent Ostler said, "You shouldn't use that word in Sunday School, son. You shouldn't use it anywhere."

"I'm sorry," you said, and sat there thinking of telling them you should have said testicles instead. "That's what they were called where I grew up."

And Superintendent Ostler said, "Where you grew up?"

And you told them about the ranch and the lambs in spring and the way the sheepherders cut them off the lambs so they'd make better wool.

And Bishop Byrne smiled at his thumbnail and Superintendent Ostler said, "There's a difference, son, between a ranch and Sunday

School."

"I'm sorry."

And Bishop Byrne said, "It's not the kind of thing you say in Sunday School. Especially not in front of young ladies."

"I'm sorry."

And Superintendent Ostler said, "As long as you understand."

"I do."

And Bishop Byrne said, "Let's leave it there. Just an accident we all know won't happen again. Okay, son?"

"Okay."

"You let us know if Brother Bird says anything to you. Okay?"

"Okay."

All the time you waited, and then when you went in, you figured that Bird would have his price, would come looking for you afterward, wanting you to pay it. And so you waited for him all week. Watched him come home from Grant's Hair Styling with his wife Nicky, leave his big Mercury in the driveway, go in his house and stay there. At the church-house Tuesday night, in your uniform, heading down the hall with Doby for the Scout Room, someone from behind put his arm around your neck, took your shoulder in his hand, yanked you hard against his side, pulled you off balance on legs that were already looking to run. It stopped your heart that it could be Bird. But it was Scoutmaster Haycock. Still stumbling, you stepped on his brown shoe, and when you looked up, he was smiling, his whole big freckled face, and then he winked, gave you a flat-handed pat on the shoulder, let you go, and kept going while you stopped and stood there, your heart racing.

"What was that about?" Doby said.

If he knew about his wife. If he knew you and her were done.

"Beats me."

"Think he heard about Bird?"

"Yeah."

"I thought him and Bird were buddies. You know. The way Bird helps with Scouts."

"Yeah. Me too."

"Guess not."

"Yeah. Guess not."

The following Sunday you looked for Bird at Priesthood Meeting. You found him, across the chapel, in his banker's suit, alone on a bench off the side. None of the other men went near him. He looked like he knew why. He looked like it was fine with him. You knew from there that he wouldn't be coming after you.

And you knew that there would be your father's price. He would have to know too, the way Scoutmaster Haycock did, that whatever happened, it was you, and that there was more to it than you just saying nuts instead of testicles in Sunday School. And so you started to wait for your father to pick his moment.

Wondering what he'd tell you when he did. That you were showing off. Making trouble. Walk you through the logic that Bird had been right about you. What you'd say back to him. Why you did it. One good reason. Not the haircut. But maybe because Bird thought he could lie to him and get away with it. Maybe because Bird had no business teaching Sunday School. Maybe because of the night in Wyoming. But you flinch away from that one because thc night in Wyoming is the only one your father wouldn't know what to do with. The one where you'd have to look away because you wouldn't want to watch what happened to his face

When was up to him. And so you kept on waiting. In the meantime, when he looked at you, it felt like you were accidental, someone he kept forgetting, someone who kept surprising him by being there, in the garage, someone who made him sad and tired of life when he got home from work and raised the door and found you standing there. You could see it. The fight go out of him. And things inside you would twist and shrink and cringe away from the way he looked at you like thread from the flame of a match.

CHAPTER 89

SINCE EARL Bird, while they've looked for a permanent one, you've gone through a string of substitute teachers, not real ones, like in school, just different men from the congregation, like Brother George, Brother Samuelson, Brother Jenkins. The class has started coming unraveled like a beat up baseball. Everyone but Jasperson and Lilly has started showing up with this attitude of mischief. Even Susan Lake has started to sit there like she's expecting to be entertained. And then, one Sunday out of nowhere, there's a new guy standing at the door, his hand out. Ahead of you, Doby shakes it, goes in, and then it's your turn.

"Morning," him saying. "I'm Elder Jensen. Your new teacher."

"I'm Shake."

"Hi, Shake. You doing okay this morning?"

"Yeah. How about you?"

"Me?" he says. "I'm rarin' to get started."

Home from his mission a couple of months ago. You were there at the Sacrament Meeting they used for his Homecoming. You and Jasperson had usher duty. You stood in back near the door while Bishop Byrne welcomed him home again, while a woman sang the Jesus in the Garden song your mother sang at home, while other men got up to the podium and gave these tribute speeches, and finally while Elder Jensen got up himself and talked about the Lord's work in the mission field of Massachusetts and the best two years of his life and told a couple of lame jokes that made the chapel explode with laughter and relief that he was finally home.

The thing you noticed most was how wide his bony shoulders were. The rest of him so thin his suit coat looked like it was hung on the crossarms of a telephone pole. You couldn't make out his legs for all the cloth his pants were made out of. He had a lumpy bony big-lipped kind of farmer face and brown hair that was crooked where he parted it low on the side.

From somewhere deep inside him there was this purified reverent luster from his two years in the mission fields of Massachusetts. This serene and benevolent attitude that made him older than his face was. Like there was nothing you could do to make him mad. Like he could never get a boner. Like he wasn't a real guy his real age, but someone maybe fifty, who counted his age not in years but in increments of his eternal progression toward godhood, someone who'd had doors shut in his face in the neighborhoods of Massachusetts, someone who could handle a Sunday School class like yours like it was a bucket half full of apricots.

"He'll be okay," West saying.

You and Doby and West and Keller and Jasperson getting the bread and water trays together for Sacrament Meeting that night in the little room underneath the organ pipes.

"Yeah. Seems like it."

"You ever tried talking and smiling for a whole hour?" Keller saying.

"Yeah," you saying. "He never let down that smile."

"How can you talk and smile for a whole freakin' hour?" Keller saying.

"Must hurt," Doby saying.

"Must take practice," West saying.

"Notice how Julie Quist just kept smiling back at him the whole time?"

"Yeah. Even when he wasn't looking at her."

"I think she scared him."

"Yeah. I'd see him look and then look back quick."

"He got a girlfriend?" says West.

"I never seen him bring one to church."

"Maybe one from another ward somewhere."

"Maybe the one that sang at his homecoming."

"Whoever she is," West saying, "she must put out good on Saturday night."

"Jeez, West." Jasperson spitting it out like what he thought was lemonade turned out to be pee. You wondering if he was ever going to get the way West went after him.

"Why?" Keller saying.

"What else is gonna put a grin on his face all day Sunday?" West saying.

This time even you cringing. But not enough to be stupid.

"You sacrilegious prick," Jasperson says. "This is the Sacrament Room."

"Wow," West saying. "Jasperson said prick. I'm gonna tell."

While you waited for your father to bring up Bird, walk you through the logic where everything you did was wrong, you started getting used to high school. The halls this chaotic flood of bigger kids. Teachers serious with homework. Hoods and greasers you and West could watch at lunch the way they idled their customized cars and hot rods out of the parking lot, laid long fat welts of squealing rubber when they hit the street, came idling back with their engines crackling and hoarse from the Dairy Ann or Wally's Burger Bar. Basketball and football jocks who ambled down the halls in their red and gray letter jackets with their fake bowed cowboy legs and moved you out of their way with the force field of their popularity. Girls with real breasts inside their pale sweaters who sometimes smiled at you. You knew they were using you for practice smiles, like some kind of human mirror, but they made your blood race anyway because you turned around and made them Carla. In the meantime you settled into being invisible and kept a lookout for the guys you knew could see you. The Jeep guys. And there was band. From a man who wrote his name in capital letters across the blackboard and left it there.

In the second class Mr. Frank groups you by instruments. On either side a kid with a trumpet. Vince on your left. Tom on your right. Tom the kid you share a music stand with.

"What kind of trumpet is that?" says Tom.

"A Bach."

"Like the guy who wrote all the organ music?"

You remember him, a kid with a trumpet case in junior high, a kid with a thick blond flattop and a face like one of those kissing fish. You wonder what he would look like underwater.

"No. Another guy."

"It sure looks old. You get it from your grandpa?"

You look down. See the long bruise in the brass.

"No. I bought it."

"How does it play with that dent there?" he says.

"I can't get it to play an A."

"Maybe you should get it fixed."

"Yeah. Someday. For now I just double flat the B."

"That's gotta be a pain."

"It's like a habit now. Whenever I think A."

"Wait. B double flat. That is an A."

"I know. That's how I have to work around it."

"It's the same thing."

"Not really."

"Sure it is."

"I'm not asking you to believe me."

"You should get a new one. Like I've got."

"I'm too used to this one."

"So if you got a new one, you'd be screwed."

"Yeah." Burning now to hear what he can do. Burning to take and run away with it. "Till I got used to it."

You figured your father would want you alone. A Sunday morning when it was just the two of you for breakfast in the kitchen. But a clock was ticking all along and its name was Karl. His birthday coming. Turn twelve in October. Get made a Deacon. Start getting up with you for Priesthood Meeting. Your father let every Sunday tick away until the Sunday morning Karl was there, contemplating his own plate of fried eggs and baloney, in the blue checked sport coat they gave him for his birthday, in his clip-on bow tie with its blue and silver stripes.

And then you get your father's price. That you don't matter. That waiting was his price and that you've been paying it all along.

From the portable radio on the windowsill above the sink, Richard L. Evans finishes his sermon, the pipes of the Tabernacle Organ go full volume, the Tabernacle Choir comes out of its idling hum and roars into the closing hymn. Come Come Ye Saints. Your father hasn't told Karl anything. You give him one more page of the Church News. When he turns it, lets it float into place, and keeps reading, you get it. He's waiting for you to do it.

"This is what we always have for breakfast," you say.

"It's good."

"Yeah."

"Does he always wear his apron?"

"Yeah. To keep his suit clean."

"How come you don't wear one?"

"I don't cook."

Karl keeps his head down except when he raises it to take a quick scowling look at the washing machine or the rugbeater or something else on the wall. You know what's on his mind. What he's scared of. What's got him scowling.

"You know how it goes?" you ask him.

"No," he says.

"You go to a room with Papa and some other men." Aware that your father's grading you on some test you don't know the questions to. "They put you in a chair and then get in a circle around you and put their hands on your head. Papa puts his on first."

"How many men?"

"Maybe five or six. Counting Papa."

"What does it feel like? All those hands?"

Twice now you've had them there.

"Just keep your head straight."

"Then what?"

"Papa stands right behind you and uses his power to give you the Aaronic Priesthood and make you a Deacon."

"Then what?"

"He says amen. And you stand up and everybody shakes your hand and says congratulations and welcome to the Priesthood. And then you go to the bathroom and comb your hair. And then you start going to the Deacon's Quorum. You'll like Brother Clark. He's the teacher."

"I mean before," he says. "When Papa gives you the Priesthood."

"What about it?"

"What does it feel like?"

"You feel pretty important. All those men and Papa giving you the Priesthood."

"No." A quick mean wild look like you're being dumb on purpose. "When the Priesthood goes into you."

Your father listening from the other end of the table. Blackwell. Electricity. Jacking off. Brother Clark making up a fake police department. Where everything you didn't know made you feel like you'd come across level red dirt and sagebrush to the sudden edge of Dead Horse Point. Where everything was just empty space in front of you and your father's voice was the uprush of air up the sudden wall of the cliff to tell you that you could walk out across it as long as you were obedient. Your father turns another page of the Church News. Karl. His question there like his bow tie. You can't do it. You'll pay the price for this too.

"It doesn't feel like anything," you tell him.

Silence from your father's end of the table. You let Karl look for something in your face, the way he looked when you pulled him off the ledge of the cave and ran him down the hill to where it leveled out before it fell away into the sandpit, where you told him about the rattlesnake, where he looked with this hostile and wild uncertainty for the same thing he's looking for now, something he can either trust or not trust.

"Not anything?"

"Nope."

"Is that true, Papa?"

"Your brother may not have felt anything," your father finally says, his voice sullen but honed on the rough stone of his anger. "But all that means is that he wasn't ready."

"Ready for what?"

"To receive the priesthood," your father says. "What else?"

"How do you know if you're ready?" says Karl.

The question you asked over two years ago when you stepped off the cliff onto air you thought you could trust yourself.

"You won't know until it happens. If you feel the spirit of the Holy Ghost, then you're ready. If you don't, like your brother here apparently didn't, then you aren't ready."

"What does the Holy Ghost feel like?"

You look up from your plate at Karl. "None of my friends were ready either."

"How can you sit there and say you know what your friends felt! By golly! Who do you think you are?"

"Don't worry," you tell Karl. "Just because you don't feel anything it doesn't mean it didn't happen."

"Doesn't mean what didn't happen?"

"It doesn't mean you didn't get the Priesthood. We all still got the Priesthood. We could pass the Sacrament and—"

"Now that's enough! You have no right to speak for your friends!"

"You think Earl Bird felt anything?"

"I said that's enough!"

"I don't want him getting scared if nothing happens!"

Your father's already folded the Church News. Now, out of his chair, he's wrestling the shoulder straps of his apron off his arms.

"Let's go."

"I'm not done eating," says Karl.

"We don't have time for this nonsense. Put it in the garbage. Come. It's your first day as a Priesthood holder." He throws you a look while he hangs his apron. "We'll settle this later."

The long bruise in the brass she ran the tip of her finger along. Like it was your bruise. Like it was something you'd done. Like it could have been sore and she didn't want to hurt it. Like it had always been yours. Pink polish on the pearl of her fingernail. A strawberry smell off hair whose color she never liked. Everything real. It would happen again. Now you knew how. Where it came from. What you had to look for.

CHAPTER 90

IT ISN'T what you thought. Half the kids can't play. The first class, when Mr. Frank had everyone play the C scale, the girl sitting next to you with the flute just faked it, just moved her fingers, kept her open lips hovered over the mouthpiece, the instrument dead in her hands. There were other kids who tried. Pacing off your own notes to the rap of Mr. Frank's baton, you could hear them, horns and guitars and clarinets and tubas, fishing for the notes, some of them behind, some of them plain wrong, to where it sounded like dishes and pots and pans spilling out of the open back of a moving dump truck.

The next class, when Mr. Frank sat you next to the kid named Tom, there were empty chairs around the room, chairs that stood there with their music stands like they held the ghosts of the kids who'd been there last time. He starts you off with John Phillip Sousa and some guy named Gustav Holst. You play from scores. You have to play note for note what's written on the page no matter how strong you feel the pull to take it somewhere else. Most of the time you sit there with your trumpet on your knees while Mr. Frank takes the flutes or tubas or guitars or saxophones or French horns through their measures, over and over, until they get the phrasing like he wants them to. The only kid who always gets to play is this drummer kid, this kid who looks Mexican except for his curly wild hair, because someone always has to play the beat.

When he gets around to the trumpets you put what you can into playing to keep him from giving your section the death glare of his glasses. When you hear Vince lagging to your left you play in his direction to pull him back on beat again. When an A comes up you can feel Tom sneaking a look at how you'll finger it. Sometimes Mr. Frank puts all the different parts together to see how things are shaping up. Sometimes he takes you all the way back to play everything through from the start again. And sometimes he explodes. Sometimes at a single kid.

Sometimes a kid you never see again. Just the ghost in his empty chair. Sometimes the whole class.

"You know what it's like to shovel snow in the middle of a snowstorm?"

He looks around the room like his eyes are chasing the vanishing echoes of the way his voice came ringing off the walls. The fluorescent ceiling lights go back and forth like lightning on the mirrors of his glasses.

"Take a driveway. You start at one end. You start working toward the other end. Nice black asphalt where you shovel. You think you're making progress. Then you turn around. Know what you see? Everything's white again! Everything's white!"

He walks a couple of circles around the stage, then stops in front of the class again, rubs his jaw, finally looks up.

"You're supposed to be practicing this stuff. Learning as we go. But then we go back and play it again from the top and it's gone. That's what it's like teaching you kids. Like shoveling snow in a snowstorm. Gone! Everything I've taught you! Gone! All that black asphalt! Gone!"

You keep going back to the drummer kid. The Mexican-looking kid who answers to Robbie Fox when Mr. Frank calls roll. He looks bored and itchy with the job of being the metronome for the class. Not like he'd rather be loafing around but like he's trapped or harnessed. Sometimes at the end of doing his metronome thing for the tubas or flutes or clarinets he'll do a thing across his snares and cymbals. Like he's ready to explode too.

"Bird say anything to you yet?"

Halloween night, out in the circle with Keller, skipping Bird's house where a burning pumpkin head sits grinning on the porch, heading for the Stones instead, you done up like a salt shaker with your mother's spaghetti strainer tied to your head and a sign around your neck that says Salt, Keller in a vampire mask and black cape, your pillowcases light, only two houses worth of candy so far.

"Nope."

"Anything to your dad?"

"Not that I know."

"What do you think he's thinking?"

"I dunno. Whatever he wants."

"You seen him in church? He just sits there. Like he's had a lobotomy."

"Yeah."

"Like he's had knitting needles stuck up his nose into his brain."

"Yeah."

"Think he's thinking about how to pay you back?"

"I dunno."

"You scared?"

"Nope."

"He's got a straightedge razor."

"Yep. I saw it."

Remembering the feel of the blade on your neck through the warm white foam he'd spread across it. Remembering the way he nicked you.

"He could sneak up behind you. Like he must of done on Germans."

"Yep."

"What'd your dad say?"

"Nothing."

"Nothing?"

"Nope."

"What do you think he'll say?"

"Nothing."

"You don't look anything like a salt shaker. Figured you ought to know."

You look for his eyes through the round holes in his white mask. For his mouth in the hole framed by bloody lips and fangs. In the dark you can't see anything.

"Sure I do."

"No. You look like you're wearing a freakin' French helmet someone used for shotgun practice."

"That's weird."

"What?"

"Hearing you talk without your face moving."

"It's a mask, you dildo."

"So maybe instead of a vampire you're just a dumbass ventriloquist who got his mouth smacked bloody."

On Woody Stone's porch, ringing the bell, waiting under the bulb of the porchlight, looking at the hinged cardboard skeleton hanging on the door.

"You ever feel bad for what you did to him?"

"They're coming. Get your pillowcase ready. Why?"

"He got that new suit and everything."

"Yeah." And then you say, "Probably cost him a shitload of hairdos."

"Think he gets paid more for the dead ones?"

And now that you're done waiting you wonder what to do with Susan Lake and the way she's started sneaking looks at you. Not just when you're talking, answering a question, but when you're sitting there, minding your own business, listening to Elder Jensen do his variation on another lesson you've heard a hundred different ways before, like chastity or tithing. The way you've started catching her just looking the way she used to catch you doing. And the way it takes her a couple of seconds sometimes to get it that you've caught her. Where suddenly you'll see her eyes go sharp and her face go soft and look down at what her fingers are doing in her lap.

And then one day at school, on your way down the hall from English to Geometry, she's there right next to you.

"Oh," she says. "Hi."

Quiet but surprised and smiling. Like it's an accident. Like you haven't spent every Sunday since you were twelve across a little room from each other. But it's the first time you've ever heard her voice when it's been meant for you, and it shoots right through you almost like she's naked.

"Hi."

Stupid the way you sound. Like it's an accident too. The residue of your stiff and stupid grin like dried watermelon juice around your mouth. She's got her books cradled up against the chest of this thin brown short-sleeved sweater. You're close enough to smell her for the first time, the trace of the Sloppy Joe she had for lunch, the thick sweet cloud of a stick of gum on her breath. Juicy Fruit. Kids coming toward you bump her up against you.

"Want me to carry those?" you finally say.

She looks at you, your trumpet case in one hand, your own books in the other, while you realize the only thing you've got left to carry anything with is your teeth.

"That's okay."

"So where are you going?"

"Science. How about you?"

You glance at the cover of her notebook where she holds it canted off her chest on top of her other books. It's covered with all these hairdos, hairdos without faces, all these blank hairdos she's doodled all over it.

"Geometry," you say.

"You always come this way?"

"Yeah."

You've never seen her chew gum. Never seen the way the muscles of her face work when she's chewing gum and smiling and talking all at once. The way she'll let the small gray wad ride her tongue and peek out between her teeth.

"What's in there?"

"A trumpet."

"Are you really from a ranch?"

It takes you a minute to get why she'd even know enough to ask you. Then you remember. Talking about sheep. Cutting their nuts off.

"Yeah."

"Where?"

"Down in southern Utah."

After a minute she says, "Were you a cowboy?"

And then you have to look at her to make sure she isn't kidding. You think what would happen if you told her yes. What she'd do.

"Naw," you say. "I was a kid."

"Oh."

"I never saw you chew gum before," you say.

"Does it bother you?"

"Course not."

"You want some?"

"Thanks. That's okay."

"Oops," she says. "This is my room." And then she says, "Maybe sometime you can tell me more about your ranch."

"Sure."

Shiny brown pearl buttons partway down the back of her sweater when she turns and goes through the door into the Science Room. In the garage that afternoon, the trumpet in your hands, you remember them. Remember the note of her voice when she first said hi. And when you hear its note again, you can hear its tone, and know how a song would start from there and then keep going. You wet your lips and draw them tight and bring the trumpet up. It doesn't happen. The smell of Juicy Fruit. The weird little ladybug buttons. Giraffes. Roy wanders in and stands there while you try line after line, stop hearing it a few notes in, then have it peter out. It doesn't happen. All this time, everything you'd expected, and now you can't get it to happen. You finally quit. Look at your brother Roy, standing there straight as a little soldier in his corduroy pants and a sweater your mother knit, arms at his sides, planted there like a hydrant. On his hands are the small cloth gardening gloves you bought him, the fingertips cut off, and around his head the red bandana he wanted too.

"Anything you'd like to hear?" you ask him.

"That fish song that Mama sings."

"The fish gotta swim one?"

"Yeah."

"You like that one?"

"Yeah."

"Can't help lovin that man of mine. That's what it's called."

"Can you play it?"

"You want to sing? You know the words?"

And he moves his feet like they itch and his face lights up helpless and shy with a grin for all the attention you're giving him.

"I just want you to play it."

"Then hold on," you tell him. "Here we go."

CHAPTER 91

NOT ONE of you meant anything to anyone when you started high school. Not Doby or West or Keller or Jasperson. Just sophomores. Invisible tenth grade kids. Through fall and into winter it started changing. West took auto mechanics and found the parking lot and some eleventh grade greasers and their cars. Jasperson and Keller joined the bowling club. Doby joined the rifle club. Strand the United Nations club. One December afternoon, in the band room, practicing Winter Wonderland for the Christmas Assembly, your turn comes too.

"Tauffler. Come up front. Bring your horn."

Your legs do it for you. The rest of you is numb. Vince pulls back his music stand to let you sleepwalk past him. And then you're standing in front of Mr. Frank, close as you've ever been to him, and for the first time you can see through his glasses to his eyes. In their thorny sockets there's too much fury gathered there to look at them for long.

"I need to know what to do with you," he says, loud, loud enough to echo. And then he takes you by your shoulder to the front of the shallow black stage and turns you around to face the class.

"Play something," he says.

"Like what?"

"Like anything you know."

"A standard?"

"A standard?" he says.

"Yes."

"A standard's fine. Which one?"

"You can pick one if you want."

More scorn and fury gather in his eyes. "All right," he finally says. "Stormy Weather."

"What key?"

"What key? Seriously?"

"Yeah."

"What key was it written in?"

"G Major."

"Use that."

"Okay."

Come in from out of nowhere. Some riff that isn't anywhere near the melody and has nothing to do with the key. Some crazy riff from a place so far away they'll think you don't know what you're doing. Just some brat kid blowing his first smartass nowhere riff on a trumpet. Sometimes piercing. Sometimes muted. Turn it human and find a way to bring it in on the melody.

And that's what you do now. Come out of nowhere and bring it slowly in on the opening phrase of the song. Don't know why there's no sun up in the sky. Let them know they can trust you to get from anywhere to where they're waiting on the well-worn path of the melody. Run through it once, hearing Billie Holiday, and then, before you reach the bridge, hearing brushes on drums, hearing the Mexican-looking kid named Robbie Fox use his drums like a question at first to ask if he can come along. Nobody stops him. At the end of the melody you come back around and this time take them far away again, far away on the journey of what you can do with the song, so far across the sky they won't care where they are, down across the huge sky of Soldier Summit and the blue-hazed mountains out the windshield of the cattle truck. Stormy weather. Since my girl and I ain't together. And now you hear the questioning notes of a bass guitar, a kid named Jimmy, asking to come along too. Nobody stops him either. You keep going. Take the song as far away as you can again and keep it out as long as you know how, all the way south to La Sal, long enough to where the twilight wind starts kicking up and night starts to fall and they start to hear the cries that animals make at night. Can't go on everything I have is gone. The coyotes around the ranch. Rex nickering in his sleep. Sheep and their troubled bleating rustling through the flock. Keeps raining all the time. To where they hear the innocent cries of the animals and get to where they're scared and look to you to bring them home and all they have to do is listen and they'll know that you can do it. That all you have to do to get them home is keep on moving. It's raining all the time. Keeps raining all the time.

Mr. Frank stands there when you bring your trumpet down to your chest. Stands there off to the side of the raised black floor you're standing front and center on and stares at you with such hard blue-jawed intensity from behind glasses blinded by light from the windows that you feel things pucker in your crotch. Stares for so long that you finally look down at your mouthpiece to hide your blazing face. There's a clap. You flinch, glance up, the chair where you saw her just now empty, just her ghost, but the damp warm skin of her yellow sweater real. There's a second clap. It's a big kid in the sax section. And then you don't know where to look.

For a minute it's just the slow insistent cadence of the one kid clapping. And then you hear the strum of a bass guitar, a single note, way down low, timed just behind the beat of the one kid clapping, and then the lone repeating crack of a single stick on a snare drum comes in and starts to play around the one kid clapping too. And before long the bass and the drum are playing all around the steady slow clap of the flabby kid's hands.

"That's enough," you hear Mr. Frank finally say.

The room goes silent again. And then you don't know what to do but stand there where you've never been before.

"I need to see you after school," Mr. Frank says.

"Okay."

"You know where my office is?"

"Yes."

CHAPTER 92

WHAT HE wants. What you did. By the time the last bell rings you've thought of everything a million times. In the halls, heading for his office, you go against the tide of the building going empty, the racket of kids whacking their lockers shut, heading for the doors.

"Come in. Sit down."

Facing his desk there's a steel chair with a naugahyde seat. Set off on the side of his desk there's a pipe. So what Naylor said was true. He goes out back to the dock to smoke his pipe. He takes his glasses off, lays them on a piece of sheet music in front of him, rubs his eyes with the heels of his big hands. His eyes are red when he drops his hands and looks at you.

"Who's your teacher?" he says. And when you look at him, not knowing how to tell him your teacher is him, he says, "Not me. I mean your trumpet teacher."

"His name is Mr. Selby."

"Selby," he says, like he needs to say it himself before he can run it through his head. "I think I know him." And then he says, "How old are you?"

"Fifteen."

"Here's the deal," he says. "I don't want you in my class."

The worst thing you figured could be his reason for wanting to see you. The thing you got ready for. The thing you spent your last class letting go of just in case. Tell Mr. Selby you tried. You look at his pipe and its chewed black stem and then quick back at him.

"Okay."

"Okay," he says. "You don't seem too upset."

"I'd just like to know how come. What I did."

Because he hated what you played. The way you played it. Because you broke his rule about showing off.

"What you did?"

"Yeah."

"You mean what you did wrong."

"Yeah."

"Listen. This school has never seen a better trumpet player. Not in my day. Not close. I knew that the first day of class."

"You could hear me?"

"It's my job to hear you," he says. "What do you think? I'm up there to hang laundry?"

"So how come you're kicking me out?"

"Kicking you out." He laughs. "My class can't do you any good. You're so far ahead the rest of them can't even see you. You're out there over the horizon."

He waits. And when you don't say anything he keeps going.

"Hook up with some real musicians. Start a band. You'll find what you're after a damn sight sooner than watching your fingernails grow in my class."

"When do you want me out?"

"You've seen your last class."

"I'm done now?"

"You played one hell of a swan song today."

He gives you time. Time to stare at him to see if he's serious and then have your stomach tell you. Time to look around and then at him again and at his pipe and then down at your hands on your biology notebook. The kid named Robbie brushing his drums while you stood there playing. The kid named Jimmy on bass who heard the sudden detour of your modulation coming and stayed with you. If they knew you were gone. Vince and Tom and the ghost chair in between them.

"What if I wanted to stay?"

"It's not up to you."

"What about the Christmas Assembly?"

"Sorry. Your parents, they'd be proud as peacocks, but I'd have every other parent pissed off, wanting to know why their kid couldn't play like the kid with the trumpet."

The big flabby kid with the sax who started clapping. And then everybody else when Mr. Frank said okay. You never were one of them. For real now.

"What if I run into kids from class?"

"I'll tell them."

"What should I do with my band period?"

"Take something else. Think about another elective you'd like to take."

The engine you and Jimmy Dennison took apart and didn't think of putting back together to see if you could make it run. Because you didn't know how to make it run. You could learn. Learn how to fix the things you take apart. You could have a class with West.

"Auto mechanics?"

"I'll take care of it. Your parents won't have a problem with this, will they? Me taking you out of band?"

"No. They'll be okay."

"If they're not, tell them what I told you. It's hurting you. It's holding you back. If they'd like, I'll tell them. Tell them that."

"Okay."

"Okay then," he says. "So tell me. What happened between you and that blond kid sits next to you? He told me you lied to him about something."

The kid named Tom.

"I was just kidding," you say. "He told you?"

"Kidding about what?"

And so you tell him. The way the kid kept needling you about how old your trumpet was. The dent in the bell. You telling him you had to double flat the B to play an A because of it.

"He believed you," Mr. Frank says.

"He looked like he did."

Mr. Frank looks down at his desk. Brings up his big bristle-backed hands and laces his long fingers through each other and stretches them until his knuckles crack. "Some days," he says, "I'd like to put a bullet in my brain."

"It just came out," you say. "I didn't mean anything."

"I keep a kid like that and have to ask someone like you to go. I'm giving you an A, by the way. Just for Stormy Weather."

Two days later you've got auto mechanics for the afternoon period where you had band. In the classroom Mr. Polk teaches you about internal combustion engines. He passes pistons and wrist pins and valves and connecting rods around. They're dry and clean this time, not slick with oil the color of blood and molasses, but your astonishment is there again, for the way they're machined, the way they fit together, the way they work together blind in the pitch dark of an engine block and the explosive furnaces of its cylinders at thousands of strokes a minute.

Sometimes Mr. Polk takes you out to the shop. An opened engine on a stand with half its guts gone. Crusted cylinder heads with their combustion domes scaled black. The crowded shining gears of an open transmission. A hoist where you look at the underside of a Chevy like your father's. Heaters hang from the ceiling and roar and turn this brooding red when they come on. The other guys in the class hold tools like they've been handed down by warrior mechanics. They treat the shop like their concept of a church and Mr. Polk like a prophet. Like if they miss a single word he says they'll be lost and gone to Hell forever.

West's period is in the morning when you have English. But soon enough you're friends with guys like Quigley and Snook and Porter. Tough guys with hard fierce currents of honesty and loyalty strong enough to carve rock underneath the surface of their toughness. Guys whose sense of right and wrong you wouldn't want to cross. Guys on the way to becoming greasers old enough to park their cars in the lot behind the school. Guys already putting their summer cash away for the cars they'll get once Brother Clark signs their permits. Guys who get your own blood going. Out in the parking lot behind the school one afternoon you're looking with West at a lowered Pontiac with blinding purple paint in the cold December sun.

"Shit color for a Pontiac," says West.

"We gotta sign up for the same period next time," you say.

"Yeah. We do. Wish I'd known."

"What's this sparkly stuff in the paint?"

"Looks like fishscale."

"Fishscale. Jesus."

"I know. On a Pontiac."

West takes one hand out of his coat pocket to shield the sun and look through the driver's window. You look back at the dock where your bike is locked to the railing. Where Mr. Frank comes out to smoke his pipe.

You never tell Susan Lake more stuff about the ranch. You knew when you came home that afternoon and tried to play. You were a curiosity. A kid who'd said nuts in Sunday School and meant testicles. A blank place in her life that she'd come across, filled in, and then moved on from, to the next blank place, the next blank accidental place that came into her life and briefly stirred her curiosity, like a pomegranate or Hawaii or maybe a giraffe. And you'd come close enough to know that there were things you didn't need to know. Juicy Fruit. The hairdos on the cover of her notebook. Maybe because of all the things you'd made up about her. Maybe because you wanted to keep them. But you knew, listening for the note she struck when she said hi, looking for the tone to give it, and the song from there, that you could never take her anywhere. She wouldn't know how to go. She'd have to pack first. She'd have to button those creepy buttons first. She'd have to make sure she had enough Juicy Fruit. In Elder Jensen's class she's back where she belongs, across the room, where you should have known to leave her.

"You ever notice when Elder Jensen turns around?"

Walking home from school in a January sun, warm enough to where the dirt and slush are steaming from the light snow earlier that morning, Keller and Doby talking.

"Notice what?"

"When he turns around to write on the board."

"What?"

"His butt."

"God, Keller, what are you, a homo?"

Dirt under your fingernails and turpentine in your nose from you and Quigley rebuilding a carburetor in auto mechanics.

"No," Keller says. "His pants butt. Not his real butt."

"What about it?"

"It's all patched. Like it got worn out from a bike seat."

"Serious?"

"Yeah. I think his suits are from his mission, man. He musta brought 'em home."

"How come?"

"Who else rides a bike with a suit on? Besides a missionary?"

"Wow. Those patches are from Massachusetts."

Going into winter you learn that Elder Jensen likes being a good guy. A guy you can have fun with. A guy where you can get away with things, not because he doesn't get them, not because he's stupid, but because he lets you. This easy and smooth and friendly smile and humored kind of look when Doby or Keller or Yenchik cracks a joke or when West brings a car into the conversation. As long as you remember that the church is everything. That's what he makes you understand. Not by saying it, the way Bird did, but by his attitude, this quiet but recognizable way the little muscles in his smile start going stiff, this calm warning all of a sudden there in his friendly eyes when you get too far from home, to where you come too close to getting out from underneath its reach.

As long as you remember. The church is everything, all around you, over your head, as far as you can think of seeing, like a second sky. Not a sky with weather. Not a sky that rains or snows. A sky with the hard iron feel of an overcast where the overcast is high and endless and made up not of the motionless gray undersides of clouds but of everything they need to keep teaching you and everything you need to keep learning. A sky where Manny and Hidalgo will stay brown and loathsome till the day they're baptized. Where the people of the world will stay that way until they accept the Prophet Joseph Smith. Where you can never stop shoveling. A sky where you can never let it show that you're angry or sad or unsure of anything. Just that smile big and fierce and eager as you can. Just that handshake, that firm grip with its tendons anchored in your heart, to show them how strong your testimony is.

It's Elder Jensen's job to keep you there. Where you can still have fun. Where you can play basketball and dance and have banquets in the gym off the back of the chapel, plays and little concerts on the stage where kids who play piano and violin and flute perform, where you could play too, if only you played the right music, if only you had the right instrument.

As long as you remember. The sky of Brigham Young. The sky of the Tabernacle Choir. The sky of your father's army. A sky you can never pedal your way out from underneath. A sky you can only get out from underneath when you put one of Mr. Selby's albums on and pick your trumpet up.

CHAPTER 93

"WHAT'S THE REST of the band doing?"

Mr. Selby comes back from lifting the needle off the record at the end of a Maynard Ferguson solo and sits at his desk again. It's an afternoon late in January. Wet rags of snow are coming down outside.

"Besides the rhythm guys?"

"Yeah. Besides them."

"Standing there. Following the changes. Picking the pretty girls out of the crowd."

"Is that what you did?"

"I'd listen. Listen for ideas. Things I could use when my turn came up."

"You never picked pretty girls out of the crowd?"

"Oh, I did that too," he says. "I'd always pick one out to play to."

You watch him smile and take another bite of his peanut butter cookie. Cup his free hand under it to keep crumbs from falling into his beard. And then, for the first time, tell him what happened in band with Mr. Frank.

"When did all this happen?"

And that's when you can't look back at him.

"Back in December."

"December," he says. "You took a while to tell me."

"I didn't know what to say."

Mr. Selby looks away from you, out the front window, past where Theo sleeps in a gray ball on the windowsill, then turns your way again.

"You must have played pretty well," he finally says.

"I don't know."

"Stormy Weather?"

"Yeah." And then you say, "He picked it."

"Out of the blue?"

"I asked him to pick one."

And now you're searching his face. If it was wrong to ask Mr. Frank to pick a song for you. If that was what you did to get kicked out. He narrows his eyes like something inside him made him sad for just a second.

"He was right. There are kids who need a class. They wouldn't know what to do. You're not one of them. For you, a class like that is a graveyard. Your teacher was telling you to keep moving. Make your own way."

"Are you sure?"

"Sure of what?"

"That that's all it was."

"No," he says. "That's not all it was. It's a big deal to have a teacher tell you you're too good for his class."

"Why did you want me to take it?"

"For the experience. For the exposure. You needed to come out of hiding. People had to know who you were. Now they do."

"Yeah."

"Here's what your teacher was telling you. Find some musicians you think you'd get along with. Get that band together. Now."

"I know."

You tell him about the kids who started to play along. He takes a long look out the window before turning back. He's got this quiet smile, warm and liquid, the way his face looks in the light from the snow outside.

"Since we're coming clean," he says, "I've got something too."

"What?"

"I've got a friend," he says. "A kid walks into his music store one day. This kid's new in town. His hands are beat up. He's got two bucks in his pocket. He's got a sound in his head from a radio. He doesn't know what it came from. So my friend sets out to help him find it. At first this kid's as shy and skittish as a chipmunk. Acts like he feels stupid for wasting my friend's time." He shakes his head and looks at you. "But my friend goes on and plays almost every instrument in the store for him until they find the right one. Know what it turns out to be?"

It comes on slow, sitting there listening, this itching heat that spreads all through you while he's talking, just telling you another story about another musician, some musician when he was a kid, this kid you don't know, this kid who walked into a music store, and then this slow exploding transformation where he turns into the kid you were that day. You look down to hide your face. Your knee was hurt. You try to get your lips to move together.

"A trumpet," you say.

"Not just any trumpet," Mr. Selby says. "A Bach. A Stradivarius."

And then he says, "One my friend used to play himself when he was young and in a band."

"It was his?"

"Yes."

"He sold me his trumpet?"

"For two dollars down and a few bucks a week from yardwork."

The smell of the worn velvet. The bruised places in the brass. The dent in the bell. Places where the lacquer was gone and the metal dull. The way you watched his hands show you how to take it apart and put it back together. What he said when you asked him about the man who owned it.

"Why would he sell it if it was his?"

"I'm not done yet," Mr. Selby says. "My friend called me the night the kid tried to bring his trumpet back."

You look at your knees again to hide your face. How you lied to him. How the instrument you lied about needing a refund for was his. This is where you leave, you think, the last Thursday, the Thursday where you get on your bike like Clark Terry when he was a kid, just get on your bike and keep on riding.

"He was upset," Mr. Selby says. "Mad as I've ever seen him."

"I know."

"I don't think you do."

"He had reason to."

"He wasn't mad at you."

"I lied to him."

"I know. You were told to. He knew that."

You concentrate on your thumbnail. On the thin black line of grit inside it from auto mechanics class.

"He knew he'd probably never see you again. He knew how ashamed you were. Said it was written all over you."

Theo jumps off Mr. Selby's desk and uses your lap to break his jump to the floor. You don't dare move.

"After that night, he kept asking if you'd shown up yet. He'd call. Or ask when I called him. Or we ran into each other. He was thrilled when I told him you'd finally come out of hiding."

It's there, all the long hunger, in your throat, on your face, the way your lips keep losing hold, but now you can't help yourself from looking up.

"He was?"

"He still asks about you."

And you have to look down again.

"I've told you this for a reason," he says.

"What?"

"You didn't do anything wrong. In your band class. Your teacher was on the level with you. Don't look for things that aren't there."

"Okay."

"I want to tell our mutual friend you're in a band. Talk to those boys you mentioned."

"I will."

"I'll hold you to it. And maybe one day you'll want to drop in on him."

There was a time when you thought if only you could outrun yourself. Who you were. Your name. Pedal to where the black mountains across the valley to the west come down in this toothed black peninsula to the desert and the Kennecott Copper smokestack pumps this shallow spreading stagnant yellow lake into the sunset. Pedal to where you could go around behind the mountains. Where they couldn't see you from your neighborhood in the foothills back across the valley even with binoculars. Where you could change into another kid. Not like Superman. Just another kid. Just long enough to pedal home, long enough to let your father see what you did to Earl Bird like some other kid had done it, long enough to stand there and feel what it was like to charge his face, feel the heat of his barefaced admiration the way your buddies always did, before you had to change back to the kid you were again.

And then it happened. You didn't have to pedal. You didn't have to ride out behind the mountains. All you had to do was listen to Mr. Selby talk about this kid who wasn't you at first. It wasn't long. Just long enough for him to stand there while you looked at him. He looked okay. This kid who turned back into you looked like an okay kid.

Jimmy the kid who picked up the bass line and started playing during Stormy Weather. Eddie the flabby kid with the sax who started all the clapping. Robbie the drummer kid who looked half Mexican. You weren't one of them. That was why, in the end, they had to ask you.

Jimmy did the asking. On a gray afternoon in February, after school, he came out the big steel door with the diamond mesh window in the back corner of the building where they kept the big garbage bins. Out on the concrete dock and down the ramp where you had your bike padlocked to the pipe railing. You looked up when the door shrieked open and then groaned shut behind him. You figured he was heading for the parking lot until you didn't hear his shoes keep going, and looked up, and there he was, where the ramp ended, not saying anything. It was Thursday. Your day for your lesson with Mr. Selby. He stood there watching you lash the case to the rack behind your seat.

"That's your bike, huh."

How he didn't have a coat on. Just this long-sleeved shirt. His fingers tucked into the tops of his levi pockets. How you wondered if he thought you might be stealing your own bike.

"Yeah."

"Good place to keep it."

"Yeah."

How an engine fired up out in the parking lot somewhere, loud and crackling, revved a couple of times, then settled into the loping idle of a racing cam the way you'd heard engines do in the shop.

"You ride it all winter?"

"Pretty much. Except when it snows."

How you didn't know what else to do except tie the last knot and then start working on the combination to your padlock.

"What happened to you in band?"

"What do you mean?"

"One day, man, you're playing in front of class, and then the next day you're gone."

"Mr. Frank told me to quit."

"Why?"

"He just said it wasn't for me."

"I quit too."

"You did?"

"Yeah. Me and Eddie and Robbie." Looking around. "We all quit."

"When?"

"We just didn't sign up for winter."

How you hadn't known they'd quit. How you forgot where you were on your combination lock and had to start over again.

"You playing with anybody?"

"Not really."

"Too bad." And then him saying, "That your trumpet?"

"Yeah."

"So if you're not in band, and you're not playing with anybody, how come you're still bringing it to school?"

"Just on Thursday. I get a lesson on the way home."

"Oh. Okay."

How your lock fell open. How you took the chain, wrapped it around the post for the seat, threaded the steel loop of the lock through the last two links, snapped it shut, spun the dial to lock it.

"You know Robbie? Robbie Fox?"

"Yeah. The drummer."

"Yeah," him saying. "And Eddie Meservy."

"Yeah."

How you took your gloves out of the pockets of your jacket. How he watched, and then when you started pulling them on, looked off, across the parking lot, like you were doing something private, not looking back until you had both of them on.

"Listen," him suddenly saying. "You don't need to be an asshole."

"What?"

"I'm freezing."

"I'm not an asshole."

"You know what I'm trying to say."

"What?"

"We want you to play with us."

You standing there, holding the handlegrips, staring at him, watching him shiver now, his arms wrapped around his ribs, his hands in his armpits.

"You guys play together?"

"Yeah."

"Yeah. Sure."

"Yeah what?"

"Yeah. Play with you? You sure?"

Him looking up, looking pissed suddenly, at the big steel door, nodding. And then the door groaning open, Robbie and Eddie coming out, standing there.

"You gotta go home right now?" Jimmy saying. You looking back at him.

"I've got a lesson."

"Can you get out of it?"

"I can call him."

"We got the band room till five. Robbie's dad is gonna come get us. He can put your bike in his truck."

That gray afternoon behind the school, just after Valentine's Day, you undoing the combination lock, pulling the chain back off the seat post, locking your bike to the railing again, unlashing your trumpet case, grabbing your books, going back up the concrete ramp and through the steel door. Robbie and Eddie standing there grinning. Jimmy rubbing his legs and arms to get warm again. Finding a phone in an office they hadn't locked. Calling your mother. You won't be home till supper. Calling Mr. Selby. You need to pass on your lesson. Him asking why. You telling him a band. Him saying he had a call to make. And then the four of you in the band room sorting each other out.

"What was that you threw in back there?"

"Just a lick from a guy named Arban."

"Who?"

"Arban. He was a trumpet professor."

"A trumpet professor. Wooooo heeeee. Hey, Jimmy, maybe I need me a drum professor."

Toward dark that night, Robbie's father picks you up, in his big gray plumber's panel truck.

"So you're a quartet now."

"Yeah. With a horn."

"Yeah. He's good, too."

"Yeah? So whatcha gonna add next?"

"Nothin. We're set."

"Well, you got Shake. What you need now is Rattle and Roll."

Jimmy and Eddie and you ride behind Robbie and his father, on wood crates back in the dark cradle of the truck, out of reach of the light from the instrument panel, your bike somewhere behind you, everything alive, the clatter and whine of the engine, Robbie's father talking about shake and rattle and roll, his knuckles colored green on the steering wheel, Eddie and Jimmy and Robbie laughing, your heart wild, your grin so big and lunatic back in the dark you can barely hold your face together.

Chapter 94

EARLY THAT MARCH, your grandfather dies, of something called a stroke like Mrs. Harding did, where a part of his brain locked up and brought everything else to a stop. The famous man who lived in a little house on an anonymous dead end street off Seventh East goes on to the mansion he's built himself in the Celestial Kingdom. The man who's the reason you're here and not in Switzerland. He never had much to say to you. He never knew that you played trumpet.

The people who come to his funeral are mixed. Some men and women from church who take your father's Sunday School class. Bishop Byrne. Some of your father's neighbor friends like the Stones and Allers and Brockbanks. And then, with their always antic wide-eyed faces, their always melodious high-strung voices like a record being played too fast, your mother's and father's Swiss friends. The Rindlisbachers, the Behrs, the Lohners, the Krausers, the Hauptlis, people you know from your mother and father taking you to performances of the Swiss Chorus Edelweiss, people you're used to seeing in Swiss costumes, yodeling, singing folk songs, blowing alp horns, playing accordions, throwing the flags of all the little states of Switzerland like sails on sticks across the stage. And then older men you don't know. But you can tell from the way they wear the slow authority of battleships and the way they talk to your father and shake his hand and then go on holding it that they're men from the higher ranks of the church. Dignified looking men in whose circles your grandfather moved. Men your father writes his letters to. In the front corner, on a small organ with a single keyboard, a woman who isn't your mother keeps repeating the same soft piece of music.

Even in this moment, with the man who raised him dead at the front of the room in a casket flanked by a chaos of flowers on easels and stools, your father can't seem to stand there and be his son. Be what you think you'd be like if it was him in the casket. Instead, he's hard at work, his big face animated, the flesh ridged and red and rough with blood with the repeating effort to make people feel good for having come, dismiss their consolation, express astonishment when one of the men from the church appears in front of him to hear him say how undeserved and humbling an honor it is that someone of his stature would remember or think enough of his father to come to his funeral. In person. By golly. You watch the men from the church stand there, shameless in the shine of his strenuous admiration, and not even try to put a stop to it.

Molly ten now. Not old enough to have learned to not go near her father when he's this possessed, this thrilled, working this fiercely at being humble. She stands there in front of his leg like it's the trunk of a tree, looking up, looking for his face in the branches and leaves of his vexed effort to ignore her into going looking for another tree. And then your grandmother notices her, goes and fetches her, propels her away from your father toward where your mother sits, talking to Bethli Graub and keeping three-year-old Maggie from running off.

And then your grandmother comes for you, and leads you to the casket where your grandfather's head rests on a pillow, where his face looks waxed and buffed, and for the first time he doesn't have his glasses on, his rimless round glasses, and his eyelids have the fragile wrinkles your father's have, and the little moustache under his nose is gone, and the crown of hair around his ears is trimmed and his bald head burnished to where the brownish spots are smoothed in with the regular skin like the stains in the brass of your trumpet, and finally you give in to your grandmother and her insistent murmuring breath, let her knuckled fingers bring your hand up to touch the hard surface of his forehead, the first time you've ever touched him you can remember.

"I'll let you say goodbye to him," your grandmother says. And then she leaves.

You take your fingertips away. But not before you feel the giving slip of your grandfather's skin on the bone of his skull. And then you just stand there, thinking of someone like Bird, scissors in his hand, snipping away, swearing his head off at the man who made it possible for people who only knew German to sing Mormon hymns and read the Book of Mormon, who made it possible for you to be an American kid in high school in a town called Bountiful. The man who raised your father. Who knew your father when he was a kid. The first time you see his eyes naked, without his little fiery glasses, they're closed, and his lips look smoother and darker than you thought they'd ever look this close.

All your cousins are there from your father's two sisters. Aunt Emily and Aunt Trudi. The ones from Provo whose father Uncle Klaus is an architect and drives a sports car. The ones from Salt Lake whose father

Uncle Bob is a psychologist who does things with mice and monkeys. In the back of the room you spot your brother Karl talking to your cousin Renata.

Roy just eight. Off to one side of the room, all by himself, your little brother stands there, in his plaid sport jacket, in his clip-on bow tie, in his Sunday shoes, just stands there, hands at his sides, like a little soldier, like an usher or attendant, except there's nobody to usher, nobody who needs attending. On a bare patch of the lush blue carpet of the funeral home, planted there in his fire hydrant posture, dressed for church, nobody notices him. Nobody sees that he's crying. Not out loud. Not where you can hear him. Just standing there crying, his little face screwed up, his mouth this open howl but with no sound, crying, too helpless and bewildered to know that when you cry you're supposed to cry into your hands, supposed to use your hands to hide your crying face, not just stand there crying in the open.

CHAPTER 95

YOU WAIT for your father to cry. Not stand against the wall like Roy in the draped room where you touched your grandfather's head. Not in the street like you when the black truck took what was left of Mrs. Harding out of the reach of your legs to catch it. Not out in the open. Just maybe with his family. Just have it hit him, like it did you, like it did Roy, that where there was someone you knew, there was nothing now. That the place where you used to see sunlight quietly explode off your grandfather's glasses is blank. That the trembling hand that used to count eight wrinkled dollar bills into your palm on Friday afternoon was always going to be gone. The sunlight caught in the ice cubes in Lupe's lemonade.

You take your trumpet to school most every day. On Thursday for your lesson. The rest of the time for the four of you to work your way together into a band. Official school bands like the marching band use the band room after school. But Mr. Frank gets you a cinderblock storage room in the basement and a janitor helps you move things back and clear the center of the concrete floor. Robbie brings an old drum set from home that he can leave there.

You keep waiting. But there's just this permanent dry overcast of sadness and his always heavy face when he finishes his plate on Sunday morning, takes his apron off, and there's his suit. At church there's the way his face transforms, comes young and charged, like his face has an apron too, an apron he wears at home or when it's just his family, and all he has to do is take it off and there's his suit face underneath, ready to go. If only he'd look at all of you. Just for a minute. And then he'd know. He wouldn't need his apron or his suit face. He could stop and cry with his real face. But he doesn't. Not at dinner. Not in his den where you make things up to ask him just to check on him. Not when you get on your knees at night for family prayer and you wait for his voice to hook on something. From when you told him about Miles Davis, you know that he could cry if he let himself, but the closest you see him come is when his face takes on this sudden wild inward stare, and he looks at his fork like he doesn't recognize what's on it, like thunder has gone off inside him, like a second from now he'll be crying. But he rides it out. At night, when he comes home from the office for good, you lie in bed and listen for him then, in bed with your mother, for her consoling voice to reach you through the closed door.

One afternoon in April, getting your bike unlocked from the rail and your trumpet lashed down for the ride to Mr. Selby's, you hear the shriek of the metal door. Mr. Frank walks out on the dock with his pipe in his hand.

"There you are," he says.

"Hi, Mr. Frank."

Standing above you, he's already fired up a lighter, and he turns it sideways, his eyebrows like a hawk's wings diving while the flame pulls down inside the pipe and white smoke starts to puff out the corner of his mouth. He claps the lighter shut and looks inside his pipe and then sticks it in his mouth again.

"We've got a spring assembly coming up in May," he says. "I want you boys to play."

"In an assembly?"

"In the gym. Three songs. You can pick them. But I get to approve them."

"Three?"

"Right."

"Anything?"

"You want me to pick them?"

"No. That's okay."

"Tell your boys."

"For sure. Thanks, Mr. Frank."

"Your folks are welcome to come. Let them know."

You've already told her you have a band. You had to. You needed to give her a reason for hardly ever using the garage to practice anymore. For not coming home from school, or from Robbie's house, till your father came home from work, till almost suppertime. With the sandpit you never came home till almost supper either. But she never asked. Maybe she got used to hearing you play from down in the garage, like the floor of the house was music she could walk on, and now that you were playing mostly at school or at Robbie's, it was just a floor again.

It was tricky telling her you had a band. You hadn't told her anything about yourself or anyone who mattered since the day she tore up Mrs. Harding's photograph and then gave you the dirty reason you wanted to play jazz yourself. It was March when you told her. A long dry wind was howling. You could hear sand trying to sift its way into the house. She wanted to know who they were. The guys in your band. From across the kitchen table she asked if they were good boys. You told her yeah. You said they were good musicians too. She asked where they were from. Around town, you told her, and then she told you she was a musician, and you suddenly saw her that way. A musician. A singer. Free of her family. Just her. A woman who played piano and sang. You didn't know what to do, except look down, and when you looked up again, she was smiling at you, her face luminous with this tender adoration, this glittering liquid shine in her eyes.

"You were my firstborn, Shakli. You had such beautiful blond hair!"

The news you need to bring home now is that your band is playing in an assembly in the high school gym. In the front yard, in her striped dress, she's moving the sprinkler that waves its high sail of water back and forth to a new position.

"You're invited. You and Papa."

"Yes, Shakli."

"I can get you a ride if Papa can't come. Robbie already asked his mom."

"Who is this Robbie?"

"He's the drummer. His mom said she could pick you up."

"I don't know this woman."

"She's nice."

"I don't know, Shakli."

"What don't you know?"

"You know, Shakli, your mother used to play in assemblies too, in high school. Oh, they had a beautiful black grand piano! A Boesendorfer! It was wonderful to play!"

A schoolgirl. In front of an auditorium of the rich kids who hated her. In her one dress whose color your father couldn't remember.

"What did you play?"

"Oh, Beethoven, Chopin, Mozart. Once a Brahms rhapsody."

"Did your mom come hear you?"

"Yah, Shakli. You know, I have asked you to play with me."

"I know."

"Don't you like the way I play?"

"Yeah."

"Then why don't you play with me?"

The way you used to quietly play along from down in the garage. It's something you haven't done since that day either. You haven't gone anywhere near her music.

"I don't know."

"Come, Shakli! Let's go inside! Let's play something! Play with your mother! Come! I just got the music for South Pacific! Come! Bring your trumpet!"

It's there, in its case, in your hand, the way you carried it up after putting your bike in the garage. You wish you'd gone through the house instead. You could have left it somewhere. Inside, from the piano bench, she props her South Pacific songbook open to a song called This Nearly Was Mine. You watch her fingers. You listen to her voice, her American voice, clean of her accent, modest and almost meek in its longing, a voice you could never hate, a voice that leaves the cold ash smell of dread down in your stomach. One dream in my heart. One love to be living for. You try to lay in some lines as she moves into the song. Close to my heart she came, she sings, only to fly away. Only to fly as day flies from moonlight. She leaves you room. You try again. And then finally let her go. Still dreaming of paradise. Still saying that paradise once nearly was mine.

It leaves you with this restless crowded dirty anger. It leaves you hungry for your bike.

"You just needed to hear it," she says, like you're still taking lessons from her. "Come! Let's try again!"

"My lips hurt. From practicing at school."

It takes her a minute. And then her face goes almost liquid with the look, the wounded angel face, the forgiving look. "Yah, Shakli. You don't have to lie to your mother. She can take the truth."

And then you're thinking. She's not coming. To hear your band. To hear you play in the assembly. You can take the truth too.

"She wasn't a tramp," you tell her. You hold her terrifying look. "She was just a singer. Like you."

Maybe when he's driving. Alone on his way to work. Or on his last drive home at night, in the dark, the highway deserted, his face in the green light from the dashboard, in the ghost light of the instruments, wet and shining, helpless like Roy's face was, his face instead, his mouth wide open howling, following his headlights home.

On a Saturday in May you're helping him put away the yard tools when he doesn't hang a shovel on its nails right. It falls and whacks him in the head. He grabs it up and throws it hard at the wall and starts cussing like a lunatic in Swiss. He yanks it off the floor and hurls it at the wall again. This time it brings the grass rake down with it. And then he stops, walks away toward the workbench, plants his hands flat on the bench, and leans there with his head down, the broad back of his yellow checkered short sleeved shirt transparent where it's wet with sweat, the undersides of his forearms black with soil from working on his roses. Over the dizzy hornet sound of a string quartet on his portable radio, you can hear him breathing, deep and hoarse and ragged, big chunks torn out of the air. You pick the rake and shovel up and hang them. He finally turns around.

"I'm sorry," he says. "You shouldn't have to see that."

"It's okay," you tell him.

Black soil lines the sweaty ridges of his forehead. There's the thin red line of a scratch he must have gotten from a thorn. His black hair is mussed and loose and dusty where it isn't wet.

"No," he says. "I'm sorry, but it's never okay."

"Other men get mad," you say.

"That's one thing," he says. "But you should never see it from your father."

"Grosspapa's in his mansion now."

It just comes out. You flinch for saying it, because there in his face again is that wild stare, thunder gone off inside him, like he knows he's supposed to know who you are but can't remember right away.

"Yes," he finally says. "That's where he is."

"The one he worked for."

"Yes. That's correct."

"Like the hymn," you say. "In my father's house are many mansions."

He looks at you. This anxious uncertain look that makes his face go soft but still keep up its guard. This look you could never forget. This look that was branded into your brain the first time you saw it, your first time in the churchhouse, from all the way across the chapel, where he sat pitched forward on the edge of a bench with his face canted at the high wall above the organ pipes, all by himself, this look in his face that held the question you couldn't look away from. If he'd be enough. He didn't know. He was your father. You could tell back then from all the way across the chapel that he didn't know. This close this time. So close you can hear the quiet clacking of his back teeth. So close you can see black flecks of soil in the deep ridged furrows of his forehead. So close you can feel your heart reach out like a hand, reach for his own hand, help him the rest of the way across a creek or ditch, pull him out of a cave away from the slithering back of a rattlesnake.

"Yes," he says. "I know the hymn well."

"I can play it for you."

From out in the circle you hear a door slam. Without looking away from your father, you know it's Bird, out of his house, heading for the wreck of his old Mercury, glancing your way just before he ducks down into the driver's door. The usual tense alertness at the sudden presence of a neighbor doesn't register in your father's face this time.

"So," he says. "How's that trumpet?"

Like he's talking to one of his friends at church. One of your buddies. Blackwell. If this is a trick you're playing on yourself.

"Mine?"

"Yes," he says. "Who else but yours?"

"It's good," you say. And then you say, "I got asked to play in an assembly. At school."

Bird takes the Mercury through the ritual of getting clanked into reverse, backed out and turned with its fan belt squealing, clanked into first, pulled out of the circle, its engine whistling through the rat holes in its old exhaust. Your father glances around. He looks back and has trouble finding you. His eyes skate anxiously across your face a couple of times before he does.

"An assembly," he says. "By golly. In front of the whole school?"

"Yeah. On Tuesday." And then you say, "You can come."

"I'm afraid I have to work on Tuesday," he says. "But maybe you can play it for me some other time."

This close. Your trumpet right there. In its case on the shelf behind you. A sudden idea sets off a fierce and eager lightning in your heart.

"What's your favorite song?"

"Mine?" he says.

"Yeah."

"I have many favorites," he says. "I couldn't name just one."

"Right now," you say. "Your favorite one right now."

You watch him look out the door into the still sunlight of the circle where the only sound is the chopping of a rainbird sprinkler. Watch his contemplative face go back through songs he can think of while you stand there barely able to wait for him to find it.

"Sometimes I feel like a motherless child," he says.

It throws you for a second, because she's still alive, your grandmother. It was his father who died.

"Wait. That's the name?"

"Yes," he says. "It's an old Negro spiritual."

"A motherless child?"

"You don't know it?"

The first time in a long time you've been asked about a song and you don't know what it is. And it's your father asking.

"If you can sing it, I can play it."

"Just from hearing it?"

"Yeah. I can."

"By golly," he says. "You can do that?"

"Yeah. I can. Just sing it."

"Sometimes I feel like a motherless child," he says, but he's not singing, just saying the words again. "A long ways from home."

"You mean Switzerland?"

"Maybe," he says, this retreating apology in his voice for drawing attention to himself. "I'm not sure. Sometimes I don't know."

All the places you've lived since then. The Avenues. Brewery Hill. Rose Park. All the work it took to keep moving you before he got you here. Any of them home. Any of them he feels a long ways from.

"La Sal?"

He shakes his head. "I don't know." And then he says, "Let's just forget it. It's nothing I can put my finger on."

"It sounds sad."

"Yes. It's a sad song. An old slave song."

"Do you know the melody?"

"Of course I do."

"Then sing it." Asking him again. "Or hum it. So I can play it."

He looks at you. And then his face gives way to such open and rough and long regret it's like one of you died instead. Maybe this is him crying. Maybe this is how he cries. It scares you to be in its face this close.

"Some other time," he says. "Right now we have to finish up in here."

"Does Mama have it? In the piano bench?"

"Whoa. Hold your horses. It's just a song. No. She doesn't. It's not one she likes."

This close. To where you've reached him but can't keep your hand closed tight enough on his to hold him from slipping off again.

"I'll look for it. I'll find it. I'll learn it."

"I don't want you to have to go out of your way," he says.

"I'm not. I want to. I will. I promise."

"We'll see."

You go back to work. Pick up the pushbroom to finish sweeping up the clippings and dirt the mower and other tools trailed across the floor when you brought them inside. To play for him. This close. Play for him the way strangers on his radio do. Take him out from under the iron sky of this place. Lift him through the hard gray overcast of everything that clouds his face to where the sky is huge and blue and it's just you and him on the steel bird of your trumpet, away from everything, from his suits and apron, from what he can do for everyone, from his typewriter, from this train station where you live, away where he can be a kid again. You sweep the clippings and dirt into a little heap on the concrete. You fetch the dustpan. Roy shows up. He wants to push the broom while you inch the dustpan back to let him catch the thinning line of dirt.

Hinkle Music.

Sometimes I Feel like a Motherless Child. If he'll have it. Or know it. The sign still there, up above the doorway, white with the name in black, quarter notes with their raised flags hovering around it. Instruments still float on air in the picture windows on either side of the recessed door. The sheet music spread across their sills is new and only barely faded. This time, in the afternoon sunlight, you know the songs and who the singers are.

What he'll say.

What you'll say back.

At the last minute you lashed the trumpet you never knew was his to the back of your bike in case he wanted to see what you could do with it. Now, in the pale shadow of the recessed entrance, on the glass door, the silver letters of his last name.

CHAPTER 96

ROBBIE FOX on drums. Jimmy Hepworth on electric bass. Eddie Meservy on tenor sax. You on trumpet. Your band. Mr. Selby said no when you invited him. You were a musician now, he said. Not a student. On the basketball court, dead center between the distant backboards and their idle nets, smack underneath the high black cage hung from the ceiling for all the lights, smack on top of the big red feathered head of the Indian they've got painted on the floor because this is the home of the Bountiful Braves. Robbie and Eddie and Jimmy are working overtime on looking loose and relaxed and bored with the whole idea. You and Eddie have stands with microphones for your horns. Robbie's got the drums and cymbals his father brought to school in his plumber's truck arranged on a patch of theater rug to keep them from sliding out of reach. Jimmy's busy tuning his tuned bass with his amp turned low. Robbie's acting like he'll never be satisfied with the way his snares are set in relation to his cymbals. Eddie keeps tonguing the reed on his sax like he'll never get it soft enough.

You're scared too. This is what it's like. The bleachers on either side are packed from the floor almost up to the steel beams of the rafters with kids. The whole student body. Spring school outfits racked like wild hillsides of dense crazily jumbled flowerbeds. The collective racket of their voices like glass that won't stop breaking. This cascade of breaking glass that just keeps spilling off the bleachers. Kids who don't know jazz from grape juice. Kids more entertained by getting out of math or speech or history than anything else. Big kids. Juniors. Seniors. Greasers. Jocks. Cheerleaders. All the class officers. All the popular kids. All the smart kids and the dumb kids and the mean kids and the smooth kids and the rich kids and the poor kids and the kids with personalities. All the sweater girls. Sandy Jenkins. Dawn Swenson. Dusty Lane. Kids not here to hear you play. Just here to put up with you. Sit through what you think you've got. Four tenth graders they've never had to notice. Four out of nowhere kids with instruments. A band the four of you forgot to name. Your auto mechanics buddies. What they'll think.

With Robbie it doesn't matter how scared he is. It won't come through his drums. Or with Jimmy through his bass. But Eddie's different. They'll hear the trembling in his sax the way it amplifies his breathing. You remember what Mr. Selby said. Get inside the tune. Forget what's out there. Pick out a pretty girl if you've got the guts to look for one. Close your eyes if you have to. Just get inside the tune with the other guys. You motion Eddie and Jimmy over in front of Robbie's drums. Eddie and Jimmy put the sides of their heads up close. Robbie's stuck on the stool behind his drum set. But then he doesn't matter.

"Remember," you holler. "It's just us. Just the tune. Soon as Robbie sets the beat."

"Okay," Jimmy hollers back.

Robbie sits there out of earshot, behind his drums, looking at you stupid.

"What about them?" hollers Eddie.

"Just pick out some girl. A cute one."

"My folks are here."

"They don't matter," you tell Eddie.

"What if they don't like us?"

"They're not gonna," you holler. "So screw 'em."

Eddie brings his face around to you. You're ready for him. Your big steel church grin except that you're showing it evil. Shock makes Eddie's face look more disorganized than ever. Turns his eyes liquid behind his Paul Desmond glasses. Makes his bottom lip look more than ever like a window shade you could just keep rolling down. And then slowly everything flexes, turns to a mean grin too, the way you're looking back at him.

"Right," he hollers back. "Screw 'em."

"Screw who?" Jimmy yells.

"Everybody."

"Why?"

"Just screw 'em."

And then the student body vice president comes across the court from the sideline, steps up to Eddie's microphone, calms the place down with his arms, introduces you, and walks away, and then there's nothing left to do but count it down and play. Scrapple from the Apple, Charlie Parker's little bebop tune, where Eddie can strut this blazing speed on the sax they'd never guess he had. Hard applause comes out of pockets of the bleachers and then loses its certainty when it spreads around the gym. You check on Eddie. He doesn't care. He's happy he made it through and came out the other end alive. Then Brubeck's Take Five because it's something most everyone's been hearing on the radio. Robbie sets the five-four beat. Jimmy gets the changes going. Applause and a couple of hollers come off the bleachers from kids who know what's coming. While Jimmy and you play Brubeck's repeating piano line down low, Eddie takes it and slides into the melody the way Desmond does, easy, full of breath, indifferent, just him and his fingers and his endless bottom lip and his mouthpiece and his reed no matter who else might think they're around. Not a breath of being scared. Jimmy takes a cut at Gene Wright's solo on his bass. Robbie goes apeshit on Joe Morello's solo on his drums. The applause is more sure this time. Shouts and whistles that get Robbie and Eddie grinning in spite of who they are and you starting to think that maybe you were wrong.

Then Summertime. This one's yours. The one you listened to a thousand times in the garage. The uptempo easy breeze of a solo where Miles plays it not like everyone else, not like some big dramatic thing where every note gets milked until it bleeds, but muted and light like just another summer day. The one you played along with till you had it copied cold, to where you could only hear one trumpet, you and Miles, just one trumpet, and then to where you did the learning, where you could lift yours away from his in places. And then, from there, your own solo, where you'll take the mute out of the bell. Eddie steps back and licks his reed and gets ready to play the repeating horn line with its fresh and lightly sour counterpoint to what you'll be doing. You take one last look at the bleachers. This one's for her. You pick up the mute, work it into the bell, close your eyes, and there she is, at your side. In the light of the paper lanterns her dress leaves her shoulders bare. Their colors play on the white flower in her dark long wavy hair. Her eyes take you in. Her smile has never been this beautiful or clearly meant for you. Around you her Negro musicians are ready to play. She raises her arm to fix something with your hair. Where it touches your ear her hand feels soft and sleek and warm. You picture water, bring the mouthpiece to your lips, raise your head, and when you bring the trumpet down to the microphone, you're playing, sending the soft notes out, no big deal, no heavy rubato, just casual and hip and liquid out across the pace of Robbie's brushes, the light stride of Jimmy's bass, the taste of lemonade in Eddie's horn line.

ACKNOWLEDGEMENTS

Tim Stephenson for the one-of-a-kind friendship and faith and coaching that did so much to make this happen. Chase Talon for opening the door on the right way to tell this story and supporting me through to the finish. Seth Ersner-Hershfield for keeping me company through the long process of earning back the freedom and sense of entitlement to write.

My kid sister Margie for her always inspiring and tireless cheerleading. My kid brother Marv for knowing enough about music theory, Mormonism, and Salt Lake to keep those aspects of the story real, and for his always defiant support.

My original agent Michael Strong of Regal Literary who for three years guided me in giving an amorphous project form and getting the muscles and bones and heart of the story right. My current agent Markus Hoffman, also of Regal, for deftly taking the baton when Michael left the agency to co-found Zola Books.

John Murray for his counsel on how to place this book where you could stumble across it. His grandson Garrett Flanagan for bringing Shake to life in the 21st century.

The magical circle of poets and writers – Nik Gruswitz, Melissa Montimurro, Carlo D'Ambrosi, Chase Talon, Bryan Straube, and others – who made up the workshop that met at my house each week for much of the 1990s. It was in the circle of this improvised family that Shake Tauffler had his genesis and spent his formative years.

The members of the New Jersey Replicar Club – men and women from all walks of life brought together by their shared lunatic appetite to build their own cars – who read my monthly newsletters and were such an incredibly real, immediate, and gratifying audience to write for.

Carolyn and Jim Youngs, publisher and editor of *Kit Car Builder*, who gave me space in their magazine for a column, the license to write about anything I wanted, and an audience of forty thousand readers.

A trumpet player on Mallory Square in Key West who let me know that you don't write about a kid who plays trumpet without knowing how to play yourself. Ed Selby, jazz trumpet player and teacher, who taught me how to play so that I could do Shake and his instrument justice, and also allowed me to model Shake's teacher on him.

The people who offered to read *If Where You're Going Isn't Home* as a work in progress. The long – and daunting – draft they read would eventually be divided to become the first two books of the trilogy. More story – the third book – remained to be told. But at 378,000 words it was time to learn how the story would play to different readers. Twenty-five people – ranging in age from 18 to 77, from all walks of life, religions, backgrounds, interests, reading tastes, and regions of the country – stepped up to volunteer. In completely random order, these remarkable people are Jean Turco, George Goetz, Kim Merklin, Nikolaus Tea, Marian Murray, Marjorie Zimmer, Debra Lynn Nicholson, Lewis Turco, Helen Tobler, Alan Merklin, Paul Mossberg, Sophie Zimmer, Edwin Selby, John Murray, Bob Smart, my son Damon Cooper, Seth Ersner-Hershfield, Marilyn Weber, Chase Talon, Fred Simpson, Theo Mickelfeld, Joan Selby, Matt Smart, Marv Zimmer, and Bob O'Connor. It is impossible to capture in words what their effort, faith, and feedback have meant to me and to the book. All I can do is thank them. Over and over.

Joan Waldron, owner and proprietor of Max's Station House, for the best watering hole a writer this side of the Hudson could ask for, and Tina, another regular there and the inspiration for the lady in the red dress who captivates Shake in Book Two.

Mrs. Whitaker, Miss Johnson, Ruth Jones, Blanche Cannon, Steve Raab, Franklin Fisher, David Kranes, Hal Moore, Richard Schramm, and all the other teachers who guided, encouraged, and championed me.

Grace Paley, Ray Carver, E.L. Doctorow, Lewis Turco, John Gardner, John Cheever, Jack Cady, and other established writers who saw promise in my work.

All the people – all my students and all my friends across more than four decades – who have had to wait and believe in me so long to finally see this happen. I hope you'll think it was worth it.

The Boys from Bountiful – George Baty, Bobby West, Roger Jensen, Mike Flowers, Johnny Rasmussen, Harold Zesiger, Steve Derbyshire, Bob Gardiner, and Johnny Greenwell – for giving Shake the fictional buddies to make the journey with.

My parents who raised me and loved me and, in the end, supported me and gave me a story worth telling.

My wife Toni for everything else.

About the Author

Max Zimmer was born in Switzerland, brought across the Atlantic at the age of four, and raised like his young protagonist in Utah in the take-no-prisoners crucible of the Mormon faith. He earned a B.A. and an M.A. from the University of Utah and was teaching fiction, working on a doctorate in writing, when he was invited east for a summer at Yaddo, the writer's retreat in Saratoga, New York. He never intended to stay in the East. But from Yaddo he took a job teaching fiction in the Writing Arts Program at SUNY Oswego. It was there, in the summer of 1978, that *If Where You're Going Isn't Home* was first conceived, as a long love story. From Oswego, Max gravitated toward the city, lived and tended bar in Manhattan, and eventually moved to the northwest corner of New Jersey, where he married his wife Toni and settled in to write *If Where You're Going Isn't Home* from the beginning. The East had become home now. Utah had become a place he wrote about.

Among Max's published works are poems, stories, reviews, magazine articles, short biographies, and liner notes for jazz albums. He was an immediate success as a writer. Following its nomination by Ray Carver, his first published story "Utah Died for Your Sins" was awarded the Pushcart Prize, and singled out in *Rolling Stone* magazine as a raw new voice in American fiction. Max has read at venues ranging from coffee shops to SUNY writers' conferences to the Pen New Writers Series. Jack Cady, Grace Paley, Lewis Turco, and John Gardner are among other established writers who have expressed their high regard and admiration for his work. E. L. Doctorow called Max's writing the best he'd seen in a coast-to-coast college tour following the release of *Ragtime.* After meeting him on a similar tour following the publication of *Falconer,* John Cheever enthusiastically promoted Max's work for the last five years of his life.

As a break from the long and ambitious project that *If Where You're Going Isn't Home* has been, Max still writes poetry, short fiction, and an anything-goes human interest column under the heading "Actual Mileage" – inspired by a Ray Carver story – for an automotive magazine with an international readership.

www.maxzimmer.com

Printed in Great Britain
by Amazon

70818381R00307